Praise for
Nicola Griffith's novel
Slow River

"A stately, measured voyage down the secret streams inside us all . . . With her first novel, *Ammonite* . . . Griffith revealed herself to be fluent in presenting realistic science and its implications, capable of cinematic clarity in her prose, insightful with emotions and character. . . . Replicating many of her debut's themes and strengths, *Slow River* nonetheless expands into new territory. . . . Packed with memorable events—including a thrilling brush with a toxic blowup in a bioremediation plant that reads like an updated version of Lester del Rey's *Nerves*."
—*The Washington Post*

"An astonishing piece of work."
—DOROTHY ALLISON
Author of *Bastard out of Carolina*

"Griffith emerges as the major new voice in the field. Displaying a mastery of craft rare to the genre, Griffith chronicles the journey of Lore van de Oest, scion of a wealthy family, from the comforts of economic empire to a marginal existence on the fringes of a near-future society. . . . In her depiction of a woman struggling for control of her life, Griffith has fashioned a paean to the human spirit, engaging both the mind and spirit."
—*The Seattle Times*

Please turn the page for more reviews . . .

AMMONITE

Also by Nicola Griffith

Slow River
The Blue Place
Stay

AMMONITE

Nicola Griffith

Ballantine Books • New York

A Del Rey® Book
Published by The Random House Publishing Group

Copyright © 1992, 2002 by Nicola Griffith
Excerpt from *Stay* copyright © 2002 by Nicola Griffith

Published in the United States by Del Rey Books, an imprint
of The Random House Publishing Group, a division
of Random House, Inc., New York, and simultaneously
in Canada by Random House of Canada Limited, Toronto.
Originally published in a slightly different form by
The Random House Publishing Group, in 1992.

This book contains an excerpt from the book *Stay* by
Nicola Griffith. This excerpt has been set for this edition only and
may not reflect the final content of the published edition.

www.delreybooks.com

Library of Congress Control Number: 2002101340

ISBN 978-0-345-45238-2

Book design by Caron Harris
Map illustration by Mapping Specialists, Ltd.
Ammonite photograph copyright © Tomonori Taniguchi/Photonica

First Del Rey Trade Paperback Edition: May 2002

147429898

For Kelley, who fills my life with grace.

Acknowledgments

I'D LIKE to thank: Ellen Key Harris, who first acquired and edited this book ten years ago; all those at Del Rey who decided it was worth giving another shot; Shawna McCarthy, my agent; and all the readers and family and friends who have helped along the way.

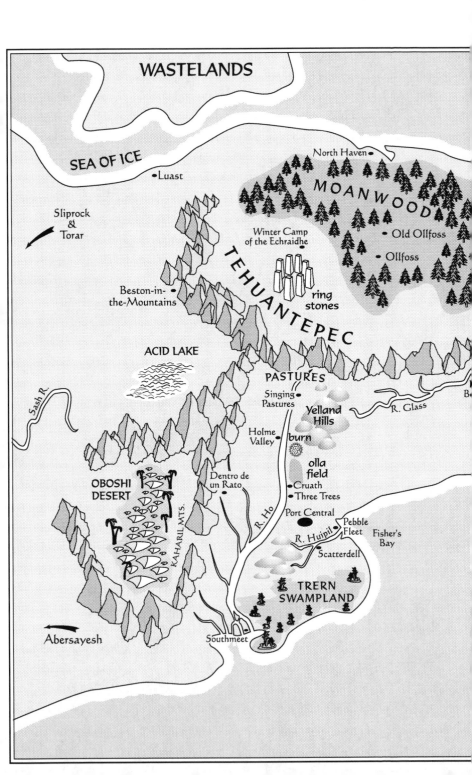

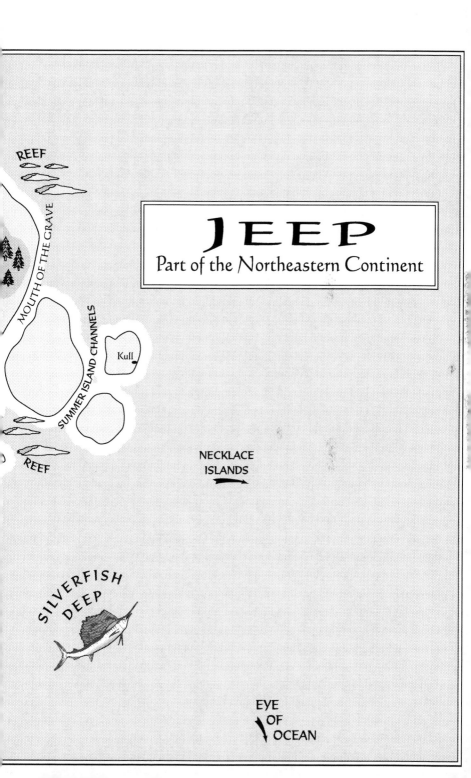

Chapter One

MARGHE'S SUIT was still open at neck and wrist, and the helmet rested in the crook of her left arm. An ID flash was sealed to her shoulder: "Marguerite Angelica Taishan, SEC." The suit was wrinkled and smelled of just-unrolled plastic, and she felt heavy and awkward, even in the two-thirds gravity of orbital station *Estrade*.

She stood by the airlock at the inside end of A Section. The door was already open. Waiting. She rested the fingertips of her right hand on the smooth ceramic of the raised hatch frame; it was cool, shocking after two days of the close human heat of A Section.

The sill of the airlock reached her knees; easy enough to step over. No great barrier. The lock chamber itself was two strides across. The far door was still closed, sealed to another sill, like this one. Four steps from here to B Section. Four steps. She had recontracted with SEC, endured six months of retraining on Earth, traveled eighteen months aboard the *Terragin*, and spent the last two days on the *Estrade* bumping elbows with the three-member crew, all to take those four steps.

"Well, Nyo and Sigrid say good luck, but they'll be out there for hours yet, fixing the satellite." Sara Hiam unclipped her headset. The slight, small woman with the atrophied muscles and club-cut dark blond hair was matter-of-fact, using her doctor persona. In the two days since she had come aboard *Estrade*, Marghe had learned that Hiam had several distinct facets to her personality, facets she rotated to face any given situation. It was a survival tactic, one way Hiam—and Sigrid and Nyo—had managed to spend five years up here without going mad. Marghe knew there was a great deal of the doctor she had not seen; she wondered what the real Sara Hiam was like.

"Life support is up and running in Section D," Hiam said. "Are you ready?"

Adrenaline, faster than conscious thought, flooded through Marghe and she had to discipline her breathing, decreasing her pulse and respiration rate, slowing blood flow and reducing the sudden over-oxygenation of her long muscles. Her face pinked as the capillaries under her skin reopened; her muscles stopped fluttering. It was a routine learned long ago.

"I'm ready."

"Very well." Hiam's voice was suddenly more measured, formal. "I'm obliged to remind you that the vaccine FN-17 now offered is still considered experimental. I also remind you that once you have taken it and once you step beyond this airlock, you will under no circumstances be allowed back into Section A: nor, whether or not you proceed as planned to Grenchstom's Planet, will you be allowed to enter any other uncontaminated Company installation until you have undergone extensive decontamination procedures." She sounded as though she was reading from a screen prompt. "These procedures consist of—"

"I know what they consist of," Marghe said. She pulled on gauntlets, closed her wrist seals. Was it her imagination or did the air coming from the lock smell different?

"This is a taped record, Marghe. Let me finish. These procedures consist of: isolation; the removal of all subject's blood, marrow, lymph and intestinal flora and fauna and its replacement with normal healthy tissues; reimmunization of subject with all bacterial and viral agents commonly found in Earth-normal human population; prior to return to home planet, further isolation at a location to be decided upon to determine the efficacy of said reimmunization. Do you understand these procedures?"

"Yes." The lock was small but, unlike the rest of what she had seen so far of *Estrade*, blessedly uncluttered.

"Further, I remind you that although FN-17 is a development of the Durallium Company, the Company in no way holds itself responsible for any adverse effects that may result from its use. Nor, though you are to be offered the utmost cooperation aboard *Estrade* and on Grenchstom's Planet, are you to be considered an employee of said Company liable to the financial restitution available to indentured personnel. Is this clear?"

"Yes." She closed her neck seal, hefted her helmet. "That's everything?"

"Yes."

"Will you help me with this?" She should have put the helmet on first; the gauntlets made her clumsy.

When the helmet and shoulder ring clicked together, the suit air hissed on. It tasted hard and flat, not like the warm, rebreathed air of the orbital station. She tongued on the broadcast communications. "Can you hear me?"

"I hear you." Hiam checked a workstation screen. "You're reading well enough." She looked up. "You?"

"Loud and clear." Through the audio pickups Hiam sounded even more remote and doctorlike. And then the only sound was Marghe's own breathing and the faint hiss of the forced air. Blue and purple readouts flickered in the lower left of her vision. Everything worked perfectly. There was nothing else to wait for.

Marghe stepped over the sill. Her boots clumped and echoed in the bare chamber, and her breath sounded loud. She touched the amber light on the control panel; the door slid shut. Hiam, arms folded, was visible through the small observation window.

Marghe studied the variety of lights, then tapped out a command sequence. A display flared red: VACUUM. Her helmet pickups were full of a hard hissing, and readouts flickered, then steadied, showing zero pressure, zero oxygen. When she moved, she felt vibration through her boots but heard nothing.

The wall display changed: AIRLOCK SYSTEMS ROUTED TO ESTRADE MAIN CONTROL PRIOR TO DECONTAMINATION PROCEDURES. TO PROCEED, INPUT SEQUENCE. Another last-minute reminder: once she started on this, there was no turning back. Marghe tapped out the memorized sequence. RAISE ARMS, RAISE CHIN, STAND WITH FEET APART. Marghe did. BLANK VISOR FOR FIFTEEN SECONDS. COMMENCING. Even through her darkened visor and closed eyes, she sensed the flare as the chamber was flooded with radiation.

EXTERIOR DECONTAMINATION COMPLETE. LOCK GOVERNANCE RETURNED TO INTERIOR CONTROL.

Marghe cleared her visor, opened her eyes, blinked away the dancing green spots. Hiam was still in the window, watching. Then, suddenly, she was gone.

Marghe watched the blank window for a moment, then took a deep breath and turned to the second door, the second panel with its red light. She reached out to input the sequence that would open it, that would enable her to take that last step over the sill that marked the boundary between what was understood and controlled and what was dangerous.

"Marghe, wait."

Marghe whirled, forgetting the two-thirds gravity. Hiam was back at the observation window, headset at one ear. Marghe had to breathe slowly, in and out, before she could speak. "What?"

"Turn on your suit comm."

Marghe tongued the channel on. "What's wrong? What have—"

"Nothing." Over the closed channel, Hiam's voice was quiet, intimate. No longer the doctor. "This is off the record."

"I don't—"

"Just listen. All those things I said before, about isolation, about spending time somewhere unspecified before going home . . . that's not what really happens."

Marghe listened to her heart kicking under her ribs. She breathed, seeking calm. *Never refuse information,* her mother had taught her when she was just six years old, *you never know what you might need.* But her mother was dead. She managed a *Go on* gesture.

"If you leave the airlock, if you take the vaccine, you'll never go home. Not ever. I had a . . . a good friend. On the planet. Was one of the initial batch taken off Jeep for study. She promised to be in touch. I think someone else wrote her mail."

"How could you tell?"

"It felt all wrong."

"If she'd been ill—"

"No. Just listen. It seemed fine at first. I assumed she just wasn't feeling good. Decon's not pleasant. Anyway, I didn't pay close attention. But once when I wrote back I put in a private joke we'd shared for a long time. A very long time. When I got her response, I knew. It wasn't her."

Marghe said nothing. She wished she had just taken that last step, not listened to Hiam—this new Hiam. *The real one?*

Hiam watched Marghe intently, then laughed, a short, hard bark. "You don't believe me."

"I'm wondering why you didn't tell me this before. Why you let me get this far."

Hiam stepped right up to the glass, close enough for Marghe to see the pleats of her irises. "Because I couldn't decide whether to trust you. But, Marghe . . . this is real, and somebody has to know. I can't prove any of it, but that doesn't mean it's not happening. You seemed . . . I just thought . . ." She laughed again. "I should have saved my breath."

Marghe did not know what to say. "You and Sigrid and Nyo have all been up here a long time. I know that must—"

"Don't patronize me," Hiam said wearily. "If you don't want to believe me, then that's your privilege, but don't patronize me."

Marghe shook her head. "I'm sorry."

Silence.

To go down to Grenchstom's Planet—GP, Jeep—would be the culmination of years of study that had started when she was just a child, first with her mother, then her father; had continued at universities, and as assistant SEC rep on Gallipoli, then Beaver. This was the reason she had swallowed her pride and set aside her misgivings about Company, why she had recontracted with SEC after they had betrayed her, why she had traveled vast distances, literally and metaphorically: to come to Jeep and study over a million people who had been out of contact with humanity for two or three hundred years. There would never be another chance like this, never.

"Sara, I have to do this."

Hiam turned away abruptly. "Then you'd better go ahead and do it."

Marghe looked at Hiam's thin back, hesitated. "I'm sorry," she said again, then tongued off the comm channel and turned slowly to face the flaring red panel. Red for danger.

The known dangers she had prepared for, as far as humanly possible. The vaccine would be waiting for her in D Section. As for the unknown dangers . . . Well, they were unknown. Nothing she could do about them.

She stretched out her hand, clumsy in the gauntlet, and tapped out the sequence slowly and carefully. The red panel blinked off and the lights around the door flared green.

The door slid open.

B Section was silent and dark. Ice glimmered in the dim sodium glow of the emergency floor lights. Marghe stepped over the sill and the door closed behind her. It was done.

The lights ran like runway flares down a narrow corridor between stripped, bare beds, each with its entertainment hookup coiled neatly at the head. Marghe's boots glowed orange as she walked. Her breathing was loud. She felt utterly alone.

She was the first person who had walked here for five years; five years since the glittering dumbbell shape that was *Estrade* had been hurriedly converted from an orbital monitoring and communications station to a research and decontamination facility. Five years since the station crew had taken refuge in Section A, leaving Sections D and C for the decontamination of occasional Jeep personnel. B Section, and the long corridor beyond—the shaft of the dumbbell—was the crew's insurance, their buffer zone, with movement allowed one way only: to the dirty sections.

Marghe watched her boots rise and fall through the orange glow; there was no dust.

The lights at the airlock blinked a reassuring green. The door opened and the wall display told her to blank her visor and hold out her arms; she keyed in the sequence on the next door, stepped through.

The corridor seemed a mile long. The familiar orange running lights gleamed on unsheathed metal and exposed wiring. Gravity decreased rapidly as she approached the center of the shaft; her suit automatically activated the electromagnets in her boots and she had to slide her feet instead of striding.

There was another airlock at the center of the corridor. She went through the dictated procedure, familiar now. The microgravity and her sensitivity to the strong magnetic field under her feet made her dizzy. She closed her eyes and took three fast breaths to trigger a meditative state, monitoring for a moment her heartbeat and electrical activity.

She went on: more corridor, another lock. C Section.

In C Section there were beds, like B Section, but each had a hood waiting to be lowered over an occupant to suck out her blood and lymph, ready to push physical and electrical fingers deep into her intestines to kill and remove the swarm of bacteria and yeasts, eager to sear away the first layers of skin and lave red, raw tissues with colorless fluids until new skin grew back. Tombs for the living. She hated them. They had not been able to save her mother.

She walked faster; she wanted to be out of C Section.

In the lock. *Hurry.* Eyes shut and arms out. *Faster.* Key sequence. *Now.*

Nothing. The panel still flashed red.

Marghe stared at it. If she could not get through into D Section, she was trapped. The lock systems would not permit her to retrace her steps without a record of her having undergone either isolation in D or fluid replacement in C.

Think.

Perhaps she had input the wrong number sequence. She had been in a rush. Yes. Precisely, accurately, she tapped in the code a second time.

No change.

She tongued on the comm channel. "Hiam, can you hear me?"

Her helmet speaker clicked. "I can hear. Go ahead."

"I'm still in lock four."

"So my readouts say."

"It won't accept the sequence."

"You're sure you got it right?"

"Seven-eight-three-six-nine." Silence. "It's the right one, isn't it?"

"Yes." Another silence. Marghe imagined the *tck-tck* of Hiam's nails on the keyboard. "How much air do you have?"

"About eighty minutes."

"There should be an emergency suit. In the locker to your left."

Marghe opened the left locker, then the right. They were both empty. "Nothing. And all the emergency blow patches have gone."

"I forgot. We had to clear everything, just in case someone infected tried to blow her way out. Let me think."

Marghe stood in the dim light and breathed precious air. Eighty minutes. She did not want to die here, alone, surrounded by nothing but dead machinery and empty space.

The audio relay clicked back on. "Nyo's back from her repair stint," Hiam said. "She knows more about the systems than I do, she's working on it right now. She—hold on." Marghe thought she heard a muttered conference. "Sigrid says Nyo's on the track of some software glitch."

"How long will it take?"

"Hold on." More muted discussion. "No guesses. But Nyo's working fast."

Minutes dragged by. Marghe concentrated on increasing her blood flow to tensed muscles, washing away fatigue acids and stress toxins. She checked to make sure her boot electros were off. She had seventy-one minutes of air left.

"Marghe, listen, I've been talking to Sigrid, and we agree. We've decided that if Nyo can't rewrite in time, then we'll EVA out from here, open up the exterior hatch of that lock, and bring you back here."

"You'd risk contamination—"

"Yes."

Hiam was serious, Marghe realized, in spite of what she believed about Company and the fate of contaminated employees. "Sara, I . . ." She floundered. "Thank you."

Hiam laughed, only this time it was not that awful bark, but longer, lighter, more friendly. "Don't thank me yet." She clicked off, and once again Marghe was surrounded by the sound of her own breath. Her breathing was strong and even: there were people on her side.

Click. "This is Nyo. Try seven-eight-four-six-nine. We'll monitor."

A four instead of a three. A difference of one digit. Marghe input the sequence: seven, pause, eight, pause, four, pause . . . The door lights flicked from red to green.

"Thank you," she said. "Thank you."

D Section was dark. She had not expected that. She switched over to suit broadcast. "Lights." Brilliant white light sliced on, making her blink.

D was square, only four beds. Two mobile hoods like slick cauls by the far bulkhead. Several workstations. Not dissimilar to crew quarters. Her visor frosted over. She scrubbed at it clumsily, scanned her readouts: external temperature 24 degrees Celsius, air composition and pressure at normal levels, no apparent toxins. Just to make sure, she sat down at the nearest workstation.

"On." The gray screen went black, ready. "Readouts of internal atmospheric composition of this sector." Figures blinked obligingly, agreeing with her own readings. She still felt nervous. "Confirm lock and hull integrity." The screen flashed CONFIRMED. "Off." The screen went back to dead gray.

Awkwardly, she took off her left gauntlet. The right was easier. The slick plastic of her helmet was still cold. She twisted it anticlockwise and cool, clean, untouched-smelling air spilled in under the opened seal. Marghe lifted off the helmet and breathed deep. She was safe, for now.

MARGHE PULLED hair still damp from the shower free of the collar of her crisp new cliptogether. She commed Hiam.

"I'm ready for the FN-17 now."

"In the food slot." Marghe padded over to the slot. Inside it were two softgels and a glass of water. "Double dose for the first day," Hiam said, "then one tomorrow, one the next day. After that, one every ten days. There's a possibility of fever the first forty-eight hours, nothing dangerous."

Marghe squeezed the gels gently between finger and thumb and held them up to the light: they were watery pink. The glass of water was the same temperature as her hand. She swallowed both gels at once, then put the empty glass back in the slot.

Marghe heard Hiam sigh. "You think I'd back out at the last minute?"

"You never know."

Marghe lay down on the bed farthest from the hoods, face still turned to the screen. "I want some privacy for a little while."

"I'll have to keep the bio telemetry."

Marghe nodded. "But no visual, no audio. Just for a while."

"Fine." The speaker clicked off.

The click, like that of the comm channel in her helmet, was deliberate, meant to reassure the subject that she was not being monitored. Either could be simulated if the observer deemed it desirable; Marghe chose to believe that this was not one of those times.

It could take up to two minutes for an object to travel down the esophagus to the stomach. She imagined the softgels dropping gently through the pyloric sphincter, the acids in her stomach breaching the gelatin of their shells, the watery pink liquid spilling FN-17. Enzymes breaking it down, carrying it into her bloodstream, into her cells. An experimental biofactured vaccine against Jeep. Jeep the virus, named after the planet.

For more than two years she had tried to imagine how it would feel to swallow the vaccine. She put her hands behind her head, staring at the ceiling.

"YOU'RE RUNNING away," her father had said, pacing his study in Portugal, wandering out of the screen visual pickup's line of sight.

"I'm not," Marghe had objected. It was spring, and the scent of grass and the sound of ewes lambing on the Welsh hillside carried through the open windows of her cottage. "This is the most fabulous opportunity for an anthropologist since . . . since the nineteenth century."

"And why do you suppose the joint Settlement and Education Councils are offering it to you? Because you're the best qualified person?"

"I'm not as naive as that."

"Then think, Marghe, think! You resigned from SEC once. They haven't changed—just as corrupt as ever. Last time you got beaten up and hospitalized. What will happen this time? There's more at stake. And this, this running away because of Acquila's death won't help anyone."

"I can do this job. I understand the risks. And Mother's death has nothing to do with it."

"Doesn't it?" Suddenly he leaned forward, close to the screen pickups. He looked concerned. Marghe was reminded of the time when she was four and had fallen down the crumbling steps of the remains of the Portuguese cathedral in Macau, and her father had appeared as if from nowhere and scooped her into his arms. *Daddy will take care of everything.* But he hadn't. Two years later he had gone to the Hammami region of Mauritania, to study the changing social structures, he said. And her mother had gone up to the moon, to teach social anthropology at the new university. All the young Marghe had had of her parents for the next two years were three battered books that lit up with their names on the fronts and their holos on the back when she thumbed them on, and a telescope through which she had watched the moon on every clear night.

She shook her head impatiently. "Mother's dead, and I'm sick of teaching at Aberystwyth. I'm good, too good to be stuck here."

"You should never have accepted that post in the first place."

It was an old argument. The fact was, she had not had much choice. SEC was the main career path for linguists and anthropologists these days; after her promising start on Gallipoli, she had gone to Beaver, the Durallium Company's mining planet, where her worldview and her face had been forcibly rearranged, and that path had no longer been open to her. Or so she had thought.

She changed tack. "Look, if you could go anywhere in the universe to study people, where would you choose? Jeep. This is a chance of a lifetime, anybody's lifetime."

"The last SEC rep died."

"Courtivron and the others didn't have the vaccine. I do."

"And maybe the vaccine will kill you."

"Maybe it will. But, John, don't you see? I don't care. The chance they're offering me far outweighs the risk. Acquila went to the moon, you went to Hammami during those awful wars . . . I'm going to Jeep."

"But they're using you!"

"Of course they are. And I'll be using them. A fair exchange."

"You'll be risking your life; they risk nothing. You'll be alone, powerless. Your SEC position as independent observer will be as much protection as an ice suit in hell. SEC's been in bed with Company for years."

"Don't lecture me on corruption and power politics. I know better than most what it means." She took a deep breath and started again, more calmly. "Anyway, I won't be alone. Two of Courtivron's team are still alive. And I'll only be there six months. Besides, what if I am Company's guinea pig? So what if SEC doesn't give a damn about my report? The important thing to me is that I get six months on a closed world to research a unique culture."

Her father had sighed. "I'd probably have made the same choice at your age." And Marghe had noticed for the first time how old and frail he seemed.

MARGHE CONTEMPLATED the smooth white ceiling of D Section. . . . *And maybe the vaccine will kill you,* her father had said.

She got off the bed, suddenly restless. Exercise, that was what she needed. She pushed two of the beds back against the wall and the edge of a workstation and stood quietly, hands by her sides in the space she had created, centering herself. She raised her hands slowly to waist level, then across, in the first move of a tai chi form. She knew several different styles, fighting and meditative, but Yang style, with its even and measured movements, its grace, was her favorite for moods like this.

When she finished, her restlessness was gone.

"Lights, low." They dimmed and the place looked more friendly. She crossed to her screen.

D Section's information storage was held separately from *Estrade's* main files, and was a disorganized patchwork of technical, anecdotal, and speculative notes added to by each decontaminee. Files ended mid-sentence and had large chunks missing. Marghe began to scroll through material with which she was already familiar, looking for the files that had been uploaded from Port Central during the eighteen months she had been aboard the *Terragin*.

Grenchstom's Planet had been rediscovered five years ago by a routine Company probe. Preliminary satellite surveys had showed a small indigenous human population living in various communities scattered over the planet, origin uncertain, though likely to stem from the same colonizing spurt that had seeded Gallipoli. Remote atmosphere testing had indicated that this could be a lucrative planet for Company's various leasing operations—

Marghe scrolled on.

Company landed its usual survey and engineering teams to lay out communications and construct the working base, Port Central. Accompanying them were a contingent of Company Security—Mirrors—and, to comply with the law, SEC representative Maurice Courtivron and his small team, entrusted with the welfare of Jeep's natives.

Marghe had not known Courtivron, but he must have been good. Jeep was a Company planet; they owned and ran every line of communication, every item shipped or manufactured there: the food, the clothes, the shelter. When Company had started setting off the burns that ruined the natives' land, he had done his best to do his job, managing—admittedly, according to the rumors, with the unlikely help of a Mirror—to bring the plight of the indigenous population to the people of Earth, sidestepping SEC corruption and forcing the Councils to bow to public opinion and set in motion the famous *Jink and Oriyest v. Company* case.

It was at that time that two discoveries were made: Jeep's natives were one hundred percent female, and there was a virus loose.

The two were connected, of course. The incidence of infection of Company personnel was one hundred percent. Eighty percent of Company's female personnel recovered; all of the men, including Courtivron, died. The planet was closed: no one on, very few off. The virus had killed the two physicians before they could unravel the world's reproductive secret—something else Marghe hoped to get information on.

She scrolled through the main directory. One of the names she had been looking for, Eagan, caught her eye. She punched up Eagan's directory. It had nine subdirectories. She called up the first: more than forty separate files. She sighed. Three days were not going to be enough to review over a year's worth of reports from Janet Eagan and Winnie Kimura, the surviving members of Courtivron's SEC team. Her assistants.

 MARGHE BLINKED and realized she had been sleeping. D Section was thick with silence. She wanted to cough, or clear her throat, just to hear something, to make herself feel less alone. She swung off the bed and padded over to the terminal. She was too tired to work, so she commed Sara Hiam.

"Quiet getting to you?"

Marghe looked around at the creamy white walls, the carefully cheerful pastels of overhead lockers, the metal bed legs, the plain flooring. "Everything's getting to me. Tell me how things are going on your end."

"Sigrid and Nyo are still debating whether the solar microwave satellite is out of synch because of a decaying orbit or faulty switching. They do agree that they can fix it. Again."

Port Central drew all its power from the microwave relay. There were several generators planetside in case the relay failed, but machinery was one thing and having the personnel to operate it another. Port Central was down to one-third of its original staff complement.

"Any other news?"

"The gig might be a day late. We relayed to Port Central the news that there are some big weather systems heading their way. We suggested that they might want to delay. Also, they're bringing someone up."

"Who?"

"You won't like it. Janet Eagan."

"But I need her down there! Can't—" Marghe shut up. Technically, she had the authority to order Eagan to remain on Jeep, but an unwilling assistant could be worse than none at all. "Do you know why?"

"Winnie is missing."

"Missing?"

"Dead, Janet thinks—"

Dead. Sweet god.

"—and Janet, quote, has more than done her duty and refuses to stay a day more when she's pretty damn sure she won't find out anything useful and where the locals are as liable to kill her as answer her questions, unquote. I'm sorry."

Marghe felt sick. She would be alone down there, unsupported, faced on all sides by hostile Company personnel. It was going to be Beaver all over again, but worse, much worse. And it was too late to back out. She had swallowed that softgel, she was here in the dirty section, Section D. She was committed. She gripped the worktable, whether to hold herself upright or stop herself from smashing something she did not know.

"I'm sorry," Hiam said again.

"I needed them," Marghe whispered. Alone with all those Company technicians. And Mirrors. Dear god.

Hiam tilted her head to one side and was suddenly all brisk physician again. "Now, I need to know how you're feeling. Have you noticed any adverse effects yet from the FN-17? My readings indicate elevated blood pressure and a slight rise in temperature."

"I'm angry." And scared.

"I've taken that into account."

Marghe closed her eyes, monitoring her respiration rate, heartbeat, blood flow, oxygen levels. "There is some impairment, yes." She felt a little dizzy. "What can I expect?"

"The usual features of fever: dizziness, nausea, headache. I've seen worse. Drink plenty of water, and rest. I'll cut visual monitoring if you like, but I'd prefer to keep audio."

"You said there was no danger."

"FN-17 by itself isn't going to do you any lasting damage, but fevers are always unpredictable. It's just a precaution."

"How long will it last?"

"Hard to say. Twenty-four, maybe forty-eight hours."

She would be well enough, then, when Eagan arrived. "Thanks."

Sara nodded and switched off. Marghe called up the language program she had worked on aboard *Terragin*. The root language spoken on Jeep derived from twenty-first-century Earth English, with some evidence of a secondary tongue based on Spanish. SEC and Company had given her access to their data bases, and she had selected a dozen of what she considered might be the most important dialects. She had studied them intently, finding peculiarities that she could trace but not explain. Several words had their root in the Zapotec spoken only by the inhabitants of the Isthmus of Tehuantepec, Mexico, generations ago. And there were some phrase constructions only to be found in Basque, or Welsh. One dialect had a seven percent incidence of ancient Greek. During the tedious voyage aboard *Terragin* she had amused herself thinking up improbable hypotheses to fit the available data.

Now she put aside the question of origins for another time. The population of Jeep was small, estimated at under one million, and its people lived in small groups, each with its own richly varied dialect. She had three days to familiarize herself with as many as possible.

After four hours her head was aching too badly to continue. She turned everything off and silence swallowed her. The light hurt her eyes. She drank some water and lay down.

"Lights, off." The dark and quiet made her dizzy. "Lights, low." She staggered back to her screen, commed Hiam. "My head hurts."

Hiam glanced off-screen, nodded to herself. "Your fever's high, but nothing to worry about." She gave Marghe a crooked grin. "You look drunk."

"I feel it."

"Take a painkiller for the headache."

Marghe went to the food slot, swallowed the painkiller, and lay down again.

What had happened to Winnie Kimura? Perhaps Eagan knew more than she was saying. Eagan would know a lot that was not in any report. She needed Eagan with her on Jeep, not up here. Six months, alone.

Silence lay like a weight on her chest, pushing her down.

Her dreams were confused. She was back on the *Terragin*, studying a language map. A word kept appearing, superimposed over her careful roots: CURSED. She tried everything she could think of to wipe the screen clean, but nothing worked. Then the walls and ceilings were whispering in Hiam's voice: *Remember the cursed*.

When she woke up, she felt hollow and light, her head full of hot wires trying to push their way out through her eyes. She lay still. The cursed. The cursed . . . What did the dream remind her of? The *Terragin* . . . working . . . overhearing one of the crew: *Supplies for the cursed*.

She sat up carefully, pushed herself off the bed, and almost fell onto the chair before her terminal.

"Sara." Silence. "Sara?"

The screen flickered into color. Sara was flushed. "Yes?"

Marghe blinked. Bad time. "Sorry." But she could not bring herself to switch off. "There's something I wanted to talk to you about . . . A dream. The cursed. Supplies for the cursed."

"Ah, yes. Our keeper. Our Armageddon."

Marghe shook her head, confused.

"The *Kurst*." Hiam spelled it for her. "Company's military cruiser hanging out there, watching us, watching Jeep."

None of this made sense to Marghe. "What?"

"Officially it doesn't exist, but SEC knows about it. We know about it. Commander Danner down on the ground knows about it. I don't think she's thought it all through, but at least she knows it's there."

Marghe wished Hiam would go more slowly. "I don't understand any of this."

"No? Wait a minute." Hiam leaned off-screen, reappeared holding a glass and a small bottle. She poured herself a shot. Drank it down. "Illegal, this. But I'm sure Company won't mind." She poured herself another. "The *Kurst* appeared a while after *Estrade* was converted. Four years ago, maybe. It's Company's insurance."

Marghe knew she must look confused. Her head hurt.

"Look at it this way, here's a planet riddled with a virus that kills all men and lots of women, almost as if it was designed as a weapon."

"Was it?"

Hiam brushed the question aside. "What's important is that it could be used as one. Don't you see? Nobody understands it, no one can control it. Except maybe those women down there. If you were a military person, would you take a chance on letting civilian technicians, even Mirrors, wander onto a world if they could come out carrying a weapon our hypothetical soldier doesn't understand and can't combat?"

Marghe had not thought of it that way. "But everyone goes through decontamination."

Hiam poured another drink. "Let me tell you something. We know nothing about that virus. Nothing. We don't know its vectors, its strength, or longevity . . . nothing. If you were to go through all those unpleasant procedures I detailed for you before you left the clean area, no one could guarantee you would be free of it. Now, given that that's the case, would you let someone off here and take them home? Imagine if the virus got loose out there!"

That one was easy. "Death, everywhere. For everyone. Eventually."

"Not necessarily. The women down there seem to have found a way." She frowned and drained her glass. "But nobody knows how."

"So what happens to those people who get taken off here, for the long-term quarantine?"

"I don't know. I don't want to know."

Marghe was tired. "Well, everything will be all right if the vaccine works." She wished her head would stop hurting.

"All right for whom?"

"I don't—"

"A vaccine is a counterweapon. It's control. Imagine: mass vaccination of the women down there. If they need the virus to reproduce, then they'll die."

"You don't know that they do." Not even Company would deal in genocide, would they? Hiam was paranoid, crazy. "You're drunk."

"Yes, I'm drunk. But not stupid. Look me in the face and tell me SEC would stand up to Company on this."

Marghe imagined her father, and what his opinion would be. Probably he would say nothing—just get up, search his bookshelves, pull down an old volume on the Trail of Tears and other, more systematic attempts at genocide, and hand it to her without comment.

Hiam was nodding. "You see now. None of us are safe. *Estrade* is probably wired for destruct. And the gigs. All because no one out there really knows who or what's safe and what's contaminated. One whiff of this thing getting out of control and *phht*, we're all reduced to our component atoms. That's why we have no contact with the *Kurst*: stops the crew from getting to know us, sympathizing. It's harder to murder people you know." Hiam stared at nothing. "Every time I wake up, I wonder: Is this going to be my last day?"

Marghe did not know what to do with this information. She did not want to think about it. Her head hurt. She felt as though someone had been beating her with a thick stick.

"Why do I ache so much?" she whispered to herself.

Hiam heard. "First-stage immune response," she said cheerfully. She seemed glad to change the subject. "The activation of your T cells is starting a process which ends up with your hypothalamus turning up the thermostat." She nodded at Marghe's shaking hands. "The shivering is just one way to generate heat. Don't worry, the painkiller you took includes an antipyretic. Your fever will ease along with the ache."

Marghe frowned. This did not fit something Hiam had said before. Something about low-level response. She tried to ignore the thumping of her head and sort out her information. SEC rules meant that Hiam was not allowed to culture the virus, or bioengineer it, so the vaccine was not made of killed virus. What she had done instead was identify the short string of amino acids, peptides, that folded up to form the actual antigen of the viral protein, map out the amino acid sequence, and then biofacture a combination of different peptides, matching different regions of the viral protein, in the hope that one or more of the synthetic peptides would fold up to mimic an antigenic site present on the viral protein. She had linked those to inert carrier proteins to help stimulate the immune system. But Hiam had not been able to fine-tune the peptides, and the immune response was supposed to be low-level.

"You said that it would be a low-level response. That's why I have to take it so often."

"The response to the peptides is low-level—"

Marghe would hate to see an acute response.

"What's happening now is partly due to the adjuvants I added to the FN-17." Marghe looked blank. "The combination of chemicals which enhance the immune response and help maintain a slow and steady release of antigen."

Marghe struggled against dizziness. Adjuvant. Chemicals. "They're toxic?"

Hiam nodded. "Cumulatively so. Which is why six months is the absolute limit for the vaccine."

Toxic. "Why didn't you tell me this before?"

"I didn't think there was any need."

Doctors know best. Marghe felt angry and uncertain; she did not know whether or not to believe Hiam. About the vaccine, about the *Kurst*. She did not want to talk anymore. "Feel sick. Bye." She felt for the comm switch, could not find it, pushed the off switch instead. The screen died and the whole room went black.

She squeezed her way through the sticky blackness to her bed. Behind her eyelids gaudy colors swam and burst. She dozed.

In her dreams her head still hurt, but it was Hiam who was going down to Jeep to test the vaccine. That seemed logical; a doctor would be the best person. Then Hiam was in D Section, saying, "But how does it all work? And why aren't the daughters identical copies of their mothers?" She got angry when Marghe could not tell her. A tree grew from the floor of D Section, a tree heavy with apples, mangoes, cantaloupes. Marghe reached for a grape the size of her fist, realized it was poisoned just as she woke to a voice calling her from the ceiling.

". . . up, Marghe. Wake up."

She tried to say something but her throat was too dry.

"Good," Hiam said. "I want you to get off the bed. Come on, that's it. Good. Now get a drink of water. A whole glass. Drink it all. Slowly, Marghe, slowly." The room swooped. "Fill the glass up again. Take it to the bed. Sit down. Good. Sip it slowly."

Marghe did. The warm water tasted metallic.

"Your reaction was more severe than I'd anticipated. I was beginning to wonder if I'd have to put a hood on you."

Marghe looked over at the medical hood. "I'm glad you didn't." Speaking made her breathless and hurt her throat.

"I still might have to if you get any more dehydrated."

Marghe sipped until her glass was empty.

"If you feel up to it, go to the slot and eat what you find there."

An apple. Marghe stared at it, confused. Had Hiam been inside her dream? She picked it up. It was cool. She felt deathly tired, too tired for subterfuge. "Are you trying to poison me?"

"Oh, Marghe. No, I'm not poisoning you. Try and eat the apple."

SHE WOKE up thirsty but clear-headed. "How long this time?" she asked the ceiling.

"Almost seventeen hours."

She sat up cautiously. She still felt a little dizzy, but that could be lack of food. The food slot hissed. It contained a glass of water and one watery pink softgel.

She opened her mouth to protest, then closed it. It was her choice; nobody had forced her to come here. The slot closed automatically when she lifted out the glass and the pill. After a moment, it slid open again. A small portion of fish, still steaming, with a bean sprout salad and another glass of water.

When she finished, she was tired again. She lay down, trying to remember if those conversations with Hiam about genocide had been real or delirium. Marghe fell asleep trying to remember what exactly Hiam had said.

 THE LIGHTS around the door to the outer access lock flared warning red, then dulled. The door hissed open. Janet Eagan was small, naked, and coughing so hard she did not have the breath to greet Marghe.

Marghe brought her a glass of water and pulled a sheet from her bed. While Eagan drank the water, Marghe draped the sheet around her shoulders. They were bony, and pale except for freckles, but her hands and face and legs were weathered. The coughing eased.

"Better?"

Eagan nodded. "For now. Thanks."

"I'm Marguerite Taishan. Marghe."

Eagan did not offer to shake hands.

Marghe gave her a cliptogether. While they ate, she found herself watching Eagan's hands, which were brown and hard, callused across the palms. She had not seen hands like that since watching a carpenter at a demonstration of old-style skills. Eagan noticed and laid them on the table palm up.

"Rope calluses," she said. "For a while I crewed a ship working the coast around the southern tip of the continent. I learned a lot."

"I'd like to hear it."

"Most of it's on disk at Port Central. I couldn't bring it with me."

"Is there anything I should know before I leave?"

Eagan laughed harshly. "Yes. It's not like anything you can possibly imagine. If I had it to do again, I'd never set foot outside Port Central, just invite the occasional native in to tell me her story. If you have any sense, that's what you'll do. I'm glad to be out of it."

Marghe said nothing. Eagan shrugged and picked up her fork. They ate in silence.

Marghe got up to get their dessert. She hesitated. "I've heard some rumors. I can't vouch for their validity, but once you've heard them, you might want to give up on the decontamination and return to Jeep with me."

"No."

"Listen, anyway." Marghe realized she sounded like Hiam. Was she beginning to believe it? "The rumor is that the people who are taken off *Estrade* are never heard from again."

"I'll take my chances."

"Take some time to think about it."

"I don't need to think about it."

"Eagan, I need you down there. I need what you know."

"It's all on disk."

"I don't want just what's on disk. I want your private thoughts, your theories, the ones that are too crazy to be put on record."

Eagan looked at her for a long time. Marghe saw the lines around her eyes. Formed by months of squinting at light reflecting on the water? "You're assuming I have some theories. I don't. Winnie had theories. She's missing."

"Tell me what you know."

"She decided to go to the plateau of Tehuantepec."

"Tehuantepec?" Marghe frowned.

"The same. Though the name is about as appropriate as 'Greenland' was. It's cold up there, nothing like the climate of the Gulf of Mexico."

Marghe went over to her terminal and punched up a large-scale satellite map of the planet. Jeep was encased in huge spiral banks of water vapor. The whole world glowed like milk and mother-of-pearl, like a lustrous shell set in a midnight ocean.

A few keystrokes removed the clouds. Marghe rotated the naked world. "Come and show me."

Eagan pointed to Port Central, on the second largest continent, then tapped a raised area several hundred miles to the north. "Here. Winnie believed she had found clues in their folklore as to the origins of these people. She was heading for a place on the plateau called Ollfoss."

"Enlarge." The screen displayed a more detailed map. Much of the plateau was forested and contour lines showed it at an elevation of almost three thousand feet. "Can you show me the location?"

"I'm not a geographer. But I'll give you some friendly advice. Don't go. Winnie headed that way, and she never came back."

Marghe stared at the screen. "How long has she been missing?"

"Fourteen months."

"She was wearing a wristcom?"

"Of course. But most places out there they're useless: few relays, and weather interferes with everything."

"What about the Search, Locate, and Identify Code?"

"A SLIC's only any good if there are enough satellites out there to scan for it. And if the Mirrors are willing to come and get you."

Marghe absorbed all that. "Do you have any ideas what might have happened?"

"Anything could have happened."

"You said that one of the reasons you wanted off was because the natives would just as soon kill you as say hello. Or words to that effect."

For the first time, Eagan looked uncomfortable. "That's not strictly true. I exaggerated, to rationalize my need to get off the damn world. They're just . . . ordinary people."

"But—"

"No." Eagan cut her off abruptly. "Winnie did not have to be murdered to die. The planet itself will do that if you give it a chance. Listen to me. Do you have any idea how many different ways a person could get herself killed? For all I know, Winnie could have fallen off her horse and broken her neck the second day out. Or she could have choked on a piece of meat. Or gotten pneumonia. Or been attacked by something." Tears, moving slowly in the low gravity, spread a wet line down each cheek. "Or maybe she just forgot to tie her horse up tightly one night and it ran off, leaving her stranded miles from anywhere. Maybe she ran out of food and starved to death. I don't know, I don't know." She brushed jerkily at her cheeks. "All I know is that she went away and didn't come back."

"She went on her own?"

"Yes," Eagan said. "I let her go out on her own. I told her she was crazy to try. So I let her go on her own, and now she's dead. And if you go, you'll die too."

Chapter Two

THE GIG taxied to a halt. Marghe stretched to relieve the adrenaline flutter of her muscles and waited for the light over her seat to show green. She stood up and fastened her disk pouch around her waist, patted the thigh pocket of her cliptogether for the vial of FN-17. Systems whined as they powered down, and from outside she heard the scrape and trundle of a ramp being maneuvered into place. The doors cracked open and leaked in light like pale grapefruit squeezings, making the artificial illumination in the gig seem suddenly thick and dim.

Jeep light.

Wind swept dark tatters across a sky rippling with cloud like a well-muscled torso, bringing with it the smell of dust and grass and a sweetness she could not identify. The gig stood on an apron of concrete roughened and rubber-streaked by countless landings. In the distance low buildings huddled against the wind.

She walked down the ramp. The concrete was hard under her soft boots. She eased her weight from one foot to another, testing her balance, feeling her muscles adjust to the difference in gravity. She sniffed, trying to equate the spicy sweet smell on the wind to something she knew: nutmeg, sun on beetle wings, the wild smell of heather.

A woman was approaching. Marghe squinted against the bright concrete light and shaded her eyes. A Mirror. For a moment the spicy breeze of Jeep became the thin air of Beaver; fear and anger flooded her system. She breathed slowly, deliberately. This was Jeep. Jeep.

The Mirror was not wearing the mirror-visored helmet that had given Company Security members their name, but the rest of her slick, impact-resistant armor was parade-ground tidy.

"Marguerite Angelica Taishan?" Marghe nodded and the Mirror made a formal semi-bow. "I'm Officer Kahn. Acting Commander Danner assigned me to show you your quarters." She paused and Marghe managed a nod. "It's a bit of a walk. If the gravity bothers you, I could summon a sled."

"Walking is fine." She followed the Mirror, stepping over a thick cable that snaked away from the gig and down an access hole. She had nothing to carry. It made her feel vulnerable and alone.

They walked for almost twenty minutes across concrete and then scrubby yellow grass before they reached the living mods. Many of their regulation doors were carved and painted in different designs. One had been framed with handmade bricks. She had never seen that before in a Company outpost.

Officer Kahn led her along a hard dirt path to the door of an untouched unit. "It needs keying," she said.

Marghe obediently put her palm on the lock and recited her name and status. The door panel blinked an acknowledge, then invited her to punch in a code for additional personal security.

Inside, the air was clean and filtered. The mod followed standard Company layout: desk and chair, bed, soft floor, bathroom niche, comm port, light panels but no heat or air controls. Filtered air was piped in at a constant seventy degrees. She pulled off her disk pouch and dropped it on the desk by the comm port. She was unpacked.

"Commander Danner thought you might wish to take a few hours to rest and refresh yourself, perhaps look around Port Central." The Mirror took a wristcom from a pocket on her belt and held it out to Marghe. "The memory already has the commander's call code, and a few others you might need today. She asks that you contact her when you're ready to meet."

Marghe fastened it around her left wrist.

"Is there anything else I can do for you?"

"No. Thank you."

Officer Kahn half turned to the door, then turned back. She cleared her throat. "Look, it's always rough coming down alone. I get off duty in five or six hours. Why don't you come along to recreation then? I'll introduce you to some people."

"I'm not interested," Marghe said harshly.

The muscles around Kahn's eyes tightened. "As you wish." She punched the door panel harder than necessary. The door hissed open and she ducked out into the wind.

Marghe sat down on the bed. She had not handled that very well. But the last time she had seen a Mirror he had been standing by with arms folded, smiling, instead of stopping three miners from beating her unconscious.

The comm port was standard Company issue. She called up a schematic of Port Central and scanned the data.

HANNAH DANNER nodded dismissal to Officer Kahn and waited for her to close the office door behind her before reopening the folder stamped FOR ATTN. OF CMDR, SECURITY PERSONNEL, ONLY: MARGUERITE ANGELICA TAISHAN.

She pulled out the eight-by-ten facsimile. The color balance was wrong, giving the complexion an orangy tint. She looked at the strong face, the broad jaw, and wondered what color Taishan's eyes really were. The picture showed them a muddy yellow. It had been taken at her recontract interview two years ago. People changed a great deal in two years.

She looked over at the picture of herself in full armor that occupied the corner of the desk. It had been taken on the day she had gotten her promotion to lieutenant and learned that she was being posted to Jeep. Her visor was pushed up and she was grinning: a younger, smooth-faced version of herself. A self who believed there was no problem too hard to solve, nothing not covered by the rule book. Sometimes she found it hard to believe only five years separated the face she saw every morning in the mirror and the face she saw in this picture.

Irritated suddenly by the idealism in that face, she leaned across the desk and thumbed the picture blank.

Marguerite Angelica Taishan was not an idealist. Once, perhaps, but no longer. She read the list of injuries Taishan had sustained in the attack on Beaver, then read the charges she had leveled at Company. Taishan had a point. It had been a careful beating and, reading between the lines, an officer could have prevented it before serious damage was done. According to Taishan's deposition, the representative had disregarded threats designed to intimidate and had submitted an unfavorable report regarding Company's operation on BV 4, recommending that the planet not be opened for long-term settlement by Company miners and their families.

Danner turned a page.

SEC had not backed their representative; they had approved long-term settlement. Taishan had fought, taking the issue as high as she could before being given an official warning. Danner frowned. That warning seemed to have knocked the stuffing from Taishan; she had stopped complaining and accepted another post. But just two days before departure she had resigned abruptly.

Danner looked at the closed face in the picture again. How did it feel to have one's trained opinion judged worthless? What did it do to one's self-esteem? She hoped she would never find out.

Taishan had become Professor of ET Anthropology at Aberystwyth. The dossier was thorough. It listed her publications: articles on subjects ranging from the evolution of Welsh to the deterioration of kinship allegiance among the population of Gallipoli since reintegration. There were two booklength works; Danner did not have to read the abstract for one, *Uneasy Alliance—SEC as Independent Arbiter?*, to guess the subject matter. Also listed were her extracurricular activities (tai chi, chi kung, various biofeedback disciplines), her credit rating (midrange), and biographical details of her last lover (no leverage possibilities noted). A note indicated that although her father was a hardline antigovernment activist, Taishan had had little contact with him since the death of her mother several months before recontract. A psychological report made several guesses as to why that might be, but Danner did not put much faith in such things. The important thing about the psych sheet was the fact that they could not come up with enough objections to outweigh Taishan's qualifications for the job of SEC rep on this kind of world. She had the ability to spend large periods of time alone, an innate belief in herself, a prodigious linguistic talent, and superb physical fitness. She was a flawed SEC tool, yes, but the best they had.

Danner had never heard of an SEC employee getting a second chance. There again, she did not know of many people who would volunteer to risk their lives for something as abstract as knowledge.

She turned to the section at the back of the report, "Miscellaneous." After reading one paragraph, she closed the dossier. There was no reason she needed to know Taishan's sexual preferences or her personal hygiene habits.

Her screen chimed and displayed the face of Officer Vincio, her administrative assistant.

"Representative Taishan is here and wishes to see you at your earliest convenience, ma'am."

"Give me two minutes." She slid the dossier into a drawer. She had time to push her desk against one wall and pull two chairs into a more informal setting around a low table before Vincio rapped on her door and ushered in a tallish, stocky woman with thick, dark hair.

Danner took her hands in greeting. They were smooth and cool. Her eyes were brown, with a hint of green, but that might have been the light. She chose the chair nearest the door, but seemed relaxed enough.

"You're well rested?" Danner asked politely.

"*Estrade* keeps Port Central time."

"Of course."

The representative wore the plainest clothes available in Company issue: soft trousers in a dark green weave and a loose-fitting brown padded shirt. No adornment. Danner suspected confidence rather than self-effacement; it took something to go in search of and requisition stores without help within—she looked at her wrist—two hours of landing on a planet.

"Is your time limited?"

Marghe's tone seemed neutral enough. Danner decided to accept the question at face value. "No," she said. "Or rather, yes, in a general sense, but this afternoon I'm at your disposal."

Her words seemed to run off Marghe's smooth exterior and Danner felt as though she were facing a mirrored glass ball. She did not have time to waste fencing. She stood up, opened her desk drawer, withdrew the dossier. "This is your file. Here." She held it out. Marghe hesitated, then took it. "It makes interesting reading, but after just two minutes with you, I feel the psychologists have made some fundamental mistakes." Marghe turned the file over in her hands without opening it. "They think you've come here for the same reason that you don't visit your father: so that you don't have to face the reality of your mother's death. The way they see it, while you're off Earth, you can believe that everything's the same back there as it was before."

"As you say, they've made a fundamental mistake." The file remained unopened in her lap.

Vincio tapped on the door. Danner and Marghe were silent as she brought in a tray of refreshments, put it down on the table between them, and left.

Danner poured steaming saffron liquid into a white porcelain cup and handed it to Marghe. Its scent was delicate, aromatic. "Dap. A local tea. It's a mild stimulant, weaker than caffeine. It's a common barter commodity, with, I'm told, a standard value, rather like a currency."

Marghe traced the smooth rim of her cup with a fingertip.

"The pottery was made by one of our cable technicians." She sipped at her own cup, rolled the aftertaste around her mouth. "It reminds me of dried apricots, though everyone finds something different in it."

Marghe took a small sip. "It tastes like comfrey." She moved the still-unopened dossier from her lap to the table.

"I want you to keep that," Danner said. "I have no use for it." She got up and retrieved another folder from her desk drawer. "I'd also like you to have this, though on a temporary basis. It's another security dossier." She held it out. "The subject is myself."

"I don't understand."

"I want you to read it, as I've read yours, so that we at least have a basis for communication. I want—" She stood abruptly, crossed to her desk, and keyed her screen to a slowly turning representation of Jeep. "Come here. Look. A whole planet. I'm supposed to oversee the safety of every single human being on this planet, and at the same time lay cables, set up communication relays, initiate geographical surveys. Hard enough. What makes it infinitely harder is the fact that I'm operating on one-third staffing levels—under a hundred Mirrors and less than three hundred technicians to do the work of over a thousand. More than half my equipment is missing or not functioning properly. Add to that the fact that the social structure here is even more out of whack than usual because every single member of my staff is female, then add to *that* a virus that might mean none of us ever leaves this place again."

Danner looked at the representative, fresh off the gig. *Do you understand?* she wanted to say. *Do you have any idea what we're up against?* "What all this adds up to is simple. Uncertainty. That might not sound too bad, but what it means is that the rules don't work here. It means that nothing has to be the way you expect it to be."

Marghe poured herself more dap—to buy time, Danner thought. "I can't just forget everything that's happened in the past, everything I know."

"I'm not asking you to forget. I'm asking you to put aside your wariness, just for a while. I know what happened to you on Beaver, but this is Jeep. I don't want to hurt you in any way—just the opposite. I need you to be willing to try. I need you on my side." Danner had no idea if she was getting through. "Please, read the dossier. I don't know how else to prove my faith."

Marghe had one hand in her pocket. Danner saw the weave of

the representative's trousers move as she clenched and unclenched her fist.

"Don't decide anything for now. Just take the dossier with you and think about it this evening." She opened another drawer in her desk. Disks glittered. "You'll need these. Janet Eagan left them for you. Read them, call me in the morning."

MARGHE WALKED alongside the ceramic-and-wire perimeter of Port Central, trying to think. Somewhere behind the clouds that at this time of year almost always covered Jeep's sky, the sun was setting, turning the gray over the living mods into a swirl of pearl and tangerine. The evening breeze faltered, then changed direction, hissing through the grass around her ankles. The grass stretched to the horizon, broken only by the occasional low bush with black, hard-looking stems and pale trails of seed fluff. There were no trees. The location had been chosen for its open aspect: easily defended.

That was typical of the way a Mirror's mind worked. Attack. Defend. Advantage. Disadvantage. Always looking for the edge, looking for a lever.

Three years ago she had walked like this for hours over the hills in Wales, seeking to forget the way her mother had tried to smile as she coughed and coughed and finally stopped breathing. Some new kind of viral pneumonia, they said. She had been sick only three days.

Walking like this when she was unused to the gravity was not helping at all. It had not helped much then, either. She walked slowly back to her mod.

It was easy to override the door controls. She sat with her legs sticking out onto the grass and her back warmed by the air streaming from inside. A woman stepped from a mod further down the row and raised a hand in casual greeting. Her hair was still wet from a shower and she wore what looked like a homemade skirt. Marghe waved back, glad they were too far away to speak. The woman walked past the mod with the handmade brick doorway and followed the path around a curve and out of Marghe's sight.

She reached down and pulled up a blade of grass. It was a flattened, hollow tube. Cautiously, she put the broken end in her mouth. It did not taste like grass, but she chewed on it anyway.

Danner's dossier had not been at all what she had expected. This was no by-the-book career officer. Most startling had been the revelation that it had been the young Danner, on Jeep on her first tour of duty as a lieutenant, who was the mysterious Mirror of rumor—the one who had helped Courtivron circumvent SEC and Company corruption and bring the *Jink and Oriyest v. Company* case to court.

Who are you, Danner? Can I trust you?

She wondered how much Danner knew about the *Kurst*, and what advice Sara Hiam might give in this situation.

She sat outside until it was dark. The heaving cloud blurred two moons to a soft silver glow; the third moon was too small to be visible through the overcast. The night was cool and silent—no insects. Two searchlights speared the grass outside the perimeter, and the unlit grass looked black. She wondered what the indigenous population thought of Port Central, and when she would get to see her first native.

Her muscles ached, from the walking, from the gravity. She went inside where it was warm and went to bed.

She dreamed that a native spoke to her, but she could not understand, and she stood by helplessly while the native rotted and died of some disease. She buried the pathetic thing, then found a Mirror kneeling by the grave. She knew it was Danner, but when the Mirror flipped up her visor, underneath there was no face.

DANNER AGREED to see her before lunch the next day. Marghe dressed slowly and checked her pockets twice for the FN-17 before she left the mod.

The cloud cover was heavy and multilayered, shades of slate blue and silver, pearl and charcoal, like a sketch washed with watercolor. The air was cool and spicy. She wondered how long it would take her to adjust to the smell, learn to filter it out of her awareness, just as the filters scrubbed it from the air in her mod. A long time, she hoped.

Again, Danner served dap in handmade china. Marghe sipped at the hot tea. "On Earth I was promised full support from Company personnel in the field. However, I now understand that you're seriously understaffed and underequipped. What can you offer me?"

Danner leaned back in her chair. "Why don't you tell me your plans."

"If there are clues to be found about the origins of these people, their common background, I need to find them. It might help with tracing the origins of this virus. It might also lead to some clues about how these women reproduce. Everything in Eagan's notes points northward. To Ollfoss."

Danner looked down into the cup she held cradled in both hands, resting on her stomach. "One of your team already tried that. She's believed to be dead."

"All the more reason to go up there and find out what happened."

Danner sighed. "At this time of year, the weather alone up there will be enough to kill you."

"I can't wait for an improvement in the weather. I only have six months."

"You'll be dealing with more than the weather. The north is isolated. The people you'll meet there won't give you any special treatment. They won't know who you are."

"I'm aware of that."

Danner put her cup down on the table between them. "I'm not happy about you risking yourself like this. You're being paid to see how well the vaccine performs, not to solve mysteries. If you get yourself killed, we're no nearer to finding out if the vaccine works. No nearer to being home."

Marghe remained silent. This was Commander Danner now, not the young lieutenant of five years ago.

Danner sipped from her cup. "I just don't understand why you want to do this. I need you here. You could teach us so much about living with these people, what to do and what not to do. You could really help us, but instead you want to hare off north and get your-self killed."

"I don't intend to die."

"But in all likelihood that's what will happen." Danner leaned forward. "I just want you to understand: I don't want you to die while you're my responsibility. I have enough on my conscience. I'll do everything in my power to help you, but that won't be much. If you go onto Tehuantepec, I can't protect you. Do you understand that?"

"I understand."

"And I can't dissuade you?"

"No." Marghe did not dare say anything further. Danner was going to jump, one way or the other.

They were both silent for a moment. Danner straightened. "Very well. When do you intend to leave?"

"As soon as possible."

Danner went around to her desk and consulted her screen. "If you can wait two days, I have a team—one officer, two civilian technicians—traveling north to a settlement called Holme Valley to install a new communications relay. It will mean an escort for part of your journey. And the community there has had contact with us before. They might be able to help you with more suitable equip-ment for further travel north than you could find here." She smiled tightly. "We have only six operational sleds. You can ride one to Holme Valley, but I'm not letting you risk it in the freezing snow of Tehuantepec."

ON HER walk back to her quarters, Marghe tried to figure it all out. Danner was going to let her go. Why? Did she believe the vaccine would not work? Or did she know too much about the *Kurst* and its intentions? Marghe reflected on this, and on the other things she had learned in the twenty hours since she had landed in Port Central.

Danner acknowledged that she was hoarding resources; she was laying a communications network as widely as she could, despite conditions. She had told Marghe, bluntly, that a SEC rep could be useful for long-term relations with the natives. Mirrors were making their own clothes and decorating their mods, like colonists.

The Mirrors did not expect to leave Jeep.

Chapter Three

MARGHE WOKE from a nightmare of drifting off the ground, spinning away from a planet with a gravity low enough to allow the muscle jerk of a sneeze to provide escape velocity.

The wind had died to a whisper and the night was quiet and inky soft. Dry ting grass scratched against the spun fibers of Marghe's nightbag as she wriggled onto her back. The cloud cover was thin and veil-like, allowing tantalizing glimpses of the moons and what might be stars, or satellites.

She closed her eyes. *Meet Jeep,* she told her senses, *a new planet.* One by one she sorted out the Earth smells: the grass-stained rubber of their shoes; the hot rotor and ozone of the sled; the thin perfume of shampoo and insect repellant; the dyes of their clothes; the metal and plastic of coiled cable. She tuned them out. The rest, the mineral-rich water vapor in the clouds, the hollow, juiceless ting grass, the sharp chalky soil under her back, was Jeep. Jeep, with its animal musk and light spice. She listened to the wind, and to the faint burrowings of unknown insects tunneling around the roots and bulbs and pods of next spring's flowers: to the breath and heartbeat of another world.

She opened her eyes again. The cloud cover over the moons had deepened, but even so their light was of a visibly different spectrum. Away from the Earth-normal artificial illumination of Port Central, her eyes would adjust in a few days. Without looking at her wristcom, she tried to judge how many hours there were until dawn. The twenty-five-and-a-half-hour diurnal cycle was just abnormal enough to be confusing. This latitude and time of year meant only eight or nine hours of full daylight; like dusk, dawn would be a lengthy affair. At least the year was shorter; winter would not last as long.

She listened to the steady breathing of the cable technician, Ude Neuyen, to the double breath of Sergeant Lu Wai and Letitia Dogias, the communications engineer, and wondered how it had been for the first colonists: listening to the breath of someone close by, waiting for the onset of the cough that meant a lover or child was going to die. How had it been—how was it—living on a world without men? From test results, she knew that the first colonists had been adept bioengineers: genetic material from Earth flora and fauna was present in indigenous species, and vice versa. The colonists had created viable crops and livestock. How long had it taken them to find the answer to their own reproductive puzzle?

From the other side of the sled, Lu Wai or Letitia sneezed and Marghe jumped, then jumped again as a pale seed drift floated by. Here, any movement in the corner of her eye flooded her with adrenaline and slicked her hands with sweat; she could not name or recognize a thousandth of the plants or animals. Or insects. She scratched the bites around her ankles, cursing under her breath as a scab came off and leaked blood. At least the insects she had encountered so far were not dangerous. As far as anybody knew.

She pushed her nightbag down around her waist to let the light breeze dry her sweat and watched the clouds scudding overhead. Gradually her heartbeat slowed, and her breathing. She slept.

She woke at dawn to a spiderweb, prismatic with dew, hanging across a clump of ting grass a handspan from her face. It was large, more than three feet across, and the strands were too thick for a spider's web: like fine, peach-tinted glass tubes. She sat up slowly, looking for the spider.

A mustardfly, whining over the tips of the ting grass, came too close. The web rippled slightly, and a strand touched the fly's triple wing. The fly struggled, and wherever it touched, it stuck. Then it stopped fighting and seemed to collapse in on itself. Marghe squinted in the cool light: the fly was dissolving, shriveling. The strand against which it was caught darkened and swelled. Within four minutes, the fly was subsumed: nothing but a glutinous lump.

The web convulsed, splitting the dark patch into hundreds of peach-colored corpuscles that pulsed in different directions down the hollow strands.

Digestion. The strands were both the spider and the web.

Cautiously, Marghe touched one of the outer strands with a fingertip. It stung. Some kind of acid, or alkali. She wiped her finger on the wet grass and wondered what would have happened to her face if she had rolled over into it while asleep. She went to wake the others.

THE MORNING was heavy and still and the sled hummed over a carpet of ivory olla flowers. The wind of their passage churned up a perfumed haze of golden green pollen; they all wore scarves wrapped around their noses and mouths. Marghe sat in the flatbed playing chess with Lu Wai on the Mirror's traveling board. Ude was at the stick and Letitia scanned the horizon for the cloud of kris flies that the pollen made inevitable. Marghe found herself looking, too.

"Your move."

Marghe studied the board, thinking about kris flies. Their stings were unpleasant, and some people were allergic. She moved one of her pawns. Lu Wai made a small sound of satisfaction and reached out for her rook; she nearly dropped it when Marghe's wristcom beeped a reminder.

Marghe took out the vial of FN-17 from her thigh pocket, popped the cap, and swallowed one.

"Can I take a look?"

Marghe hesitated, then handed them over. Lu Wai tipped one out onto her palm. "Such little things," she murmured through the scarf. She rolled it back into the vial, closed it, handed it back. She watched Marghe slide it into her pocket and double-check the pocket seal. "I'm glad to see you're being careful. Just make sure you're at Port Central when that stuff runs out."

"You think it would make that much difference?"

"With a one in five chance of not surviving, you need any edge you can get." She tapped the medic flashes on her shoulder. "Someone like me can make a difference. Your move."

Marghe moved her bishop.

Lu Wai sighed. "You're not concentrating. Check."

Marghe pushed the board aside. "Tell me about the virus."

"You're resigning?"

"I'm resigning." She felt restless and it was hard to breathe. Her head itched. She pulled her scarf off, let it hang loose around her neck. "Tell me about the virus." She wanted to know how the Mirror felt when she tried to heal people and they died; she wanted to know how it was to get sick and not know whether or not you were going to die. She needed to know what to expect.

Instead of switching off the board's field and pushing the pieces flat to close it up, Lu Wai pulled each piece free one by one and laid them down carefully in some pattern Marghe could not follow. "The virus has a long incubation period, very long," the Mirror said, intent on the little pawns and castles, "so we'd all been down here a while and settled in before anyone got sick. The first one I saw was called Sevin. He was a plastics engineer. Started coughing one day out by the perimeter, and didn't stop. I gave him, tried to give him, emergency CPR, but he died. Took just six hours. His death was the easiest I heard of." She examined the pieces critically, closed the box, ran her finger along the seal, and slipped it into a belt pouch. She untied her scarf, began to fold it into smaller and smaller triangles. "The next one I dealt with was a woman, named Margaret. She liked to cook, she told me. I remember that because I hate to cook. That's all I could think of, how I hate to cook, while she coughed and her eyes swelled up and she screamed with a headache not even mycain would help. She survived, though." She tried to smile. "Made me a thank-you dinner.

"By then we knew it was some kind of virus that integrates with human cell DNA, a bit like a retrovirus. People, mainly men, were dead all over the planet. Communications were bad, still are, so we couldn't call everyone in for medical attention. Lots of people are still officially missing, that's how we lost such a lot of equipment, sleds and such, but we know that most of them are dead. We tried everything against that virus we could think of, but none of the usual nucleoside analogues made a dent in its multiplication. We tried the interferons and synthetic analogues of $2',5'$-oligoadnylate; nothing worked. When we figured out that the female mortality rate was around twenty-three percent—"

"I thought it was less than twenty."

Lu Wai smiled again, but this time it was a hard sliding of muscles like tectonic plates. "Officially it is, if you don't count those 'missing.' " She paused. "You want me to go on?"

Marghe nodded. Her skin was tight and cold, as though someone had rubbed her down with a handful of ice. It was different down here, in the close, perfumed air, with the clouds massing overhead; Lu Wai had seen it on a scale Sara Hiam could not even imagine.

"So, we saw that more men than women were dying; we tried hormones. Didn't work. Maybe it's some kind of estrogen metabolite that inhibits the virus, but we don't know which one. There might even be more than one. We were desperate. We tried isolation. It didn't work, of course—Jeep's a hard, mean little virus, uses everything and anything as a vector: air, water, saliva, sperm, food, feces . . . everything."

"Does it affect animals?"

"Doesn't seem to."

"So where does it come from?"

"That's what I'd like to know. If we had the records of the first settlers, maybe it would turn out that it was a genetically altered virus that got transferred from an animal to a human, and became something else."

"It would have to have had much more than one crossover point. That seems to preclude accidents."

Lu Wai smiled, that hard sliding of muscle again. "You haven't seen a man stuck out in the boonies for weeks on end. He'll fuck anything after a while."

Marghe wanted to believe this was Mirror humor, but Lu Wai did not seem amused. "I didn't know there were any large animals here."

"I haven't heard tell of any. Maybe they all died, too. But it doesn't matter to me where the virus came from. I'd just like to know how to kill it so we could all get off this planet."

"I didn't think you were so unhappy."

"I'm not. I'd just like to be able to go home, leave this place where so many friends died."

There was nothing Marghe could say to that. She thought about the *Kurst* riding in orbit, some young officer with her or his finger on the button that would detonate *Estrade*. If Hiam was right, none of them would ever go home.

"You haven't told me how it felt when you went down with it," she said.

Lu Wai leaned back against the side of the sled and stared at the clouds. "Everyone's symptoms are different. Mine started with a rash on the underside of my arms. A couple of hours after my arms started itching, my eyeballs began to hurt, then I knew. I didn't bother with the medical station; I went to my mod instead. I figured if I was going to die, it may as well be in peace, away from all that hustle. It's only about a mile from the station to my mod, but I had difficulty walking those last few yards, it hits that fast. My joints ached, knees and hips mostly, though they didn't swell up like some people's do, and then the headache started, and the itchy eyes and throat. Then the cough."

"How long were you sick?"

"Three days. I was weak much longer."

Marghe wanted to reach out and take the Mirror's hand, something, but Lu Wai had them both clenched around her scarf, remembering. "If I got it," she asked her gently, "what would you advise?"

The Mirror looked at Marghe speculatively. "I saw the vaccine specs; it's your basic artificial antigen, but weaker than killed virus, because it's not very specific. The adjuvants should make up for that. It should work."

"But just suppose it doesn't."

"Complications are almost always respiratory. Make sure you're warm and dry, move your arms around a bit, give your lungs a chance to pump out any phlegm that might collect. Drink lots of fluids. Water's best, but boil it. Dap would be okay because of that, but remember it's a stimulant—not a very good idea when your body's already weak. Eat lots of fruit and vegetables if you can get them. Commonsense precautions."

Marghe nodded her thanks, but the Mirror was not finished.

"If anything happens, if you lose your pills, or it doesn't work, get back to Port Central, to a medic. Don't mess with it. That's the best advice I can give you."

"Kris flies!" Letitia called, pointing.

Marghe pulled her scarf back up and tightened the knot. She breathed steadily through her nose, in and out, and followed Letitia's finger. They were dark on the horizon, like smoke. She breathed more deeply.

Lu Wai squatted next to her and unfastened her medical roll. "Are you allergic to any of the antihistamines or bronchiodilators?"

"No." She watched the swarm grow bigger.

The Mirror nodded, satisfied. "I've never heard of a swarm attacking without cause, but there's always a first time. If they come close, curl up and expose as little of yourself as you can. And try not to panic."

"I won't."

Letitia had already altered course to the shortest route off the olla carpet, but the kris flies were getting closer. Marghe hunched down and concentrated on her breathing. If she did get stung, she was confident she could neutralize the worst of the venom herself, or at least keep the effects localized. She closed her eyes and listened. A thousand, a hundred thousand pairs of wings beat the air, whisking it to a whining froth that blew into her ears and made her throat itch. It sounded wrong, and Marghe realized she had been expecting the drone of hornets or bees. The volume did not increase. She raised her head cautiously.

The swarm poured by almost close enough to touch, undulating and shimmering in the diffuse light like a silk scarf in the wind, gold, green, and black. The colors did not trigger Earthlearned fears; they were beautiful. All four women watched the swarm pass over the horizon, and were quiet a long time afterward.

THE EARLY morning sky was mother-of-pearl; in its light, the chevrons and gray medic flashes on Lu Wai's shoulders shone almost silver as the Mirror pointed a free hand westward. "Look over there."

At first Marghe could see nothing different; then the grass changed from yellowish green to black. Letitia put down her schematic and clambered up into the front. "The blasted heath," she said. They watched the black plain spread out to their left like a pool of charcoal dust.

Marghe leaned out to take a closer look. She thought she saw fresh green shoots pushing through the withered remains. "I'd like to go in closer."

"Not advisable," Letitia said, "at least in the sled. It's not a good idea on foot either, unless you're with someone who knows about burnstone."

Burnstone could smolder under the ground for years before sighing into ash. Company had triggered several serious burns before they had learned to listen to the indigenes and avoid these unstable areas.

"This is the big one," Letitia said. "The one that got SEC's knickers in a twist."

Marghe nodded. The *Jink and Oriyest v. Company* case. "I wonder what happened to the owners."

Letitia leaned against the waist-high siding of the sled and watched the ruined grass flow beneath them. "Nobody owns this land," she said.

"For now, the journeywomen are letting Jink and Oriyest use some land to the north and west," Lu Wai said. "Not far from here."

"If it's not far, I'd like to visit."

Marghe felt the women in the sled tense. Letitia and Lu Wai almost looked at each other but did not, and in the back of the sled, Ude sat up. No one said anything.

"What have I said wrong?"

"Nothing. It's just that they'll be busy right now, getting in their flock," Lu Wai said easily, without taking her eyes from the horizon.

Letitia nodded. "We'd waste a day or two tracking them down, and we need to get these cables laid and the relay in place before the weather turns. You're operating under a tight schedule, too."

Marghe looked at them one at a time. They had closed ranks against her, but why? What was going on? "Are you saying you refuse to take me to find Jink and Oriyest?"

"No," Letitia said, "just that we'd search for days and more than likely not find them."

Which meant the same thing, Marghe thought. If they did not want her to meet Jink and Oriyest, there was nothing she could do. She was angry, and did not bother to hide it. "I don't know why you don't want me to find them, but I'm not stupid enough to waste my time trying to force you. Perhaps on my way back."

She pushed her way past Letitia and stared out across the burn. A faint speck hovered over the western horizon: a herd bird. Marghe watched it for a long time, feeling like an outsider again.

THE WIND was strong, driving tall, sail-heavy clouds across the gray sky. Lu Wai and Ude were both asleep, and Letitia was making notes on her wristcom.

Marghe held the sled's stick in both hands. In the west water flashed silver, surrounded by large dark shapes. She eased the stick left and the sled veered. Letitia looked up.

"Ah. The river Ho."

Marghe ignored her. She was still angry.

"The people around here call those tall things skelter trees. When you get nearer, you'll see why." She must have sensed Marghe's hostility, and went back to her calculations.

The Ho was broad and flat but the banks were steep. Long-fronded water plants trailed downstream like bony green fingers. Something leapt into the water with a plop. Marghe slowed the sled to an easy glide and cruised up to a skelter tree. It was tall, over fifty feet, and she could see where it got its name: branches of uniform thickness grew in a spiral up and around the charcoal black trunk, like a helter-skelter. The single-fingered leaves were arranged symmetrically along both sides of the branches and were broad as Marghe's outstretched hand, the delicate green of lentil sprouts. They hardly moved in the wind. She brought the sled to a hovering standstill and reached up to touch one.

Something shrieked and chittered, shaking the branch until the leaves shivered.

"It might be a wirrel," Letitia said. "I think they live in these trees. They're small, but they've been known to bite."

Marghe wondered if Letitia was waiting to see if the SEC rep wanted to touch an alien leaf badly enough to risk a bite from an equally alien animal. Well, Letitia would be disappointed; there were other trees, and she would not always have an audience. She backed up the sled.

"The river winds a bit, but it runs all the way to Holme Valley," Letitia said. "If you want to see lots of wildlife, just follow the bank."

"No." Lu Wai was awake and looking at the sky. "That would add hours to our journey, and I don't like the look of these clouds." She clambered into the front and gestured Marghe aside. "I'll take the stick. Things are going to get rough."

Clouds gathered on the northeastern horizon, greasy and heavy, an army wearing unpolished mail. Marghe relinquished the controls. Lu Wai slammed the stick as far forward as it would go.

Marghe lurched and had to cling on. Once again she felt like an outsider, a stranger who did not know what was happening, what to expect.

Letitia scrambled into the front. "I don't think we're going to make it to Holme Valley before the storm." Marghe wondered why she was grinning so hard.

The wind grew stronger. It flattened the grass and slid its hand under the sled, tilting it sideways on its cushion of air until it skittered like a bead of water on a hot skillet. As they headed north, outcroppings of gray rock became more frequent and Lu Wai had to ease back on the stick to maneuver safely. Ude woke up, took one look at the sky, and started to tie down the cable coils and clip lids on the storage bins.

They raced over the grass; the rotor hum deepened and the sled slowed as they began to climb a steady incline. Halfway up, the turf was scattered with rocks.

Lu Wai hardly slowed. She took them right over the first few, cursed as she swerved around the boulders. Letitia tapped Marghe on the shoulder and pointed ahead to a grayish red clump of rock.

"See it?" She had to yell over the wind. Marghe nodded. "She's making for that crag. We'll ground the sled there, take shelter." She grinned again. "You'll get a good view."

A good view of what?

They both clutched the siding as the sled bucked and twisted and narrowly missed scraping its hull on a jagged overhang. The incline was steep now, and the sled groaned and rumbled, vibrating through Marghe's bones and making her teeth ache.

They edged past a tumble of broken boulders and between two leaning stacks of sculpted and striated stone; the wind followed them, thrusting its tongue into every hollow and crack, making the rock sing and scream like a crazy woman in restraints. Lu Wai backed them right up against the rock. Then the wind died.

"Do you feel it?" Letitia sounded eager; her head was tilted back as though she were drinking rain.

Marghe began to say no, but then she did. It was like being lowered slowly into water, feet first: the hairs on her ankles lifted, then on her legs, her stomach, her arms, the back of her neck. Electromagnetic disturbance.

"We're far enough from the epicenter to be safe and sheltered here," Lu Wai said as she cut the power. In the absence of the wind, the tick and sigh of the plastic settling slowly to the ground was eerie. An insect hummed past in a blur of wings, hovering over the tiny yellow flowers amongst the brown spikes of moss that spilled from the crevices at the base of the rock.

Letitia jumped down and scrambled up and around the overhang. Lu Wai and Ude slid covers over the instrument panels and clipped them down, then began securing the plastic storage bins with all their supplies. They were quick and efficient; there was nothing Marghe could do to help. She hesitated, then climbed up after Letitia.

The technician was lying on her stomach behind the remains of a dead tree that pointed up from the sparse soil like a bony finger. She looked up and grinned when Marghe joined her.

The sky was slippery with cloud massed in ranks of zinc and pewter. Lambent. Marghe could feel the atmosphere curdling, twisting in on itself, pulling the air from her lungs like a fire. She was slick with sweat. The static grew, crawling through her hair until she thought her scalp would creep right off her skull. An ache started behind her eyes and in the hinge of her jaw.

The world lit up like a silent photograph, flat and grainy, limning the tree stark as a charcoal slash against a parchment sky. Lightning exploded like blue-white cat-o'-nine-tails until sound rolled and cracked and splintered and Marghe could no longer tell if it was the ground shaking or her muscles; she felt deaf and blind and exposed to her core. Electricity and exhilaration surged and hissed over her bones. The storm held its breath a moment and she heard Letitia laughing, whoops and rills and great ringing ululations, and when the lightning cracked again Marghe laughed too; they held each other with heads back, mouths wide and open from the throat down to the stomach, laughing and shaking with exultation.

The storm dropped to silence, leaving Marghe blinking and Lu

Wai shouting up at them. "Get down! The wind will hit any minute."

Marghe looked at Letitia; the engineer's grin had stiffened to a muscle spasm and her eyes were rolled back in her head. Marghe heard the rattle and scramble of the Mirror climbing the scar. Without letting go of Letitia, she peered over the edge.

"Get her down. Please, Marghe, get her off there right now."

Marghe took a slow, steady breath. "All right. I'm all right. Letitia's . . . If you're steady where you are, stay there. I'll see if I can lower her over the edge."

Lu Wai's face was pale and indistinct. "Go as fast as you can."

Marghe wrapped both arms around Letitia's waist. The technician was stiff and unresponsive but still fizzing with silent laughter. "Letitia. Letitia, can you hear me?" She tightened her grip and half lifted, half trundled her to the edge of the rock. She changed grip, holding Letitia under the arms, and closed her eyes. Breathed in through her nose, out through her mouth, in and out, harder now, deeper. In, out. In. Out. She pumped strength around her body. She would pay for this later.

"Hurry, Marghe. Please."

Marghe opened her eyes, then walked Letitia off the edge of the cliff, holding her up using the muscles in her legs and back and arms. She lowered her as fast as she dared; bending a little, going onto her knees, then down on her elbows until only her back and shoulders and arms held the technician's weight. She lay on her stomach and hung Letitia down like a plumbline.

Lu Wai reached up and took the stiff woman by the hips. In the quiet, the Mirror's grunt was loud as she steadied herself and the engineer. "I have her. Get yourself down. Fast."

Marghe swung herself over the edge, hung for a moment, then dropped. The grass was dry and prickly, the yellow moss flower sharp smelling in the still air. She helped Lu Wai drag Letitia into the shelter between the crag and the sled.

The wind hit like a sledgehammer swung low and slow and easy, thudding into her ribs and roaring over her ears until all she could hear was air. A heavy plate of tree bark flew out of nowhere and smashed down onto the sled; the plastic storage bin burst open and the wind tore the packaged rations to shreds, whirled them away. Her traveling food.

Marghe did not dare move. The rock under her shoulder shuddered as boulders rolled and crashed against its other side. She hunched down into the warmth of bodies. Someone put an arm around her waist; she leaned her forehead against a shoulder. She no longer felt like an outsider. The boiling clouds brought rain that pattered, then drummed on the torn food wrappers.

MARGHE WOKE to the distant thunk of a mallet. A wooden mallet. Her coverlet smelled comfortably of use and herbs, tempting her to stay in bed a while longer, resting the muscles she had overused the day before. Ude's bed was empty. She looked around, wondering how late it was. The ceiling was low and domed; its longitudinal rib arched from the floor, over her head, and back down to the floor at the other end of the lodge. Lateral ribs of black wood were chinked with wattling and daub, decorated in earth tones. Morning seeped through the weave of the door hanging and filled the lodge with air and sunlight. She sat up. Sunlight.

She swung herself off the sleeping shelf and pushed aside the door hanging.

Beyond the trees, Jeep's sky was Wedgwood blue. Sunshine poured into the valley, filling it with a light like rich yellow cream, sliding over her skin, turning the hair on her arms to gold wire. She just stood there, letting the sunshine push sweet, warm fingers into her aching muscles.

Under her bare feet the grass was cool and luscious with dew; still early, then. She could see no one, but the sound of mallets floated downstream like underwater knocking, and from one of the stone-walled barns near the bank she heard the soft hiss and thump, hiss and thump of threshing.

The edge of a cloud veiled the sun and shadow raced down

one side of the valley, blurring the wide glitter of the Ho to a dull gleam, then running up the other side. Her feet were wet and cold. She turned to go back inside. And stopped.

Last night she had been exhausted, and the hot swirling torches of the women who escorted her and Ude to the lodge had only smeared the dark with red. She had noticed the roughness of the roof and walls but assumed it was thatching. She had been wrong. The outside of the lodge was alive with greenery. It looked like a small hill nestling amongst the trees. She reached out and touched a pale green leaf. Cool and silky. Another leaf fluttered as a beetle the size of her thumb skittered out of sight. A wirrel shrieked, then another. This time she did not jump.

Curious, she ducked inside the lodge to take another look at the central rib and the branching lateral spars. Branches. The structural skeleton was a skelter tree.

She dressed, then prowled the lodge, picking up the wooden bowls, polished with use, looking under the table, noting the way the underside was not planed but still rough with black bark, the leg joints fastened with wooden pegs. There was a knife on the table, its blade made of a smoky, vitreous substance: olla, named after the flowers that grew over the raw olla beds. She tested it against the hair on her arm. It was extremely sharp. The pitcher of water was made of red-glazed clay; the cutting slab was stone, like the pestle and mortar. A shelf ran around the lodge at waist height, piled with neatly folded clothes. She ran her hands over them, under them, between them. They were smooth and rough: cotton and canvas, leather and wool. They were warm. Her knuckles bumped on buttons of horn and wood, caught in ties and laces—no cold shock of metal fasteners. The door bar slid back and forth on greased wooden blocks that were glued and pegged into place.

Marghe followed the winding path between lodges toward the river and, she hoped, Lu Wai and Letitia. She popped a memory chip from her wristcom, inserted another, touched RECORD, and continued her notes from the day before. "Holme Valley has a population of about four hundred women and children. Sometime in the next ten days this will swell by another hundred or so as the community north of here drives their herds down from the pastures to winter in the valley. The women of Singing Pastures and those of the valley form two distinct communities. They even use different calendars dictated by different moons: the valley people divide the year into fifteen months of eighteen days each; the women of the pastures reckon with a ten-month calendar, each month twenty-seven days long."

She hit PAUSE. She wished she could spare the time to stay and observe the mingling of the different populations, watch how they interacted. It would be like being able to go back in time and observe the early symbiotic interactions between people from human history on Earth.

A wirrel shrieked. Marghe went very still. This was not Earth; this was Jeep, a planet of alien species, a place where the human template of dual sexes had been torn to shreds and thrown away. This was something new. She knew these people had evolved cultures resting on bases very different from those of any Earth people; she did not know whether that made these women human or something entirely Other.

She shook herself. The question, What was humanity? was as old as the species, one she never expected to answer. She resumed her walk through the trees, but more slowly, thinking and occasionally making notes.

"If skelter trees grow at approximately the same rate as Earth trees, then to shape such a tree into a dwelling place must take forty or more years." She imagined a family group selecting a tree, bending it, pruning it judiciously as babies were born, girls grew, and old women died. Did the lodge retain its integrity when the tree died? She exited RECORD and looked up botanical records. Skelter trees lasted two hundred years. "The use of such building methods must be indicative of the social temperament of these people: patient, planning for the long term. Also willing to experiment."

The trees ended a few yards from the river in a grassy slope, hammocked and tufted here and there where it grew over old tree stumps. Marghe wondered whether the tree fellers had used axes with stone or olla blades.

Someone was walking through the trees toward the path she had just left. Color flashed. Marghe recognized the fatigues.

"Lu Wai!" She waved and the Mirror saw her. "How's Letitia?"

"Angry with herself and a bit shamefaced for making you risk yourself like that. Otherwise, she's fine. I was coming to see if you'd join us for breakfast."

"I'm breakfasting with one of the women who farm the biggest field here. Cassil. I hope to trade for some travel rations. But thank you." She paused. "This thing with Letitia, I gather it's happened before."

"More than once."

"Is it organic?"

"I haven't been able to find anything." Lu Wai shrugged. "Which doesn't mean it's not there. The diagnostic tools we have are primitive." She sighed. "But what do I know? I'm only a medic."

Marghe heard the hours of tests and record-searching in the Mirror's voice and could find nothing to say. She watched Lu Wai walk away and wondered if Danner knew about Letitia. Yes, the Mirror commander would know; she would have to know everything in order to make Jeep work. She would know, too, that Lu Wai would do everything in her power to keep Letitia safe.

CASSIL HAD hair the red-brown of strong tea, and gray eyes. She also had a baby on her hip, which, judging by its fair hair and brown eyes, was not hers. She looked tired and utterly human. She spoke slowly and with much repetition for Marghe's sake.

"What we have isn't mine or my kith's to give."

"But you farm the land?"

Cassil sighed, as though she had tried to explain this many times before and failed. "My kith farms well. Everyone sees that. So the journeywomen give us more land to work. We work it well, produce more food, leave the land fresh for the next season's growing. Everyone benefits. We use the food to feed ourselves, and for trata." The word she used did not mean trade, exactly; it meant trade as the first step on a journey whose outcome was uncertain—an opening gambit in a game that might continue for generations. Trata could be between two people, between two or more kiths, or between several communities. Frequently it was all three, each exchange resonating with another in the web.

The baby squirmed and Cassil switched it to her other hip. "If I give you food, or good boots, a woman might say to me, 'Cassil, if you had given me that food, I would have made you two fine hangings for your lodge, and given you first pick of my next catch. But you gave it to that stranger woman and neither of us has gained anything from each other. Tell me, Cassil, what did this stranger woman give you in return?' And what would I say to that?" The baby wriggled again, more determinedly this time. Cassil jiggled her up and down, gave her a finger to suck.

Marghe was acutely conscious of her fatigue, the ache in her muscles, as she opened her empty hands. "My kith is large and very powerful."

Cassil regarded her a moment. "Then why not return to your large and very powerful kith for more supplies?"

Because they might not give me any more, because Danner might not let me go again, Marghe wanted to shout. *Because I am utterly alone on this world.* She had nobody; no kith, no kin, no community. Danner, Letitia, Cassil . . . they all sat in the center of a webwork of colleagues, friends, lovers. Family. She was alone, and scared. All she had was herself and her breathing exercises and her FN-17. Sitting here, across from a woman secure in her own community, all of that came home to her. She was alone on a strange and dangerous world, and she knew it showed on her face.

Cassil tilted her head. "You are an orphan here," she said softly, and touched Marghe's cheek with the tip of one finger.

The warm, dry finger against her cheek pulled memories up from the well: her mother laughing and throwing away a batch of burned bread, saying, *Never mind, we'll buy some;* ripping the computer plug from the wall, furious with some review; making her a fan from yellow tissue paper when she had a fever, then folding it up into a paper hat when she realized it wouldn't work. Her mother singing a nonsense song, telling her stories of Macau, and of Taishan where she had been conceived; trying to smile before she died. It hit her all over again: she could never come back from Jeep and tell her mother how useful her organizational techniques had been in analyzing her notes for publication; she and her mother could never share tea and a funny story of misunderstandings with an alien people. Her mother was dead.

Marghe found herself hunched over, arms wrapped around her stomach; they were wet. She was crying. Fatigue, she told herself; her blood sugar was down. She breathed, hardly hearing Cassil moving around, tucking the baby into a blanket on the sleeping shelf, poking the fire into a blaze, swinging the dap kettle over the flames. Busy alien sounds. Water rumbled in the stone pot.

She felt the warmth of Cassil standing over her and turned her head, then took the worn square of cloth and wiped her eyes in silence. She thought about Danner saying *I don't know how else to prove my faith*, of Kahn saying *I know how rough it is, coming down alone*. She had thrust their offers of friendship back at them.

Then she thought of Hiam, and of the *Kurst*, and of Danner's unspoken certainty that the Mirrors would not be leaving Jeep. Here, now, with Cassil, she had a chance to help them, in her own particular way, at the same time as she helped herself. Trata was the key.

Cassil put two steaming bowls of dap between them. "So," she said quietly, folding her hands, "you're an orphan."

Marghe did not want to distract them both by trying to explain the concept of *father*. She nodded. Her face felt hot and swollen. "But not entirely alone. I have been . . . adopted, into a rich and powerful kith, but I'm new to their ways, and yours." Cassil smiled as if to say that was not news. Marghe chose her words carefully. "Someday, they—we—may be your neighbors. We could be useful to you."

"There's no burnstone in this valley, but perhaps your friends will find some other way to hurt a land they don't understand. How will that be useful to us?"

"We've learned a lesson, and how to listen."

Cassil appraised her. "Perhaps that's so."

Marghe opened a pocket and slid out a thin strip of copper. She put it next to Cassil's bowl. Cassil picked it up, rubbed it, weighed it in her hand, but Marghe could not tell what she was thinking. She opened another pocket and took out a similar strip of iron. Cassil compared the two, then put them back on the table. She looked down at them a long time, then nodded abruptly. "Talking is thirsty work." She drained her bowl, refilled it.

They ate breakfast, and they talked, and ate lunch. It was late afternoon by the time they agreed: three months' travel food, a pair of fur leggings, and a small sack of dap in exchange for one kilo of copper, two of iron, and guaranteed special consideration—if not quite friendship—from all Company personnel presently at Port Central. Trata. She would need to bargain for furs and a horse from the women of Singing Pastures, if they were amenable to trade.

"The trata must be witnessed by a viajera." A journeywoman teller of news, Marghe translated, though obviously with some ritual function. "We expect T'orre Na soon." Cassil's face rounded with pleasure, and perhaps a little worry. "She comes to lead the pattern singing for Rhedan's deepsearch. I'm Rhedan's choose-mother."

Marghe mentally compared this with Eagan's notes: the ritual name-choosing by pubescent girls, and the concept of different mother roles within a kith. But what was pattern singing, and why did it give Cassil cause for concern? "Congratulations," she said cautiously. Perhaps she could observe the ceremony. But her time was limited, and there would be equally interesting ceremonies on Tehuantepec. "How soon do you expect the journeywoman?"

Cassil shrugged. "Not before the women of Singing Pastures drive their herds down. She's a few days down the windpath, with Jink and Oriyest's flock, and that one of your kith, Day."

Marghe did not know what she meant. "Who?"

"Your kith who is called Day, the one adopted by Jink and Oriyest. The one Jink saved when the burn went." She looked at Marghe curiously. "You don't know the story? It's a good one. T'orre Na could sing it for you."

A woman called Day, her kith. A Company woman . . . It made sense now. This was why Lu Wai and Letitia had not wanted her to meet Jink and Oriyest. Day would be there. Day, a Mirror who had gone AWOL. One of the many missing, presumed dead. How many of the others were alive?

She would have to talk to Lu Wai about this. Later.

"I can't wait for T'orre Na. Perhaps one of my adopted kith can witness for me." It would take several days to get the relay up and working. Lu Wai could be her proxy.

IT WAS another two hundred miles north to Singing Pastures. While Letitia and Ude worked on the relay, Marghe rode north with Lu Wai on the sled. She watched the Mirror's gloved hands gentle on the stick, her indecipherable face beneath the quilted cap, and wondered what would drive a Mirror to go native.

To go native. She rolled the phrase around her mouth. It tasted of scorn. And fear. Why did the idea make her so afraid? And how many, how many Mirrors and technicians were out there, living in these strange cultures? They could tell her so much.

"How many people know about Day?" she demanded when they stopped to eat and relieve themselves.

"Officer Day is listed as missing, presumed dead," Lu Wai said calmly, and carried on peeling a goura. She cut the fruit and held out half. Juice ran over her wrist. "Want some?"

"I want to know what happened to Day. Have you seen her since she . . . since she left? And are there others?"

Lu Wai put down the fruit. "I haven't seen her, no, but Letitia saw her last year, and she leaves messages now and then. Usually written ones, but sometimes message stones, or a knotted string. She does that as a joke, I think. She knows we can't read them."

Marghe thought she sounded wistful. "Would you like to go, too?"

Lu Wai thought about that, then shook her head. "I think she gets lonely."

Perhaps she was lonelier before, Marghe thought, among a people who did not understand her.

"Tell Danner," she said suddenly. "Tell her about Day. She needs to know." She thought of the *Kurst*, of the vaccine ticking away like a bomb in her pocket. "And if there are any others, find them, talk to them. You won't be betraying them. Persuade Danner to offer them amnesty, even let them go back to where they've been all this time. Just get them to talk to you. You're going to need what they know."

And the connections they've forged.

At least she had been able to set trata in motion, for Danner, for Lu Wai and Letitia.

For all of us.

She wondered what this woman Day was like, and where she had found so much courage.

Chapter Four

Singing Pastures howled. Splits in the chalky rock bounding the easternmost pasture funneled icy gusts into a river of air and sleet. Marghe sat with her back pressed against a rock wall, huddled so tight between the herders, Holle and Shill, that she looked like the midsection of some strange fur-clad mammal.

In front of them, tethered nose to tail, three horses formed a living windbreak. Their winter coats were growing in and their manes were stiff and black. They were oddly proportioned to Marghe's eyes: thick necks and barrel bodies, like brown zebra. She wondered what their gene map would look like.

The saddle on the middle mount, Marghe's, was unadorned leather, as were the reins; the stirrup irons were unpolished wood, and the bit a four-inch sausage of poor-quality brown olla. The mare herself, Pella, was fit enough but old and beginning to lose muscle. Holle and Shill's mounts were hard-legged, their leather work finely tooled and polished, stained rich reds and purples, and stitched with green and gold thread. Marghe supposed the herders had very little else to occupy their time once the taar herds were corralled for the winter.

The noise made conversation impossible. She huddled down a little further in her furs that smelled of horses and women and cold air, and wished the wind would drop. Holle and Shill had seen by now that she could ride well enough to be trusted with one of their horses, and she was eager to get back to the cave, hand over the metal as trade, and prepare to leave. Every hour was precious. The sky was heavy, the color of wet ash.

The lead horse lifted its head and whickered. Shill listened hard, then tapped Holle on the shoulder. They stood, leaning into the wind, and began untethering the animals. Marghe stayed where she was, pulling her muscles tighter against the expected fist of wind when the horses moved. Holle squatted in front of her.

"We must . . ." The words were lost in the wind but Marghe understood her gesture. They wanted her to mount up. Shill was already mounted, holding the reins of the other horses. Marghe gritted her teeth and swung herself up.

The hot stale smell of animal filled the gully. Pella stiffened beneath her. Shill leaned half out of her saddle and grabbed Pella's headstall, pulling hard to make the mare high-step backward.

A river of four-legged flesh thundered by, eyes rolling and neck tendons straining. Here and there mounted women flicked whips, but it seemed to Marghe that the taars ran from something more frightening than the crack of plaited leather.

When the strangers were passing, Shill released the headstall and leaned to shout in her ear. "We follow!" She pointed to make sure Marghe understood.

Marghe thumped her heels into Pella's ribs and clung on as they jounced down the twisting trail. It had been a long time since she had done any prolonged riding. Her thigh muscles trembled and the wind whipping under her hood made her ears ache with cold, but the two women ahead of her lashed their horses into a headlong gallop and she knew she could not have slowed Pella if she had wanted to. She wondered what they were running from, then stopped wondering to concentrate on staying in the saddle.

The slope steepened and Pella skidded on loose shale, nearly sending them both facefirst. Marghe remembered Janet Eagan's warning: *Do you have any idea how many different ways a person could get herself killed? For all I know, Winnie could have fallen off her horse and broken her neck the second day out.* The ride became a nightmare.

Then, miraculously, the wind died; they were in a high-walled side cut. With an effort that made her hiss, she swung out of the saddle. Her boot dislodged a pebble, sending it clattering on bare rock. The cut was sharp with the smell of limegrass. It made her eyes sting.

"The cave's ahead." Holle slung a leg over her horse's neck and slid down with an ease Marghe envied. "There'll be food and dap." Shill took the horses.

The cave was dim and hot with animals. The herd milled and lowed restlessly.

"Why's the herd sheltering in a cave?" Marghe asked.

"Hyrat."

"What Shill means," Holle said, "is that a swarm of hyrat were spotted, so the droving started early. We don't know how big the pack is. If it's small, then we can fight them off at the cave entrance and the herd will be safe without having to run the flesh off their bones."

"And if it's big?"

"We'll run."

The pack turned out to be small. Marghe helped herd the taars out of the cave, and when she dismounted outside she saw a pile of dead hyrat. Their pelts were shades of gray, like the rock, and looked soft. Marghe wanted to touch one but was wary of vermin. Each strand of hair seemed unusually thick. Perhaps they were hollow, like ting grass. Their forequarters were heavy, the pelt matted around the chest and throat of male and female. When she saw their fangs, she understood why. The upper canines were grayish yellow and long enough to leave matted channels in the fur of the lower jaw; if they fought amongst themselves, they would need the protection. No tail to speak of. It was the eyes that looked alien: silvery, with horizontal slit pupils.

HOLLE AND Shill strapped Marghe's belongings behind her saddle. Marghe pulled out her map for a final check. Without a navigation satellite, she would have to reckon with map and compass.

Holle looked at it over her shoulder. "Those who don't know their way around Tehuantepec have no business going up there in winter."

"It's not winter yet."

"It will be up there." Holle picked up the map and stroked its smooth plastic surface with her fingertips. "This is your path?" She pointed to the broken line that stretched northeast from Singing Pastures to the forest and Ollfoss. Marghe nodded. "You'd be wise to avoid the tribes that move south for the winter." She traced a new route with her finger. There was dirt under her nail. "Take a more easterly path the first few days, then turn north."

"How much longer will that take?"

Holle shrugged. "A day, two days."

Marghe frowned, weighing the delay against Holle's seriousness and others' previous advice. She rolled her sleeve back, touched RECORD, and indicated new headings into her wristcom, then re-set her compass reminder. Holle watched, curious.

"That will help you find your way?"

Marghe pressed REPLAY and Holle laughed at the sound of Marghe's recorded voice. "Like a southern mimic bird!" She looked at Marghe slyly. "Maybe those stories are true."

"Which stories?"

"That there are people here from another world."

Later, repacking her map, Marghe wrapped her fingers around an unfamiliar shape. She pulled it out: a knife. The flint blade was short and ugly. She pushed it to the bottom of her pack.

SNOW SLANTED across the mouth of a smaller cave. Beyond a brake of tanglethorn, the clouds were dirty yellow, heavy with more snow. Shivering hard, Marghe shaved slivers of bark from the dry tanglethorn and heaped them in a pyramid around a kindling pellet. Then she peeled back the metal strip and waited for the chemical reaction. A curl of bark puffed into flame. She blew on the tiny blaze, adding bigger stems of the thorn until the fire crackled. Pella snorted and backed as far from the flames as she could.

Her shivering eased and her face and hands tingled and ached as blood squeezed through previously closed capillaries. The scratches on her hands stung. She slapped her arms around her body a couple of times and tried not to think of what might have happened if she had not found the cave before the snowfall had become a blizzard.

"Your turn now, Pella."

Her fingers were thick and red and felt as though they belonged to somebody else. She struggled with the clumsy wooden girth buckles and staggered a little as she dragged the saddle off. There was a cloak in her pack. She pulled it out and rubbed the mare down with it as best she could. Pella sighed and leaned against her. Marghe thumped her on the withers until the mare grumbled and straightened up. She draped the cloak over the horse's back, dragged her pack over to the fire, and sat down, exhausted by the cold.

Food would help. She could name only half the items she pulled from her pack: goura, sun-dried until shriveled to the size and color of large apricots; moist wild rice, pressed into squares and wrapped in crumbly rice paper; honey cakes; thick succulent leaves, like vine leaves, rolled to finger size; nuts; strange crunchy shapes that tasted vaguely of bacon; strips of smoked wirrel . . . She chewed various combinations and decided that the green fingers were good stuffed with the rice, and dried goura went well with honey cake.

She filled a nosebag for Pella, then lay down and listened to her heart beat and the wind howl over Tehuantepec.

When she was young she had lain awake in the sticky heat of Macau and listened to the chirrup of insects and the beat of her heart. It had frightened her that her life depended upon such a fragile organ, that a lump of muscle hardly bigger than her fist was all that kept the blood pumping around her body. She wondered how thick the heart walls were, and if it ever just got tired and gave up, decided it had had enough of sucking and pushing and squeezing blood around her veins. She lay with her hands over her ears, only to discover that made the sound more distinct. Humming herself to sleep worked, or drumming little rhythms on her futon.

As she grew older, she learned to listen more to the beat that underlay her whole life: how it speeded up when she was tense or tired; how it was smooth and confident when she exercised regularly; how she could make it change if she breathed fast and hard, or slow and easy. It fascinated her. She took up yoga, then chi kung and tai chi, until she could increase blood flow to various parts of her body at will. Then she went to Beaver, and had all her confidence beaten out of her.

The months in Wales afterward were full of anxieties and short breath, phobias and panic. Her doctor referred her to a meditation specialist; he said to do this, and do this, but she could not relax enough to try. The specialist referred her on to the experimental-psychology department in Llangelli.

They hooked her up to machines that measured her alpha waves, her blood flow, her temperature, the electrical activity of her skin, the gaseous content of her blood and its pH, the dilation of her pupils. With different words, they helped her relearn that her body was an intricate mechanism made of interconnecting parts, a homeostatic system: change this, and this alters, which changes this. And she relearned: with breath and exercise, music and self-hypnosis, until now she could cut blood supply from a hand or a foot, channel pain, slow or speed her metabolism, and more. Once, at a party, she had amused a friend by blushing and paling at will.

Later, on her own, she took her training further, experimenting with sensitizing her body to magnetic and electrical fields. She had hoped to write a paper on biofeedback, autogenics, and the supernormal experience in myth.

Pella snorted, too hot under her makeshift blanket. Marghe took it off, checked the nosebag, scratched the mare behind her ears. The blizzard howled.

WOMAN AND horse were hunched and dark against the snow; veils of cold mist filtered the afternoon to pearl. The only sound was the crunch of hooves and the creak of leather as Marghe's weight shifted with her mare's walk.

"Faster now, Pella."

Her quiet voice was sucked away, swallowed by the silence. Not for the first time, she swung in the saddle and peered into the mist behind her. There was nothing there, nothing but white quiet and the snort of her mare's breath.

Her nose began to drip. There was nothing to wipe it on.

Something was different. She lifted her head, reined Pella to a halt, turned her head this way and that. There, to her left: a darker patch. The air seemed to thrum, tickling the fine nerve endings under her skin as though she was in the presence of a strong magnetic field. She clucked the horse into a walk.

A megalith loomed before her; others curved into the mist. She nudged Pella closer and leaned from the saddle to run a gloved hand down its side. Where she rubbed away frost, the stone was dark and pitted. She dismounted and walked around it. It was twice her mounted height, three times the thickness of her waist.

Who had made this? And why?

Not bothering to remount, she led Pella from one stone to another. The sleeve of her overfur was stiff with frost; with difficulty, she uncovered her wristcom, touched RECORD.

"There are twenty-seven stones ranged in a circle but I can't judge how perfect its dimensions are. The purpose of these stones is unclear, but it should be noted that the tribes in this area utilize a twenty-seven-day lunar calendar." She ran her fingers over the pitted stone, wondering at the tingle she felt. She looked more closely and the electric tingle was replaced by excitement. "The tool marks appear weathered to an extent incompatible with the surmised landing date of the first settlers. These stones are very old."

They were impossibly old. These stones should not be here, unless humans had landed on Jeep hundreds, thousands of years earlier than supposed; or unless whoever, whatever, had quarried these megaliths, carefully shaped them with crude tools, and raised them up, was not human.

She stood in the snow, rubbing absently at her cold-numbed buttocks. Who made this? The large animals of Lu Wai's theories? But then they would be sentient animals. She stopped rubbing, cocked her head to the mist. All she heard was Pella pawing at the snow to get at the grass.

The day was fading. Marghe uncinched the girths and swung the saddle into the snow. It was lighter than it had been. Just outside the circle, she scraped away a big patch of snow for Pella. The tent took two minutes. It was dark inside; when her wristcom beeped she had to fumble for the FN-17, which she swallowed with a mouthful of icy water.

She popped the memory chip from her wristcom, replaced it with one on which she kept her personal journal. "I don't know what to make of these stones. Even here, in the tent, I can sense their presence. It's not quite like anything I've felt before. I wonder what their significance was, and to whom. Perhaps I should say *is*. Even assuming their makers are long dead, I feel sure they'd still be a focus of ritual activity. On a plain like this, stones this size would really mean something."

She rubbed her forehead. Of course they meant something. She hit OFF, curled up against the pack and saddle, and pulled her furs closer. She was tired. Outside, Pella munched loudly on half-frozen grass. They were both tired, tired and sick of the monotony of the almost-void where the only changes were ones of brightness, a brightness that dimmed as they plodded north.

Maybe she would be more coherent in the morning. She sighed and pressed CHIP EJECT. Nothing happened. She tried again. Nothing. Perhaps it was the cold. She took the wristcom off, held it between her palms, tucked her hands between her legs. While she waited for it to warm up, she breathed deep and slow, concentrating on finding a still, calm place in her center. She came out of her light trance and tried the eject button again.

Nothing. She tapped in a request for diagnostics. The chip was still accessible, but it suggested she take the wristcom to a reliable service outlet, as the port was jammed. She turned it over in her hand thoughtfully, then requested a chip map. The chip was almost full. She tried to run an erase, but the jam had triggered automatic erasure protection. There was room for perhaps fifteen hours of dictation. The operating memory would add another hour or so.

Fifteen hours was not enough to keep a decent record. Her trip would be useless. How much time would she lose by going back? She slid her map from its pocket and studied it. It would take weeks to get back to Port Central, weeks to return here. Not an option. She tried looking at the problem from another angle: how else could she record her observations? She had a little paper, not much. Perhaps she could persuade the women she met to give her cloth, and dyes to use as ink.

A sudden thought occurred to her. She tried the compass. The stones sent numbers flickering at random; useless. She was alone on Tehuantepec, plateau of myth and magic, strange beasts and wild tribes, with a malfunctioning compass, out of range of any communications relay, and with a SLIC that for all practical purposes was useless. Was this what had happened to Winnie Kimura?

 SHE AWOKE to dawn and hard-edged thoughts. She was not going to end up like Winnie. The compass damage might be as temporary as her proximity to the stones. There was only one way to find out. She slithered from her nightbag. If the damage was irreversible, then she could probably retrace her path. Even with bad weather, it should not take her more than twenty days to get back to the valley. She would be safe there until either a satellite came in range of the new communications relay or the spring came and she could make her own way back, somehow, to Port Central.

Pella whickered.

She rolled the nightbag into her pack. The sooner she left, the better. She dragged her pack through the tent flap, stood and stretched, and looked around.

Fear slapped the breath back into her lungs.

She was surrounded by riders on motionless horses. Shrouded in mist, with only their eyes visible under frost-rimed furs, they looked like apparitions of otherworld demons.

Marghe lifted her arms to show she was weaponless and walked stiffly toward the nearest figure. When she stepped within the cloud of breath wreathing the horse, its rider snapped down her spear. The stone tip brushed the furs at Marghe's belly, and she realized that stone could kill just as effectively as steel. The rider's eyes were heavy-lidded and light blue.

The point of the spear did not waver a hair's-breadth as the rider pulled back her hood to show flame-red braids and cheeks shining with grease.

"Stranger, why do you stand in the ringstones of the Echraidhe?"

The accent was difficult, but Marghe heard the cool lack of interest in her questioner's voice and her throat closed with fear.

"The penalty for soiling the stones of our ancestors is death."

The spear moved as the rider balanced it for a belly thrust. Fascinated, Marghe watched the point pull back for the disemboweling stroke.

"Uaithne!"

The spear before Marghe hesitated.

"I forbid, Uaithne." The voice was low and harsh.

"Levarch, she is nothing. A burden."

A woman of middle years kneed her horse forward until she sat eye to eye with Uaithne. "I forbid."

Uaithne shrugged. "I obey the Levarch in all things." She shouldered her spear.

Marghe realized she was not to die alone and unremarked in a heap of her own entrails, and her legs sagged. The Levarch leaned down and supported her under the arms. She shouted at another rider. "Aoife, take up the stranger. Uaithne, bring her horse and goods."

Marghe hardly had time to understand the Levarch's words. She saw a woman with dark features and a broken nose galloping at her, and then she was heaved across the bow of a saddle, bouncing uncomfortably on her stomach and clinging to the horse's shaggy withers. She could barely breathe and thought she might vomit, but when she tried to struggle upright, the rider named Aoife thumped her over her right kidney. She stayed still, face rubbing against the rough wool saddle blanket.

The riders made swift time over the snow. Marghe hung on, sick and frightened, eyes closed against the thunder of hooves just below her face.

The day wore on. Shock, cold, and hunger impaired Marghe's control. She could not maintain an even blood flow around her dangling body and drifted in and out of consciousness. Once, swimming out of a daze, she struggled until Aoife struck her a ringing blow to the temple.

The horses' slowing roused her. One side of her face was scraped raw. The horses came to a halt, pawing and snorting, and Marghe heard Pella's distinctive whicker. Aoife swung down from the saddle.

Marghe lifted her head. There was no thump, no shout of warning. It was almost dark and she could not see much. She felt a hand on her belt and flinched.

"Dismount." Aoife pulled, hard. Marghe slid backward onto her feet and crumpled onto the snow. She stared at her legs stupidly. Someone laughed: Uaithne. Aoife hauled her upright. Standing, Marghe towered above her.

"Open your clothes." Aoife had a knife in her hand. "Open your clothes or I'll cut them open."

Marghe pulled off her gloves. With the tip of her knife, Aoife pointed to the snow; Marghe dropped the gloves. Her fingers were stiff and she fumbled open the ties of her overfurs.

"And the rest."

The buttons of her fur waistcoast and densely woven shirt were easier.

"Hands on your head."

Marghe did as she was told. Aoife stepped in close and ran her free hand expertly over, between, and underneath the layers of clothing.

"What's this?" She pulled back the fur from the wristcom.

"It . . . I talk to it, and it remembers. Like a mimic bird." She hoped this tribeswoman had heard of the southern bird.

"Show me."

Marghe touched RECORD. "Weapon violence is obviously a feature of these people's lives," she said. She played it back. The sound was tinny in the cold, thin air, but recognizable.

"Give it to me."

Aoife felt around it for sharp edges, sniffed it, weighed it in her palm, hesitated, then slipped it into her belt pouch. She stood on Marghe's boot tips, pinning her to the ground, and palmed her way down the inside and outside of both legs. She found the FN-17. "This?"

Sweat beaded on Marghe's upper lip. She did not know the word for medicine. "It stops me becoming sick."

Aoife tucked it away with the wristcom. Hands back on her head, Marghe struggled to keep her face expressionless. Aoife stepped back and sheathed her knife. Marghe did not see where it went.

"Fasten yourself up."

The tribeswoman marched her over to a mound of snow, then walked off.

Marghe panicked. Were they going to leave her there without food or horse or vaccine? Wild-eyed, she looked about her. No. They were hobbling the horses. Relief made her want to grin. She closed her eyes, trying to make sense of what was happening.

"Do you enjoy freezing?"

She jumped. Aoife stood there.

"Here, under the snow—" the tribeswoman bent and brushed at the snow mound, "a shelter. It's warmer." She spoke slowly, as though to a half-wit.

That stung, but it was something Marghe could make sense of, something that had happened before, that she could respond to. "How was I to know you covered your tents with snow?"

Aoife looked at her, then shrugged and walked back to the horses. Marghe wondered if it was her accent the tribeswoman had found difficult to deal with, or her ignorance. She resolved to watch, listen, and learn. Out here, ignorance might be a capital crime.

When she thought no one was watching, she squatted and

wriggled through the tiny entrance flap headfirst. It was light, and did not smell, which surprised her, and had room for three or four if they stayed prone. She lay there for a while, grateful for solid ground and a place away from curious eyes.

She breathed in deeply through her nose, exhaled through her mouth. And again. Her heartbeat began to steady and her fear lessened. The basics always helped.

What was her status: hostage, guest, slave? What would happen to her? She had no idea. She tried, instead, to organize her thoughts around questions she might be able to answer. Where was she? If the stones had not scrambled her compass irreversibly, she might be able to guesstimate her position. If she could get back her map. Where was her pack?

She lay there listening to her heartbeat, reassuring and steady. If she was left here alone, it might be possible to creep out in the night, find her pack and her horse, and leave.

In the dark, a dark without stars or moon?

No. Tomorrow, then. For now, she would have to stay calm, wait and watch. And think. She spoke the strange words aloud, *Eefee, Waith-nee, Lev-ark, Eck-rave*, rolling them over her tongue, tasting them, testing: Gaelic names that had not been used on Earth for thousands of years.

Aoife wriggled into the shelter, followed by two others. Not Uaithne. Marghe accepted the nightbag flung in her direction. Her own, she noted.

"Sleep."

She followed the others' lead, stripping off hood and boots and sliding fully clothed into her bag. She thought she saw a look of approval on Aoife's dark and broken face.

They were up the next day in the thin gray light before dawn. Marghe was not offered food, nor did she see any of the Echraidhe eating. They rolled up their nightbags, donned hoods and boots, and began unpegging and stowing the leather tents. Marghe wondered if Aoife still had the FN-17. She could not escape without it.

The small muscles over her ribs and stomach tightened in dread as Aoife walked a horse toward her. The bruises from yesterday's journey were just beginning to show and her face was red as skinned meat.

"Hold him."

Marghe took the rein. She did not know what else to do. Aoife strode off and returned with Pella. The tribeswoman stood by with folded arms while Marghe patted her mare and ran her hands down her neck. Her gear was neatly slung behind the saddle. She checked her pack and found it was all there, her FN-17, her wristcom, her map. Only the knife and the food were missing. Her relief was so great, she nearly turned to Aoife and thanked her.

The tribeswoman mounted and gestured for Marghe to do likewise. The other horses were wheeling and thundering northward.

As they rode, Aoife pulled strips of dried meat from the pouch by her thigh. She handed some to Marghe. They slowed a little to eat and Marghe took the opportunity to strap the wristcom back across the pale skin over her left wrist. With it back in place she sat up straighter, could regard Aoife coolly, and she understood suddenly that her relief at the presence of the wristcom on her wrist was not just the practical comfort of having the compass: while she could record things, she still had a professional persona. She was Marguerite Angelica Taishan, the SEC rep; she was not lost and alone, helpless as any other savage on a horse.

Aoife had the power to take away from her that so-slender thread of identity any time she wished.

She touched the compass function key. It seemed to be working. Good. She turned a casual circle in her saddle. She had horse, vaccine, map and compass. Aoife's spear was strapped down securely and her small, shaggy mount was probably no match for the longer-legged Pella at full stretch.

Aoife was watching her. She tapped the sling at her belt. "I can kill a ruk with this at nine nines of paces. You—" she looked Marghe and her mount up and down, "you I could bring down before that summer mare lengthened her stride."

Marghe said nothing. Perhaps, if it came to it, Aoife would hesitate to kill.

"A stone can stun a rider, as well as kill," Aoife said.

Marghe turned her face away, winced as the wind bit into her raw cheek.

"Here."

Frustration made her angry, and stubborn. She refused to look at what Aoife offered.

"Grease for your face."

Marghe ignored her. Aoife swung her mount in front of Marghe's and wrenched them both to a halt. She pulled Marghe's face to hers by the chin. Her eyes were flat and brown.

"You will take this grease."

Marghe stared at Aoife's broken nose, the thick white scar that writhed over her cheekbone, nose, and mouth, and made no move to take the small clay pot.

Aoife sighed and pulled off a glove. "Hold still." Strong blunt fingers smoothed the grease delicately over Marghe's face. Nose first, forehead, chin, then cheeks. Marghe flinched, then relaxed. It did not hurt.

"Close your eyes and mouth."

This time she obeyed, and Aoife stroked the thick, milk-colored stuff onto her lips and eyelids. Then she stowed away her pot.

Marghe touched her lips, the sore place on her cheek; the grease was a kindness. "Thank you."

Aoife nodded. "The others are far ahead." They kicked their mounts into a gallop. Marghe checked her compass and saw that they galloped northwest. Ollfoss, and the forest, lay northeast.

 THEY RODE hard for three days and Marghe began to understand Aoife's contempt for Pella. The mare looked gaunt and dull-eyed, while the shaggy horses seemed tireless. They ate on the move, strips of dried meat, and drank a sour, half-frozen slush called locha. It was made from fermented taar milk. Marghe hated it, but she drank it; it put warmth in her gut.

As they neared the main camp, the tribeswomen seemed to relax. They talked more among themselves. Marghe listened and learned: the triple handful of riders were returning from the annual ceremony at the ringstones.

"Did I interrupt your ceremony?" she asked Aoife as they swung back into the saddle one afternoon.

"It was finished. The Levarch was showing us the southern pasturelands. We were on our way home when Uaithne found you."

She remembered Uaithne's threat. Intrusion in some religions carried an automatic death penalty. "Have I disturbed the . . . rightfulness of the stones for you?"

"No." Aoife paused. "It's happened before. Twice."

Marghe's heart thumped. Winnie? She licked her lips, swallowed. "What happened to the women?"

Uaithne galloped past. Aoife shook her head and would not answer any more questions.

At the end of the third day, they came to the winter camp of the Echraidhe.

Chapter Five

DANNER TURNED away from the lists on her screen and looked instead at the tapestry on the wall behind her. It was an abstract of blues and golds about a meter square, a present from her deputy, Ato Teng, about a year ago. She wondered if Teng had made it herself, this marvelous picture that made her feel hollow inside, like homesickness. Or had the artist given it to Teng? In exchange for what? It bothered her that she did not know the answers to these questions, that she did not know her deputy well enough to even guess.

Her office had no window. Port Central followed Company design: the nerve center, her office, was protected by myriad other rooms, corridors, and storerooms. There were no external signs for indigenes to read and follow; the usual procedure. More than one Company security installation had suffered sabotage. But here on Jeep, the precautions were ridiculous. The natives simply stayed away. Port Central had become a sophisticated prison for its inmates, while the natives roamed a whole world.

She wished she had a window because sometimes, sitting here

in her box of an office, with the air always the same temperature and officers all wearing the same uniform, she could believe that this was a normal situation, one that could be resolved by the application of all those wonderful scenarios and procedures taught at the academy in Dublin. But Jeep was not normal. What other Company planet was under the charge of a lieutenant?

She fingered the insignia sealed to her epaulets. She might wear the two stars of a commander, but in her head she was still a lieutenant, playing at command, as though it were a test after which the real brass would unplug her from the simulator and point out all her mistakes, patting her on the back for any smart moves. But here there was no one to tell her if she had made any smart moves, no one to talk to about anything. Command isolated her more effectively than a deadly disease.

When she had first realized how it was going to be, that she was the superior officer, she had been scared. Hundreds of people relied on her. Hundreds. In those first weeks she had been too scared, shaking too hard, to spend time with anyone. In front of others, she was not allowed to be Hannah Danner, the newest lieutenant on Jeep; she had to be Acting Commander Danner, the one with all the answers, her orders crisp, clear, and fast as the breaking of a bone. It reached the stage where she could not even bring herself to eat or drink in front of other officers. It took her a long time to learn that patterns of command were well laid; as long as what she asked people to do made some kind of sense, they would be glad to have someone in charge. Then she relaxed a little. But the habit was already formed: isolation, loneliness, solitude.

Her older sister, who had had more to do with bringing her up than her parents, had said it was never too late to start over. But Claire had been wrong about many things.

Claire had taken her side against liberal parents who had been horrified when Hannah had announced she wanted to join up. It had been Claire who came to graduation and hugged her, then apologized for rumpling her dress uniform; Claire who told her, tears in her eyes, that there was nothing she could not do, if she wanted it badly enough, even to changing the world. She had believed that, then. That day in Dublin, with the air soft and green after an Irish rainfall, she had believed that she could make a difference—that in a few years she would be commander on some Company world, defending the rights of those who could not speak for themselves, making the opening up of a new world a thing of pride and wonder, not horror. Oh, yes, that day in Dublin she had believed, and had been proud to wear this uniform.

Her desk chimed. Danner turned away from the tapestry as her screen windowed on Vincio's face. She sighed, and touched the window, which expanded to fill the screen. The philosophy could wait.

"Sergeant Lu Wai and Technicians Dogias and Neuyen are back, ma'am. Lu Wai and Dogias request a personal debriefing."

"What's wrong with just putting the report on my desk?" Vincio, who always seemed to know when a question was rhetorical, said nothing. "They specifically asked for me, not Lieutenant Fa'thezam?"

"Yes, ma'am. The sergeant said that what they wanted to talk about was more than a communications issue."

Lu Wai was a reliable officer, a good sergeant. If she was in such a hurry to get to the commander with this story, it meant trouble. "Tell them to be ready in one hour."

The screen reverted to lists of figures. In the last two years she had become well acquainted with the needs of many disciplines, how their smooth functioning depended upon seemingly innocuous items such as *suture reels, case 12 × 20* or *cable clips, heavy, Cu and Al, sheathed.* The little things always ran out first.

She looked carefully at the medical supplies. The one-shot subdermal diffusion injectors were low. Allergy shots accounted for much of that. She tapped in a request, nodded thoughtfully. There were hypodermic syringes available, but they too were disposable. The medics would have to find a way to reuse their injectors, or stop giving allergy shots. Sophisticated antibacterial and painkilling drugs were no use without the means to inject them. Lu Wai was a medic, wasn't she? She made a note to talk to her about it.

The hour passed quickly. She rubbed at her eyes, turned off the screen. Her back ached. She was spending too much time in this damn chair.

Vincio tapped on the door, brought in a tray. Danner could not help glancing at the time display on the corner of her desk.

"I scheduled them twenty minutes late," Vincio said. "You need lunch." She put the tray on the small table near the door.

Danner ate potato soup, crackers, and salad, beautifully presented on matching china. She accepted the service that went with her rank because it was efficient use of her time, but sometimes she thought she would not keep either long enough to become accustomed to it.

THE FARTHEST Danner had ever been from Port Central was during the first week they had been on Jeep, when she was still a lieutenant. Captain Huroo had taken her and a squad to fight the burn that lay halfway between here and what they now knew as Holme Valley. He was dead now, of course. It was at the burn that she had met Jink, the one who had saved Officer Day. The skinny native had been half-dead with concussion, burns, and loss of blood, but she had still escaped, then recovered well enough to come back into Port Central to find Danner weeks later. Had anyone been sick by that time? She could not remember. She wondered what had happened to Day—another name on the missing list.

When the virus began to kill, everyone had been confined to base, and she had been here more or less ever since, first taking captain's rank, then acting deputy, then commander as they died, one by one. Hell of a way to get promoted. Just like a war. And now she was stuck. Her job was to protect the welfare of her personnel; that could best be done from Port Central. From right here, her office. Sometimes she longed for a change of scene.

Nights were the worst, spring nights, when the air was soft and blew in from across the grasslands full of alien promise. At those times she ached to be Out There, walking through strange country, seeing a new world for herself, meeting challenges that were not administrative. Once in all this time she had toured the area surrounding Port Central, riding a sled accompanied by a score of officers. It was not enough. What she wanted was to be headed somewhere definite, with a purpose, toward a situation only she could handle. She wanted to do the job she had trained for, not stare at damn screens all day and make notes on whom to speak to about what. She was bored.

And so when the sergeant and technician were shown into her office, Danner gestured to the low table on one side of the office. "Please, sit."

The sergeant hesitated before complying. Danner came round from behind her desk and joined them. She thought about asking for tea, but that would probably only make Lu Wai more uncomfortable. Sergeants did not usually take tea with commanders.

"I hope you've both eaten, because we might be here some time. You have some news to impart, I believe, and I have curiosities of my own to satisfy."

Tell me what it smells like out there, she wanted to say, *and how the sky looks, what the air feels like.* She could not quite bring herself to ask, but some of her hunger must have been apparent. Lu Wai's face smoothed into the bland look Danner remembered well from her own days as a cadet, the expression assumed by junior officers when one suspected the commander was about to say or do something particularly bizarre.

Danner sighed, and Letitia flashed her an amused glance. Danner was momentarily disconcerted. Dogias was an odd one.

"You traveled in the company of Representative Taishan for several days," she said briskly. "I want as accurate a description of the journey as possible—what you talked about, how she responded, what she was particularly interested in. I would also like your general impressions."

"General impression of everything in general?" Letitia Dogias asked.

The woman was teasing her. "Yes," Danner said firmly. "Try not to edit. I need to know how she responds to things here. Whether or not she likes it, and us."

Us. The word hung in the air between them. *Us.* Danner wondered what was the matter with her today. She felt restless, insecure, shaken loose from all her normal patterns. *Us.* She tasted the word again: *Us.* It felt right. Perhaps she should talk to these two again sometime. And others. Perhaps it was time to start breaking down her isolation.

Unexpectedly, Dogias smiled. Danner smiled back, allowing herself, just for a moment, to feel part of a group. *Us.* She noticed Lu Wai had relaxed enough to let her fatigue show. Dap might be a good idea, now. She had Vincio bring it in.

It was Dogias who did most of the talking at first: about Marghe's discovery of the web that was the spider, the kris flies, the storm. Danner did not miss Lu Wai's tight expression while Dogias talked about the storm, or the way her hand almost reached out for the technician's. It must have happened again. She wondered what it was like to love someone like that, and found herself enjoying being near them.

"How was her attitude to Company in general, and to you, as a Mirror, in particular?" she asked the sergeant.

"Reserved," Lu Wai said slowly, "like she was withholding a decision. I'd say she was fair-minded."

Danner waited, but the Mirror did not explain why she thought so. "And how does she feel about the vaccine, the virus?"

"She's scared," Lu Wai said simply. "I don't think she's entirely convinced the vaccine will work."

"Are any of us?" Dogias asked.

Danner thought about that. Was she convinced? "I think it might work, yes."

"But do you want it to?" Dogias asked softly.

The question reached right inside Danner, but she was not ready for it, and pretended not to hear.

"Tell me about Holme Valley."

They described the lodges made of skelter trees, the slow-moving river, the preparation for the arrival of the women and herds from Singing Pastures. Dogias told her how she and Ude Neuyen had laid the northern relay, and Danner once again wished her job felt more constructive. Most of what she achieved could only be measured in negatives: less sick leave, fewer emergencies due to good planning, no sag in morale. It was hard not to feel jealous of the satisfaction in Dogias's voice as she talked about solving one practical difficulty after another.

". . . and we might have been back a day early if we hadn't had to take the time to witness the pattern singing. And the agreement."

This, then, was what they wanted to talk about. Or at least part of it. She gestured for them to continue.

"The storm we ran into," Letitia said, "it destroyed Marghe's—Representative Taishan's—rations. She had to bargain with the natives for more food to take with her. They gave us some, too, though that wasn't strictly necessary. The bargain she made was something called trata."

The term was unfamiliar. "Go on."

"As I understand it, Marghe told them that we"—Letitia made an all-inclusive gesture—"are all part of one social unit, a family. A family for which she is empowered to speak. She offered them the everlasting favor of her family in return for food and clothes."

Danner found that she had been holding her breath. She let it out. "That doesn't sound so bad." She looked at Lu Wai. "Or is it?"

Letitia shrugged. "We're not sure. I think what she offered is an alliance of some kind."

"An alliance." Danner steepled her fingers, looked at the ceiling. The last thing she needed: worry over a group of people who might look to her in situations she knew nothing about. In her peripheral vision she saw Lu Wai sit up straighter and realized she had shifted back into commanding officer mode. "And you, Sergeant, you witnessed it, not Marghe?"

"Yes, ma'am. My orders were to offer any reasonable assistance to the representative, to obey her instructions as long as they did not conflict with our task. As this seemed to be the only way for Representative Taishan to continue her mission, and as she requested that we undertake the witnessing so that she could be on her way, in my judgment it was appropriate to comply."

Danner nodded; she had done the right thing. "How formal do you judge the agreement?"

"It was witnessed in the presence of a viajera, ma'am."

Not a spur-of-the-moment thing, then. "Marghe left a report?"

"Yes, ma'am." She gestured at Dogias, who pulled a chip from her belt and set it on the table.

Danner picked it up. Such a tiny thing. "I need to take a look at this. Go get some rest. If I have further questions, I'll call you later."

At the door, Lu Wai half turned, hesitating.

"Yes?" It came out sharper than Danner intended.

"Nothing, ma'am. Sorry." They left.

Now what had that been about? Perhaps she should not have been so sharp. Well, done was done. If it was important, Lu Wai would get around to telling her. She dismissed the matter from her mind.

Two hours later, she levered herself up from her chair and paced, trying to think. Trata. She could still hear Marghe's voice: "Trata is a serious matter. For a complete reference, see Eagan's field notes, file K17-9a I think, but I can give you the essential idea. The most important thing is that, to the women of Holme Valley, we are no longer strangers. This means that if something terrible happened, for example the microwave relay failed, or we ran out of food, Holme Valley would be bound to help us. Of course, it also means we have to help them, but the major point is we are no longer alone on this planet. We have allies. The alliance cannot be dissolved until there's been some trading— that's a loose definition, see Eagan's notes for more detail—by both parties. What will probably interest you most is this: we are now involved in this world. We have a stake in the culture. Because of that, we will be considered when and if the journeywomen make any changes that could affect us. Danner, do you understand this? It's important. We've become part of the social network, here, like . . . oh, part of the cultural food chain. We're linked with these people. From now on, what they do—all of them, any of them, because the trata network is woven right through these communities, linking each with another—will affect us, so they'll consider us and our needs before they do anything. They won't consult us, no, but they'll be careful not to incur our outright wrath. It was a risk, but it seemed a good one: we have a base here of sorts, if we need it."

Part of the cultural food chain. Damn that woman. She paced harder. Her bootheels made no sound on the restful, absorbent tile, which irritated her further. They already had a base. Did Marghe think Port Central wasn't good enough? Obviously. *Part of the cultural food chain . . .* Didn't that damned woman realize Company personnel were not supposed to get involved at all with the indigenous population?

Of course she knew. It was her job to know.

Danner dropped into the chair Dogias had been sitting on just two hours ago. What was Marghe saying to her? She played back the last sentence. "We have a base here of sorts, if we need it."

Why would they need it? If the vaccine did not work. But the vaccine would work.

But do you want it to?

She shoved Dogias's question aside, began to pace again. The vaccine had to work. It was their only chance.

She stopped, stood very still.

Their only chance? What did she mean by that? The vaccine might be the last chance for Company to profitably exploit Jeep, of course, but it was not *her* last chance, or that of her staff. If the vaccine did not work, Company would lift them off. Marghe, and Sara Hiam on the *Estrade*, were civilians . . . bound to lose faith now and again. But Company would not abandon them.

Thinking of Sara Hiam reminded her that she should let *Estrade* know that the relay at Holme Valley was up and running. No doubt the doctor would have more to say about Company, and the *Kurst*, which she referred to openly as "that engine of death," but it would be good to talk to someone who did not have to call her ma'am.

What time would it be now up on the *Estrade*? Late. But not too late.

After a moment, a woman Danner recognized as Nyo filled her screen. She smiled at her. "Hello, Nyo."

Nyo did not smile back. "Good evening, Commander."

Maybe the woman was just having a bad day. "I'd like to speak to Dr. Hiam."

The screen blanked, then flared again. Sara Hiam's face was set and unwelcoming. "Yes?"

Danner wondered what was wrong. "It's me," she said.

"I can see that."

"Is anything wrong?"

"You tell me." Her voice was flat, hostile.

There was no excuse for this kind of rudeness. Muscles along Danner's jaw bunched. "I didn't call to spar with you, Doctor. If there is some problem up there, I'm unaware of it. Perhaps you could apprise me of the situation."

"No." Sara Hiam's face was taut with anger. "You should tell *us* what the hell the situation is, Commander; you should explain to *us* what all this crap with codes is about."

"Codes? I don't understand."

"You should."

"Obviously. But the fact remains that I don't." She was too tired, too confused to stay angry. She rubbed her face. "Look, Sara, I honestly have no idea what you're talking about. I'm sorry you're angry, but unless you tell me what you think I've done wrong, we can't clear up this misunderstanding." She hesitated. "I thought we had each other's trust."

"That's what I thought, that's why I'm so angry. So you explain why you're sending tight, coded messages up to the *Kurst* and not telling me or anybody else what the hell is going on."

"Coded messages? From Port Central?" It did not make sense. "You're sure?"

"I'm sure."

Danner frowned. "I didn't send any messages."

"Somebody did."

"What did they say?"

"They were coded, remember?"

"Did you record them?"

Sara Hiam shook her head. "It was pure chance Sigrid caught them, and we weren't set up to record."

"I don't understand." What was going on? "Messages, you said. There was more than one?"

Sara tilted her head. "You really don't know anything about it, do you?" Danner shook her head. Hiam was suddenly businesslike. "Sigrid said they were multibursts. Or something. Apparently it's something the military does: send several communiqués in one compressed burst."

Military. "And they went to the *Kurst?*"

"That's right. From Port Central."

"When?"

"Eight days ago."

Eight days, eight days. Nothing unusual had happened then. Someone was sending messages in code, military code, from Port Central to the *Kurst*, and she knew nothing about it. Her head began to thump. "I assume that this is the first time you've intercepted this kind of communication."

"Yes."

"Why now?" Danner muttered half to herself.

"It might have been going on for some time," Hiam offered. "Sigrid was trying some new frequencies for the satellite, ones we haven't used before. For all we know, the spy could have been sending information up for months. Or years."

"Spy?" The thumping in Danner's head became a hot ache.

"Why else would someone send transmissions without your knowledge?"

There was no other reason. None at all. Danner felt as though someone was pushing a hand inside her stomach and squeezing.

"Who would want to spy on Port Central—on me?"

"Company," Hiam said gently.

"Company?" Danner was bewildered. "But I'm Company."

"Perhaps they don't think you're Company enough."

She tried to think, and her confusion slowly heated to anger.

Hiam was right. It had to be Company spying on her. Company going behind her back after seven years of faithful service. But it still did not make sense: if the people on *Kurst* wanted to know something, why not just ask her? She would tell them. She had nothing to hide. Nothing. She had always been loyal, above-board. Always. Only now they seemed to think she was not, that she could not be trusted, that she needed to be watched. Who, who the hell, was doing this?

"Can Sigrid find that frequency again?" She was breathing hard.

"I'll check with her. Hold for a moment." Hiam paused, finger poised above a key. "You might like this"—she smiled wryly—"or you might not. It's one of Nyo's." The hold screen was a cartoon: a knight in medieval armor balanced on the hull of the *Kurst*, aiming a catapult at the planet below. In other circumstances, it might have been funny.

The cartoon flicked out and Hiam's face reappeared. "Sigrid says yes. Apparently she's already monitoring it, just in case."

Danner's anger was mounting, but she kept her voice steady. "Please convey my gratitude and ask her to continue to do so. When our spy uses that frequency again, I want it recorded." The code could come later. First, catch whoever it was. Then find out why. "Another thing. Tell her that finding the originating locus of this signal takes priority over its information content."

"What if there isn't a next time?"

"There will be," Danner said grimly. That damn spy would want frequent reassurance from the powers above. She would need it. The muscles in her face felt tight.

"I wouldn't like to be in her shoes when you catch her," Hiam said dryly.

"No," Danner said, and wished Sara was beside her, at Port Central, instead of up there.

After they said good-bye, Danner sat very still, trying hard to grasp the slippery idea that someone in Company did not trust her. *Her.* Now she knew how Marghe must have felt to have her judgment questioned. Who was the person who smiled, and said, "Yes, ma'am," and then went running behind her back? She wanted to tear out of her office and destroy something, anything; shout, line everyone up against a wall and force the truth out of the spy with the sheer power of her rage.

Wait until you've calmed down, she told herself. *Do some work, then figure out what you're going to do.* She took a couple of deep breaths, turned on her screen of lists, and tried to concentrate. No good. She was just too angry.

She strode to the door, opened it. "Vincio? I'm leaving. Unless a situation occurs which Deputy Teng can't handle, I'm unavailable for the next three hours."

She wished the office had the kind of door she could slam on the way out.

She marched across the grass toward her mod, then abruptly changed direction. She would take the long way back, around the perimeter. Walk some of this off.

It was cool, getting toward winter. Her uniform began to heat up, getting hot around the small of her back first and making her sweat. She switched it off. This time she wanted to get warm on her own.

How had Marghe dealt with the challenge to her judgment?

The sky was gray, full of hard rain. The wind in her face felt damp and cold. She shivered, walked faster. It would be even colder up north, where Marghe might be stuck in a snowdrift, or sneezing miserably inside her tent. Or maybe she had already reached Ollfoss and was snugged up in a log cabin with a cheery fire and some smiling woman bringing her soup.

Some smiling woman bringing Marghe soup.

Danner reached the perimeter fence and stopped. It was the first time she had really, deep down, thought of the indigenous population of Jeep as women. Not aliens, or natives, or beings to be taken into consideration from a humanitarian point of view, but women like her, like Marghe, like Teng or Vincio or Letitia Dogias. *Like us.* Women who lit fires against the cold and made soup for their loved ones.

She remembered, long ago, her meeting with the journey-woman T'orre Na. The journeywoman had held out her hand. *Look at this hand,* she had said. And Danner had. *This hand can birth children. This hand can make music. This hand could kill you.* And Danner had been shamed into risking her career, shamed into taking the part of T'orre Na and the herders Jink and Oriyest against Company.

Against Company . . . Was it this that Company held against her now? One act of humanity?

And then she understood why it was only now that she was able to acknowledge the humanity of Jeep's natives: because it was only now that she understood that Company, the ones with the power, held her, a Mirror commander, in as little regard as they held the inhabitants of this world. It was only now that she understood, for the first time, that despite her title, her uniform, and the two stars on her shoulder, she was as helpless as any native herder or farmer or sailor.

She touched her fingers to the slick ceramic-sheathed chain-link of the perimeter fence. It did not seem like four years since she had ordered it turned off to save power. Time seemed to be a very slippery commodity, like these links, greasy with moisture.

She stared out at the endless grass. Marghe was somewhere out there, Marghe and the vaccine. *But do you want it to work?* Dogias had asked. Did she? If the vaccine did not work, then this would be all she would have for the rest of her days. Grass and wind, and month after month of wearing her uniform, until it came to mean nothing, and no one listened to her anymore.

Her hands hurt. She loosened her grip on the fence. That would not happen. This was not one of those legendary lost outposts turning to dust, with tales of which new recruits frightened each other on lonely, predawn guard duty. She shook her hands at her sides until the white marks faded. If the vaccine did not work, then Company would close down the operation. She and her personnel would be transferred to some orbital hospital facility. There might be a few tests, yes, but after suitable decontamination and quarantine, and no doubt tedious debriefing, they would be sent home on well-deserved furlough, then reassigned.

Would they? That was not what Sara Hiam thought, nor what Marghe seemed to believe.

Danner did not know what to think. Until an hour ago, she had believed that Company trusted her, that it looked after its own. But that was what Marghe had thought about SEC. And she had been wrong.

Clouds scudded overhead. She tipped her head up to watch. They looked like the giant sea skates she had seen easing past above her the time she had gone diving off the Great Barrier Reef.

A cold, fat raindrop splashed on her forehead at the hairline. Another hit her hand. On impulse, she lifted her wet knuckle to her mouth and sucked. The rain was sweet, unspoiled. She remembered a day when she was eleven, standing scrape-kneed with her friends on a heap of used car tires, tasting polluted rain and trying to guess what the different chemicals were. Afterward, they took some home and tested it to see who had identified the most. There were far more than any of them had thought.

The rain was coming down steadily. If Sara Hiam was right, if Marghe was right, she might never see Earth again, might never get to taste rain eaten up and spat out, partially clean, by tailored bacteria. She walked slowly along the fence. The grass was getting high here, hard to walk through. She should order it cut. It could provide cover for hostiles.

Hostiles. Sometimes she felt like a bit player in one of those old, bad movies about the American West. Only, in this movie, some of her cavalry soldiers were spies, and the good ones left the fort, went into a reservation, and were never heard from again. Perhaps, as in the old movies, they died.

"Stop this," she said out loud. Her voice sounded small and lonely against the hissing of the rain. She leaned her forehead against the chain-link. Maybe she was lonely, maybe there were spies, but she was not small and she was not helpless. She would find these spies, and she would not let Company use her up and leave her for dead like a broken-winded horse.

EXCEPT FOR the piles of printouts awaiting her attention, the neat chip racks, and the framed hardcopy of her promotion fixed to the wall above the computer, Danner's mod was as bare as the day she had first come to Jeep. She stripped off her uniform and showered. Halfway through drying herself, she threw the towel on the floor next to the discarded and crumpled uniform. She did not want anything next to her skin that reminded her of Company.

She sat naked in front of her screen. What was Company, really? A profit-making organization. Whatever the situation, they would make their decisions based on the accounts. Very well.

She pulled up lists of plant and equipment, compared their costs to transportation costs; tried to figure in months of full pay for personnel who did nothing but sit around in decontamination, and added to that the cost of such a facility; weighed all that against Company's control of public opinion through the media. The answer was clear.

If the vaccine did not work, Company would find it more expedient, more cost-effective, to simply abandon her, her staff, and Port Central. No one would find out: Company controlled the media.

She wondered why she had never understood this before, then realized she had, deep down; just like Marghe, just like Sara Hiam, just like all those Jeep personnel, Mirror and civilian, who were busy decorating their mods, making their own clothes, and weaving beautiful tapestries. Adapting to the realities and necessities of their new home, as she had been: worrying over supplies of suture reels and hypodermic needles, pushing, always pushing to get more communication relays up. Yes, she had known all along.

A new thought struck her. She tapped at the keys for several minutes, then sighed in relief. No. It would cost too much to sterilize the planet as a precaution against the virus. All Company needed to do was destroy *Estrade*, and that was that, planet sealed. The only question was whether or not they would take off Sara Hiam and the rest of the orbital crew first. They were uncontaminated, but they knew too much. She set that problem aside for later.

Supposing the vaccine did not work, and Company really did abandon them all. How would they survive? How would they replenish their food, their clothes, their medicines? The microwave relay satellite would not remain in orbit forever; they would need to find new ways to heat and light their homes. They might even need to build new homes, closer to suitable agricultural sites. And what would they use to make plows, and barrels, and sacks and bottles and plates and shoes and beds and combs?

She stared at the screen, then blanked it. This was not something she could fix in a few hours. This was more, far more, than an exercise in resupply. Marghe was right. To survive here, they needed to be part of the cultural food chain.

First, she needed information on Company and its plans. Information. The only person likely to know more than she did was the spy—or spies. Find them first, proceed from there. After all, the vaccine might still work.

To catch a spy, or a rabbit, or a thief, one needed a trap. To set a trap, she would need assistance. Who could she trust?

The transmissions had been sent eight days ago, from here, Port Central. Eight days ago Letitia Dogias and Lu Wai had been at Holme Valley. They could not have sent them. They might still have had something to do with it, but she dismissed that; she had to trust somebody, sometime. The more she thought about it, the more it made sense. Dogias was a communications technician, so she would be able to think of ways to track the signal. Both she and Lu Wai often left Port Central for weeks at a time, so any necessary absence would not attract suspicion. Perfect.

She dressed rapidly, returned to the screen.

"Vincio?"

"Ma'am?"

"Please inform Sergeant Lu Wai and Technician Letitia Dogias to meet me here, my mod, in two hours."

"Yes, ma'am. Are you available to take calls now?"

"Not for two hours. In an emergency, I'll be at the fencing hall with Private Kahn."

Ana Kahn was a championship fencer, good enough to give her a workout that should drain the last of the anger from her body. She could not afford anger. For what lay ahead, she needed a clear, focused mind.

Outside, the rain had stopped. Danner strode briskly, leaving bootprints in the wet grass.

Chapter Six

THE WINTER camp of the Echraidhe huddled under a fast-moving winter sky: fifty or more tents surrounding three animal pens and a thin, ice-rimed spring that ran fifteen yards before disappearing back into the ground beneath the snow. Blue-gray smoke, sharp with the smell of animal dung, trickled from several of the low black tents. One of the tents was much larger than the others. As they rode closer, Marghe could see the roofs sagging with snow. Winding from tent to tent, to stream and corral, paths had been worn through the snow to the mossy grass beneath. In places there was no moss, and Pella's hooves rang on the iron-hard ground. A windswirl blew snow up off the ground into Marghe's face.

Two of the pens were empty. A third held a handful of horses standing nose to tail at the far end near a trough that was beginning to scum over with ice. Their breath steamed. The wooden uprights and cross-planks looked dark and old but were fixed together with rope—a temporary structure, like everything else.

Behind an outlying tent, two children played a game with polished bones. Their heads were bare, hair matted and tangled, and one had some kind of rash on her face. Vitamin deficiency, Marghe thought. The ragtag collection of furs, leather, and felt they wore hid their shape and made it difficult to judge their age. When they saw the riders, one hooted with glee, scrambled up, and trotted alongside the Levarch's stirrup; the other paused to pick up the bits of bone with a chapped hand before running off into the center of the camp, calling out their arrival. People began pushing aside tent flaps, blinking up at the riders. Greetings screeched through the cold air like the cries of hungry birds. Marghe found the sharp vowels and harsh consonants difficult to follow.

The riders slowed to a walk. Their horses were soon surrounded by old women with brown eyes, smiling through their wrinkles; women holding babies and touching passing saddle leather and fur-clad thighs; girls calling up to the riders, grinning.

Many women pointed at her big horse, and children darted out of the crowd to touch her boots. After the silence of the plains, Marghe felt bewildered by the bright eyes and flashing red mouths. *I am an anthropologist,* she told herself, *not a prize of war,* and steadfastly returned their curiosity.

Every few feet, a rider reined in by a tent and was surrounded by a knot of family and friends who almost dragged her off her horse and inside. The further they went through the camp, the smaller their group became, until by the time they reached the big tent, the Levarch's, Marghe, Aoife, Uaithne, and the Levarch herself were the only ones still mounted. Marghe followed Aoife's lead and reined in Pella to let the Levarch and Uaithne approach the tent alone.

Six women—one very old, two adolescent—pushed through the flap to greet them. One of the young ones tied up the flap and the other took the reins from the Levarch and Uaithne when they dismounted. Marghe noticed that the girl smiled at the Levarch, but seemed afraid of Uaithne. That difference was mirrored in the greetings of the others: the old woman barely nodded at Uaithne, but her face split into splinters and cracks of welcome when she turned to the Levarch. Uaithne was not ignored, but Marghe could see how formally she was greeted. When she ducked inside the tent, none followed her. The Levarch was still outside, her arm around a woman her own age, grinning and clasping the outstretched hands of others. Marghe wondered why these women, especially the Levarch, shared a tent with someone they did not like.

Aoife sat her horse patiently. Marghe wondered how many times the tribeswoman had watched this ritual, and if anyone was waiting for her at her own tent.

Eventually the Levarch disentangled herself from her family. Her boots crunched in the snow as she walked back to where they sat.

"Aoife, take the stranger woman to your yurti. I'll argue you an extra taar from the herds to take the strain."

Aoife bowed her head. "I will teach her, feed her, replace worn clothes."

Marghe, alert to nuances, heard the ritual acceptance in the tribeswoman's response. She had just been disposed of in some way, become Aoife's responsibility.

"Levarch . . ." she began, but Aoife was already wheeling them both into a canter.

"Never address the Levarch unless she questions you."

Marghe could not think of a suitable reply.

Aoife's tent was set a little apart from the others and close by one of the empty pens. The tribeswoman gestured for her to dismount, then followed suit. No one pushed back the tent flap and smiled.

Aoife took off her gloves, began to unfasten the girths. She looked at Marghe. Marghe pulled off her own gloves, stuck them through her belt, and began to untie her pack. It looked like most of her teaching was going to be by mime show. When she lifted the pack free, Aoife nodded at the tent. "In the yurti," she said.

Like the others, this tent was low, made of black felt supported by two wooden poles along its long axis. Two other poles, smaller, set side by side about six feet apart, supported an awning with its own entrance flap; this was shoulder height, and laced closed.

Her hands were cold and the flap's leather thongs were stiff with ice, and the fact that Aoife was watching made her feel clumsy and incapable, but Marghe managed to untie them. She pushed her head through uncertainly and found herself in a tented

antechamber with one white wool wall of the inner tent before
her and black felt on the other three sides. She had to stoop to get
inside, and when the flap fell back into place it was dim. She could
make out pots and sacks and other things stacked neatly along the
walls. She wondered what they held; the air was acrid with some
kind of chemical that made her nose run. There was nothing to
wipe her nose on, so she sniffed. The felt and wool absorbed the
sound and made the walls seem too close to her face for her to
breathe. She dumped her pack down by the far wall and pushed
back out into the hard cold.

Aoife had the saddle off her own horse and was loosening her
pack. Marghe carefully rolled the flap up and tied it back out of
the way with the thongs, as she had seen the young woman do at
the Levarch's tent. Aoife nodded curtly and turned her attention
back to her horse.

Marghe was surprised and angry at Aoife's lack of acknowledgment of her initiative. She jerked hard enough at Pella's girth for
the mare to whicker in protest. Why was she so eager for Aoife's
approval? Because she was scared; because she already understood
that this was no longer an exercise in anthropology and that she
was no longer studying in the field, she *was* the field; because now
this woman controlled her life.

They took their mounts to the corral by wrapping fingers deep
into the manes and tugging the animals in the right direction.
Marghe's arms were still shaking.

The corral was now almost full of horses standing patiently
while children looked at their feet, felt their legs, and curried
muddy snow from their coats. One group of girls sat on the fence
and watched, calling out to one of the grooms now and again, and
three or four very young children dashed about, getting in everyone's way. One ran by Aoife and Marghe, shrieking, her nose
plugged with thick green snot. The air was wreathed with the mist
of talk and hard work.

A young woman, about fourteen, saw them coming in and
clambered down from the fence to meet them. Aoife relinquished
her horse without a word, but Marghe found it hard to let go of
Pella.

"Look after her," Marghe said to the thin-faced girl. The girl frowned at her accent. "She feels the cold more than your horses."

"She'll be warm enough with all the others," the girl said. She looked Pella up and down, mouth pursed. "Her coat'll thicken up soon enough, and she looks a good size for foals. Bit old, though." She wrapped the thin fingers of her right hand around a tuft of Pella's mane, took a handful of the other horse's mane in her left, and led them into the corral. There she released Pella with a slap on the rump and tended to Aoife's mount first. Pella trotted into the herd as if she had never belonged anywhere else. The only way Marghe could pick her out at this distance was that the mare was a little longer in the leg, less shaggy in the coat. She wondered if she would be assimilated as easily into the Echraidhe.

MARGHE EXPECTED the inside of the tent to be dark and oppressive. She was surprised. The light allowed in through the rolled-up entrance flap, already filtered through cloud and reflected back from snow, was further thinned and clarified by the white wool. The result was light like skimmed milk seeping into dark spaces and wetting to a glisten the deep colors of the tapestries that hung on the interior walls. It was a large tent, perhaps sixteen feet long inside, and every wall was covered in weaving of bold, geometric designs. The effect was warm and rich, with twilight purples and hot reds layered like sunsets over thick golds and greens. To Marghe, it was like cutting open the gray exterior of a geode to discover the jeweled crystal inside. She wondered if Aoife's seamless exterior concealed any such surprises.

Aoife started unfastening her overfurs. Marghe shivered and stepped further in. The floor was a mix of rough and smooth: coarse felt, worn cool and smooth in places, covered here and there with old furs. She stood on one of the furs, glad to get her feet warm, and looked about.

Where she stood, near a wooden tent pole, the roof was high enough that she did not have to stoop. Directly ahead, two pallets heaped with more furs lay to either side and slightly to the front of a hearth which looked as if it was heaped with dead ash. Two pallets, both used—Aoife did share with someone, then. Such a large space for two people, given the subsistence living of the Echraidhe. Behind the hearth stood a second tent pole. The space beyond that was taken up with several bowls and pots, some in use, some empty.

She shivered. It was cold enough to see her breath.

From the roof hung a bewildering assortment of mosses, a string of shells, semi-tanned leather, herbs, skeins of dyed and undyed wool, strips of drying meat, and bottles made of clay and leather. The smells were smoky, human, rich. Standing free by the right-hand wall was a loom with a wooden shuttle tucked into the half-finished weaving. She did not need to look closely to see the same geometric patterns that were repeated on the hangings.

Where the hangings did not cover the walls, the felt had been reinforced by thick strands of what looked like rope that arced down from the tent poles to the floor. Marghe touched one. Horsehair. Sewn onto it were pouches, each a patchwork of leather, brightly dyed cloth, and felt. They bulged with odd shapes. Marghe could see that at regular intervals, where the walls met the floor, the tent had been pegged down from the outside.

Although she knew that the tent was designed to be dismantled and packed onto horseback in a matter of hours, the whole thing felt secure, lived in, permanent. But cold. She shivered again.

Aoife slung her overfurs across the foot of her pallet and stretched out with her eyes closed. "Fire needs building. Plenty of taar chips outside."

Marghe waited for more, but Aoife did not open her eyes. She went back through the white wool hanging to get her boots. The foretent was well organized: sacks of grains and legumes stood against one wall, separated from some sealed clay pots by bits of wood. She poked the wood, picking up small pieces. Out here where there were no trees, wood meant wealth. Next to the wood was a neat pile of leather scraps; plumped on top were two tied sacks the size of her fist. She untied one and sniffed at the greenish gray powder. Her nose flooded and stung, her eyes ran. She tied it up again quickly and did not bother with the second.

Her shivering was now a constant shudder. She jammed her boots on and pushed through the outer flap.

She walked around the tent twice, flapping her arms to keep warm, without seeing anything that looked like taar chips. She looked out between the taar pen and the other tents, across the tundra. There might be satellites and orbital stations and a military cruiser wheeling across the sky, but this cold and lonely place, this wasteland, belonged to the Echraidhe. Holle had tried to tell her: Tehuantepec belonged to the wild tribes, to the ghosts of magical beasts. She had no place here. And she had no idea what would happen to her now. Already this plain made her think in terms of things happening *to* her, not her *acting*. Tehuantepec could drain a person of everything but what it took to stay warm. She wanted to run, as far and as fast as she could.

One thing at a time, she told herself, one thing at a time. First, find these taar chips, then get a fire going and get warm. If she could stop shaking, she could think; if she could think, then she would get Aoife to tell her what the Echraidhe wanted of her; if she knew that, she could find a way out of here, somehow.

Walk, she told herself, walk and think. Keep body and mind ready. Every minute you have to spend here, spend it learning, stay supple-minded. She forced herself to look at the tent she was walking around. The forward poles were topped with leather caps; the rear support was left bare. Why, she asked herself roughly, think why. To let out smoke. And the tent pegs, what were they made of? Bone, sharpened bone.

It was getting dark. On her third circuit of the tent, she kicked something that rolled a little way through the snow. It looked like an olive-gray stone. She bent and picked it up. It was the size of a plover's egg, smooth, hard. Frozen droppings. A taar chip. She sniffed it cautiously, but all she could smell was snow and the wet fur of her glove.

The taar chips were stacked in three snow-covered cairns against the left wall of the tent. She took off her gloves, squatted next to the nearest cairn, and tried to pry a few lumps loose, but it was like trying to tear apart concrete with her fingers. She needed something long and thin, a rod or a knife, to lever the lumps free.

She thought for a moment, then began to feel through the snow at the base of the cairns. She found it: a piece of bone a foot long, sharpened at one end. When she brushed away the snow, she found a leather sack.

Back inside, what had looked like ash turned out to be carefully banked and covered embers. She used the bone stick to hold a lump of dung over the embers long enough to partially thaw, then crumbled it into slivers. She dropped a sliver on the embers. It kindled, a tiny blazing thread. She added another, and another, fanning the threads to busy tongues. Then she added two frozen lumps. They spat and hissed as they thawed, then gradually began to burn with a soft lavender flame that yellowed and filled the tent with a ripe, sweet smell. She sat back on her heels and added more, until there was a good-sized fire and her purple hands turned red and began to itch. She rubbed at them absently, enjoying the animal comfort of warmth. A good fire.

Aoife still appeared to be asleep.

She enjoyed the fire a little longer, then cleared her throat. "Why am I here?" It came out softer than she intended. Aoife did not stir. She tried again, louder. "Tell me why I'm here."

Aoife opened her eyes. In the firelight they glimmered like the eyes of a beaten-bronze statue Marghe had once seen in a Macau temple. Shadow played over her broken face.

"You are here to learn to be Echraidhe."

"I'm not Echraidhe. And I wish to leave."

Aoife looked at her so long that Marghe wondered if she had gone to sleep with her eyes open. "You are Echraidhe," she said again.

"I need to know why you have brought me here against my will." She searched Aoife's face for an expression she could understand. Aoife said nothing. "You can't do this to me." She took a deep breath, exhaled. Another. "It's important that you understand. People will be looking for me."

Aoife shrugged. "In winter, tracks fade and the cold stops even the closest of kin."

"But my . . . kin . . . track by a means unknown to you. They and I are from another world. A place far away, in the sky, like . . . like the moons." Even to her, it sounded ridiculous.

"You are Echraidhe," Aoife said flatly.

She shook her head. "No. I'm not even from your world. I—"

Aoife, unfolding like a mantis, sat up, cracked Marghe across the face with her open hand, and was back on the pallet before Marghe understood what had happened. "You are Echraidhe. Never say differently, or you will be whipped." She stood up. Marghe flinched. "Stay here. Wait for Borri." She walked through the wool flap.

Marghe blinked, touched her hand to her stinging cheek. She had moved so fast. Just like those miners on Beaver. Marghe breathed hard. This was not Beaver, and she would not let this happen. She surged to her feet and ripped open the hanging, but Aoife was gone, swallowed by the gathering dark.

She breathed harder, deliberately focusing her anger, husbanding it, trying to think. Aoife was gone; to hand was fuel for fire, and food and water; she had her FN-17. She could run, now. She pulled on her boots in the foretent, then came back in with her saddle pack. First she pulled down one of the bulging skins of locha, then grabbed food and the half-full sack of taar dung. She stuck her head out of the flap. No one. She heaved the saddle up onto her left arm, supported it with her right, and ran to the horse corral.

It was guarded by two women. One, mounted, laid a hand on her knife. The other straightened from breaking the ice on the trough and folded her arms. They watched her in silence.

Marghe wanted to run at them, smash them out of the way, ride into the cold dark. But there were two of them. She stood there, feeling angry and stupid, weighed down by the saddle. The woman on horseback nudged her mount forward. Marghe turned around and began walking back to Aoife's tent. The rider followed her all the way.

MARGHE CALMED herself with breathing and meditation. When Borri entered the tent, she was sitting peacefully by the fire, staring into the lavender and yellow flames.

"So, you're the stranger." Borri was taller than Aoife, and older, too, rangy under her furs. She untied a belt hung with tiny pouches and packets and dumped it on the bed.

"Marghe."

"Marghe, then," the woman acknowledged. "And I'm Borri." She sat down, held big-wristed hands out to the fire. "Ah, that feels good. It's a cold night and they ache from rubbing the phlegm from little Licha's lungs."

The talk unsettled Marghe. She had not realized how accustomed she had become to Aoife's silent gestures. She wondered if she was supposed to do something for this woman, and if she would get beaten if she did not.

Borri was looking at her, head tilted to the side. Her eyes were gray and widely spaced. "I've got something for that cheek. It won't soothe the pain much, but it should ease the bruise away quicker."

"Thank you," she said cautiously.

"We'll need to heat some water."

Borri filled a pot from one of the skins and showed Marghe how to settle it securely on the fire. "Aoife doesn't mean to be cruel," she said suddenly. "You mustn't let her treat you as badly as she sometimes treats herself."

Marghe was not quite sure how to respond to that. She wanted to grab this woman's hand and shout, *I don't belong here, on this world!* Instead, she asked, "Where's Aoife?"

"With the Levarch."

Marghe wondered if it was anything to do with her. "Does she go there often?"

Borri nodded. "She's Agelast." Marghe looked blank. "Agelast. The next Levarch."

Marghe searched her memory for the word. Agelast: one who does not laugh.

 MARGHE STOOD in her stirrups to scan the taar herd. In the distance, Fion lifted her palo stick and flicked it to full length, slicing the air horizontally in a question; Marghe raised her hand in an *all's well* gesture. Overhead, clouds raced by in tatters and streamers, and for the first time since Holme Valley Marghe caught glimpses of hard, deep blue sky. A pensel sky, Borri called it, after the pensels the riders wore fluttering from their spears during bollo games in the spring. Sunlight glittered on the snow that had fallen fresh the day before. Here and there, piles of taar droppings glistened, dark and smooth against the white.

It was her fourth day at the winter camp, her second riding with the herd. While she rode, Fion always kept her in sight. Aoife had told her that the younger tribeswoman was not as good with the sling as she: if Marghe tried to escape, Fion would go for a chest shot, perhaps breaking ribs, or worse.

Marghe was careful not to make any sudden moves. In time, she reasoned, Aoife and the others would relax, just a little. A little was all she needed. Whenever she could, she replenished her saddle bag with food. When the opportunity came, she would be ready. Until then, she would be patient and win their trust.

Meanwhile, there were things here to be observed.

She hooked her leg over her saddle horn, pulled off her right glove, touched RECORD. "The Echraidhe number one hundred and eighty-three, and occupy fifty-four tents, or yurtu. Although age is difficult to judge, I guess that about thirty are under fifteen, twenty-eight or -nine over sixty—two of whom are or appear to be very old. More than half the rest are between about forty-five and sixty. There is some evidence that the yurtu hold many fewer people than they were originally built for. I believe their population is declining, and suspect that the absence of trata has led to diet deficiencies which—"

Movement caught her eye; she touched OFF, slid her foot back into the stirrup, and pulled her pony after the straggling taar.

"Haii!" She did not have the extra reach of a palo, so she had to lean half out of the saddle to whip the animal across the rump. It leapt nimbly to rejoin the herd. Fion gave her a thumbs-up and Marghe smiled to herself. Human cultures kept the oddest gestures. Many too, were lost: in the minimal gravity of space communities, people did not nod or shake their heads; it caused inner ear disturbances.

She wondered if she would ever see any of those communities again. *Don't think of the future,* she told herself, *stay in the here and now.*

In the far distance a woman sat on a horse, watching. Uaithne. After a while, the rider wheeled away. Marghe was glad. Uaithne's constant scrutiny was unnerving; she did not understand it. She went back to her report.

"The yurtu and their occupants form economic and social units, each laying claim to, and having use of, a variable number of taars and horses. As the Echraidhe subsist on these animals, such divisions of property are vital. They are kept and tended in a communal herd; I am not yet sure at what point individuals or families take responsibility." Or whether the women watching the herds day and night guarded them from more than just her escape attempts.

They drove the taars back into camp in the late afternoon. They passed a young woman heading out, empty sacks flapping behind her saddle: dung-collection detail.

Fion helped Marghe pen the animals. Children waited to groom their mounts. Finally Marghe edged sideways into the yurti with the saddle. Aoife was squatting on the floor, feeding the cookfire, one chip at a time. She looked up and nodded. Borri stood near the entrance, filling her medicine belt with pouches and bundles of herbs. She smiled briefly at Marghe, and the deep frown line above her nose disappeared and reappeared.

"It's little Kaitlin this time." She tucked her single braid down under her overfur and pulled up the hood. "Don't save food."

Marghe laced the flap after her, for the warmth. The fire would give enough light. "Kaitlin?" she asked over her shoulder. It was a kinship question, one of the few Aoife would answer.

"Mairu's youngest. Licha's soestre."

Marghe nodded. Soestre: those children, two or sometimes—rarely—more, born at the same time to different mothers who shared the same yurti—though not all children born this way were named soestre. The concept held a special significance which she had not yet been able to unravel. Marghe wondered if it was linked to the fact that the tribe celebrated the anniversaries of their children's conception, not birth. Some yurtu were organized around two or more soestre and their tent sisters, who might or might not be biologically related. Borri and Aoife were tent sisters but not soestre, nor, as far as Marghe could tell, otherwise related.

By the light of the fire she checked the saddle over for wear. Scooping a gobbet of grease from the jar by the hearth, she began to rub it into the leather. Aoife had some water bubbling and was dribbling it over shavings of dap into a clay bowl. One braid hung down her back, the other dangled in front of her, almost dipping into the bowl; the firelight picked out strands of silver, staining them to red gold. Her eyes were soft with concentration. While the drink steeped, she ground coarse grain into meal, her movements graceful and precise. When the dap was ready, she strained it through a cloth into two smaller, wooden bowls.

Aoife dropped a handful of meal into her bowl and stirred it with a finger. To that, she added a scoop of taar butter, then mixed the mess until it formed a doughy, greasy ball the size of her fist. She tweaked off a piece and chewed it.

Marghe set the saddle aside and wiped her hands down her thighs before reaching for the tea. She preferred to drink half her dap down, enjoying the earthy, fragrant warmth, before adding the grain and fat she needed to survive here in winter. She longed for fresh fruit, or vegetables.

Aoife pulled off another piece of dough, rolling it through her fingers into a small ball. "Soon," she said, "my daughter Marac, and Scatha, the daughter of Aelle, will bring their beds to this yurti. You will become their tent mother, like Borri. Aelle stays choose-mother."

Marghe did not know what to say. "How old are they?"

"At the Moon of New Grass, they celebrate their sixteenth life day." She put the dough in her mouth, chewed, and swallowed.

Marghe sipped from her bowl. Sixteenth. She would be joint mother to two twelve-year-olds. She tried to think of the right thing to say. "Marac and Scatha are soestre?"

"No." Aoife stared into the fire. "The old Levarch wanted kinship ties between my yurti and Aelle's, to strengthen the tribe.

Aelle and I are not soestre, not even tent sisters, but we tried." She bowed her head. "We failed."

Marghe put down her bowl, tried to work out what Aoife was telling her. "Soestre only come from soestre?" she asked slowly.

"No."

"Usually from soestre, then." Aoife nodded. "So soestre from tent sisters is rare."

"It has been done."

Marghe ignored the warning in Aoife's voice. She leaned forward. "But the old Levarch was asking you to do an almost impossible thing, because you weren't soestre?"

Aoife looked right at her. Brown eyes met brown, but Aoife's were cold, igneous, compressed by years of hard living. "The Levarch asked, and we obeyed. It has been done."

 IT WAS dark and cold. Marghe crouched in the snow behind the yurti, where the women usually relieved themselves, and lifted her wristcom closer. "So," she whispered, "although at first I suspected these simultaneous births were the result of menstrual synchronicity of some kind, there's obviously more to it. Perhaps, then, the term soestre has biological as well as social significance."

So many people would give so much to understand how these women reproduced. A bitter smile cracked open her lip: she would trade the professional opportunity of a lifetime for an operational SLIC and the sight of Danner and a squad of Mirrors humming over the snow on their sleds.

Her mouth was bleeding. She wiped at it. Snow, crusted on her sleeve, broke open her lip in half-a-dozen other places. She had the foresight to take off her gloves before wiping at her tears.

FIVE OF them ate around the fire. Aoife sat on her own pallet and Marac shared Borri's. Scatha shared Marghe's, and whenever either of them moved, it rustled. Borri had shown her how to weave together the flat, dry ropes of horsehair and stuff the pallet with dried grass and scraps of felt. It was still new enough to be uncomfortable. Scatha and Marac would bring their own pallets, along with the rest of their belongings, from Aelle's tent after the meal.

Marac was named after the small black knife of a healer, the marac dubh. Like her mother she was dark and slight, her eyes the same brown; she lifted fingers full of spice-yellow rice to her mouth with the same precision. Next to Aoife's flinty strength, however, Marac was lighter, thinner, and her hair, untouched by silver, was pulled back from her face into a single braid. Marghe looked over at Aoife's face, all hollow and muscle, and wondered if it had ever been as soft as her daughter's, even before the scar. Aoife and Marac were identical twins, separated in looks only by time and circumstance. She thought about that for a while. Marac was no one's soestre. But Mairu's daughter Kaitlin looked nothing like a twin to her mother, and Kaitlin *was* soestre, to Licha. Being soestre must have something, somehow, to do with the alteration of genetic information passed from mother to daughter.

Aoife was looking at her. She returned her attention to her food.

Scatha lifted her bowl to Borri. "This is good."

Marac smiled shyly. "We'll eat better here than with Aelle."

And Marghe was struck by the similarities between these two adolescents and herself at that age. She remembered a meal with her mother's aunt, Great-aunt Phillipa; she had felt the way Marac did now, a little cautious, a little shy, on her best behavior, but not really ill at ease. These people were utterly human. But what was human? Human was not just family dinners, human was also the Inquisitions of Philip, the extermination of the Mayans, the terrible Reconstruction of the Community. Human meant cruelty as well as love, human was protecting one's own at the expense of others. Human also meant having the capacity to change.

Borri helped herself to another portion. She nodded at Marghe's almost empty bowl, raising her eyebrows. Marghe shook her head.

"It's not to your taste?"

"It was good, very tender. I'm not very hungry."

Borri frowned. "Are you well?"

Marghe glanced at Aoife, considered. She did not have to tell it all. She pulled the FN-17 from her pocket. "Every ten days I take one of these. When I do, they take away my appetite for a while."

"What are they for?" Marac asked.

Borri held out her hand. "May I see one?"

Marghe hesitated, then twisted open the vial and laid one of the softgels on the outstretched palm. Aoife watched Marghe intently.

"I'm not from here, the north," Marghe said carefully. "I take these so that I don't catch a virus, a sickness, from you."

"Why did you come up here?" Scatha asked. "Where were you going?"

"I was going to Ollfoss. In Moanwood."

Borri rolled the softgel around on her palm and nodded. "A bezoar. Prevention. Just as we used to dose ourselves with ellum root when we went south to trade, to stop bowel rot." She picked up the softgel, sniffed it. "What sickness is it you protect yourself from?"

"I don't know what you call it. It takes forty to sixty days to develop and can start with a cough and itching eyes."

"Followed by aches in the joints, sore gums, high fever?"

"Yes," she said, surprised. "Sometimes." She looked at Marac and Scatha, who were smiling. "Do you know what it is?"

Scatha laughed. "Baby fever!"

Marghe looked to Borri for confirmation, and the healer nodded. "It's not common, but sometimes a baby is born early and two moons later comes down with fever. Rarely, they bleed from the nose or the eyes and then their hearts run away, beat themselves to exhaustion. If that happens, they die. Otherwise they cough a few days, and scream enough to try their mothers' patience, but recover fast enough." She looked at the softgel thoughtfully. "I've never heard of a grown woman getting it. Not Echraidhe or Briogannon, not at Singing Pastures or Ollfoss." Her eyes were very bright when they met Marghe's. "Not even in faraway places across the Oboshi Desert or the Western Ocean."

Scatha leaned forward. "Where are you from?"

Aoife stirred. "Marghe is Echraidhe now." She held Scatha's gaze, then Marac's. There were no more questions.

After the meal, Aoife and the two younger women left for Aelle's tent. Borri stayed where she was, rolling the softgel absently between her fingers while Marghe banked the fire and collected the bowls to take outside and scrape clean in the snow.

"Put the bowls down," the healer said mildly, "and come sit with me."

Marghe settled cross-legged opposite her. The healer held the softgel up to the light.

"This is like nothing I know of. Here, take it back." Marghe dropped it into the vial, stowed it away in her pocket. The healer watched her. "Marghe, where do you come from that you're so afraid of baby fever, and Aoife is afraid to let you speak?"

Marghe said nothing.

"Don't fear Aoife on account of me. What you say here is between us two."

Marghe wondered if that was true. "What do you know of the world?" she asked eventually.

"Much," Borri said dryly. "What is it you think I don't but should?"

Marghe felt her cheeks go red. "I meant, what do you know of the physical shape of your world?"

" 'Your' world?" Borri said thoughtfully. She leaned back a little, but Marghe saw the muscles around the healer's eyes tighten.

She decided to trust Borri. "There are many; the moons in your sky are worlds, but nobody lives there. The world I come from is something like this one, but the people are different, and the diseases."

"Have you told anyone else this?"

"Only Aoife. Will you tell me what's wrong?"

"Listen to me." She laid a hand on Marghe's knee. "Aoife was right to protect you. You must never, never speak to anyone of what you've just told me. No one."

The hand on Marghe's knee was brown; a vein blue-snaked across it from below the base of the thumb. Marghe lifted her eyes from the hand to Borri's face and could not keep the bitterness out of her voice. "*Aoife* protect me? Who from?"

A draft blew a spark from the fire. Borri sighed. "Aoife's soestre. Uaithne."

Aoife and Uaithne? "But I thought . . ." She thought Aoife had no family; she thought that, like her, Aoife was alone. But soestre usually lived together as family; as tent sisters, if not lovers.

"What happened?" she asked.

"Ask Aoife," Borri said. "It's not my story to tell."

Aoife would never tell her, they both knew that. She tried another approach. "Why would it be dangerous for me if Uaithne found out I'm from another world?"

"Not just dangerous for you. For all of us." She glanced at the entrance flap, and Marghe hoped Aoife and the two younger women would be a long time at Aelle's.

"Something happened to Uaithne a long time ago," Borri said eventually. "It disturbed her mind. She believes she's the Death Spirit returned. We have a story, an old story, about the goddess of death and how we came into this world."

IT WAS quiet and dark outside, with wind slow and steady from the northeast. Marghe wondered what the stars would look like this far north: Jeep's sun was one of a huge constellation. Beyond the clouds, the sky probably blazed. She wished she could see it.

She levered a few taar chips free and shoveled them into the sack. Aoife, Borri, Marac, and Scatha were inside rearranging the tent. She had volunteered to refill the sack; she did not want to be near Aoife at the moment, not until she had time to think over what Borri had said.

She touched RECORD. "The Echraidhe have a legend that clearly links the virus with their reproduction, and with their retention of languages and customs already dead a thousand years before they left Earth. They tell of a death world, a spirit world which contains all the peoples and monsters there ever were."

Marghe found herself adopting the same singsong cadence Borri had used. "In this spirit world, death is the goddess of all. Or almost all. Long ago, some of these spirit people renounced death: there must be more, they said. Yes, said the goddess, you shall find out. And she cast them forth. At length, they came to a place where the goddess in her normal guise could not follow, a place of strange beasts and too many moons.

"But in this place where the goddess was not, her spirit still lived, though sleeping, in the hearts of fully half the people, and in this place, her spirit awoke and claimed them in a great sickness. But the goddess is ever-merciful. To those who survived was given a miraculous gift: children. It is said that the spirit of these people lives on in their daughters, and their daughters' daughters, so that all who come after may remember back to what once was, and what may be again. However, it is also said that the spirit of the goddess of death has come to live within all who survive, waiting. It is said that she will rise again in her chosen one, and that there will be an accounting."

To Marghe, most of the story was clear enough. It was a fable of the original settlers' journey from Earth and their arrival here, the place of strange beasts and too many moons. The goddess of death was, of course, the virus. According to the story, the virus somehow made it possible for the survivors to conceive children. The memory references of the fable were not clear, though the allusions to a Chosen One were not too different from the kind of messiah myth found in scores of cultures.

What was unusual was that Uaithne, Aoife's soestre, believed that the Death Spirit had returned within her. Borri had not told her how Uaithne had come to believe this, but apparently the tribeswoman was adamant, saying she was only waiting for a message. Borri, like Aoife, believed that if Marghe let it be known she was from another world, Uaithne might think she was the messenger. And nobody knew what Uaithne would do then.

Thick indigo clouds moved overhead like a school of whales.

Borri and Aoife had both told her: stay quiet. For their own sakes, or hers? Was this something she might turn to her advantage? And did they know Uaithne was already watching her?

She sat back on her heels and watched the sky. It matched her mood: slow-moving, benthic. What had happened between Uaithne and Aoife, the two soestre? She needed to know.

OVER THE next few days, Marghe watched Aoife. In a tribe where women prided themselves on self-sufficiency, Aoife was more alone than any. She was liked and respected, she was Agelast, but Marghe never saw her smile, never saw her reach out and pat someone's hand while they talked, or lean her head on another's shoulder. None shared her bed. Even the Levarch and her family, Borri, and her own daughters, Marac and Scatha, were kept outside, unable to reach through her solitude.

Out on the plains with Marghe, Aoife seemed content. Marghe understood that, too. Grief was not a spectator sport. After her mother had died, she had spent hours roaming the Welsh hillsides, her only company the sheep that still lambed on the bleak hills in spring. But Aoife's was a constant grief, a wound that could not heal: Uaithne was still alive.

Once, when they were alone with the herd and the wind, Marghe cut out a limping taar from the rest and dismounted to check its hooves. Aoife reined in and joined her. Marghe lifted the beast's forefoot to look at the tender spot.

"Tell me why he's limping," the tribeswoman said.

"I think it must have been ice. Gone now." She let go of the leg and slapped the taar on the rump. Aoife nodded approval and then went to her saddle pack and took out a palo. She held it out to Marghe.

"You know enough to have this."

Marghe hefted it in her hand. It was as long as her forearm and thick as a spear shaft, made of polished hardwood. Near one end was a carving of a horse. Not a shaggy Echraidhe mount: Pella.

"You made this for me?"

Aoife said nothing. Marghe flicked it experimentally; it snapped into a slender pole almost two meters long. Another flick of her wrist telescoped it back in on itself. She did not know what to say. Wood was precious, but it was not only that: Aoife had made this, carved it, polished and stained it in secret. For her.

Aoife held out her hand for it, showed Marghe the tiny leather strap at the end. "This is to secure it for traveling."

Marghe did so, then fastened it to her belt. It hung to midthigh. She ran her finger down the carefully stained wood. "Aoife, thank you." But Aoife was already swinging back into her saddle.

On their way back that afternoon, they saw a figure galloping away into the stretching white at a furious pace. Aoife bowed her head, as at some old hurt, and Marghe knew it must be Uaithne.

"Where does she go at such a pace?"

Aoife turned her face away as if she had not heard.

Chapter Seven

EACH DAWN brightened later and later. Aoife started taking Marghe far out onto the plains, past the grazing grounds, beyond the sight of smoke from the fires. They used their palos to clear away patches of the hard-packed snow and the tribeswoman showed Marghe a world she had never dreamed existed. A world of frozen ice moss, of fist-sized scuttlers called ruks, of the snow worm. She learned how to catch the worm, how to bite off the tail and drink down the viscous, sugary fluid until all that was left was an empty, flaccid skin, like a lace. That could be toasted and eaten, or used like a leather thong. They ate ruks, too, but these Aoife had to catch. Marghe, though she was learning to use a sling, was hopelessly slow compared to the hard-shelled snow crabs. Perhaps because they did always defeat her, she disliked the taste: the flesh was greasy, acrid enough to bring tears to her eyes. Aoife made her eat it because it was good for her bones. Marghe, remembering the vow she made herself to stay as fit as she could, complied.

Sometimes they just rode, eyepits stained dark against the snow glare, while Aoife told stories of Tehuantepec before the coming of the tribe. Tehuantepec, she said, had long ago been a plain waving with grass, peopled by dark spirits. Marghe wondered about climatic change. On cold nights, Aoife continued, when these spirits still roamed, they might trick an unwary rider from her horse, then eat her, or the horse.

Marghe asked about the stones.

"They have always been," Aoife said, shrugging. "They were there before we came, will be there long after the plain has returned to a sea of grass." Every year, she said, they went there to feel the magic, to thank the spirits that sang every spring and made the grass grow and the taars quicken. The spirits in the stones sang all year. Listening, Marghe remembered their electromagnetic hum.

Sometimes Aoife told stories of tribal honor, of raids on the Briogannon, another tribe who dwelt on the plain; of raids on the herds of Singing Pastures and, in times past, on the forest gardens of Ollfoss.

"But why not just make trata with other communities?" Marghe kept wanting to know. "You'd both benefit." She had seen how small their population was. They needed trade, cultural diversity. Genetic diversity, too, though she did not know how that worked. Without the taking of strangers like herself, they might die out. They might die out anyway.

"Echraidhe do not stoop to trata."

"Why not?"

"We take what we need, not bargain like farmers," Aoife would say. "The old ways work well enough."

"Old ways are not always the best ways."

And Aoife would shrug and fall silent. Moments later, she would begin an instructional tale about the Echraidhe code of tribe before self. In such a hostile environment such a code was necessary for survival, Marghe knew; she had encountered it on the harsh world of Gallipoli, in old Scottish clan ties of Earth. She wondered what needs Aoife subjugated for the good of the tribe. She found the complexities of such an honor code hard to sympathize with. Aoife was always patient. "Selfishness is for younglings," she would say.

Sometimes, when even Aoife admitted the weather was bad,

they would sit in the yurti. Marghe held the wool for Aoife while she wove, or helped her mix with water the acrid powder that was stored in the foretent: Aoife told her it was made from the dried leaves of corax, a black, leathery succulent found in the northern forests in summer. It made a powerful bleaching agent.

Marghe listened carefully to anything Aoife told her, not knowing what might prove useful later. Despite the fact that Aoife was partly responsible for her capture, for her remaining a virtual prisoner, Marghe watched the tribeswoman enjoy having her there to teach, and felt unhappy; she knew she would be prepared to do this woman injury, if necessary, to escape. At these moments, she would take a deep breath, put aside the confusing thoughts, and help Aoife smear the bleach paste onto raw wool with a bone spatula.

Borri, and Marac and Scatha, also spent more and more time in the yurti, for as the Echraidhe reckoned it, this was the Moon of Shelters. Soon it would be the Moon of Knives, when only the unwary or the desperate would ride far from the hearth.

The Moon of Knives, Aoife said, was the time of great blizzards, of the howling cold that swept over the Ice Sea from the north. Strange beasts traveled on the breath of the ice wind. From the wastelands they would come, across the frozen waters. While the land lay quiet under the days of dark, nine days of night barely lightening to gray before deepening again to full dark, the beasts would roam northern Tehuantepec. The creatures of the Great Forest—the tree-dwelling yanomao, the glimmer flies, the rare and beautiful jewelfeet—would be driven deep into its snow-shrouded fastness by the cyarnac and the goth. Cyarnac, it was rumored, were four-legged, smaller than a horse and swifter than the wind. Those who had seen one and survived said they were as alien and cold as the great mountain glacier, and that they drew heat from a woman's body and soul as swiftly as meltwater. Thick-furred and white as bleached bone, they kept their hairless young in pouches and ate anything that moved.

Marghe listened, appreciating the storytellers' art, analyzing the content.

The goth were different. Tall they were, half as high again as a big woman astride a big horse. Gray and gaunt, they were creatures of the cold mist and the dark places under trees. They stood on two feet, and a woman who had seen one, Aoife said, told of strange, flat eyes which she swore on her mother's blood were intelligent. Intelligent or not, the goth were said to live on lichen and bark scraped from the sides of trees and under the snow. Their faces were round, like platters, their mouths horny-lipped. Their fur was shaggy and streaked and it was said that a woman could stand next to one in a forest and not know it was there until it moved.

Marghe wondered if these half-mythical goth could be the builders of the stone circle, driven from their usual habitat by warm-blooded aliens. But none of the Echraidhe would admit to having seen one themselves. It was all tales from the past. Perhaps they were long dead.

NEAR THE end of the Moon of Shelters, when foul weather had penned the Echraidhe in their yurtu for more than two days, the tribe gathered in the enormous yurti of the Levarch, the story tent. Most were drinking. The circular tent was low and the air heavy with the smell of unwashed women, their fur and leather clothes, grease, and the animal stench of taar chips. It was very hot.

Marghe took a long swallow of ale; her face was already flushed but she filled her bowl with more of the dark, slightly bitter stuff. Cuirm, the Echraidhe called it; a great improvement on the ever-foul locha. She looked around the tent. The former Levarch, Nehu, whose old voice was like the whispering of dry leaves, was telling a tale of a young Echraidhe adopted by the beasts of the forest. Even to Marghe it sounded well-worn, the phrases ritual and well-practiced. And the Echraidhe were restless.

She sipped at her ale again, licked foam from her lips. Even the Levarch was flushed and wild. Aoife sat a little apart, knotting bright colors, occasionally looking up from the thick strands under her hands. A half-full cup stood on the floor by her knee. Borri lay with her head on Aelle's lap. On the opposite side of the hearth, Uaithne stared fixedly at a point two handsbreadths above Aoife's head. She did not drink from her cup. To Marghe, unused to so much ale, it seemed that Uaithne's hair flamed with violent thoughts. The air was bright and thick with sexual tension.

Nehu's tale wound to its ending and, as was then her right, the old Levarch requested a story about a raid from Mairu. Mairu stood and held her palms outward for silence; the Echraidhe quieted. She struck an over-solemn pose and told the tribe she would tell of a time, last spring, when she and her soestre had, by trickery, parted the women of Singing Pastures from the possession of four sacks of grain, a sack of dap, and a saddle. She pranced and postured and pulled faces, exaggerating her cunning and her victims' stupidity. Roars of laughter, and shouted interruptions from Fion, her soestre, accompanied the story as Mairu ruthlessly reduced the women of Singing Pastures to creatures with no more wit and wisdom than snow worms. Though the end of the tale was greeted with stamps and shouts of approval, Marghe heard the heat and wildness surging and building in the tent. At the back of the tent, two women were kissing in endless, slow intensity; their furs were undone. Marghe watched a weather-dark hand stroke soft breasts and became aware of her own muscles coiled sleek and plump under her too-tight skin, of hot air rubbing at her throat and widening her nostrils.

She could have taken her sexual energy and smoothed it down, but she wanted to let it burn through her, she wanted to enjoy being alive. She turned away and gulped from her bowl. The ale made her reckless.

She scrambled up and held out her palms for silence. The tent quieted abruptly.

"Women of the Echraidhe . . . Though the snow lies but a finger-width from these walls, though the air is cold enough to freeze the milk in a taar's tit, let my words take you to a faraway place where women sweat in the heat and bathe naked in mountain springs to cool their skins."

Oh, she had their attention now. They were leaning forward, bowls halfway to mouths; even Borri was sitting up. She winked at Aoife, took a huge swig of cuirm, and realized she was drunk already. Haii! What did she care?

"Tonight, I will speak to you of strange lands and beating hearts, of stone that burns under the ground like dry dung, and of passion, power, and intrigue."

And so Marghe spoke of her recruitment and passage to this world. She dressed it up as a legend-quest: a powerful tribe of one country discovers the richness of a neighboring country and determines to take what it needs. But those who enter this strange new country with their arrogance and superior weaponry suffer through ignorance. They set off great burns in the unstable south and western grasslands and many die; they ignore the wise women of the country and fight the burns in such a way that they get worse. As if this was not enough, many of the newcomers begin to fall sick and die of a mysterious disease.

Marghe was enjoying herself. She transformed Company into a group of bickering tribal elders arguing over the selection of a suitable daughter for a trading mission. This chosen one was then prepared for her task. The initial survival training she had undergone years ago on the deserts of the Kalahari and the cold crags of the Rockies needed no significant changes, nor the laborious learning of another language. She did not have to force her eyes to sparkle with tears when she told of the death of the woman's mother, or the final leavetaking from the beloved green hillsides and gray stone of her country.

The Echraidhe traveled with her through memories of the alien smells and tastes, sounds and sights, of the ugly slashed land around that outpost in the strange country, Port Central. They listened while she spoke of grasslands that still smoldered, of the determination of the herders there to claim reparation, of the wonders of Holme Valley and her own passage through Singing Pastures. She made them feel, as she had felt, the exhilaration and fear, the freezing cold and stifling heat of her journey alone over the years to reach here, this place. Tehuantepec.

It was a great success. Marghe leaned against the wall of sound, the roar and stamp of approval, swaying. It felt good to be seen as human. She looked over at Aoife and saw the scar twist in a slight smile. Before she knew what she was doing, she held out her palms again. She looked at the Levarch.

"I've told a tale. Now it's my right to ask one to be told?"

"It is."

"Then I ask that Aoife speaks of how she came by her scars."

Silence congealed around her. She looked about in confusion. Several women looked away. "Aoife?" she said, swaying.

"I will not." Aoife's eyes were flat and hard, like stones.

Marghe did not understand. She had expected Aoife to tell some tale of daring, of wounds heroically gained, of being named Agelast. Instead . . . this.

The Levarch cleared her throat. "Marghe asks only her right. But this story rightly belongs to Uaithne."

Heads turned, waiting.

"I obey the Levarch in all things." Uaithne's voice was light, unperturbed. Marghe felt sick. How could she have been stupid enough to get drunk? Uaithne held out her palms in the ritual gesture and began. The tale she told was plain, without exaggeration or mime, and in third person:

"At the end of the grazing season nineteen summers ago Uaithne and her soestre Aoife made a pact that when the time came for them to choose their real names, they would join together in the deepsearch and go back further along their memories than any of their tribe had searched before. A common youthful declaration.

"The time came. They withdrew to their yurti, linked together in the deepbond of soestre, and tranced together for the deepsearch into the memories of their mothers and their mothers' mothers. As everyone gathered here knows, deepsearch is exhausting. No matter what one swears in youthful exuberance, one usually does not go farther back than three or four generations. But Uaithne and her soestre were fine and brave, strong young women who believed that together they could do anything. And so they tried. They tranced deeper and deeper, further and further back, to the foremothers of their foremothers' foremothers. And further. Back to when Echraidhe and Briogannon roamed Tehuantepec as one tribe, back to before the tribe left the forest for the plain, back to the Beginning when all peoples lived together in one place, Ollfoss, deep in Moanwood.

"For Aoife, this was enough, more than enough. She had seen all the women who had given life to each other, generation after generation, in a long line leading to the present, and herself. She knew her place in the world. She had chosen her name.

"It was not enough for Uaithne. She wanted to go further back than any woman had gone before; she wanted to see what was on the other side of the Beginning. She dived deep, then deeper. Aoife struggled, tried to stop her soestre, scared for both of them: if they went too deep, they might be unable to come back up to their true place in the world, to themselves. And neither had the strength for much more. But the two women were soestre, deep-bonded so that when one hurt, the other suffered; it was a bond that was knitted into their lives and experience, as necessary as breathing.

"Uaithne dragged Aoife further down.

"Aoife knew that if she did not stop this, they were lost. She did the only thing she could: she broke the deepbond.

"Somehow, Aoife dragged herself back to the present. Uaithne lay still and white and silent beside her. Aoife tried to wake her, to call her back, but she was young and did not have the skill. Uaithne, deep in trance and not expecting the dissolution of the bond that had kept them close enough to share dreams all their lives, had been unprotected. Now her mind wandered alone amongst the strange herd of memories, unable to find the path home.

"Aoife ran to find old Macha, Borri's teacher. It took many days for Macha to find Uaithne and bring her back to herself. When she did return, she screamed herself raw. She was ill for a long time. And afterward, she could not bear the sight of her former soestre and she was taken to live in the Levarch's yurti.

"Time passed. To those who were concerned it seemed that the estranged soestre did begin to heal, in their own separate fashions. While Aoife spent much time not talking to anyone, Uaithne seemed to recover from the broken deepbond and took to riding out to visit the Briogannon.

"At the time of the new Moon of Sweet Grass, Uaithne and a woman of the Briogannon, Fellyr, went before the elders of that tribe and swore themselves to each other. Afterwards, as is usual for those of different tribes, they decided to start a child each as evidence of good faith. Now, although they were lovers and soon to be tent sisters, they had neither skill nor knowledge of one another to trance together deeply enough to mutually quicken each other and conceive soestre. They would link together just deep enough to quicken together, Fellyr decided. But Uaithne had not tranced since she had chosen her name, and was afraid. When Fellyr tranced and quickened, Uaithne did not, but said nothing. Thus deceived, the Briogannon woman was happy to say a temporary farewell to Uaithne, who was to journey back to the Echraidhe for the blessings of her family and Levarch, and to collect her share of horse and herd, before traveling back to the Briogannon greengrounds.

"At that time, the greengrounds of the Briogannon were three days' ride from the Echraidhe yurtu. On the second night of her journey back, Uaithne was lying in her nightbag, composing herself for sleep, when a patch of cloud uncurled itself from around the spring moon, and light poured down from the sky and through the open flap of her tent. 'Try once again,' the moon seemed to say, 'and I will watch over you.' And so Uaithne did. She deepened her breathing and slowed her heart, and fell into trance.

"At first, all was well. She heard the voices of her foremothers calling but did not listen; she was here to pay heed to her body, to listen to the rhythms of blood and egg, to quicken life. But one voice, stranger than the others, called and for just a moment Uaithne listened. The moment stretched to hours, the hours to days as the voice drew Uaithne deeper into the past and through the barrier that is the Beginning. To this day, no one knows how long Uaithne stayed in deep trance, rigid and hardly breathing. When she came to, the snows lay heavy on the roof of her tent and her skin hung loose on her bones.

"When she came at last to the yurtu of the Echraidhe, all marked how thin and strange she looked. To those few who asked, she said nothing. When the Levarch, worried, spoke to her sternly, Uaithne said only that she had spoken with the goddess of death, that she was her chosen representative in this place, the Death Spirit, and that she awaited the sign to begin the accounting long spoken of. She would not be gainsaid. She resumed her life with the tribe. She made no mention of Fellyr of the Briogannon nor of her oath; thus, no word was sent, no message knot delivered to her lover, still waiting at the Briogannon greengrounds.

"Time passed, and Fellyr grew worried at her lover's absence. Without pausing to consult the elders, she saddled her horse and rode hard. After two days without rest or sleep, crazy with worry and hunger, she came to the summer camp of the Echraidhe. She saw Uaithne working alone by the taar pens and slid from her horse, into her lover's arms, sobbing with relief. But Uaithne thrust her aside and told her that she no longer wished to partner a Briogannon, that she had other tasks, that she withdrew her oath.

"Now, when Fellyr the Briogannon realized she had been cast aside with as much thought as one would discard a worn boot, her worry turned to rage and grief and she slid her knife free. Uaithne, as no one would dispute, is a fine fighting woman: she knocked Fellyr aside and took the knife in her own hand.

"Fellyr lay sobbing and broken on the sweet new grass and, instead of pity, Uaithne offered violence.

"Aoife, who had caught the Briogannon's panicked mount out by the Levarch's tent and was searching for its rider, came upon the two a heartbeat before murder. Uaithne had her knee on Fellyr's chest, oblivious to anything but the keen-edged knife lying across the soft throat beneath her. There was no time to call out. Instead, Aoife leapt and knocked Uaithne aside.

"Uaithne fought like a demon, as though she did not know she struggled against the woman who had been her soestre. The blade caught Aoife across cheek and nose, the haft smashed into bone. Half blinded by her own blood, Aoife fumbled in the grass for a stone and swung at the side of Uaithne's head. She had to hit her twice more before Uaithne dropped the knife and collapsed onto the white-faced Fellyr. . . ."

Someone added a chip to the fire. It spat into the silence. Marghe felt the ale ungluing her world, slipping it free from its moorings. If she moved her head, the world would spin. Uaithne raised her bowl and tilted it toward Marghe in mocking salute. "Did you enjoy your tale?"

"It is not finished," the Levarch said heavily. She turned to Marghe. "The Briogannon woman returned to her tribe. There she renamed herself Ojo, which in their speech means evil eye. A year later, when her daughter was born, she named her Ojo also. The elder Ojo and her tent sisters have sworn blood feud against Uaithne. They have raided us many times. I fear there will soon be tribe feud between us. Now, instead of Echraidhe and Briogannon exchanging news and lovers, we guard our herds day and night."

MARGHE WOKE up long before dawn with the splitting head and stretched-tight feeling of a hangover. The tent was cold and filled with the soft breath of four sleeping women. She was thirsty, but the water jug was empty; her bladder was full.

Shivering, clutching the jug, she staggered outside to relieve herself. Snow crunched under her boots, loud in the predawn quiet. Her urine smelled hot, toxic; it pattered and steamed as it burned into the snow. She stood up, kicked more snow over it, and laced up her furs. If only she could dispose of last night's mistakes as easily.

The herd trough was thick with ice, and she had to bash it through with the bone propped against the fence. She dipped the jug in; icy water made her hands ache to the bone. She drank, thought she might throw up, then drank again and refilled the jug. She tucked her hands under her armpits, glad of the ache. She deserved it.

One of the Echraidhe guarding the herd, a fur-wrapped bundle on a horse, nudged her mount over.

"It's a while until dawn," she said, curious.

How they hated to ask direct questions, Marghe thought, and just nodded, hoping the woman would leave her in peace. She idly considered knocking her from her horse and riding out of here. But the guard always stayed just out of reach, hand on knife. Elementary precautions. Even if she could escape, it would be pointless. Aoife would track her down within hours.

"You're the second one up so early," the woman volunteered. "Uaithne rode off north and east before the moons set."

The tribeswoman had been guarding the herd all night, Marghe realized, and had probably not heard about the stranger woman humiliating Aoife in public. She could not know that Uaithne's was the last name Marghe wanted to hear. Marghe borrowed one of Aoife's tactics and simply ignored the guard until she clucked her mount back into the middle of the sleeping taars.

Marghe contemplated the snow on her boots. Uaithne often disappeared for days at a time; no one knew where she went. Why should this be any different? But she sensed that it was.

She had other things to think about. After another drink of water so cold it burned all the way down to her stomach, she set the jug back down in the snow and pulled her wristcom from a pocket.

"As the Echraidhe use it, the term soestre means those who are born after their mothers somehow synchronize their biorhythms and, through a process which I assume bears similarities to the control by a trained person of her otherwise autonomic nervous system, stimulate each other's ova to divide." It sounded bizarre, but the Echraidhe reproduced somehow, and unless the entire tribe was crazy or lying, then some of the daughters of these women, the ones they called soestre, were not genetically identical to their mothers. Which was impossible. Except it happened. How? "Tentative theory: that this ovular stimulation by another somehow encourages genetic information that is recessive to become dominant." That might account for some of the differences like eye and hair coloring. But what about height, or bone structure? She did not know enough to be certain whether or not these could be explained by the differences the fetuses encountered in the womb.

She drank some more water.

"The deep trancing necessary for reproduction has acquired mystical aspects for the Echraidhe. The rite of passage is attended by a ritual trance, called deepsearch, which, the Echraidhe claim, allows the adolescent to somehow access the memories of her ancestors. The trancing is so deep that psychosis may occur, or may go on so long that it becomes physically detrimental to the subject."

The Echraidhe accepted access to memories of past lives as casually as others believed in their gods, in reincarnation, in hellfire and damnation. She would not make a judgment on the matter.

She clicked RECORD again, then changed her mind and hit OFF. There were only a few hours of chip space left. She could speculate any time. When the chip was full, she would have to lift her face from the here and now, from her perspective as a woman researching a primitive tribe, and face her future. But the chip was not full yet.

Inside the tent she laced the flap closed behind her. There was just enough light to make it back to her nightbag without treading on anyone. Aoife stirred.

"Aoife?" There was no reply, but she could feel Aoife watching her in the dark. "I'm sorry. I . . ." There was no way she could explain how she felt. "I'm sorry," she repeated.

The next day, and the day after that, Aoife got her up before dawn and kept her out on the plains until after dark. Marghe wondered if the tribeswoman was keeping her out of harm's way.

This time, there was no storytelling. Aoife was grim, speaking only to explain how to tell the difference between the vein and artery in a taar's neck, and which was the right one to cut if she needed a quick kill, or to explain how to hold the skinning knife to take a skin whole from a just-butchered taar. There were endless lessons, and it seemed to Marghe that Aoife was trying to teach her in one winter everything there was to being an Echraidhe. She wondered at that. Before the night in the Levarch's tent, Marghe would have thought Aoife's actions arbitrary, but now she wondered what the tribeswoman saw ahead to prompt this hard, uncompromising work.

Marghe still resented Aoife, because she was her guard, the one who watched her constantly, the one who stood between her and freedom. But as they labored on the plain, Aoife patiently repeating what must have seemed to her a basic lesson, Marghe trying over and again to master something any Echraidhe child could do with ease, she came to see that they were not that different. Aoife only did what she thought was right—and Aoife, too, was alone.

At night, they both lifted their heads at the sound of hoofbeats, lowered them again when the hoofbeats passed and it was not Uaithne.

Five nights after the incident in the Levarch's tent, Marghe woke up in the dark, listening. Hoofbeats. Uaithne. Pulling on her boots was difficult; they were as stiff as her arms.

The sky was almost clear of cloud. It was the dark of the moons, but stars were strewn in a thick twist, like old jewels, across the sky. The air was crisp and bright. She could hear the horse clearly. Others did, too; tent flaps were unlaced, and feet stamped in the snow to warm hastily donned boots.

Aoife appeared at her shoulder, stood close.

"It's Uaithne," Marghe said, and felt the tribeswoman nod. Suddenly she wanted to put her arms around the small, fierce-faced woman and hold her close, protect her from more hurt. A rush of loneliness made her throat ache.

The drum of hoofbeats got louder; they heard the harsh breathing of an animal pushed too hard. Then it was there. Someone held the horses while Uaithne slid from the saddle and held up both arms.

"It has begun," she shouted. In the starlight, the blood on her hands looked black.

Chapter Eight

THAT NIGHT the sky remained clear, fading from black to a dark, almost navy blue near morning. The air was bitterly cold, brittle as glass. The change in the weather signaled time for the herds to be culled, the old and weak killed that the fodder might last the rest of the herd over winter and that their flesh and bones and blood keep heat in the tribe's veins during the Moon of Knives and the Moon of Silence, when the world itself seemed to slow to a stop and hesitate before spinning on to spring.

Shards of light thrown up by the snow had the taars shying and skittish as Marghe and Aoife and others, on foot, herded them all into one pen. The women called to one another, shouted at the stupid beasts that milled in confusion, cursed when one enterprising animal made a run for the open plain. Uaithne's braids burned in the sun like rivers of hot Irish gold as she chased it and brought it down in a tangle of legs.

Marghe wondered how the taar had felt, running to freedom one moment, brought crashing to the snow in a gust and swirl of laughter the next.

Marghe surreptitiously did her best to keep the herd between herself and Uaithne, Uaithne whose teeth flashed whiter than snow as she laughed and lunged her horse this way and that, Uaithne who was strong and healthy and unconcerned about what she had done. A few laughed with her. The shocked silence of last night had given way to mutterings which had become resignation, then calm acceptance: Uaithne had killed a Briogannon, yes, had plunged them into a feud with another tribe that might be the death of them all before spring, but she was also Echraidhe, one of them, their sister, and her madness—if it was madness—was bright and proud and beautiful.

Aoife said nothing. She had remained silent since the night before.

The Echraidhe separated out the culls. It was hard work, and confusing: women slapping at rumps with palos, twirling nooses, cutting out taars from the rest seemingly at random and herding them to one end of the pen. Marghe watched Aoife and tried to follow her lead, using her palo to nudge an old or thin or limping taar away from its more healthy siblings. Once she almost got trampled by two taars running blindly from the swinging palos and had to scramble on all fours across the dung-spattered snow. She looked up to find Uaithne watching her with an almost sexual intensity. She flushed. Uaithne laughed and turned away.

The morning wore on and Aoife still said nothing. Marghe was nervous. She stayed too fast and light on her feet, blinking too often, throwing her noose and missing, jerking her head up at every shadow, thinking it was Uaithne. By the time Mairu whistled and stopped everything for food, Marghe was exhausted. Marac and Scatha and two other youngsters she did not know brought around bowls of dap and grain. She ate.

Someone stood next to her, her shadow sharp against the ice-granule snow. She looked up, expecting Aoife. It was Uaithne. She leaned against the fence; her hood was down and snow clung to her hair. Her skin was creamy, fresh, with a delicate flush of exertion, and very smooth. Her gloves were tucked under her belt, next to her knife. The carving on the bone handle was worn smooth with use. She smiled.

"You should eat that before it freezes," she said, and nodded at the fingerful of grain and butter Marghe still held halfway to her mouth. Marghe, knowing she would be unable to swallow it, put it back in her bowl. Aoife was nowhere in sight. Uaithne took out her knife and began picking dirt and grease from under her nails. "Why do you stay?" she asked conversationally.

"Why do I stay?" Sun gleamed on the tiny golden hairs on the backs of Uaithne's fingers and ran like bronze along the polished black blade. Marghe wondered if she had killed the Briogannon with the same knife, pushed it deep into her stomach and twisted.

"Yes," Uaithne said. The knife twitched, drawing blood. She did not seem to mind. "Why do you stay, and why did you come?"

Because you forced me, Marghe wanted to say. *Because you pointed your spear at my stomach and Aoife threw me across her horse.* But Uaithne was staring out across the snow, and Marghe sensed she was no longer waiting for an answer, that she already had her own.

"And why did you send the other one? To test me?"

Other one? Where was Aoife? She dared not turn her head away to look for her.

"But I passed her tests," Uaithne went on. Blood dripped onto the snow, perfect round ruby drops. "Oh, she threatened me, searching for weakness, but I laughed at her promises of demon voices that curve around the belly of the world, of light that kills, of rafts that glide on rivers of air faster than the fastest horse can gallop."

Sleds. The woman was talking of comms and lasers and sleds.

"I showed her the ways of the Death Spirit. I showed her I was worthy. I ignored all her pleas and killed her slowly, one piece at a time. One piece at a time." She seemed to shake herself back to the present. "So why have you come? To test me again?"

One morning when Marghe was eight and running through the door on her way to play outside in a hot, steamy rainfall, her mother had caught her by the arm and told her she could not play until she had tidied her room. Marghe had pulled free and said plaintively, "But I already did that." She must have sounded a lot like Uaithne did.

Unthinkingly, she said the same thing now as her mother had said then. "I don't believe you." But she did.

Uaithne dipped her bloody hand in a pocket and pulled free something that glittered in the sunlight. Marghe reached out reflexively and took it. After so long handling only bone and wood and leather, the metal felt slick and slippery.

A wristcom. Broken.

"See, the same as the one you wear."

Marghe examined the wristcom. No way to tell whose. Fear pushed at her guts like an expanding bubble of air. "When did you take this? How long ago?"

Uaithne shrugged. "Sixteen moons, perhaps less."

Winnie. She had killed Winnie. "You killed my assistant." She was angry now.

Uaithne shrugged again. "I cut off her fingers, then her toes, but she kept testing me, threatening me with the light-killing demons on rafts, to see if I would stop. So I cut off her arms, to show I was worthy—"

Marghe shook her head, trying to shake the world away, but the sun stayed in the same place, her breath still steamed in the cold, this woman was still talking about murdering Winnie Kimura, torturing her to death.

"—she died squealing like a two-day-old foal until I cut out her tongue. She lived a long time. You send strong messengers."

Deep breaths. In. Out. "I sent no one," she said, then remembered she had just told Uaithne that Winnie was her assistant.

Uaithne smiled slyly. "She said you would come, and here you are. You almost fooled me, too, coming on a horse instead of a raft. But I know who you are. I've met you before." She shifted the knife to her other hand. Blood stained the hilt. A ritual cadence crept into her words. "You have spoken to me in my waking dreams, for I have tranced and I have seen Death. Now we are in a living trance, and you have come. Speak to me, sing to me, tell me what you need of me."

Madness and worship glittered in her eyes like chips of ice, and Marghe was afraid. Fear spiked under her ribs and fluttered under her skin. Sweat burst out on her face and began to freeze.

"Marghe." The voice came from behind her. Marghe only dared turn her head slightly. Aoife was standing there empty-handed, balanced like a dancer, ready, eyes fixed on the knife in Uaithne's bloody hand. "You are not needed here, Marghe," she said softly, still not moving. Uaithne was swaying now. "Go help Borri in the yurti."

Marghe backed away slowly, out of reach and out of earshot, until her legs threatened to give way and she had to stop. Aoife spoke to her soestre softly, moved a step closer. Uaithne stopped swaying and Marghe wondered what she had said. Aoife rested her hand gently on Uaithne's arm, still speaking. She pointed to the taars. Uaithne nodded, listening. Aoife talked on. Uaithne smiled, clapped her hand on Aoife's back, returned her knife to its sheath almost as an afterthought. She laughed and walked away. Aoife joined Marghe.

They walked back to the yurti in silence. Marghe was perturbed by her sense of security in Aoife's presence, recognizing the feeling for what it was: the passing of responsibility for her personal safety from herself to Aoife. That scared her almost as much as Uaithne had.

SHE DREAMED of the cull: red knives flicking, blood pumping over well-muscled arms wrapped around the necks of terrified taars and running into clay pots. Only fill them half-full, Aoife said, or the pots will break when they freeze. And Uaithne picking up a bowl, nodding to her and smiling, and drinking, drinking until sticky red poured down her chin, slicked her furs, began to fill the tent like a dark whirlpool. Learn to swim, Uaithne whispered, learn to swim, and the children of the Echraidhe laughed and splashed and played as the blood rose higher and higher until it lapped thickly at her chin.

Marghe surged up out of her nightbag, panting. Everyone was asleep. The hearth still glowed; the inside of the tent was red and full of other people's breath. She groped in the dim light for her overfurs.

It was snowing, a soft, silent fall. She walked away from the yurtu, away from the pens, past the Levarch's tent, until she was alone in the dark quiet. Soon it would be time for the days of dark—nine days of twilight. She hated Tehuantepec.

According to her wristcom, it was still early, hours before dawn. She could just keep on walking out here, forever, until she was exhausted. The snow would cover her tracks. She would probably die of hunger and exposure before Aoife found her. Maybe dying was better than staying here, like this, like some domestic animal kept for its breeding potential—its ability to bring fresh blood, new genes to the pool.

Breeding potential. She laughed out loud as she walked and the laugh was swallowed by the soft snow, the same empty dark that waited to swallow her. The dark was many things: the cold, the alien world, the virus, her own fear. Her FN-17 would not last forever. But if she managed to escape, she would die of cold or be caught. She stopped walking. Snow fell on her face, her hair. But if she stayed here, she might die anyway. She walked again. But if she ran, they might send Uaithne after her, with her knives that cut off toes and fingers and tongues . . .

She sat down in the snow, careless of the freezing cold, and pulled out her wristcom. She would externalize her thoughts. She was a rational woman. All she needed to do was list her options, then make the most sensible decision.

"Problem: the long-term survival of SEC representative Marguerite Angelica Taishan. Options: to give up and stay here in the camp of the Echraidhe; to attempt escape right now; to attempt escape at some point in the future when the Echraidhe may be less vigilant. Pertinent information to be considered: One, assuming escape is possible, where does she go? She's lost. Even if, by some miracle, she managed to reach Port Central before the experimental vaccine is all gone, she might still die. However, medical facilities will be available." She paused, thought a moment of the conversation with Lu Wai about the virus. "The most important thing to consider, direction-wise, is that she must be under shelter when the vaccine runs out and the virus hits."

She pulled the FN-17 from her pocket, tipped the softgels carefully into her palm, and counted them one by one back into the vial. "Assuming the incubation period is thirty days, and reckoning in a safety factor, estimated onset of the virus is approximately four moons from now. If, therefore, she attempts to escape, she should head for the nearest shelter, wherever that may be."

It was too dark to look at her map, but she had examined it many times before. It did not help much. She had tried to estimate the distance covered on horseback from the ringstones to the Echraidhe camp, but she had spent much of that journey upside down over a saddle and without access to her compass. The camp could lie anywhere within a circle whose radius might be seventy or more miles. Using a discarded leather thong, carefully marked to her map scale, she had measured possibilities. From everywhere but the most southwesterly segment of the circle, Ollfoss, or at least Moan-wood, was closer than Holme Valley. Practically, then, it would make sense to head north and east, to Ollfoss. How far north, and how far east, depended on her exact position, which she did not know.

"Second consideration: should she wait out the onset of the virus here, in the camp of the Echraidhe? Borri seems to be a competent healer. Weighed against this is the danger posed by the tribeswoman Uaithne."

Her legs were going numb. She closed her eyes, took the three deep breaths that triggered light meditation, and sent blood pumping around her veins, squeezing into the capillaries in her fingers and toes. Her legs began to warm. She shivered.

"Third consideration . . ."

The wristcom blinked amber: no chip space left. She stared at it. It carried on blinking. She turned it off, put it in her pocket, took it out again. Maybe this was a dream, too. She touched RECORD. The tiny amber light blinked, making her fingertips glow orange. It blinked for nearly a minute, then automatically shut itself down.

Marghe sat in the snow thousands of millions of miles from home, alone. Now there was nothing left. She did not weep: this far north, her tears would turn to ice and cut her cheeks.

MOON OF KNIVES.
Marghe and Aoife rode less often. Even with extra clothes

on under her overfur, Marghe froze. Now she understood the moon name: the cold slashed at her lungs like a thousand knives. Aoife made her a snow mask, a pad of taar felt to fit over her nose and mouth. It was still hard to breathe, but she went out as often as possible. Whenever the fire glowed in the yurti, she saw her dream of Uaithne, and of blood. Out here she could forget Uaithne for a while, gaze into the endless white and the ever-changing sky, listening to the soft crunch of their horses' hooves, the creak of leather.

Once, when they were out riding, Aoife leaned forward and Marghe saw her attention flow to a single point on the horizon. It was like watching a rough river funnel into a gorge. She followed the tribeswoman's gaze and saw a black speck that might be a rider. Aoife's hand hovered by her sling. A rush of adrenaline took Marghe by surprise and she had her own sling out and her reins gathered tight under a thigh to leave both hands free before she figured out what she was frightened of: Uaithne.

The black speck disappeared over the horizon. Aoife spoke without looking at her. "There is no danger."

Marghe tucked her sling back into her belt, took up the reins. They rode on in silence for a while.

"Aoife, Uaithne killed a . . . member of my family. Now I think she wants to kill me." Her voice was muffled behind the snow mask.

Aoife did not stop scanning the horizon. Her reply was mechanical. "You are Echraidhe. Your only family is Echraidhe. Uaithne is Echraidhe. She will not kill someone in her family."

"You wouldn't, no. But, don't you see, Uaithne isn't Echraidhe anymore, not in her head. She thinks she's the Death Spirit, beholden only to the goddess of death herself. Right now, the only thing that's kept me safe is that she can't quite make up her mind whether I'm here to test her or whether I'm the great goddess herself."

Aoife said nothing.

Marghe tore off her mask. "Listen to me. The woman is insane. She's already tried to kill you, her soestre, a member of her family, an Echraidhe, and now she's plunged the entire tribe into some kind of feud that none of you want. What more proof do you need before you do something to stop her?"

"There is nothing to be done. Uaithne is Echraidhe, I am Echraidhe. You are Echraidhe."

Marghe tried to marshal her thoughts. "Think of it this way: for the good of the horse herds, you geld the young stallions and kill the ones that persist in fighting. Uaithne is like a mad stallion; she's pulling the tribe apart. She must be curbed."

Aoife looked troubled. "She is Echraidhe, not a horse."

"Yes, which means you will have to think how to deal with her. Find a new way. The old ways sometimes aren't enough."

"They have always been enough."

"No. No, they haven't." Marghe could feel words bubbling under her tongue like lava. "How many yurtu are there pitched for the winter camp?"

"Fifty-four."

"How many were there pitched at the winter camp when the old Levarch was Agelast?"

Aoife was silent. Marghe pressed her advantage.

"More than fifty-four, and probably all were crowded, not half-empty the way they are now. Look at what that means, Aoife, face it: the Echraidhe are dying. They've always been dying. Ever since they split from the Briogannon. Ever since the tribe stopped trading, stopped mixing with others. There's a . . ." How could she say *minimum population density*? "A small tribe needs trata. Look at the health of the children, little Licha and Kaitlin. They need more than taar butter and grain to keep them well in the snows. They need green stuff, fruit, fish. Things that can only be found in trata." She took a deep breath. "You're Agelast. Stop Uaithne. Trade with the Briogannon instead. Old ways are not always the best ways."

They were still walking the horses forward through the snow. Aoife stared sightlessly at the horizon. "We are at feud," she said finally, "done is done."

"Change it."

"It has not been done before."

Was Aoife asking her how? "Take Uaithne to the Briogannon,

say to them: Here is the Echraidhe who did this thing. What she did was wrong. We're sorry. We'll pay reparation and make sure it never happens again. Let's find a way to stop the feud." Aoife was still listening. Marghe felt her way carefully. "Situations change. Sometimes people have to do new things, things that have never been done before. Everything your foremothers did was new once. You will be the next Levarch. Take this opportunity to save your people."

Aoife was silent a long time. "I am Agelast. It is my part to uphold the Echraidhe way." And Marghe heard the rush of bitterness in that voice, the burden of always having to do the right thing, always having to uphold the Echraidhe code, even when she was hurting. "We are at feud," she said, and did not look at Marghe.

ON SOME days as they rode, Aoife spoke so little that Marghe found herself drifting into thoughts and daydreams about her childhood in Macau. But as the days passed, Marghe's daydreaming turned to escape. She imagined herself sneaking from the tent at night and somehow stealing two horses from under the noses of the guards, saddling one, using the other as a pack animal. There was always snow in this scenario: warm snow that would hide her tracks, keep her out of sight of Aoife and Uaithne, snow that drifted with her, showing her the way to Ollfoss.

Sometimes, Aoife rode at her side and they were both escaping.

ONE DAY, a day when it was less cold than of late, Marghe surprised herself by reining her horse in front of Aoife and forcing them both to a halt. She pulled off her snow mask. "The two women, the two you said had been captured in the ringstones before me, tell me what happened to them."

Aoife considered. "The first was caught in the time of my

foremothers. The Levarch then was wild and cruel. They say the stranger was slaughtered and butchered, the pieces of her body hung over the stones until they rotted."

Marghe wondered if this was the example, the memory that Uaithne had used to guide her torture of Winnie Kimura. "And the other?"

"She is dead also."

"When was she taken?" Had they given Winnie to Uaithne to play with?

"I was there. I was very young."

Not Winnie, then. "How did she die?" Marghe asked softly.

"She took her own life."

She took her own life. If the Echraidhe did not kill you, despair would. "How long was she held hostage, Aoife?"

Aoife looked at her a moment without speaking. "When a woman trespasses amongst the stones of the ancestors, she belongs to the Echraidhe. She becomes Echraidhe. Like horse and herd, she belongs to the tribe. Like me, like you. The woman we took lived in our yurtu as one of us for twenty-six winters."

Marge imagined how it would be to live amongst these people for almost twenty years. She stared sightlessly at the snow between the horses' hooves. Her throat felt tight and strange.

"Thank you," she said to Aoife.

Aoife shrugged helplessly. "Put your snow mask back on."

Marghe considered that. "Before I do, answer me this: Which direction is Ollfoss?"

"An Echraidhe does not need to know this."

"No." Marghe hesitated, then lifted her eyes to meet Aoife's. "If I tried to escape now, would you kill me?"

Aoife pointed to the sling at her belt and shook her head: she would not need to. Her face had the set look that Marghe had learned meant she was unhappy.

Her snow mask halfway to her face, Marghe paused. "You care, don't you, Aoife?"

A small silence.

"Then why don't you simply give me directions and let me go?"

"I can't." Her voice was harsh. "You're not mine to give away. You belong to the tribe."

"I don't belong to *anyone*! I'm not a thing, to be kept or ordered or driven to such despair that I open my own veins. Look at me, Aoife. Look at me! I'm a woman."

Aoife raised troubled eyes. "No." She turned her horse, brushed at her face. "Put your snow mask on before we ride back."

Without warning, Marghe thumped her mount into a gallop away from the camp.

Time seemed to stretch oddly, and she felt a fierce exhilaration. She was going to get away. Aoife wouldn't stop her! Laughing, she leaned forward over her mount's neck and urged it to fly, to put the Echraidhe forever behind it. The gelding stretched his stride and Marghe burned with the hot joy she had not felt since the first time she was able to slow her heart rate.

Then her horse stumbled and the snow came flying up to meet her. She lay for a moment on her back, winded.

This was not happening. She was on horseback, galloping to freedom, not lying in the snow.

This was not happening.

Aoife cantered up and peered down whitely. "Are you hurt?"

Marghe saw her slip her sling back into her belt. Of course. How had she been so foolish as to think otherwise?

Aoife had to help her back onto her horse. She had sprained an ankle in the fall. They rode back in silence, Marghe too numb even to weep.

THE HOURS of daylight grew less and the days darkened, along with Marghe's hopes. Sometimes she forgot about her injured ankle and tried to walk, then was puzzled when she fell over. Borri would find her and rebandage it, tutting over the swelling, trying to tell her that if she did not take care, the ankle would never mend properly. Marghe did not care.

Now Marghe's dreams were not of escape, but of all the kinds of death she had touched upon in her life: the death of her father's radical dreams and of his warmth to her; the death of her own ideals; the death of her childish self on the way to becoming adult; the death of her mother; the death of all those thousands here on Jeep. Sometimes, in waking dreams, sitting by the fire in Aoife's yurti, she would weep over a bowl of blood-rich soup, imagining the silver-slit eyes of the taar that had died to feed her; only the eyes of the taar in these dreams were always brown, like a cow's.

The days of dark wrapped Tehuantepec in a seamless twilight. With no hard daylight to anchor her, no sharp shadow edges to keep the world of the Echraidhe a real world where people ate and breathed and relieved themselves, Marghe slipped and spun inside her dreams. These people had abducted her, submerged her in this timeless otherworld that was no more real than the underwater palaces of those other abductors, the Sidhe, the unearthly faerie who stole human children, twisted their souls from their bodies, and filled them instead with dark glamour. Nothing was real.

She tried to run away twice more, hardly knowing what she did. Each time, Aoife brought her back and Borri shook her head, wrapped her up, and tried to make her eat. At these times she did not hear Borri when she spoke to her; she ignored Aoife's gentle hands that rubbed life back into her feet after half a night on the plains without her boots. She did not hear Borri say to Aoife that she should not be allowed to have her knife in this state, or hear Aoife tell the healer that the knife was Marghe's, and not theirs to take away.

There was no escape from here, except in her dreams.

When she was out on the snow with the taars, she did not see the herds. Sometimes she imagined they were sheep, like the ones on the Welsh hillsides where she had walked while her mother was dying—dying and coughing her lungs up and crying, and always, always saying, "I'm sorry, Marghe, I'm sorry," and making her feel even worse, making her feel even more strongly that it was all her fault.

There was no escaping death. When her FN-17 ran out, she would die here among the Echraidhe, coughing up her lungs like her mother. Alone. She no longer cared.

THE DAYS of dark passed and gradually a few minutes of daylight became an hour, then two hours. It grew still colder, and clouds covered the sky like a caul.

Marghe patiently coaxed her ancient mount to a trot. This was the last day before the taars were driven into their winter pens and she and the young woman who herded them had not bothered to take them far.

She could not remember the young Echraidhe's name. She must have been told it three times but she could not be bothered to make it stick in her mind. What did she care for a name?

Marghe sighed as a taar wandered in search of more plentiful grazing. She resisted kicking her horse into a faster pace. The mare was an old one, on her last legs. Since her last attempt at escape she was refused young, swift horses. If she or her mount had to be killed, the Echraidhe would prefer to waste a less valuable animal.

She slid her palo to full length and goaded the taar back to its herd mates. She glanced at the reddish patch of sky where the sun was sinking toward the horizon, hidden by cloud. The taar settled comfortably back amongst its fellows and showed no signs of wandering off a second time. Marghe unstoppered the skin of locha at her saddlebow and took a swig. She looked at the sky again; it was brighter than before. She looked at it a long time, took another swig. That was not right. She wiped her mouth with the back of her hand, restoppered the skin, and called to the young Echraidhe, pointing.

"Haii! The sky!"

The tribeswoman stiffened. "Fire!"

Marghe wondered at that. Fire? On Tehuantepec's snow? The Echraidhe woman was standing in her stirrups. "The Briogannon raid at last. The yurtu burn!" Then she was off, thundering toward the glowing sky, loosening her sling as she rode.

Marghe sat still a moment, considering, then wheeled her mare in the opposite direction and jabbed her heels into its ribs.

The snow flew in clods around her ears. Marghe refused to allow herself to think; she would just ride the ancient animal to its limit. She kept her mind blank, aware only of the heaving flanks between her thighs, the thick reins running over her fingers. She rode easily, as disconnected from what was happening as a child bobbing on her back in the ocean, lost in the sky and cloud. Then it was dark and the horse had slowed to a stumbling trot. She blinked and reined to a halt. Again, the sky was clear, utterly silent and still. The moons hung two-thirds full, and she was cold. She twisted in her saddle. Nothing but white quiet. Where was she?

With her eyes closed, it was easy to picture her map. Then she revisualized the taars, the setting sun, and the direction of the burning yurtu, and calculated. She had fled due north. Ollfoss lay north and east; she would find it, somehow.

She turned the mare's head in the right direction and kicked her to a walk. All she had to do was keep going, not think about the fact that she had no food, no shelter, no sling, no spear, and no fuel; that even being a captive of the Echraidhe might be better than dying out here, alone, in the frozen wastes. For now, it was enough to be free. That was important. Freedom meant something, didn't it? Her furs tickled her chin and she pulled the snow mask tighter.

When the moons set, she was still riding. She realized she had been searching for a suitable stopping place: a stream, a bush, some shelter—anything that stood out on this endless stretching white. There was nothing. There would be nothing. She reined in and dismounted, and the mare hung her head while she uncinched the saddle. When she pulled off the headstall, the icicles hanging from the mare's shaggy mane broke off. She started to rub the poor creature down with her gloved hands before she remembered something Aoife had told her: the snow and ice in a horse's coat could act as insulation the same way a snow tunnel could shelter and insulate a person.

She squatted, pulled off a glove, and rubbed snow between her fingers. Dry snow. Good building material. She took a careful swig of locha and began.

First, she took off the headstall to hobble the mare, who could scrape up snow from the moss and find her own grazing. The saddle went on the snow. Marghe knelt next to it and began scraping snow up around her. She managed to curve the walls in slightly, but when she tried to make a roof the way Aoife had shown her, it kept collapsing under its own weight. She tried several times, first with lightly packed snow, then with snow she had packed almost solid, finally by trying to form a cement of ice by running her blade along the snow. Nothing worked. Stubborn, her father had always said, stubborn as a Portuguese donkey. Not today. She curled herself into a tight ball, laid her head on the saddle, and went to sleep.

She woke about two hours later, rippling and shuddering, her muscles pulled so tight against the cold that her bones ached. No more sleep tonight. She did some breathing and stretching before saddling the mare. Even that made her dizzy. She needed food. She had none—all she had was a half-full skin of locha. She leaned her forehead against her mount's shaggy flanks. There was still time to retrace her tracks to the yurtu. Her stomach did a slow roll forward. No. Not again. She had plenty of furs, her palo, a knife, the locha, a horse. A few days, just a few days. She could last that long. She pulled herself into the saddle, set the mare's head toward Oll-foss, and nudged her into a walk.

The second night, she simply lay on her back and wriggled until snow covered everything but her face. She woke to a world of seamless white and hunger sharp as a rodent's tooth. The sky was soft and milky, like the plain; it was as if she stood inside a hollow pearl. It made her dizzy. She finished the locha and hung the empty skin back on her saddle. If she found nothing to fill it with, she could always try to eat it.

This time she had to kick the mare to get her moving.

Marghe woke on her third morning alone to find that her hunger had passed from pain to a dull ache; she knew she was hungry, but she no longer minded so much. The snow underfoot was as soft and white as the furred back of the mythical cyarnac. Today, it was beautiful. She smiled to herself as she looked around. Everything seemed dusted with crystal. When she brushed snow from her sleeves, every fiber of her overfur was magically clear. She studied her saddle dreamily: every pore on the leather was distinct. She could have spent hours watching the light in tiny droplets of ice on the mare's coat. Hunger was no longer important. She heaved the saddle onto the mare and blood flowed warm and strong through her veins. Her limbs felt smooth and light. Today, she felt . . . fine.

The mare kept her head down, cropping the frozen ice moss, while Marghe tightened the girth. The wooden buckle slipped easily into its usual hole and the buckle itself nestled comfortably into the slight bed it had worn into the leather. But the straps were too loose. Too loose. She took a step backward and forced herself to see loose skin and jutting ribs instead of individual hairs. Her horse was starving. So was she.

The mare pawed aside more snow, cropped. Marghe watched and licked her lips, thinking of ice moss. When it was cooked and dried it could be ground like flour and made into flat cakes. Raw, it would not be poisonous, but probably indigestible. But she had to eat something.

She squatted and scraped bare a small patch of moss. She yanked it up, a clump at a time, and set it aside. There was something else she wanted to try first. The ground was hard as iron; she had to lean her weight onto her knife blade and twist the point until she loosened a tiny lump of soil like frozen gravel.

It took hours to cut a vertical hole about the size of her forearm. Her mare kept cropping and pawing, cropping and pawing.

Marghe rolled up her sleeve and thrust her bare arm down the hole. She closed her eyes against the searing cold, began her breathing. In and out, in and out. Hold. In. Out. Hold. In the left nostril, out the right. Hold. The extra oxygen made her dizzy. She visualized the corpuscles rushing red and busy through her arm to her finger, back up to her shoulder, through the pulmonary vessels, the heart, and out again in a gushing rush. Hot red. Hot. And full of information. She sank her entire awareness into her arm. Listened with it, extended her own electromagnetic field as she had learned to do, dowsing. Out and out, thinner, diffuse. Wait.

There was nothing at first. No trace of snow worms, as she had hoped. Then she sensed a far-off scratching, pushing. A ruk.

She opened her eyes. What had Aoife said? *The need breeds the skill.*

Keeping her breathing soft and her movements slow, she unfastened the palo from her belt, pulled it to about half its length, and wedged her knife behind the fastening strap. Then she crouched over the hole, makeshift spear poised.

The ruk came, beetling its way through the stone-hard ground. Every sense open, every muscle ready, Marghe waited. The ruk came closer; she could hear the rasp of its thick armored skin against the dirt. A snout pushed through one wall of the hole and Marghe thrust. Hunger made her slow. The ruk scuttled away, back the way it had come.

As SHE had known she might, Marghe vomited up the raw moss as soon as it reached her stomach. The mess steamed in the brittle air for a moment before beginning to ice over. The temperature was still dropping. She sucked snow to take away the foul taste in her mouth and willed her breathing steady. She must think now, or die.

Aoife had told her tales of tribeswomen who punched holes in the neck veins of their mounts and drank the blood. But she was un-skilled, and the horse would probably bleed to death before cold plugged the vein. It was an old, half-starved beast; it could not afford to lose even a cupful of blood. She needed it alive. Her only hope was to get to Ollfoss, or at least the boundaries of Moanwood where she could make a fire, collect nuts, shelter herself from the snow . . . Even with the horse, she might not get there. Without, she certainly would not.

There was nothing to eat here and the temperature was drop-ping. She would head east and hope.

Before she pulled on her gloves, she took a long look at her hands. The bones showed gaunt through white skin. There was not an ounce of fat left on the whole of her body; the cold had melted it away. In a matter of days her body would be scavenging upon it-self, absorbing muscle until she was nothing but loose skin and bone. A generous estimate would give her another four or five days' survival, if she carried on as she had been doing. To reach the forest she knew she needed to stretch those four or five days into at least seven or eight. She would have to close parts of her body down when they were not needed. It was possible, theoretically; she knew how. But this was not a controlled environment with monitoring hookups and attendant medics, and she was already seriously undernourished.

She climbed into the saddle. The clouds were low and rounded, as featureless as a basket of eggs. An alien sky. All alone under an alien sky. Somewhere up there, Sara Hiam was sitting in the *Estrade*, wondering if her vaccine worked. Somewhere up there, too, was a satellite that if it just came nearer and lower could pick up her SLIC, beam it to the nearest relay, to Danner. A sled could get here in four or five days. Oh, and then she would have hot tea, or soup, and bread, and the smiles of a woman she knew. And all the time she ate and drank and had her hands bandaged she would be heading back to Port Central, to safety.

No, she had done enough dreaming. The only reason she should look at the sky was to determine the weather. She was alone. No one was going to rescue her. Not Sara or Danner, not Lu Wai or Letitia. Not even Aoife. As Cassil had said, she was alone, an orphan under this sky. No one knew her. Here she was Stranger Woman, or the SEC rep. Not Marguerite Angelica Taishan, not Marghe. She wondered if that person existed anymore.

Once she had her mount headed in the right direction, she began trance breathing.

MARGHE NEVER really remembered the next few days. She rode in half trance through the white and cold and silence. Sometimes there were brief flurries of snow. Twice each day she would swim up from her trance to swing from the saddle and dig out ice moss for the horse, which was getting too tired to find its own. While the horse ate, she would concentrate on opening and closing veins around her body, sending her blood pounding into hands, feet, and face where patches of skin were white and dead from frostbite. Each time, it became harder to shake off her trance and force her body to move.

When she slid from the saddle on the sixth day, her legs would not hold her. She crumpled onto the snow and had to persuade blood around her body before she could stand and clear snow for the horse. When she tried to remount, she could not. The leg in the stirrup trembled and shook but could not lift her body. Fear, sudden and sharp, flashed under her skin, setting a muscle by her eye twitching. Her breath whistled. She had to get back into that saddle. She leaned her face against the mare's ice-shagged withers and rested a moment. She could do it. Blood to her upper arms, to her thighs and calves. Breathe. Gather.

She part jumped, part hauled herself up by the saddle horn until she lay belly-down across the mare's back. She dragged her right leg over and was astride and upright. She swayed as the horse started its slow, plodding walk.

IT WAS the wind that woke her, driving hard and cold into her left cheek from the north, from a sky the gray yellow of lentil scum, a sky full of snow.

The horse was stumbling and weaving; Marghe could feel it tremble and sag at each step. The wind died and the first flakes of snow wobbled down like moths. Within minutes the wind was back, driving the flurry into a blizzard of ice blades. She could think of nothing to do but force the horse on. Ice and snow whipped through fur and hair, past eyelashes and under fingernails, to reach places Marghe had thought long numb. The horse staggered, but righted itself.

Marghe tried to guess at how long the storm would last; at least a day, maybe two. She doubted she would survive it. It would take too much effort to stop her mount and climb down, so she simply allowed the horse to wander as best it could. She felt very peaceful.

When the mare fell, she did so without warning, her front legs crumpling like scythed wheat. Marghe fell free and looked at the wreckage, then crawled over to touch the mare's neck in apology; the horse was alive, but would not be getting up again.

The blizzard hissed around her. Her hands were so numb with

cold that she could hardly feel the bone haft when she pulled out her knife; she had to hold her eyes to slits, and the snow gathered on her lashes made it impossible to see if she was grasping it properly. Spicules of ice clung to the mare's mane; she stroked it, and sang. Singing seemed like a good idea. It was some wavering tune she remembered from her first childhood visit to a temple. She wanted the mare to hear something other than the blizzard before it died.

While she sang, she scraped a mound of snow up against the big vein that snaked along the thin neck. Then she showed the old mare her blade, smiled, and pushed the knife in.

The blood was impossibly red, pumping onto the white snow. The mare sighed and her eyes glazed as the moisture froze. The pumping blood slowed to a trickle. Marghe cursed and scrambled to the saddle to get the empty locha skin. She held it up to the vein, but the container's mouth was too narrow; the skin stayed flaccid, with only about a cupful of blood inside. Marghe scooped up a mouthful of bloodied snow. She held it on her tongue until it melted and warmed. It was sweet, metallic. She waited a little while before her next mouthful. It stayed down.

There was already a drift of snow gathering by the carcass. Not much time. She picked up the knife again and sawed at the dead mare's belly. Her hands were clawed with cold and the knife was small. She kept dropping it. Again and again she picked it up and hacked. It was very messy, very tiring. She could hardly see. Now and again she stopped to rest, wipe the ice crystals from her eyes, and swallow another mouthful of bloody snow. By the time she was finished, her furs were slimed from cap to boots, but she had several slices of raw meat lying beside her in the snow. She opened her furs and dropped the red, slithery strips inside against her skin where her body heat would stop the meat from freezing.

The blood had given her a little energy, but there was still hard work to do. She shoveled at the snow, dragging great armfuls alongside and between the forelegs, then the hindlegs, of her dead mount. The saddle had to be cut free; she hauled it to lie halfway between the stiffening, outstretched legs. Then she pushed snow against legs, carcass, and saddle until a waist-high wall rose around her. Using her knife again, she made a great, three-sided cut in the mare's hide. With all the subcutaneous fat gone, it was easy to shear the skin away from the internal membranes in one piece. It was more difficult to drag the flap of skin, about two feet square, over her head and pull its edges down to meet the snow wall.

The result was cramped and stifling, but a shelter of sorts. It was all she could do. She huddled down around her precious cupful of blood and few tatters of meat, all that kept her from death, and breathed deep into her belly. There was nowhere to go from here.

MARGHE'S FEET were numb now and the blizzard still raged. She chewed on her last strip of meat, knowing that this one, like all the others, would not give her enough energy to keep warm.

The day wore on. With her snow mask pressed tight against nose and mouth, and her face pressed against the fur of her hood, she could hardly breathe. She could not get rid of the persistent image of herself as a blowfly egg, waiting to hatch into a maggot in the rotting flesh of the horse's carcass.

The numbness in her feet crept to her knees. She was not sure if it was frostbite or a result of her restricted circulation, but moving would mean lifting the skin flap, and the wind would whip away all her hoarded warmth in a heartbeat. She was too weak to survive that. If the blizzard did not stop soon, she would grow weaker and weaker until her heart stopped.

She did not want to die. Even now, half suffocated and starving, with patches of skin dying on her face and hands, she refused to give up. This was not how her life was meant to end, frozen and stinking and alone, forever listed as missing, unless she turned up entombed in an iceberg drifting down the eastern coast between the mainland and the Necklace Islands. She refused to die.

Think.

There was a story her father had told her once, about the organic chemist who had been searching for the solution to the structure of a certain molecule and had fallen asleep and dreamed up

the answer: the benzene ring. Her father had used the story to il-
lustrate several of his annoying sayings, like *Where there's a will there's
a way*, and *Westerners teach their children how not to think*, and *Relax,
let it come in its own time*. Right now her hunger and fear were blot-
ting out everything else. She needed a clear mind, a relaxed body;
she needed to be still, and let it come. Perhaps there was a solution
to all this, a solution as perfect, elegant, and obvious as the benzene
ring.

Her hands were numb now, as well as her legs. When she unstoppered the locha skin, the tiny movement sent agony into all
fingers except the third and fourth on her left hand. She drank the
last mouthful of thick, clotted blood and then rubbed her hands as
best she could inside her gloves. Feeling did not return to the two
fingers. Frostbite—a clear signal that parts of her body were now
shutting down permanently.

Think or die.

But could death really be any worse than this pain in her back,
pain from curling around a bottle of blood almost inside the belly
of a dead horse? Might it not be preferable to feeling bits of herself
die of frostbite, and rot? Death, whatever else it was, would surely
be peaceful, not like this constant diamond hiss of cold, this endless
grinding fear and pain and struggle. If she just gave up, gave in,
who would know, and what difference did it make?

She did not have the answers.

Why was she trying so hard to stay alive? If she lived through
this, she might not live through the virus. If she survived the virus,
Company might blow the planet to pieces. Life was nothing but a
series of fruitless struggles. A sudden memory of herself as a three-
year-old dropped into her head like a screen menu. She was in the
roof garden of their house in Macau, high above the sweet smells
of rot and rice wine, squatting next to an old plastic pail in which
she had placed a handful of earthworms. The worms wriggled and
humped their way up the sides of the pail, slipping now and again,
but persisting, getting closer and closer to the rim, and freedom.
She watched them with the utter concentration of all three-year-
olds. Every time one reached the top, she leaned over and carefully

flicked it back down to the bottom. It was not cruelty that prompted her; she simply enjoyed watching things try. And those worms kept trying, blindly, stupidly, stubbornly, and eventually her three-year-old self got bored and tipped the pail up, and the worms slithered out and burrowed safely into the dirt.

Very well. She would try to wriggle out of the pail; there would be time to worry about the quality of the dirt afterward.

Her first deep breath triggered a coughing fit that wracked her body enough to momentarily crack open the frost-rimed skin flap, admitting a slice of air so cold her eyes streamed. She rubbed her face into the fur of her hood to dry them—ice would blind her. She was well-practiced; her second deep breath, then her third, triggered deep muscle relaxation.

The trick to meditation was to let the mind sit in a quiet soft place full of ease and warmth. Marghe imagined that she was curled up, not under a piece of skin covered in blood-smeared snow in the middle of a blizzard, but on the mauve and green rug that lay in front of her fireplace in Wales. She could smell the applewood logs burning; flames rubbed themselves lazily up against the soot-stained bricks, shimmering with distant hot worlds in yellows and reds. She stared into the flames a while to see what she could see.

Hours passed. Occasionally, she put on another log from the basket, or threw on a handful of salt and sugar and watched the flames burn lavender and spring green. Then the basket was empty, only wood chips left, and the logs were burning down to embers. The embers dimmed.

She wanted to stay curled around the last remnants of warmth, try to sleep. *Get up,* her inner voice said, *get up,* but she did not want to leave. *Get up,* said that voice again, *there are no ideas here. You must get up.*

Oh, but it was hard. The door from her familiar room led to a high flight of dank stone stairs. No railing. Each step seemed taller than the last, and the higher she climbed up out of her trance, the more slippery the stone became. It would be so easy to lean backward just that little bit too far and go tumbling down, back into the room that was still warm. She set her teeth and climbed, and gradually her legs became numb and she felt her fingers turning blue and cold and curling into claws. All except two. Her ears hurt.

SHE WOKE to dark, sour quiet. Although she was too weak to move, her head was very clear. Meditation had produced no magic formula, no elegant solution to her problem. There was nothing more she could do. It was midwinter, the last day of the Moon of Knives here in the wild Echraidhe country of Tehuantepec, and the only thing left for her to do was to choose her way of dying. The warm room would be a good place in which to die. Perhaps she should go back there, put on the last of the wood chips and just fall asleep forever. There was nothing noble about dying a slow and painful death, surrounded by nothing but empty silence.

She took a slow, deep breath, let it out gently. Took another. Exhaled abruptly.

Silence?

When she breathed the next time, it was strong and deep, a breath that pumped her blood vigorously through those blood vessels that would still open, dragging with it oxygen, life. Her arms tingled with the effort of pushing up the snow-covered flap. She peered out. Snow and sky lay pearly white and quiet. The blizzard was over.

Moving sent pain shooting through her legs. There was no way she could stand up yet. She crawled out from underneath the flap; when she was halfway out, it cracked and broke. The light was blinding after so long in the dark. She had no idea what time of day it was. Late afternoon, maybe. On all fours, she looked around. She began to laugh. She leaned back against the carcass and laughed at the sky, laughed until icy air tore into her lungs and set her coughing and she had to pull off her snow mask and smother her mouth with her hand. Even then, her shoulders shook.

To her left, looming dark on the horizon, lay the forest. Food, shelter, and firewood lay a couple of hours' walk away. If she had gotten to this place just a little before the blizzard started, she would have seen. She would have smelled it, as she did now: an alien green smell, the smell of strange trees unfurling in the dark, furtive and strong. Just two hours away. Half an hour on a horse. But her horse was dead and it was all she could do to sit without collapsing.

Hope gave her the strength that would have come from food, or warmth. The worm prepared to try one last time to wriggle up out of the pail. She pushed herself from sitting to kneeling, from kneeling to balancing on one foot and one knee. She had to lean against the carcass before she managed to drag the other foot up to join the first. She stood, and swayed, but did not fall over.

One step at a time, she told herself. However long it takes. She put one foot in front of the other. Not so bad. Then the other one. Look at me, she wanted to shout, look at me! It was like learning to walk all over again, with legs that did not belong to her. Her heart thumped soggily inside her ribs, but it did its job. She took another step and nearly fell over. Don't think about it, it's easier if you don't think about it.

She opened her mouth and began to sing the first thing that came into her head: a nursery rhyme she had learned when she was five. *I know a teddy bear, blue eyes and curly hair, roly-poly round the town, knocking all the people down . . .* She sang all the verses. The song faltered often and her legs trembled like reeds, but she refused to stop. The trees drew nearer. Or what looked like trees. What if an alien forest did not have nuts, or berries, or anything she could eat? Never mind that, just put one foot in front of the other, and sing.

Each step became a test of will. Eventually, she lost the struggle and fell over. She crawled. She had sung all the verses of the nursery rhyme. She began to make them up. *I know a dinosaur, green of eye and red of claw, romping stomping round the town, having fun chowing down, I know a dinosaur . . .* Her world narrowed to the stretch of ground under her hands and knees, the eighteen inches she could see before her without lifting her head. Her voice wavered like a newborn's while she crawled on, over roots and fallen tree debris, not seeing.

Something moved.

She looked up, blinked, tried to focus. There, behind a tree. Sweet gods. It must be seven feet tall. Goth? Cyarnac? Had she come all this way just to get eaten by something like a huge teddy bear? *I know a teddy bear, silver eyes and lots of hair, zipping ripping on the plain, killing until we're all slain* . . . Maybe she was imagining it. Yes, she had imagined it. No such thing as giant teddy bears. She crawled on.

A woman stepped out from nowhere.

Marghe blinked again, waited for the mirage to disappear. When it did not, Marghe reached slowly, painfully for her knife. The woman's taar skin boots and cap, the sling and palo on her belt, were all too familiar, even if the carved disk of bone at her belt was strange and her face was one Marghe had never seen before. She would kill, the woman or herself, before being taken hostage again.

The woman stepped closer, but not within knife range.

"I am Leifin. Daughter of Jess and Bejuoen and Rolyn. Sister to Kristen."

"Where are you from?" Marghe's voice was a whispery croak.

Leifin leaned forward, trying to catch what she said. "I am Leifin. There is no need for your knife." She took another step forward. "How are you named, stranger? Who are you?"

Marghe thought about that. Who was she? She was not sure. "Where are you from?" she croaked again. The knife point glittered before her eyes.

"Where am I from?" Leifin gestured behind her. "Ollfoss. Three days' walk away or more."

The knife point wavered. Ollfoss. Ollfoss. Marghe fell on her face in the snow.

Chapter Nine

THE GYM'S neon strips were too bright after the cool grays of Jeep's winter light. Danner stripped out of her fatigues and into fencing whites. Time now, she thought, to lay aside the question of what trap to set for the spy in their midst. Kahn was already warming up, whipping her foil back and forth, shadow-lunging. Danner pulled a foil free of its holding field on the wall, tested it. She had been mulling over the spy problem for weeks now, getting nowhere. She clipped on her face guard. Later.

Kahn waited, her *en garde* perfect but for a slight overextension. Danner studied her. That overextension had to be bait—but if she did not take it, she would never learn the lesson that Kahn obviously intended. She could take the blade in a bind, *quarte* to *sixte*; that should at least make her seem not wholly naive.

Neon swam down her blade, twitched as Kahn effortlessly cut over and landed the buttoned tip against Danner's throat guard.

"The derobement," Kahn said. "I'd like you to try it with a disengage, then lunge."

This time it was Danner who assumed the slightly overextended *en garde*.

"You're bending your wrist again." Danner straightened it. "Better. Don't lean forward so much."

The world focused down to the two blades, her own steady, waiting, Kahn's moving closer, reflecting light like the scales of a predatory pike. Danner moved. Point under, feint, lunge. Kahn parried, beat aside Danner's foil, bent her own blade against Danner's chest.

They parted.

"Again."

Kahn's mesh mask glittered like the compound eye of an insect. Metal mask, metal foil. Metal.

Danner assumed the *en garde* mechanically, thoughts elsewhere.

Metal. If Company abandoned them, these foils would be useful, not as weapons but as trade. She extended her arm. The blades were steel, on these foils at least. Some of the others were composites, some energy blades, some smart blades. Kahn was a traditionalist: learn the basics first, she had said, you can always adapt a sound technique. So they used steel-bladed foils with aluminum bell guards and brass pommels. Three different metals.

Kahn laid her foil alongside Danner's. Danner started the automatic derobement.

All different kinds of metal: different trade values. And there were other metals available, like the chain-link of the fence.

Kahn beat aside her blade, thrust hard. "You're not paying attention." She feinted and thrust again, forcing Danner to parry and retreat. Then she came in with a corkscrewing motion. Double bind. Danner disengaged, managed to parry Kahn's thrust to the low line, riposted. She was panting.

"Better." Kahn drove her back.

The fence. It was important, but she could not concentrate with Kahn's blade flashing. The fence. Metal. If they took it down, melted it . . .

Kahn's button punched into Danner's solar plexus. Kahn tapped her foot. "You need to—"

Danner held up her left hand, trying to get her breath. "Wait." Kahn stepped back, head tilted to one side.

Danner transferred the foil to her left hand and used her right to pull off her mask. "The fence," she said. "That's how we'll do it. It's perfect. And it's metal."

"SO WHEN we take down the perimeter fence," Danner explained to Sara Hiam, who peered out from the tiny screen in Danner's mod, "our spy, whoever she is, should find that worrying enough to call the *Kurst*. We'll be listening—Sigrid up there, Letitia down here—we'll catch her. Or them. And . . . well, it would just make me feel better if we took down that perimeter. There's no history of violence from these natives; it simply serves to make us feel like we're trapped inside, while they have the run of the entire planet. Makes good sense from a psychological point of view."

"You don't need to sell it so hard."

Danner leaned forward. "But you know what the real beauty of it is? The fence is metal. Tons and tons of metal we can use as trade goods. If we get stranded here. I thought about it while I was fencing with Kahn. All the metal in those foils. We could melt it down—"

"I'm surprised you didn't think of sharpening up the foils and using them as weapons."

Danner did not know how seriously Hiam meant that. "The metal would be more useful as trade goods, I think," she said carefully. "And we have plenty of other material available for weaponry. Projectiles are our best bet in a world like this: bows, slings, spears. All of which can be made without metals. And we have ceramics people who can figure out how to work this olla, for blades, if we need them. What metal we do use will go on things like plows, adzes, scissors, needles, chisels . . . tools." Sara was looking at her with a curious expression, almost fondly, and suddenly Danner felt embarrassed. All her ideas suddenly sounded like the fantasies of a young girl who had once dreamed of riding a horse over the plains, yelling, waving her bow and arrows, and challenging the wind.

"You've done a lot of thinking."

"Yes."

"Good. So have I. Danner, you need to find a way to get the three of us off this platform without the *Kurst* finding out. Just in case. I have one or two ideas, but there are problems."

IT WAS night, and Vincio was off duty, when the call from Sara aboard *Estrade* came through to Danner's office.

"Hannah, we have the signal." The doctor looked over her shoulder, said something. Danner's screen split: Hiam on one side, Sigrid on the other. Sigrid was a pale woman, with washed-out eyes.

"It's the same frequency, Commander."

"Hold on." Danner used her wristcom. "Dogias. It's coming through. Same frequency. Keep this channel open." She spoke to Sigrid. "Any direction yet?"

"No. But a preliminary scan shows it at the north end, maybe northwest end of Port."

Danner spoke into her wristcom. "Dogias, Sigrid says north, northwest."

"I hear and obey."

Danner sighed.

"Problems?" Sara asked from the screen.

"No. Just Dogias being herself." She shook her head. "Hold a moment." She punched up Lu Wai's call. "Sergeant, we have the signal."

"Yes, ma'am. I heard. I'm here with Letitia. I'm on it."

"Initial direction is north, or northwest. Take Kahn."

"Yes, ma'am."

"And keep this channel open."

"Yes, ma—"

Dogias interrupted. "I think the signal originates about three hundred meters in from the perimeter."

Danner pulled up a map of Port Central. "There are a lot of buildings there."

"Not all on the net."

Danner looked at the screen. "Sigrid, can you tell us whether it's a net signal or personal relay?"

Sigrid smiled faintly as she worked. "Not net," she said eventually.

"Damn," Dogias said. "Could be anywhere, then."

Danner knew better than to tell her to keep looking. Dogias knew her job.

"Lu Wai here. Suggest Officer Kahn and I run standard enter-and-search pattern."

"Negative. Repeat, negative. Leave it to Letitia and Sigrid to pinpoint. Where are you now?"

"About five hundred meters from the perimeter. Between guard posts six and seven."

"Any activity?"

"Plenty. We're right by Rec."

"Status?"

"Conspicuous. Both in full armor."

That was not good. She wanted this action to be inconspicuous. Two armored Mirrors were unusual enough to excite comment from the women going to and from the bars and screen theaters of Rec. "Keep Kahn armored up but out of sight. You strip to usual guard attire. I want this kept quie—"

Sigrid interrupted. "I have a bearing. Using you as zero, signal emanating from north 336, west 42. Give or take five meters."

Danner split her screen again, added the coordinates to her schematic of the complex. Three small buildings directly behind Rec. "Dogias, we have a possible in the Rec area storage and office row. Can you confirm?"

"A moment." Dogias hummed to herself. "Well, well, well," she said, sounding pleased. "I can tell you exactly where she is. Tell Lu Wai she'll find the spy hiding behind the beans."

Danner bit back her irritation. "Sergeant, Dogias—"

"Understood, ma'am. I overheard. Suspect in dry goods storage. We'll apprehend."

"Negative. Take containment positions, and hold." She hesitated, then reached for her helmet. "Sara, Sigrid," she said, as she checked her equipment, "I'm going out there. Keep monitoring. All communications from now on come via my command channel." She clipped down her helmet, pulled on gauntlets, and tongued on the in-suit comm system. "Dogias. Keep monitoring. All comm through command."

"Thought you sounded like you're talking from the inside of a garbage can. Will do. She's still talking, by the way. Want to hear what she's saying?"

"It's not coded?"

"Well yes, but I've had a couple of minutes. She's used a fairly simple variation on—"

"Negative on that suggestion." Talking would only distract her. "Record only. Unless in your judgment the communication suggests immediate danger to any of my personnel." She thought of Sara. "Or those aboard *Estrade*."

It was snowing. Her suit warmed rapidly, and the starvision visor turned the world smoky gray, ethereal, with the snow drifting down in black flakes. The grass was frozen, but she could not hear the crunch of her footsteps: all sound, all vision, all sensation was filtered by her suit. She was isolated from the world, just as though this were one of her first virtual-reality training missions as a cadet.

She walked through the night, her mouth dry with the familiar taste of adrenaline. Once she saw a small mammal scuttle through the grass, a lighter gray against the grainy background.

Kahn was standing perfectly still by the north wall of Rec. Without Danner's starvision, she would have been invisible.

"Kahn, I see you." Kahn slowly scanned the area, then raised a hand in acknowledgment. "Stay put. From now on, if you see anyone pass by here, detain her."

"Acknowledged."

Lu Wai was crouched underneath one of four lit windows.

"I'm fifty meters behind you," Danner said quietly, walking. "Is she in there?"

"Yes."

"Exits?"

"Just one, east of the building. And the windows. We need Kahn up here."

Danner squatted next to Lu Wai and slid up her visor. "Agreed."

On the command channel, tinny now because of the outside air, she heard Lu Wai ordering Kahn to join them beside the window. The sergeant turned to her. "Suggest Kahn and I take the entrance, bring the spy into custody."

Danner nodded. "I'll send Kahn along when you're in position. Wait for my signal before you proceed. And do it quietly."

Lu Wai nodded, and slipped into the dark. With her visor up, it seemed to Danner that the sergeant disappeared. Good. The whole thing should be contained. She risked a look over the windowsill. The light was dim; she saw vague shapes—sacks, she supposed—and what had to be the spy, holding a comm to her mouth. Talking. She could not see who it was.

She tongued for a channel change. "Sara. She's still talking. Is the *Kurst* talking back?"

"Sigrid says there's definitely two-way communication. She also says, and you should find this interesting, that the *Kurst* transmission comes directly from their bridge."

Danner nodded to herself. It was the confirmation she needed: whoever was in there was talking to and spying for Company hierarchy, with everyone's full knowledge and consent, except the command on Jeep. It was a relief; now she would no longer wake up in the night, wondering if she was being paranoid. Danner was surprised at the sudden bitterness she felt at the confirmation. After all, she had expected this.

Kahn arrived. Danner sent her to join Lu Wai.

The spy had not moved. What did the woman have to talk about for so long? Danner began to wish she had had Dogias patch it through. Was the spy talking about her?

"Dogias, do you recognize the voice?"

"Nope. No one I know. But judging by the way she's talking to the first officer up there, she's a Mirror, and not a lowly foot soldier either. Lieutenant, maybe."

Danner only had six lieutenants. She knew all of them, had promoted all of them personally. The betrayal bit deep. She wanted to know who it was, *now,* but she restrained herself. They had to let the woman finish her message; the longer the *Kurst* was kept in the dark about Danner's discovery of their duplicity, the more Danner could learn, the more time she would have before . . . whatever was going to happen happened.

"This is Dogias. Sounds like she's winding up the conversation."

"Sergeant, any minute now." She flipped channels. "Sigrid, please monitor the *Kurst.* I need to know the instant they switch off." She flipped back. "Sergeant, I want you both armored up, just in case." She risked another glance through the window. "I don't think she's armed, so be quiet, be smooth. I want her silenced and subdued inside this building. Not a whisper to escape. Acknowledge."

"Acknowledged."

"I'm right here outside the window if she chooses to come this way." She slid down her visor. The world turned gauzy. Her heart pumped.

"That's it," Dogias said suddenly in her ear.

"*Kurst* transmission ended," Sara confirmed.

"Go," Danner said. She edged away from the window to give herself the space to maneuver if necessary. It had been five years since she had been involved in any kind of action. She had forgotten how adrenaline made legs wobble and defied the suit thermostat. She shivered.

Nothing happened. Surely Lu Wai and Kahn should be there by now?

Yellow glare flooded her vision for a split second before her visor compensated: in the storeroom, her Mirrors had turned on the lights. One armored figure, Kahn, Danner thought, had her weapon out and was covering Lu Wai as the sergeant confiscated the spy's wristcom and wrapped a cling around her arms and waist, then her ankles.

"Subject immobilized." Lu Wai's voice was calm.

Danner slid up her visor and strode to the door. Her thigh muscles felt too big, too tight: adrenaline reaction, rage. Now she would see.

The storeroom smelled of dust and grain and the faint ozone hum of clings. The spy was not wearing a helmet.

Lu Wai saluted. "Sublieutenant Relman, ma'am."

The spy was half sitting, half lying on some sacks. Young. Short black curls. Round face that normally looked relaxed, but now reflected her physical discomfort.

"Sit her up straight," Danner said to no one in particular. Kahn obeyed. Helen Relman, who worked under Captain White Moon. Who answered directly to Ato Teng. How far did this go?

"Lieutenant Relman, you are being held on suspicion of behavior likely to endanger fellow officers. You will be taken to an appropriate holding place and questioned. Do you have any questions of your own at this time?"

Tell me it's all a mistake, Danner wanted to say. *Explain everything.*

Relman said nothing.

She was pumped up with adrenaline, with over-oxygenated blood hissing through her veins; that silence was too much for Danner. "Goddammit, Relman!" She wanted to shake the woman until her teeth rattled, but settled instead for pacing up and down. "Why in hell did you do this? You think I've treated you badly? What?"

"You said I would be taken to an appropriate holding place before being questioned."

"This is as appropriate as anywhere." She hit the wall stud that darkened the windows, then folded her arms. "I've got all night."

Relman appeared to think. "I would like my partner, Bella Cardos, informed of my whereabouts."

"She's involved in this?"

Relman looked startled. "No. But she'll worry."

Danner turned to Lu Wai. "Sergeant, find Cardos, bring her to an adjacent office. Tell her only that she is to be questioned in regard to an offense that may endanger the safety of fellow officers."

"I told you she's nothing to do with this."

"I don't believe you," Danner said mildly. "You may choose, of course, to try and convince me otherwise with some pertinent information."

No reply.

"We have all the time in the world," Danner said, knowing it was not true, knowing that now that they had Relman, things would move very fast indeed. Relman's cheeks were pale except for some broken blood vessels around her nose. Danner thought it made her look like she had a bad cold. The woman was just realizing what kind of position she was in.

"You have a choice, of course. Tell us everything, let us verify it; we'll take that into consideration. Or you could keep quiet and hope that something happens, some miracle to change the situation in your favor." Danner kept her voice steady, calm, reassuring. "That hope, in my opinion, is not only unreasonable but foolish. I don't think you want to continue being foolish." Surely the woman could not believe that the *Kurst* would come down just for her.

"We've got nothing to tell you."

" 'We'?"

Relman flushed, but said nothing.

Danner sighed. Stupid woman. "I don't really know why you're behaving like this. You've nothing to gain from it, and a lot to lose." She looked around, found a folding stepladder made of slippery gray plastic, pulled it opposite Relman, sat down. "In all likelihood, you will never leave this world. None of us will. Think about that: we're the only people you will ever see, ever again. And we're not happy with you, we won't forgive you. Not even Bella. And no one will forget. Is that what you want?"

Danner stopped. She was not getting through: Relman did not yet see the seriousness of her situation. She stood up. "I'll be back, when you've had some time to think."

Outside, the air was cold and wet and smelled of snow. Danner nodded to the women who were leaving Rec in ones and twos. Halfway back to her office, she called up Lu Wai. "Sergeant, I want

you to take Relman over to sick bay and check her over. She
might be suffering some shock. See that she gets something to eat.
Don't talk to her until she starts talking to you. When Cardos is
found, explain to her what's going on; if you can persuade her to
help us, give them five minutes alone. Whether or not Cardos is
cooperative, keep them both in sick bay. Separate rooms. Use the
usual procedure for reporting sick personnel to their superior.
Give out that both Relman and Cardos seem to have contracted
some rare infectious illness, no visitors allowed. If Captain White
Moon kicks up a fuss, refer her to me."

Let Relman stew a little in her own juices.

Her outer office was dark. The lights came up automatically
when she entered, but the room still felt dark around the edges, the
way empty spaces always did. In her inner office, she stripped off
her gauntlets, flexing her hands a couple of times. Her head ached.

She massaged the bridge of her nose and called Dogias.

"Letitia, I need that conversation as soon as you can get it to
me. Don't send it over the net. Bring me a disk by hand."

"If you can't protect the net, what makes you think you can
protect your system? I'll transfer it to audio disk and wipe my
comm. Your office in twenty minutes."

Dogias was infuriating, but right as usual. Twenty minutes. She
went through the empty outer office to make herself some tea.

A four-year-old memory superimposed itself behind her
eyelids: the smile of victory on Helen Relman's face as she stood
straight while Danner attached the sub's shoulder pips. What had
Relman been thinking that day? Danner sighed. She doubted she
would ever get the same pleasure from a promotion ceremony
again.

She would probably never hold another promotion ceremony.

Her eyes stung. She rubbed at them impatiently. She had better
things to do than indulge in old memories.

Back in her office, tea steaming in front of her, she punched in
Sara Hiam's code. "This is Danner. We have a woman called Helen
Relman. Sublieutenant. She's not talking, but there's at least one
other person working with her. Name or names unknown. Dogias

will have the tape to me in just a few minutes; that might help." She took a sip of her tea. "Or it might not."

She put down her tea, rubbed at her forehead. "Sara, what if this woman won't talk?"

"Make her," Hiam said bluntly. "There are several drugs available to your medics that are efficient and painless."

"I don't like the idea of drugs."

"Who does? But do you have the right to not use them to get information that might be vital to the survival of hundreds of people, just because of your squeamishness?"

Danner sighed. This was the last thing she needed. "I thought you might be a little more sympathetic, both to me and to Relman."

Sara laughed, a flat, ugly laugh. "Sympathetic? Danner, I'm feeling too damned scared to be sympathetic. Every time I start to fall asleep I imagine the gunnery officer aboard the *Kurst* hitting the trigger by mistake. When I do sleep I dream about never waking up. Drug the woman, find out what you can."

"I may not have to."

"Maybe not. But don't spend too long trying it the other way."

 OVER THE next day, Danner tried everything she knew: threats, cajolery, sympathy. Relman stayed silent. Time was running out. She decided to give Cardos, who seemed to understand the danger of Relman's situation better than Relman herself, one more try.

When Danner brought Cardos over from her secured room in the medical wing, Kahn stood up from her chair outside the glass-paneled sick-bay door and prepared to go in with Cardos.

"Stay here, Ana. Let her go in alone." Danner gestured for Cardos to go on in.

"Ma'am?"

"We'll just wait out here." Danner refused when Kahn offered her the chair.

Time passed slowly. The sealed skin patch in Danner's pocket felt larger than it was. She brushed it with her fingertip. *Don't make me use this, Relman.*

When Cardos came back out, she was shaking her head. "Nothing. I could try again."

"Would it do any good?"

"I . . . No."

"Officer Kahn will escort you to your room."

"Shall I call Sergeant Lu Wai here first, ma'am?" Kahn asked.

"That won't be necessary. And when you return, take a position at the other end of the corridor."

Kahn looked surprised, Cardos scared. "You won't hurt her?"

"No." She would not have to. She stepped into sick bay.

The room was small, low-ceilinged; the walls were a soft spring green. It held two beds, a screen, and a framed print on the wall opposite the door. There were no windows. Relman was clinged to the nearest bed; she looked better, not the awful pinched white of the evening before.

Just you and me, Relman.

"One last time, Relman. Tell me what I need to know."

Relman ignored her.

"This isn't a game, Lieutenant, and my time and patience have just run out. I don't want to drug you, but I will."

This time Relman looked at her. "No, I don't think so. Using drugs against another's will is illegal and unethical. I know you, Danner. You won't do it."

Relman really believed that, Danner thought, and then was angry: with Company, with Hiam, with Relman herself for forcing her to do this.

"Goddammit, Relman. Listen to me. Really listen. Forget what you know about fair play and employee rights. Right now, above our heads, people aboard the *Kurst* are trying to decide whether or not to kill us all or simply abandon us. I need what you know. Hundreds of lives may depend upon it, and that supersedes all my notions of right and wrong. Believe me, I will use drugs."

Relman paled a little. "Then go ahead. I'm not telling you anything."

Stupid, stupid woman.

Danner took the foil package from her pocket. When she tore it open, it released a faint antiseptic smell. *Use a pre-op patch,* Hiam had said, *a muscle relaxant. She'll stay awake for twenty minutes or more, and she won't care what she talks about. I've had people tell me the weirdest things while they're under.*

Danner rolled up Relman's right trouser leg and slapped the patch harder than necessary behind her knee. *She could have saved herself this,* Danner thought fiercely, *it was in her hands. I'm not to blame. I'm not.* But as she waited, she wished she were a thousand miles away.

After two minutes, Relman began to hum. Danner recognized the tune as one that had been popular on Gallipoli about eight years ago.

"Did you know, Hannah," Relman said conversationally, "that clings are erotically stimulating? Something to do with the electricity, I think. Makes all my nerves feel alive, and my body—"

"I don't want to know about your body. I want you to answer my questions. Who is the other spy?"

"I don't know."

"Of course you—" She would try another way. "Is there another spy?"

"Oh, yes." Relman nodded. "Oh yes, yes, yes." She could not seem to stop nodding.

"How do you know?"

"She talks to me. On my comm."

"Is she someone you know?"

"I don't think so. The voice is all funny—comes through a digital coder. But I always know it's her because she uses a code number." Relman smiled brightly, eager to be helpful.

"How often does she contact you, and why?"

"Now and again. To tell me who to listen in on, stuff like that. I have to do what she tells me, but not only what she tells me. I called the *Kurst* on my own initiative. I thought, 'Why should Danner be able . . .' "

Relman's voice trailed off, and she frowned. There was a sudden stink of feces. She giggled. "Oops." Then she smiled again, as though it was a tremendous joke that she was incontinent and incapable.

Danner gritted her teeth. It was not her fault; she had needed this information. She had had no choice. Relman had.

"Why did you do it, Relman?"

"Well, ma'am, you didn't seem quite right." Relman grunted; urine pooled on the bed, dripped slowly to the floor. "First of all, you sided with SEC and the natives against Company. Then it, well . . ." She trailed off, smiled at nothing in particular. Danner waited. "We've been here almost five years, and the last four all we've done is mark time: no serious exploration, no mining. And then there's the mods. The mods the mods the mods."

Danner waited. "The mods?"

"You know, officers and technicians are decorating them. It's not like anything I've ever seen before. Disturbing. Yes. Disturbing, disturbing, disturb—"

"Why?"

"And you've been reducing the guard complement. And Mirrors wear armor less and less, and off-duty civvies are handmade. Think of that, a Mirror wearing handmade clothes . . ." Relman suddenly seemed to focus. "And when I heard you'd ordered the fence down, what was I supposed to think?"

"You could have come and asked me."

Relman went on as though Danner had not spoken. "It just seemed to me that you've been undermining us, ma'am. Gradually making us seem less and less different to the natives." Her words were slow now, and slurred. "Maybe you want us to be natives. But we're not. We're not. Only this bit of the world's ours. And you wanted to take down the boundaries, muddle it all up, let them in. We are who we are, but you're letting it all get confused. We don't know why we're here anymore."

Silence.

"Relman?"

"So confused . . ." The words trailed off into a snore.

Danner stepped closer, looking down at her officer. Relman, who had seemed so young, so eager. Whom she had led to this. *So confused . . .*

Danner did not want anyone else to see Relman like this; she rolled up her sleeves.

When she left, the clings were at her belt, and Relman, clean and naked, was covered by a light sheet, sound asleep. Danner dropped the used pre-op patch in a receptacle and used her command code to lock the door. When she reached the end of the corridor, Kahn stood to attention, face carefully bland.

"Relman's locked in. Check on her visually in about twenty minutes, then join us in the convalescent room."

We don't know why we're here anymore. Was Relman right? she wondered as she turned down another cheerfully painted corridor to meet Lu Wai and Dogias.

The pastel-toned room with its huge picture windows was empty. She watched the snow falling outside. *We don't know why we're here anymore.* She had not been able to answer that at the time, but now, watching the snow, the alien sky just beyond the fragile glass of the window, she could. They were here to survive.

"Any way we can," she murmured, as the door behind her opened.

"Any way we can what?" Dogias swung off her jacket, began to brush the melting snow from her hair.

"Survive." Danner turned back to the window. She saw Dogias's reflection sling her jacket over the back of a chair.

"Well, survival's always a good place to start." Dogias combed through her hair with her fingers. "Why do they keep these places so hot?" She wiped her wet hands down her hip shawl. "So, did our caged bird sing?"

"Eventually."

Dogias gave her a hard look. "But?"

Danner sighed. "But I hated it, Letitia." She would not tell Dogias about the drugs. That was between her and Relman. "What she said disturbed me. She thinks that what I've been doing, all the sensible precautions like reducing the guard duty—because who needs guards when the natives just want to stay away?—like letting things relax a little because we're going to be here for . . . well, a long time at least . . . She thinks all my orders are designed to undermine us. To demoralize and confuse everyone. I'm beginning to think she might be right."

"Well, I'm not confused."

"No, but . . ."

"But what? Everything you've done has made sense to me."

"But is it the kind of thing another commander would have done?"

"Who cares? You're the only commander we've got. You can have my opinion, if it matters to you. I think you've done much better than any other commander I can think of. After all, you've learned on the job; you've got the right skills; you haven't tried to apply irrelevant rules to an extraordinary situation. You've put common sense and compassion before policy. The way I see it, that makes you a superb commander for the people here on the ground. It might not look too good to those who aren't here. To Company hierarchy." Dogias raised an eyebrow. "But we kind of knew that already."

Danner's smile was halfhearted. "I always thought that what I was doing was for the best. Relman's a good officer. I wouldn't have promoted her otherwise. But she doesn't like what I've been doing. It scares her. How many others does it scare?"

Dogias tucked a strand of hair behind her ear. "The situation scares us all. Those who are less brave than others will look to something, someone, concrete to blame. Which means you: you're the one giving orders that won't let them hide behind the idea that this is like any other tour of duty. But some of us are brave, or at least brave enough not to blame you for everything."

Dogias had a point, but there was more to it than that. "Everything I've done I've justified with logical-sounding reasons. But I'm beginning to suspect my own motives." She took a deep breath. "I think, deep down, I wanted this to happen. I wanted to stay here, on Jeep."

"You think you're the only one?"

Danner did not know what to say to that.

Lu Wai and Kahn came in together. "I've been thinking," Danner said abruptly, before they could do more than nod in Letitia's direction. "We have a sublieutenant out of action. She needs to be replaced. Lu Wai, you are now promoted to sublieutenant, effective immediately."

"Thank you, ma'am." Lu Wai stole a glance at Dogias, who shrugged.

"Officer Kahn, you are to assume the duties, rights and responsibilities of sergeant. Also effective immediately."

Kahn nodded. "Ma'am."

"Both of you will report directly to me, until I say otherwise. Your immediate superiors will be informed."

Danner said nothing about formalities. They did not ask. Given Company's recent actions a ceremony, with its pledges of loyalty, would mean nothing.

"Sit down, please. All of you." They did. Danner felt momentarily lost. *Company doesn't matter anymore; my commission means nothing.* She took a seat among them: Letitia and Lu Wai sitting close together, Kahn picking something out from under a nail. Good women. Her silence lengthened. "I trust you," she said eventually. "I hope you trust me." Another pause. "I need . . . I need your help to make some decisions." Danner waited for the looks of pity or contempt—decision-making was her job, her burden, no one else's—but their attentiveness did not waver. She wondered why she was finding this so hard. Trust them, she thought. Just trust them. "Dr. Hiam, on *Estrade*, and her two crew need to be brought down from orbit. I thought that between us, we could find a way to do it safely—without anyone on the *Kurst* being any the wiser. It goes without saying that the longer we can keep things here looking normal, the longer we have to organize ourselves before Company does whatever it is they're going to do. Every extra day helps."

Silence.

"Basically, we need to get the gig up there, on an apparently normal mission—"

"Taking someone up," Letitia said.

"—and back down again, containing four people when it should only contain one pilot, without *Kurst* getting suspicious."

"Why don't we just ask around and see who wants to get off-planet, there's bound to be someone, then send her up with the pilot?"

Danner shook her head. "I daren't. The fewer who know about this and are in a position to communicate with the *Kurst*, the better."

"Are you asking for one to us to volunteer, then?" Letitia said.

"Not yet."

The silence was long. Danner watched the snow fall outside. Last winter, the snow had formed drifts of eight or nine feet in places. Hiam had assured her that this winter would be milder.

"What's *Kurst's* position relative to *Estrade*?" Kahn asked suddenly.

"I'm not sure." Danner tapped a request into her comm. "Variable, according to this."

"A regular variable?"

"Yes."

"And are the two sometimes out of line-of-sight, obscured by Jeep itself?"

Danner tapped some more. "Yes."

"Ha!" Dogias crowed, reaching over and poking Kahn on the thigh. "Ana, you're a genius." She turned to Danner. "How long would the two be out of line-of-sight?"

Danner sighed, and requested that information. "Six hours."

"Long enough?" Dogias asked Kahn.

"Maybe," the Mirror said thoughtfully. "Tight, though."

"Maybe you two would like to explain."

Kahn gestured for Dogias to take it. "The *Kurst* is a military vessel, equipped with the best in sensors and detection equipment. I should know, my assignment before Jeep was working on a cruiser's systems. The only thing is, when the object you want to scan is obscured by a large body, you have to use a separate set of sensors, which need careful and exacting reprogramming, or"— she grinned—"rely upon rough data. Very rough data. If we send up the gig during this six-hour period, they'll have to choose. So what they'll do is check their rough data first." She looked to Kahn for confirmation. The Mirror nodded. "All we have to do is make sure their rough data will satisfy them enough so that they don't

feel the need to go through all the trouble of the second, more accurate scan." She stopped, pleased with herself.

"And?"

"And so as long as we stick something alive on that gig, they
won't know if it's human or not."

"An animal?"

"As long as it's big enough," Dogias said.

Danner wondered where they could find an animal big
enough.

"Would it have to be one large one? How about several small
ones?" Lu Wai asked.

"That should do it."

Danner considered. It could work. They could even pilot the
gig up by remote. The less personnel risked, the better. Tapes of
conversation should satisfy audio requirements. Yes, it could work.
For the journey up. "What about the rest?"

"How badly do we need the station's systems?"

"We need them. They control the satellites: our communications and microwave relay, weather information . . ."

"More than we need the *Estrade* crew?"

"Personnel come first," she said firmly to Letitia. *Do they?* a
little voice whispered. *What about Relman?* "Why, what were you
thinking?"

"If we rigged the platform to explode a few minutes after the
gig took off Hiam and the others, then it's likely that no one
would bother with a complicated check of the gig on its way
down on a routine mission. They'll be too busy trying to find out
why the platform blew."

"There must be a better way."

"Maybe we could rig some other explosion—maybe one of
Estrade's OM vehicles or something."

Kahn nodded thoughtfully. "That might be possible."

Danner looked from one to the other. "Any other ideas? No?
Right, Kahn and Dogias, I want you to work up the details of
what we've discussed. Bring them to me by . . . day after next?"

Dogias and Kahn nodded.

"Good."

"Ma'am?" Lu Wai asked.

"Yes, Serg—" Danner smiled. "—Lieutenant."

"What about Relman?"

"Let her go."

"Ma'am?"

"She's suffered enough. Confiscate her wristcom, and Cardos's, and send them off on some make-work mission. As far from here as possible."

"Cardos is a cartographer."

"Then have them start mapping the area south and west of here. That should keep them busy for a while, and give Relman time to think. She's safe enough as long as she can't communicate with the *Kurst*." She stared out of the window. "We need every healthy woman we can get. There's so much work to be done. We'll have to prepare for wholesale evacuation of Port Central, in case the *Kurst* decides to sterilize this area." Sterilize. How easy it was to use euphemisms.

The sky was solid gray; the snow was still falling.

"I miss the sky," Danner added, to no one in particular. "The thought of never again seeing a light blue Irish morning above wet green fields makes me want to weep."

"I like it here," Dogias said.

"I miss home," Lu Wai admitted, "but I don't think we'll ever see it again." She touched Letitia's hand. "This isn't such a bad place. It could become home."

Danner suspected that for Lu Wai, home was wherever Dogias was. "And you, Ana?"

"I was born on a station orbiting Gallipoli," Kahn said. "Earth isn't home. The place they'd send us if we ever left here certainly wouldn't be home. This may not be, either, but it's a good enough place."

Yes, Danner thought, it may be a good enough place, but how would they live here? And when the dust settled, what would be her place on this new world? She was a military and security commander; all she was good at was giving orders. She knew nothing of communities and the way they worked. She wished Marghe were here; an anthropologist would be invaluable.

"If only we really knew what it's like to live amongst these people," she said, frustrated.

Letitia and Lu Wai exchanged glances. "But we do," Letitia said slowly. "Kind of. Or, at least, Day does."

"Day? Officer Day, the one that got rescued from the burn by that skinny native, before the virus hit?" Dogias nodded. "But she's dead. Isn't she? The virus."

"I believe she's listed as missing, ma'am," Lu Wai said.

"You mean she's not dead?" The truth hit her. "You know where she is!"

"Yes."

THE SLED hummed next to what was left of the northern perimeter gate as Lu Wai ran it through ground checks. Though it was only midmorning, it was dark enough for twilight; wind drove thick snow almost horizontally through the gloom. Inside her hood, Danner kept her eyes slitted against the flakes and half walked, half ran across the grass to the sled. Dogias was on the flatbed, securing the last of the supply cases.

Danner tapped her on the shoulder. She had to shout over the wind. "Remember, tell her it's all unofficial. According to the records, she's still listed as missing, and it'll stay that way no matter what, unless she wants it different. Tell her anything you think will persuade her, but just get her here."

"Do my best," Dogias shouted.

The foul-weather cab hatch slid back and Lu Wai leaned out. "Let's get going. The weather will only get worse."

Dogias jumped down from the flatbed and slid into the front seat; Lu Wai pressed the hatch-seal button, cursed, and began to crank it down by hand.

The sled lifted off the ground with a whine. Snow hissed underneath it and bit at Danner's ankles.

The sled eased forward, gathering speed. Within two minutes, all Danner could see to the north was snow.

She felt suddenly lonely. Two weeks would be a long time

without Dogias's irreverence—maybe three weeks if the weather got worse. Danner had ordered them to return immediately if there was any problem with communications; it was too danger-ous to be out in this weather if they lost touch, or if their SLICs went down.

That made her think of Marghe: no SLIC, no communication, hundreds of miles to the north where the weather, according to Sigrid, was brutal.

She started to walk away from the perimeter. Half-dismantled, and deserted because of the weather, this part of Port Central already looked like a ruin.

DANNER SPLIT her screen: Nyo on one side, Sara on the other. "Is it, or is it not, possible to move that damned satellite to pick up Marghe's SLIC?"

"Well," Nyo said, "we could move it, yes, but we might not be able to get it back. And that would screw up what comm you've got down there."

"The SLIC might not even be operational," Sara pointed out.

Danner ignored that. "Let's just assume that it is."

"It really wouldn't be wise at this point," Sara said. "What would the *Kurst* think when they saw a satellite being moved? We can't afford to do anything alarming, nothing that looks like change."

Hiam was right. Danner would just have to forget Marghe, trust to the representative's luck and toughness. And the vaccine. When Day got to Port Central, Danner could see if there had been any word through the viajeras on Marghe's progress. Without Marghe to negotiate trade and friendship between Port Central and the natives, to gain a foothold on this world she would have to rely for now on the personal link between herself and Day, and the natives who had saved her life, Oriyest and Jink. And upon the more impersonal trata agreement between Cassil of Holme Valley and herself as commander of Port Central. And on hope.

Damn small things to base a life, many lives, on.

Chapter Ten

MARGHE AND Leifin were three days traveling through Moan-wood to Ollfoss. Later, Marghe could not have said whether it was a year or no time at all. She remembered little: occasional fractured snapshots of trees that were not quite trees, whose roots were greater around than their crowns or which possessed no crowns at all; musty, sharp smells of small nesting animals; pain in her hands and feet and face. Most of all she remembered one day falling down on the snow-dusted floor of the forest and lying on her back, dizzy, while leaves, or what might have been leaves, whirled around her head. She had laughed aloud, but the forest swallowed her thin bright ribbon of laughter and she quieted as she realized it was she who was the alien here; that the dark and the green around her would remain unaffected by her, could not digest her if it tried. Like cellulose in the gut of a carnivore, she could not be assimilated. Alien.

The rest of the journey was a jumble: Leifin climbing on top of her, keeping her warm; soft wet stuff in her mouth that Leifin had already chewed for her; Leifin sneaking something from her pocket then shouting at her to stop, stop, and Marghe realizing she had Leifin's hand between her teeth and her gums hurt, but refusing to let go until Leifin put the vial back into Marghe's pocket.

She remembered nothing of arriving at Ollfoss. She had imagined how it might have been, since: stumbling out from under the dark canopy onto the blinding white snow; past the open-walled shelter that housed nothing but a small metal gong; along the snow-covered path that ran between the bathhouse, built over the hot spring, and the famous vegetable gardens of Ollfoss; on to the houses and outhouses and gathering places that looked like stone versions of the tents of the Echraidhe, with horizontal slit windows and wooden shutters under their eaves of sod, and careful stone channels running down the corners of the sloping roofs. Low houses, sturdy houses, built to survive snow and the rushing, runneling thaws of spring.

More days followed spent tossing in fever; shouting in hoarse Portuguese for someone to turn the lights on; trying hard to swallow soup and crying when she spilled it; feeling pain in her hands and feet and face. Being tied down. She remembered faces looming over her, serious or smiling, but all strange.

So gradually that she could not have pointed to one day in particular and said, *There, that was when I began to really recover,* Marghe realized that what she thought were restraints on her arms and legs were bandages of cloth and moss. Her spinning dreams steadied down to a world where certain faces reappeared again and again in connection with lifting her over to the fire, bathing her with warm water, feeding her, trimming the wick on the horn-shaded lamp that sat on the trunk by one whitewashed wall.

The face that appeared most often, the one accompanied by pain in her smeary fever dreams, was a dark, walnut-faced woman, Kenisi, who untied the cloth and removed the moss, rubbed something into the pain, replaced the wrappings with fresh moss and clean cloths. She was smaller, quicker than Borri, but she had the same eyes as the Echraidhe healer. Marghe tried to smile the first time she realized what Kenisi was doing, but split open her healing lip.

After a while she began to stay awake long enough to sit up on the narrow bed she occupied, and to greet by name the other faces: Leifin, of course, the one with the shifting-sea eyes and the thin mouth, who often brought a knife and sat whittling wood; Hilt, a tall woman whose hair, just a fraction darker than the coffee color of her skin, was the shortest Marghe had yet seen on this world. Hilt was a sailor, from North Haven, in Ollfoss to visit her blood sister Thenike, a viajera.

As Marghe began visibly to gain strength, Kenisi allowed other visitors, women from neighboring families. Some, like Leifin, wore the cap, furs, and sling of the tribes; others, like Hilt, wore felt cloaks and knit caps; still others, a mix of homespun, pelts, and felt. Many wore jewelry: bright olla beads in strings around necks and wrists or dangling from wooden earcuffs, brooches carved and painted in strong colors. Some lived in Ollfoss; others were either living in Ollfoss for the short term or visiting kith or lovers for the winter. All were curious: here was a woman from somewhere totally other, who had survived the Echraidhe and won through Tehuantepec in the winter.

Marghe ignored all their questions. She found she could not think about the Echraidhe, the snow and ice, the way she had nearly let herself die. She still did not know why she had made herself struggle to survive, nor if she was glad she had.

Instead, she concentrated on her body. The next time Kenisi came to change the wrappings on her hands, rather than staring up into the thick rafters that sloped to a point over her head, Marghe asked some questions of her own.

The two crusty scabs where the two smallest fingers on her left hand should have been needed no explaining, but Kenisi pointed to the mottled finger on that hand, and the little finger, missing its nail, on her right. "This one, and this, should heal." She let Marghe look, then rewrapped them carefully and started to unwind the cloth around Marghe's head and ear. "There'll be scars here"—a cool touch of her finger above the left eyebrow—"and here." Where she touched just behind the ear, Marghe flinched. "Hurt?" Marghe nodded. Kenisi rubbed it gently with the ointment. "You've lost part of that ear, too. Nothing your hair won't hide."

Marghe was grateful for the healer's matter-of-fact tone. It gave her the courage to ask, "Is there anything else? My feet?"

Kenisi smiled, fissuring her face. "They're a mess, but they'll heal." She stopped rubbing ointment into Marghe's face. "Think we'll leave these wrappings off for now, see how it goes," she said, and started on Marghe's feet.

Marghe was glad Kenisi had already told her they would heal: they reminded her of half-flayed baby seals, an unhealthy mix of purplish black skin and red raw flesh. She turned away, glad, suddenly, that she had not been able to look into a mirror since she had woken.

Later that day, Leifin brought in a young girl with long, unbraided hair. They were both carrying food. Stewed fish, fruit, water: soft stuff. Marghe's teeth still rocked in her gums. It would be a while before she was up to chewing meat or fibrous vegetables. Leifin introduced the girl. "Gerrel, daughter of my blood sister, Kristen."

Gerrel, Marghe saw, was trying hard not to stare at her. Her face. She touched it gently. "What does it look like?"

"Like you ran into a tree," Gerrel said. She appraised Marghe frankly, shook her head. "Like you ran into a tree twice."

"Well, it could be worse."

Gerrel's expression said she doubted it. Marghe concentrated on eating the food while Leifin and Gerrel took out her pot and brought it back freshly scrubbed with snow and smelling of some aromatic.

After that, Gerrel often brought Marghe's food by herself, and helped wash her down, or moved her to the fur-draped trunk against one wall while Kenisi and a woman called Ette laid fresh covers on the bed. When Marghe asked, Gerrel went to get lukewarm water and a cake of hard soap. While Gerrel washed her hair, Marghe tried to fill in some of the gaps in her knowledge.

"Who is Ette related to?"

"She's from Kristen's family."

Marghe frowned, remembering. "Your mother and Leifin's blood sister?"

Gerrel carefully teased out a tangle. "Kristen's my blood mother."

"But you don't live with her?"

"No. Her family lives in the house with the two chimneys: her and Namri, Ellyr, Rathell, young Hamner, and baby Gin."

Marghe shook her head, still uncertain about who belonged in what house.

"Careful. You'll get water all over the place."

"So who do you call your family?"

"There's Wenn, she's the oldest, and Kenisi, of course."

"The healer."

"She's really a cook. She's the one that makes most of what you eat. Bakes bread for other families, too. And during harvest, it's always our family's cookpot that everyone lines up at. You should see her festival cake!" She scooped Marghe's soapy hair up in one hand, pulled the bowl of water closer. "Lean forward so I can rinse this off."

Marghe did.

"Leifin and Huellis have baby soestre, Otter and Moss. Then there's Thenike, who's here right now but not often, because she's always off viajering in that boat of hers, and her blood sister Hilt. This is the first time they've both been home together for ages. And then there's me."

"So why do you live here?"

"Thenike's my choose-mother. Wenn said I should come and live here with Thenike's family because she said I'd end up clashing with Kristen. Something like that, anyway. I've been here since I was an infant."

Adoption, or fostering. "And who's Thenike related to? Apart from Hilt."

"I don't know. But she's been part of the family since before I have."

Gerrel was a mine of information. Huellis, she said, was Leifin's partner, but everyone knew that it hadn't started because of love: Leifin had wooed her because of the bad trata agreement between their family and Huellis's, years ago. Now that they were part of the same family, the trata agreement had to be renegotiated, and their family was richer than it had been. Huellis and Leifin seemed to like each other well enough now; at least, Huellis had stayed.

Gerrel was not afraid to ask her own questions. Marghe did not always answer them, but the girl seemed to accept that there were some things Marghe was not prepared to talk about.

Gerrel asked one question Marghe knew she would have to find an answer for, eventually: "Leifin rescued you and brought you here. The family's caring for you. How will you repay us?"

TWO DAYS later, on a morning when sunlight slid now and again through the window slits set up near the roof and made her want to be outside, Marghe was sitting up in bed and pondering that question. Across her knees lay several objects: the vial of FN-17, her fur mittens, her knife, her palo. All gifts from women she had barely known. All she had in the world.

She touched them one by one.

The vial was almost empty, and there was one less softgel than there had been. She hoped that somehow, during her delirium, her subconscious body clock had told her when to take it. She was unsure how long she had been here, but it felt as though it was almost time to take another.

The mittens that had been tawny brown when Cassil first gave them to her were dark, crusty with blood and slime. They stank. Unless they could be cleaned along with the rest of her furs, wherever they were, she did not even have any clothes.

The knife, too, was stained; the hide wrappings around the haft looked splotched and diseased. The stone blade had a new chip she did not remember. That should be possible to grind out. She touched it gently with her fingertip. Cold. Rough. Like Shill and Holle, who had given it to her.

She picked up the palo last, hefting it in her right hand. In the light, a long way from the harsh Tehuantepec snow, the carving seemed cruder than it had amongst the tents of the Echraidhe. Aoife had made this, for her.

She put it down next to the knife.

All the gifts had been made for her; not bought in a bright hive of commerce in one quick afternoon, but crafted on cold winter nights by the light of tallow, or cut from the steaming bodies of animals while the sky rushed overhead. The wood had been seasoned, whittled, carved, polished, stained. The knife had been old when she received it: a comfortable, familiar friend to someone, given with love. Even the FN-17 was the product of personal sweat and effort by Sara Hiam.

These things were all she had. These things had kept her alive. She would never be able to repay the givers in full.

When Gerrel came in with soup and a dish of the rough gray-brown Ollfoss bread, Marghe was still staring at the things on her lap. Gerrel put the tray on the floor and cleared them away. "They smell," she said, and tugged the coverlet, smoothing it. She laid the tray on Marghe's lap. "Neat's-foot and onion soup."

It smelled like asparagus, and was almost clear, with a hint of brown that could have been the wooden bowl, or caramelized onion. Cheese, just beginning to melt, floated on top. It looked too hot to eat right away. Marghe picked up one of the small loaves.

"It's best if you soak the bread, then scoop some cheese on," Gerrel said.

Marghe tore off a piece of bread. "What's neat's-foot?"

"I knew you'd ask that." Gerrel pulled two leaves from her pocket. They were the size of bay leaves, milky with pale green veins. "When you first pick them, they're clear, like olla, and these bits"—she pointed to the veins—"are dark green. But if you don't use them right away they go cloudy. Like this."

Marghe was having a hard time with the stringy cheese.

"No, like this." Gerrel broke off her own piece of bread, dipped it in the soup, twirled it expertly until it was wrapped in cheese, and popped it in her mouth.

"Ah. Like spaghetti."

"What?"

Marghe explained about spaghetti. Gerrel listened carefully. "Gerrel, do you believe anything I tell you?" she asked suddenly.

Gerrel looked confused. "Why? Isn't it true?"

Marghe suddenly wanted to cry. "Yes, it's true. It's all true."

Later that afternoon, Marghe had a visitor.

She came in quietly, smiled, gestured to the end of Marghe's bed with a raised eyebrow, and sat when Marghe nodded.

"I'm Thenike." Her voice was textured, rich with harmonies.

Marghe dredged her memory. "Blood sister to Hilt." Like Hilt, she was taller than average, though not by much. Her skin was darker than the sailor's, and differently textured: close-pored. Her features were planed to bones and hollows and looked strong, like the exposed roots of a mature tree. Unlike Hilt's, her hair was long, coiled up on her head, dark and glossy, like the wood of massive trees that were too dense to float: mahogany, teak, silkwood.

"Gerrel tells me you're a viajera."

Thenike smiled. "I bet that's not all she's told you."

"True. Though she couldn't tell me how I can repay your family for my care."

Thenike said nothing for a while. "As you say, I'm a viajera. Your story would be worth a great deal to me. If you feel up to it, telling me how you came here would pay part of the debt to the family."

"My story in exchange for all this?" Marghe gestured around her.

Thenike studied her. "Mine isn't the only say. If it was, then, yes, it would be your story in exchange for all of this. It's not always easy to give a story to a viajera. But I do have some say, and if you give me what I need, then part of your debt will be discharged."

"Who decides the rest?"

"The family. All of us. In this instance, because Leifin was the one who brought you, she will have a great deal to say. But back to your story. It won't be easy, but if it's done right, both of us will benefit, I think. Are you willing?"

This was a good opportunity to see firsthand the way a viajera worked. "Yes."

"Then we'll begin today." She looked up at the shutters of the unglazed slits that passed as windows. "It's stuffy in here. Outside, it's cold, but sunny. Perhaps you would like to breathe some fresh air, see the sky?"

"Yes." She would have to do better than just *yes*. She made an effort. "I'd like that."

"I'll find you some clothes."

Thenike lifted the lamp off the trunk and rummaged for a while. "Here." It was an enormous tent of a cloak. She pulled back Marghe's covers. "Swing your legs out. There. Yes. And I'll help you with these." Marghe recognized the fur leggings: her own, cleaned. "Now, put this on. Over your head. Put your arm over my shoulder, no, lean on me, and up." And Marghe swayed onto her feet, draped in the felt cloak.

"How's that? Can you try a step?"

Marghe nodded, and did. Her feet hurt ferociously. It must have shown on her face.

"It'll hurt, but a few steps won't do any harm. Time you were up and about."

Marghe took another step, winced. "Lean on me," Thenike said.

After being inside for so long, the sharp, clear air made Marghe cough, which hurt her feet even more. The sun shone—a thinner yellow and from a lighter blue sky, but it was sunshine and the world was still here. She stood and wheezed and not all the tears that she wiped from her cheeks were from her coughing.

"I've prepared a place for you, as you see."

Thenike helped her sit on the pallet that waited on a sun-lit patch of moss by the wall. Marghe leaned back, eyes closed, and soaked up the illusion of warmth. She knew Thenike was watching.

"Do you get a lot of sun here in Ollfoss during the winter?"

"This will be the first winter I've spent here for four years," Thenike said, "and the last time it was nothing but cloud until the Moon of Aches." Marghe opened her eyes to find Thenike smiling. "But, yes, all the other winters I've been here, the clouds unwind now and again, and the plants in our gardens and nurseries unfurl their bright new leaves, and we eat well. How is the winter where you come from?"

"I come from many different places." So many.

"Whichever you choose. It's in my mind that I'll have seen none of them. Tell me what you wish."

And Marghe told her of winters in Macau when the sky was the gray of an upturned fish pot and the air smelled to her six-year-old self of rice wine and sea, and carried with it the excitement of the casinos and the sharp fear-sweat of men gambling more than they could afford to lose. She told of the winter hills of Portugal as she remembered them from the last time she had visited her father: the cold blue skies, the wind that slid through her clothes when she walked a goat path in the morning. She did not know what winter would be like at Port Central.

The sun disappeared behind a bank of cloud that looked as though it had been carved from slippery gray soapstone. Marghe watched, tired after so much talking.

"A suke sky," Thenike said.

"Suke?"

"Like the belt sukes some of us wear." Thenike reached under her cloak and pulled out a round disk, drilled through at the top and threaded with a thong. She untied it, handed it to Marghe. "My suke."

It was half the size of Marghe's palm and unpainted, smooth on the back, slightly rounded, carved on the front with a fish. The carving was clean-lined, stylized, well-executed. An emblem of some kind.

"You did this?"

"It was my mother's."

"She's dead?"

Thenike smiled. "No. Her lover carved her another one, this time with two nerka instead of one."

"Nerka?"

"This fish. Blue-backed fish that live at sea but come back to High Beaches every spring to spawn." As if sensing Marghe's fatigue, Thenike seemed happy to take over the talking duty. "Hilt and I were born in North Haven; that's where she makes her home, when she's not at sea. My home is everywhere." She gestured around her. "Ollfoss, North Haven, High Beaches, Pebble Fleet. Up the Ho and down the Sayesh, along the Huipil and on the banks of the Glass."

"Sounds like you still like to stay on the water."

"Yes. I have a skiff, the *Nid-Nod*. You know the nid-nod? It's a silly bird that lives in the marshes out by the river Glass, and in the Trern Swamplands. She has long legs and a longer beak too heavy for her head, which she's always lifting up and down to see what's happening. The nid-nod, the story goes, is convinced that something good is happening somewhere close by and she's missing it."

Marghe smiled, remembering a number of people who acted that way.

The sun came out again and they enjoyed it quietly.

"Time to get you back in, I think."

Marghe did not demur; she was tired. It hurt more to get back to her bed than it had leaving it. Thenike helped her onto the bed, but let her take off her own cloak and fold it. "I'll come back tomorrow. Early if the sun's shining."

When Thenike was gone, Marghe realized she had not once mentioned Wales, or her mother. Or her mother's death.

The next day the sun was shining; Thenike came while Marghe and Gerrel were sharing a breakfast of goura chunks and pulpy nitta seeds. "Ugly plant, the nitta," Gerrel had told Marghe, "all waxy pods and roots, and the seeds are hard to get. I don't know why we bother with them, taste like wirrel droppings." But Marghe liked them, and accepted Gerrel's share.

"You should eat those," Thenike observed in her rich voice, "they're good for you."

"You eat them if they're so nice," Gerrel said, unconcerned.

"Unfortunately, I don't like them any more than you do." She smiled. "But I value my health. If you don't eat nitta, make sure you put extra gaver pepper in your soup, like I do." Gerrel pulled a face. "Maybe it's time for me to tell the story of Torren and the healer again."

Gerrel sighed, and spooned some seeds from Marghe's dish to

her own. Thenike pretended not to notice. "No need to rush your food on my account," she said to Marghe, "the sun will wait. It's warmer than yesterday."

When they were outside, Marghe looked at Thenike. "The story of Torren and the healer?"

Thenike smiled. "Torren was a young girl who thought she knew best and did not always eat her nitta seeds, or wear her cap in the middle of winter. One day she got sick and went to the healer. The healer turned her away, saying, why should she help Torren when Torren always refused to help herself?"

"So what happened?"

"It depends. Sometimes Torren repents, sometimes the healer relents, sometimes Torren dies."

Marghe pondered that. "So viajeras teach. What else do they do?"

"Depends on the viajera. We witness agreements between kiths and communities; we judge disputes; sometimes we allot land to herders."

"Land that you hold?"

"No. There's a great deal of common land. When a family moves, or hits a burn, or simply splits into two, they need to use other land. Viajeras remember which land is in use, and which of that available land would be suitable for the family that's asking for it. We remember. We remember which family might quarrel with which, and make sure they're given the use of lands that don't adjoin. We travel and tell news, we sing songs and spin stories; we lead pattern singings and deepsearch, we heal broken bones and old resentments, but mostly we remember."

Marghe got the feeling that she was missing something, but had no idea what.

Thenike grinned. "But being a viajera is not all of who I am. I'm also a bad cook and a good sailor, and dangerous to meet over a game of knucklebones." Marghe did not look satisfied. "Did you expect more? I'm not a sage or a holy woman. I have skills that I use as a viajera. Just as you have skills that you use as an anthropologist." She said the word carefully, only having heard it once, the day before. "Everything I do can become part of that work, if I choose. Just as it can and does for you, if you choose."

She stared up at the sky, which was swirling like scum on top of a boiling pot, letting the sun through for brief moments. "If I wasn't a viajera, didn't have the skills of a viajera, I'd be someone different. A sailor, perhaps, like Hilt, leaving North Haven in the spring and only coming back in the autumn after crossing Silverfish Deeps as far as Eye of Ocean and back again." She sounded wistful. "And you. What would you have chosen to do if you had not come here, to be an anthropologist?"

Marghe thought about that. "I don't know."

"What do you like to do? In the winter when you walked the hills in Portugal, or lay on your stomach on the roof watching the fisherfolk of Macau"—again the careful words, strange in her mouth—"what was it that you wished you had the time to do?"

"Explore," Marghe said, surprised. "Go places I'd never seen before. Exciting places, where dragons might just be real." She laughed, delighted at her discovery. "I always liked to follow paths, see where they went, who they led to. A map, a new world, a strange country—they're all like puzzles where I have to put the pieces together to feel comfortable, to understand how things are. Once I understand, I feel too comfortable. Then it's time to move on, find a new place, new people. New discoveries."

"Always?"

"So far," she said slowly, suddenly unwilling to go any further with this.

Thenike nodded. "And these places you go, the people you find, do you come to care for them? Or do you only study them, like strange shells you might find on the beach?"

Marghe forced a smile and waved the question aside. *Like strange shells that you find on the beach . . .* She did not want to think about it. "What kind of sky would you call this?"

"A chessel sky," the viajera said. "If I was in my skiff, I'd be looking for a place to put in. We'll see a bit of wind."

"Chessel?"

"If you feel up to a little walk, I'll show you."

Marghe had to breathe deeply, steadily, and lean on Thenike as they walked the snow-dusted path to a building half-hidden under the trees. The sloping roof was covered in old snow, icy and gray, and the slit windows were shuttered from the inside. Unlike most of the other buildings of Ollfoss, much of it was underground.

The steps leading down to the sturdy-looking door were not steep, but Marghe took them one at a time, like a child.

Inside, it was cool and dim, full of barrels, slablike tables, sacks and stacks and huge clay jugs. She ran her hands over one: stoppered with a rough clay seal. Food storage. Thenike used a wooden pole, curved into a hook at the end, to lever open a couple of window shutters. There was a milky, sickly smell Marghe could not identify, and overlaying that, something thin and sharp.

"A chessel," Thenike said, pointing.

It was a wooden cheese vat. Thenike leaned her pole up against a whitewashed wall and pulled off the gauzy cloth covering, sending a gust of sharp not-quite-cheese smell in Marghe's direction. In the vat, the whey looked scummy, rancid, like the sky.

"This is where we make butter and cheese, and store what milk we don't use on any day." She slid the stone lid off a good-sized bowl. "Yeast. For the bread." She slid it back. "Through here are the vegetables." There were mounds of roots and tubers, leaves drying in bunches and bulbs hanging from the roof. Thenike reached into a barrel, pulled out a small, round fruit, sniffed it. "Soca. Here. Can you smell the spice? That means it's not ready yet. We pick them at the end of the Moon of Shelters, leave them here in the dark until they're ready. When they're ready they smell terrible, like bad feet, but they taste like rain after a drought, like wind on a calm sea."

To Marghe it seemed that the storage cellar was full with enough to feed a thousand people for a year, and it occurred to her that she had never really seen whole-food storage before. At Port Central, there was probably more protein, more vitamins, stored in a tenth this space, all in the form of concentrates, flash-frozen choice cuts, and prepeeled mixes.

The chessel sky was wrapped right around the sun by the time they emerged. A cold wind bowled snow dust along the paths. Marghe's scars ached. She shivered. Here she was in Ollfoss, the place she had been traveling toward for two years in order to . . . *study the people like shells found on a beach.* She was not sure she wanted to do that anymore. Suddenly she was not sure about anything anymore, and that was frightening. If she did not want to do what she had set out to do, then what did she want? Something had changed. Some part of her was gone.

"Marghe? Are you well?"

"No," she said.

"Lean on me. It's not far." The arms that Thenike wrapped around her waist for support were strong and hard. Marghe wanted to lean into them and weep for what she had lost, though she did not know whether her loss was good or bad, or even real. Instead, she started the painful walk back to the guest room.

She allowed Thenike to help her into bed, grateful when the viajera stooped to add wood to the carefully banked fire and stoked it into a blaze. When she turned back to Marghe, her face was ruddy. "That should keep you warm. Do you need anything else?"

Stay with me, Marghe wanted to say. *Don't leave me alone with my thoughts.* "No."

"Then I'll check on you later."

Marghe was tired. The fire was hot. She fell asleep.

In her dream, she walked along a long, bleak shore littered with bladderwrack and feathers and seashells. Someone was down by the surf. Thenike. She held something out to Marghe, something hard and bright, crusted with wet sand. A chambered nautilus. "Do you see, Marghe," she said, opening it as though it were on a hinge, "shells are not empty." Chamber after gleaming chamber was filled with soft, wet life. Such a fragile and beautiful thing. Precious. Then the shell and Thenike were gone, and Marghe was running up and down the beach, listening desperately for the cries of her mother, who was trapped inside one of the shells and being swept away on the tide.

But something caught her attention, something dark and wet, gleaming in a nest of seaweed. She stooped for it. A fossilized shell, an ammonite. It was cold and heavy in her maimed hand, like stone. But her mother was being swept away. *You can't lose me now,* it whispered, *you've only just found me.* And while she watched, it sank into her palm and disappeared. When she looked up, all the other shells were gone.

Marghe jerked awake. Her left hand was numb; she had slept on it. She shook it until it began to tingle, shivered as her sweat dried. She remembered her dream, the fossilized shell . . .

Or do you just study people like shells found on a beach? Thenike's question had passed Marghe's barriers and gone deep; it demanded an honest answer. To herself, at least.

Very well.

She had lived alone for as long as she could remember, her father and mother had always been so busy. She had buried herself in study, in observation and analysis. People were there to be watched, not related to. And now her mother was dead and her father estranged, and she had no friends. She had no friends, because whenever she began to get close to someone it felt like unknown territory, and it scared her; she ran away to a new place, to find new people to study, people to whom she did not necessarily have to be a person back.

To be a person back. She was not sure she knew how.

She was staring at the coverlet, trying to digest that revelation, when Thenike came back.

"How are you?"

"I don't know."

Thenike sat on the end of the bed. "What is it?"

Marghe did not dare look up from the coverlet. But she had to talk to someone about this, make it real. "There are some things I haven't told you." So many things. "About my mother. About what happened to my face." She touched her nose, the break that only she could see. "About . . . about why I feel so alone."

Thenike took her hand. "You're not alone. I'm listening."

"Sometimes . . . sometimes I feel that all I've got is my job. I study people, that's who I am: studier of people. What you said this morning was true. I treat people like interesting specimens, not like humans. And I do it because . . . because I don't know how else to behave. It's as though all I am is my job. All I am is an empty shell. I look all right from a distance, but up close there's nothing there, nothing behind the pretty whorls and brittle exterior. But I don't have that job anymore. No shell. But if I don't have that, then what do I have?"

She did not mention her dream of the ammonite, sinking heavy and solid, complete, into the bones of her hand.

"What did you have before your job?"

Slowly, Marghe told Thenike about how her mother, Acquila, had been an anthropologist before her, how Marghe had taken up the studies because it was a way to be close to her mother when she wasn't there, which was often. She told her about Company. About her beating. About the death of her mother and her fear of the virus.

It was not everything, not nearly everything, but it was a start.

They were sitting peacefully, watching the fire, when Gerrel came in with lunch for herself and Marghe.

Thenike looked up. "That smells good."

"There's some left in the kitchen. Do you want me to get it for you?"

"Thank you."

"Here, then. You two start in on these and I'll bring another bowl for me."

"If you put them by the fire, they'll stay warm. We'll wait for you to rejoin us," Marghe said. She suddenly needed the company of this unconcerned child and the woman who denied she was wise. She felt depressed and uncertain, not yet ready to be alone with her new and fragile thoughts.

MARGHE AND Thenike talked every day. Marghe learned of linn cloud, the waterfall cloud in multilayers which brought very heavy rain; of n'gus, queen daggerhorn sky—stately and slow-moving like the beasts of the forest; of pilwe sky, soft, white undulating cloud that could hide the sun for a whole moon.

She did not know what Thenike learned, but Marghe told her of coming to Jeep, of the trata agreement with Cassil in Holme Valley, of how Holle and Shill had lent her Pella and given her the knife that helped keep her alive. She spent one whole afternoon talking about Aoife.

"She made this for me"—she showed Thenike the palo—"but she hit me more than once. Sometimes she treated me like I wasn't human, but sometimes . . . Thenike, I know she cared! Sometimes I think she came to care more for me than she had done for anyone for a long time. But she wouldn't let me go. There was one time when I thought she might, I really thought . . . I tried to ask why. But it was as though she was two people. The tribe, the tribe, nothing but the tribe. It was all she knew. I just didn't matter to her, in the end. I belonged to the tribe, I was subhuman, even though everything in her heart told her otherwise. How can people do that?"

"Perhaps she did what she could to help."

"She was my jailer."

"She taught you how to survive."

"So that I could be a good and productive member of the tribe!"

"Nonetheless."

Marghe brushed that aside impatiently, winced as her healing hands banged on the edge of her cot. "She kept me like a caged animal. Until I didn't know who I was anymore. Thenike, there were days on Tehuantepec when I wished Uaithne would kill me, just to end everything. No, that's not true. I didn't care enough about anything to even bother to actively want anything. I just didn't care. I was nothing. A blank. Have you ever felt like that? It's the most terrible thing in the world." She was crying, but did not bother to brush away her tears. "I nearly didn't try to run, when I had the chance. I saw the fire and the first thing I thought was, Why bother to run, why not go back, at least it'll be warm." She laughed, heard the pain in it. "And you know what the worst thing is? I thought, It won't be fair to Aoife if I run away. Not fair to Aoife. How can I live with that?"

"But you did decide to live."

"Yes. I did, didn't I. I wonder why."

"Do you think it matters why?"

"Yes. No. I don't know." She was quiet awhile. "It was hard,

Thenike. I had to fight and fight and fight. All the time. When my compass broke. When I escaped. Through the blizzard. To keep moving, to get to the trees. To keep living. There has to be a powerful reason to stay alive through all that."

"You're a survivor."

"I don't know what I am." She wiped away the tears that were drying, cold, on her cheeks. "I don't want to be Marghe the anthropologist who examines seashells on the beach and moves on. I don't think I am her anymore. But I don't know who I want to be."

"Do you want to know?"

Marghe thought carefully. "Yes."

"Then in a few days, when you're stronger, there's something you can do that might help you find out."

IT WAS the last day of the Moon of Silence, and the air was still and cold. The structure that sheltered the gong stood near the edge of the forest. It was rough, four timber posts holding up a shingled roof, and lay open to any woman of Ollfoss who might walk by. None did. This was Marghe's place for the next day and night.

Marghe, tented inside her felt cloak, knelt on the patch of moss she had swept free of snow and contemplated the gong. It hung from the roof by two weathered ropes and was made of hammered metal that caught the light like copper but turned buttery silver in the center where the hammer dents of its making were almost worn smooth from generations of use. Thin morning light cast a blurred reflection of her face onto its uneven surface. Like a moon.

She studied the pale silent face before her, remembering Aoife naming the moons. Moon of Silence: Aoife's name for this month of midwinter; now Marghe's name for her own face.

The cavity formed between a planetary body and its ionosphere acts as a natural resonator; most people who lived on Earth were unaware that they lived on a gigantic gong that boomed out exactly sixty-nine times every day. On Gallipoli, a much smaller body that pulsed more frequently, the colonists were equally unaware. Here on Jeep, the people knew. Three times a year—before sowing the gardens with their seed and bulbs, when the fruits and grains were ripening, and as the last of the harvest was being gathered—a woman of Ollfoss was chosen to sit by the gong all day and all night, sounding it in time to the pulse of the world. The rhythm, Thenike said, helped the crops. It would also help Marghe; if she could still herself enough to hear, she would learn what she needed to know of herself.

Extended meditation. Marghe knew it would not be sound that she would hear, but something she would sense, as she had the Tehuantepec stones. She sat by the gong and breathed gently, slowly, long, long inhalations and steady exhalations, and sank her awareness down into her own electromagnetic field; when this world rang, her body would tell her.

At the right moment, when she felt her lungs would fill forever with the no-longer-alien sticky resin smell of green and dirt and small mammals' nests, when it seemed the world waited for just a brief hitch of time, when she heard and felt and was the electromagnetic pulse of Jeep, its laugh, its breath, she rose up onto her knees, lifted the wooden rod she held in her right hand and struck the gong with the padded end. Vibration seeped through Ollfoss like the smell of grass after rain, resonating with the pulse of the world, its heartbeat. She sat back down on her heels. Long after the sound faded, she sensed the air humming as the gong quivered on its ropes.

The metal's vibration slowed. She sat and breathed and watched the reflection of her face reform. The reflection watched her back.

She was not who she had been. Like dull, raw glass in the hands of a skilled blower, she had become something different. Something cold, brilliant, and still. On her left hand were two fingers, a thumb, and two scars. The face that had been beaten into a different shape on Beaver carried new marks. Once again it was no longer her face.

She contemplated that while she listened to the waiting green silence of Moanwood, to the slow breath of the world: the muscle of its dirt, the bones of its rock, the blood of its seas. She heard the world humming deep in its throat, and when it rang with its soft pulse, she leaned forward to strike the gong.

Again and again her face shivered to splinters; again and again it re-formed.

Marghe knew that this meant something: she listened to the world with her body; she hit the gong; her new face swam apart and came back together.

Strike the gong.

They were connected: the world, her body, her face. Perhaps she should not be asking who she was but, rather, of what she was a part. The world was telling her: her blood, the tides in her cells, and the fluctuations in her nerves already beat to its rhythm, just as they had once resonated to the electromagnetic surges of Earth. Her body rang with this world. She had a place here; she could take it up, if she chose.

Strike the gong.

Marghe drank down the cold, still air, felt it suck heat from her lungs. She expelled it gently through her mouth in a deliberate cloud of breath crystal that dulled the surface of the gong. Her mark.

She raised her head. The sky was covered with endless round humps of dark cloud, like a shoal of blue-backed salmon broaching the sea, poised forever before diving. A nerka sky. Those clouds were made of her breath and the breath of a million women who had made peace with the world; women she had set out to study, like seashells.

No longer.

It was possible now for her to put aside that person she had been and choose to accept Thenike, or Cassil or Holle and Shill, even Danner and Lu Wai and Letitia Dogias, as nothing more and nothing less than equals from whom she could learn and derive comfort, to whom she could offer advice or a strong hand. If she chose.

Strike the gong.

She struck it harder than she needed to and set it dancing on its rope. The sound clashed and jarred around the clearing. Choose, it seemed to be saying. Choose. But there was no real choice; that decision was made already. All she had to do was accept it: Jeep the world, Jeep the virus, would become part of her now whether she wanted it or not. There was not enough FN-17 to last her back to Port Central. Even if she was fit enough to travel, even if the tribes and their feud were not making it impossible to cross Tehuantepec, even if the weather didn't mean no ships could make the passage south until the Moon of the Aches, there was not enough. There was not enough. The virus was going to invade her, cell by cell, sliding cold fingers into her cells and curling around her genes. She would never get rid of it. Never.

She could stop taking the FN-17 voluntarily, let Jeep in with open arms. It was coming anyway. This way she could prepare herself. It might make a difference, Thenike said; she might stand a better chance of living if her mind was not fighting her body, if she was struggling toward the possible, toward staying alive, rather than fighting for the impossible, to keep the virus out, right out from under her skin.

To make that choice, to voluntarily set aside the FN-17, she would have to take a step into the unknown; she would have to step out from behind her professional persona and be naked, vulnerable. Herself.

Marghe squirmed. Maybe she should keep taking the vaccine. After all, it was possible that Danner even now might be working miracles, might be establishing new relays, or moving satellites, or sending Mirrors north to track her SLIC. Then she could go up to *Estrade* before the six months were over. She would not have the virus. She . . .

No. All dreams. She would contract the virus; she would be infected and survive, or she would be infected and die. The rest was just details.

Strike the gong.

The face that re-formed was gaunt and pale, and reminded her of her mother.

At the back of all her fears lay her mother. Her mother coughing and sweating. Dying. There were no decisions to be made after dying.

Her mother had died on the bed in the cottage's spare room, the one that was not really big enough. She had lain there, looking as though she might still take a small tearing breath and start coughing again, and Marghe had waited, holding her own breath, hoping. But her mother remained quiet. Marghe had stood there for almost an hour, not believing what had happened. It had taken just three days to turn her mother from a laughing woman striding along the Welsh hillsides to this waxy, thin mannequin. There was nothing left of that vital, bright woman now, except the memories buried deep within her daughter.

Marghe stared at the gong, at the pale, featureless reflection. If she died here, who would remember her, and how? She had been Marghe the SEC representative, or Marghe the vaccine guinea pig. No one knew Marghe the woman.

Except perhaps Aoife. Aoife, who had carved her the palo and given her the knowledge she had needed to stay alive, but who had tried to keep her captive in a place where she would have died slowly of being less than human.

Marghe had asked Thenike why the Echraidhe were so inflexible, so bound by tradition.

"Because they are so few," Thenike had said. "Because their sisters' mothers are also their choose-mothers' sisters. They're born too close. All their memories interlock and look down the same path to the same places. Each memory reflects another, repeats, reinforces, until the known becomes the only. For the Echraidhe, it's not real if it can't be seen elsewhere, in their mother's memory, or their mother's mother. For them, perhaps, there is no such thing as the unknown." Thenike shook her head. "It's a danger to all who are able to deepsearch into their memories well, or often."

"Viajeras."

"And those who might have become viajeras," Thenike agreed. She seemed focused somewhere deep inside. "You can see so much of the world through others' memories, places you've never been, faces you've never seen and never will, weather you've never felt and food you've never tasted, that sometimes it's hard not to want to just feel, taste, see those familiar things over and over. Truly new things become alien, other, not to be trusted. There are those who know their village so well, through the eyes and hearts of so many before them, that they can't leave it to go somewhere else, they can't bear to place their feet on a path they have never trodden, on soil they have never planted with a thousand seeds in some past life as lover or child. Some become unable to leave their lodge or tent, or can't sail past the sight of familiar cliffs. Many who can deep-search powerfully enough to be a viajera end like this."

"And you?"

Here Thenike had smiled, though Marghe saw memories of bitter times written on her face. "I'm fortunate enough to have the memories of a thousand different foremothers, some clear, some not. Fortunate, too, to become bored with the past and eager to sail over the horizon or walk over the crest of the hill and see what's on the other side."

Strike the gong.

It was just after midday. Marghe shivered, cold after sitting all morning.

The results of the virus, the abilities it conferred, could send a person mad. Uaithne had been proof enough of that. How would it affect her? Would she be able to see into her past, the past of her mother, her aunts? Her father? No one at Port Central had mentioned any of this to her, no strange memory effects . . . but how many had tried? It was not a thing that just happened. It involved ritual and discipline. Perhaps, though, it involved more than that. Perhaps the virus had to be part of the cells from birth, even before birth.

Strike the gong.

Early afternoon. Marghe saw a tiny figure walking out of the gathering dark and across the snow toward her. She could not spare the figure her whole attention; part of her body was always listening, attuned to Jeep. Waiting. The figure grew, stepping carefully. Carrying something. Food. Gerrel put down the covered tray an arm's length from Marghe's feet and withdrew without speaking. It struck Marghe, then, just how much she knew about Gerrel:

not only her name, her house, soestre and antecedents, but what foods made her wrinkle her upper lip in distaste, what stories she liked to be told when it was cold and gloomy outside, what made her laugh or blush. That knowledge told her a great deal about herself, about her attitudes to this place: these people were becoming real to her.

She could live here, for a while.

Marghe ate, listened, struck the gong. Listened and felt and struck the gong. It grew dark. The stars came out, and the moons, but the clouds reduced them to shimmery blurs. The blurs sank down into the horizon, faded. The smell of the forest changed, grew wilder, darker; Marghe thought she heard something large prowling along its edge.

Gerrel brought her breakfast before dawn. She did not eat it. The world seemed very wide and thin.

When the sun came up, Marghe waited, struck the gong one more time, then stilled its vibration with her fingertips and laid the padded stick along the top. She stood, swaying a little, then bent and took the half goura from the bowl on the untouched tray. The trees seemed to call her. *Listen,* they said to her, *we ring to the same beat as you, to the same beat as the virus, the same beat of the world.* This might be the place to stay and finally learn what it meant to have a family and friends. She wandered off into the forest; she did not want to see anyone just yet.

WHEN MARGHE came out of the trees, she walked through the gardens and up the path that led through Ollfoss to Thenike's door. She lifted her hand to knock and realized she was still holding the half-eaten fruit. She knocked with her other hand. No one answered. She knocked again.

Thenike came to the door. Her eyes sharpened when she saw Marghe.

Marghe spoke without preamble. "I want to stay here, at Ollfoss. There are things I have to learn. Help me."

Chapter Eleven

"If you want to stay, you need to talk to Leifin," Thenike had said that morning. "She found you and brought you here. If she didn't have a good reason for it at the time, then she does now, though I couldn't begin to guess what. She always has a reason for everything, a plan, an explanation." She paused to rake out the ashes and blow the embers to a glow. "She found you; in that sense, she's responsible for you and will have a large say in what happens next."

"Do you like her?"

"Huellis said to me once that she thought Leifin spent too much of her time thinking and not enough feeling."

"That doesn't answer my question."

"No. But it's an answer you'll have to wait for until you've made up your own mind. Go see her. Talk to her. Tell her you want to stay. See what she has to say."

Marghe suddenly felt reluctant to talk to Leifin. "There's no other way?"

"Of course there are other ways." Thenike sounded irritable. "Nothing will get decided without the whole family's approval, and yours. But it'll help you to know Leifin's reason, or reasons. She's the right place to start."

LEIFIN WAS sitting on a stool by the south hearth in the great room, carefully shaving layers from a small block of wood on her lap. Stone and olla tools lay in a neat row on a worn strip of leather; shavings curled in a heap at her feet. Marghe could smell the new wood from the doorway. The infant soestre, Otter and Moss, were lying on a beautiful fur rug near the fire; one— Marghe could not tell them apart—was awake, with her fist in her mouth. The great room was long and slope-ceilinged. It took up the whole of the west side of the house and was the only room Marghe had seen so far in Ollfoss that had a vertical window. In proportion to the room, the window was small, but it was glazed— thick, wavy olla glass stained with hints of cream and rose. The floor was polished wood, like the heavy furniture, and there was a hearth at both ends.

The room was full of beauty: wall carvings, tapestries, furs—on the floor and the walls—intricately patterned doorframes, and gorgeous wooden candlestick holders. But the centerpiece of the whole room was a huge sculpture, low on the floor—the torso and arms of a woman swimming, arching her back as she reached as far as sinew and bone would permit for her next backstroke.

When Marghe stepped into the room and closed the door behind her, Leifin looked up briefly, nodded, then returned her attention to her carving. The expression on her face was the same one Marghe had seen when she had first stepped out of the trees just behind the goth: intent, focused. A hunter's look.

Marghe went to the fire and sat down next to the sleeping baby, content to wait. Eventually, Leifin put down the knife she had been using and selected a chisel.

"Is that your work?" Marghe asked, gesturing at the floor sculpture.

"Yes."

She stroked the fur she sat on. "And this?"

"No, that's an old one. Some of these others are mine." She pointed her chisel at a magnificent blue-gray fur hanging over the back of a bench. "I did that one before I chose my name." She waited to see if Marghe would ask anything else, then went back to her work. If she was curious about Marghe's reason for staying there, she did not show it.

The chisel was sharp and Leifin worked deftly, skimming the blade again and again down one side of the block. Rich golden brown slices fell at her feet, and gradually Marghe saw a curve developing in the wood. Sawdust clung to the dark hairs of Leifin's forearm.

After a while, Leifin paused, put down her chisel, lifted the block of wood, and turned it this way and that in the light. Marghe wondered if Leifin studied a dead animal that way, too, before cutting for the hide.

Leifin looked up and misinterpreted the question on Marghe's face. "I'm tracing the grain, trying to follow it with my tools to bring out the best in both the wood and the sculpture. To give it strength."

She found what she wanted and went back to work, lifting one tool after another, always replacing them in the right place on her leather roll. She worked methodically, patiently, like a trapper noting the strengths and hunting out the weakness of her prey. The pile of shavings grew.

The baby who was not asleep took her fist out of her mouth and began to cry, waking up the other, who joined her.

"They're hungry." Leifin carefully put the curving piece of wood next to her tools and brushed the worst of the sawdust from her arms. She scooped up the one who was screaming the loudest and jiggled her on her knee while she unlaced her leather-and-fur tunic. "There, little one." The baby sucked lustily. "Rock Moss, would you?"

Marghe picked up the infant gingerly, remembering to support her head. "How old are they?"

"They were born just after the harvest."

Four moons ago, or three and a half months. "They're lucky. To have a family."

Leifin nodded, waiting.

"You helped me. The family's caring for me. I like it here." Marghe hesitated. "I want to stay."

"Go on."

"That's it. I want to stay, here, at Ollfoss."

"With this family?"

"Yes," Marghe said, surprised. Who else would she stay with?

"Why?"

"You're the ones who have helped me. And I'm beginning to know some of you: Thenike, and Gerrel, Kenisi . . . I've hardly met anyone from the other families. Not yet."

"And you don't want to wait until you're well enough to get to know the others first?"

"No."

Leifin was looking at her with that intent, hunter's look. "Good. Then I don't see any reason why you shouldn't. Soon." She smiled and held out her hand. It was warm and firm; it should have felt friendly, but it did not. Leifin, Marghe thought, had an agenda of her own.

 ON THE second day of the Moon of Cracking Frost, the family of Leifin and Thenike, Gerrel, Hilt, Kenisi, Kenisi's partner, Wenn, and Huellis and the infant soestre Otter and Moss met to discuss Marghe's petition to join them.

The day outside was dull and gray, and the light that struggled through the milky glass of the single unshuttered window did not do much to thin the fire shadows that danced over the women sitting around the hearth on their rugs. A pot of dap simmered by the fireside. Even though fire was burning at both ends of the room, Marghe was cold. She huddled between Gerrel and Thenike, her allies, pulled her furs closer, and listened.

"You taught me," Gerrel said to Wenn, "and you, Kenisi, and

you yourself, Leifin, you all taught me that actions lead to responsibility. Leifin found Marghe, saved her life. Marghe allowed her life to be saved. These two are, now, responsible to each other. How else could it be?"

Marghe slid her hand into her pocket in an automatic search for reassurance, and for the second time that day was shocked to find the pocket empty. The vial of FN-17 was still in the guest room, where she had laid it aside. She breathed deep, in and out, keeping her anxiety down. She was safe, safe. This was Ollfoss; these women were not Echraidhe. No one was going to pull a knife or hit her for no reason.

"Perhaps we can fulfill our responsibility another way," Huellis ventured.

Kenisi sighed. "Marghe, Leifin brought you here. We acknowledge the responsibility to feed and shelter you until you are well enough to leave. Is this not enough?"

"I ask to join your family."

"You haven't been here long. Will it not wait?"

"No." She had tried to explain, earlier, tried to tell them all how much she needed to belong, belong now, before the virus crept in and started to lever her away from life. Thenike, she knew, understood, and Gerrel would be happy to have a new sister. Leifin was on her side for reasons she neither understood nor trusted, but the others . . . They understood her danger, but not her fears.

The next question was inevitable.

Attention shifted around the circle, came to rest on Wenn. The old woman was blunt. "Why should we give you a place with us, a place in our hearts, when in two moons from now you could be dead?"

Because I'm afraid, she wanted to say. Afraid that she had used up all her self-reliance surviving Tehuantepec, afraid that there was nothing left inside her but empty space. To face the virus, she needed to be able to put down one taproot, to be able to say, *There, it would matter to these people if I died.* She needed to know she belonged somewhere, that the virus would not simply sweep her up in a vast, dark undertow and carry her away forever, with no one to remember, no one to mourn. She needed and was afraid of needing, because if she was refused now, she might never get the chance to try again.

She sat helplessly, not knowing how to say any of it.

"We should admit Marghe formally into our family because she is already in our hearts." All eyes turned to Leifin. "Already, Gerrel feels as though she has a sister to replace the soestre she lost—" Marghe looked at Gerrel; she had not known that. Gerrel managed to grin and blush at the same time. "—and Thenike has someone to focus her teaching to stop her fretting while she's trapped here for the winter."

Thenike smiled faintly, but Marghe already knew her well enough to see that it was not a particularly friendly smile.

"There's nothing to stop Marghe staying with us for the winter, earning her keep until she wants to leave in spring," Wenn said irritably. "Longer, if necessary. And if she wants to ask again to join us in a year or two, then maybe we'd be more inclined to say yes."

"I didn't have to earn my keep first, nor Thenike," Hilt said quietly.

"That was different. We knew your family."

"No, you didn't." Thenike's voice was soft.

"Well, we knew where to find them, anyway. What do we know about Marghe?"

Being talked about in the third person reminded Marghe of the Echraidhe Levarch assigning her to Aoife like so much baggage. She felt something hot and brittle move under her ribs, but did not know if it was anger or desperation.

She stood up. They looked at her. She felt horribly vulnerable. These women could accept her or reject her, and there was no professional facade to hide behind, no separate place to which she could retire and remain aloof. She looked at Thenike, who smiled, very slightly, and Gerrel, who was frowning. She cared for these people. Two of them, anyway.

Her voice shook. "I accept that my need does not equate to yours, but I ask nonetheless that I be taken in as one of your kith. I have nothing in the way of possessions, but I have my knowledge, which is varied, my limbs, which are strong and willing, and my heart, which is true. Will you take me?"

"I'll accept you," Thenike said immediately.

"And I." Hilt.

"Me, too." Gerrel.

But Wenn was shaking her head. "We don't even know where you come from, Marghe, who your people are, nothing."

"But we do." Leifin again, sounding calm. "At least, we know she has powerful friends who have trata with Cassil in Holme Valley. These women won't stay where they are forever; there's not enough land there at their Port Central for them to grow food. When they move, we need to know what they might do, where they might go. Who they might trade with. If Marghe becomes a part of our family, then it's *us* trata families will come to in Ollfoss; they'll know we have the ear of a powerful new kindred from the south. Think about it."

Wenn looked thoughtful.

Marghe looked at Huellis, who was nursing Moss. Now she had an idea how the poor woman had felt: like a pawn in the greater game of trata. She remembered what Thenike had said—*She seems happy enough with it now*—and almost did not say anything. But she wanted to be accepted for herself, not for something she might not be able to provide. "I can't negotiate trata with you on behalf of the women in Port Central. Asking to join you means I'm no longer part of their . . . family."

She sat down. Wenn's thoughtful expression had not changed.

"Perhaps not," Wenn said, "but we could learn a great deal from you."

"And you're strong and healthy. Or you will be; you heal fast enough," Kenisi added.

Leifin's words had done their work. Marghe looked at Gerrel, at Thenike and Thenike's blood sister Hilt. At least they would be accepting her for the right reasons. Maybe Leifin liked her, as well as seeing her as a way for their family to spread its trata tentacles; and Wenn and the others did not exactly dislike her, they were just wary. She would have a family, of sorts. Perhaps love would come later.

Wenn was nodding now. "Yes, yes, this might work. I don't see any reason why not. Huellis? Kenisi?" They both nodded. "Very well, then."

One of Wenn's knees cracked as she stood up. She held out her arms to Marghe, who scrambled to her feet. "Welcome, Marghe, daughter of . . . ?"

"Acquila. And John," she added, "my father." They did not understand the word; there was no word for father in the Ollfoss dialect. She did not want to use the approximation *sire*; it did not mean the same thing at all.

"Daughter of Acquila and John, sister to . . . ?"

"I have no sisters."

"You do now," Gerrel said, and leaned forward to lay a warm hand on her foot.

"Welcome, Marghe daughter of Acquila and John, to our hearth and home, to your sisters Gerrel and Thenike and Hilt"—they stood up, one by one, and surrounded her and Wenn—"and Leifin and Huellis, Moss and Otter, and Kenisi." She stretched out one gnarled hand and helped her partner stand. "And myself, Wenn."

"Thank you," was all Marghe could think to say.

"We will feed you, and clothe you, share everything that's ours with you, without reservation, without condition. You in your turn must do the same. Will you do that?"

Marghe looked at Gerrel's eager face, knew that behind her Thenike would be smiling. Family. Yes.

They ate together. Gerrel was full of herself, and Hilt told a story of her last voyage, but Marghe was too shy to say much. She huddled next to Thenike, who seemed to understand her need for quiet. She felt tired, and a little ill.

They were talking about her again. Gerrel leaned over and tugged her sleeve. "You're not a guest anymore," she said, "which means you can't really use the guest room. You'll have to share. Do you want to share with me?"

Gerrel was pleasant to be with, for a little while, but Marghe simply did not have the energy to deal with her all the time. She tried to frame an answer.

Kenisi saved her the trouble. "Gerrel, Marghe's not healed yet. She'll need the peace and quiet of the guest room awhile longer."

"But she could decide now whether or not she—"

"Gerrel, the poor woman's almost falling on the floor with fatigue."

"But—"

"Later."

Thenike touched Marghe's shoulders. "I'll help you back to bed."

Now that Marghe felt safe, or at least safer than she had felt before, she started to question Thenike in earnest: How had Ollfoss come to be? How long had it been settled? What about population fluctuations?

"There's a map in Rathell's house you might want to see."

Rathell and her family lived in one of the bigger houses in the west of Ollfoss. Rathell herself showed them into the great room. "There it is. When you've seen all you want to see, come and find me. I'll probably be in the kitchen. We'll share a pot of dap."

The map hanging on the western wall was huge, perhaps four meters wide and three deep, and old. The paper was stiff, and close up Marghe could see where sections had been glued together. The inks, here and there brilliant blue or gold, were mostly faded to the color of old blood, brown on brown. From what Marghe could remember of the precise computer representations of the planet she had called up aboard *Estrade*, the map looked surprisingly accurate. It was crammed with tiny representations of villages, herd grounds, rivers, caves, and dangerous currents.

Significantly, each picture was labeled in tight, careful script. It was English, the variety that had been spoken three or four hundred years ago.

"You can read this?"

Thenike shrugged. "Where the writing is clear, yes. Look, here." She pointed to a picture, a waterfall just inside the southern edge of the forest. "Ollfoss."

"Can everybody read this?"

"Most people here, perhaps, yes. Not everyone wants to learn."

"You did. Why?"

The viajera smiled. "I like to learn everything. How to sing olla, how to dye cloth, how to throw pots and chip stone. How to hum to a herd bird and skin a taar. Everything."

"So you didn't learn to read just so that you could understand this map, so that you had accurate directions?"

"No. All I have to do is ask."

"What if you forget?"

Thenike's eyes were very soft, light brown. They reflected the sepias and dark ivory of the map. "Viajeras don't forget."

Marghe thought back to Thenike telling her *We remember* and wondered if, somehow, the virus conferred extraordinary memory on those who called themselves viajeras. Thenike was watching her. "Are there other writings?" Marghe asked her. Maybe there would be some kind of ship's record, something that would say where these people had come from, and when. How it had been for them.

"Some. Not many. Paper doesn't last as well as message stones or knots. Or as long as memory."

"Are there any records from the beginning? From when your ancestors first came here?"

"What is it that you wish to know?"

"Many things." Thenike was offering to tell her, from her memory, from the oral tradition. "But I want to also see the records. The records themselves are important to me, as important as the account they may contain. Are there any?"

"Rathell keeps many old things in here, handed down from mother to daughter. She showed me, once . . ." Thenike moved over to a wooden chest, old enough to have had its corners rounded by time and polishing. "I don't think she'll mind." Inside were several bundles wrapped in cloth. Thenike opened one: it held a broken pot. She rewrapped it, unfolded another. "Is this what you're looking for?"

Disks. But big ones, as big as her palm, cheerful with refracted color. They were like nothing she had ever seen before, except in old records. Useless. There was no way she could read these.

Unless . . . Perhaps Letitia Dogias could do something with them, if their notoriously fragile information storage had not been long since destroyed. Disks. What a wealth of information there might be here. "Wrap them, put them back. I can't read them. Perhaps, in time, someone who can will come and take a look."

Thenike wrapped them carefully and laid them back in the chest. Marghe tried to set aside her disappointment and wandered back over to the map. South of Ollfoss there was a picture of standing stones. Anxiety hit her like a fist in her stomach. She breathed in and out. She was with family now. She looked at the map again. There were two or three communities near where she imagined Port Central to be. She pointed. "I didn't know these were here."

"They're not. Burnstone moved them on a long, long time ago. They're here now, at Three Trees and Cruath." She pointed with a long brown finger. Her nail was glossy pink, and a longish scar ran from the thumb joint over the back of her hand.

Thenike seemed to be enjoying her interest, so Marghe examined the map more closely. She thought she could still detect a faint hint of blue in the picture of the waterfall at Ollfoss. Waterfall, foss. Ollfoss. "I haven't seen the foss," she said.

"It's no longer here. Or, rather, we are no longer there. The soil was poor. When you're well, I'll show you the old valley and foss."

And the way Thenike said it, something in the way she tilted her head and accented *when* to leave no possibility of *if*, Marghe knew that the viajera meant not only *after you have recovered from walking out of Tehuantepec* but *after you have been sick with the virus, and have lived.* Thenike had said more than once that she, Marghe, must save all her energy, hoard it until the time came to face the virus.

Thenike, she had discovered, was as much of a healer as Kenisi. "All viajeras are healers," she had told Marghe, "to some extent or other." She had not explained further.

 MARGHE HOBBLED, then limped, along the paths that ran between the gardens of Ollfoss where women from different families worked, sweeping the dirt free of snow, breaking in the ground with hand hoes—preparing the huge communal plots for the snarly nitta and goura shoots, the squat soca bushes that were harvested and traded every summer in North Haven. She waved at those she recognized. Sometimes she helped Gerrel and Kenisi carry their family's share of bread and soup to the kitchens in Ette's house where the women would gather for lunch.

The weather improved, as did Marghe. Gerrel, seeing the improvement in both, took it upon herself to show Marghe the small family garden and teach her what needed to be done.

THE SKY was blue and clear, and an end-of-winter wind gusted from the treeline, filling her hair with the smell of snow and green. Marghe moved her tatty mat of what had once been taar skin a few feet along the furrow and knelt, glad to get the weight off her feet. Her sharp stone hand hoe cut easily into the first few inches, but she had to work to dig deeper. The hoe slipped; she added her three-fingered left hand to her right, bunched her muscles, and pushed.

The pressure made the scar tissue on her left hand ache. She shook her hand. Such little things, fingers; she wondered if she would ever stop missing them, mourning them. At least she had her feet. And her life. She was still here to enjoy the cold, wet roughness of fresh-turned dirt and the sharp wind on her face. She would not dwell on her scars. She would not.

She dug into the loosened dirt with her right hand, plucked out small stones and tossed them aside, pulled up weeds. She was alive. Alive. She paused and felt carefully around the bulbs that were just beginning to root, found another stone. She yanked up a clump of creeping lichen and shook it vigorously, freeing the dirt from the roots. The lichen had to be gotten rid of, but the soil was rich, and had to be kept.

"Are you trying to kill it?" Thenike grinned down at her. The viajera was holding a steaming mug. "This is for you."

Marghe gave the handful of greenery one more shake, then

threw it onto the pile that would be kept for compost. She took the offered mug, sniffed. More of the foul brew Thenike cooked up for her every day; it would remove the poisons in her body put there by the vaccine, she said. The viajera had broken one of the softgels open into her hand and touched the oily pink mess delicately with her tongue. Marghe wondered how she had been able to tell about the cumulative toxic effect of the adjuvants just from that test, but had not doubted that she could, and was glad to find someone who thought she could help her body get rid of them. She set the brew aside in the snow to cool and went back to her hoeing.

"What's this?" Thenike asked, gesturing at the newly broken ground.

"Right now, a mess," Marghe said, "but if I get rid of all these weeds, by midsummer it should be a patch of cetrar."

Thenike knelt beside her and watched. Marghe dug up a bulb by mistake.

Thenike picked it up, weighing it in her hand. "Such small roots."

They did look too flimsy—lacy, almost—to do the job. "The purple bits, growing out of the top, here"—Marghe pointed with a dirt-rimed fingernail—"will be the stalk, and these tiny buds will be the sprouts."

Thenike looked at it carefully. The buds were the size of aphid eggs, almost invisible. "It's hard to believe that a lumpy vegetable comes from such a delicate-looking thing." She pushed it back into the dirt.

Marghe dug it back up again. "How long is it since you planted something?"

"A long time."

"Too long. Cetrar needs loose dirt. Like this." She dug a hole, dropped the bulb in, pushed dirt back on top with her hand, gave it a quick pat.

"You've learned a lot."

Marghe sat up and lifted her face to the weak sun. "I have, haven't I?" After a moment she started digging again, but with her hands. She enjoyed the feel of soil between her fingers. Thenike watched. Marghe looked up. "If you want to help me, you could start on those weeds."

They worked together quietly for a while.

ALL THROUGH the Moon of Cracking Frost, Thenike gardened with her, bathed with her, sat next to her when the family ate, and listened. Marghe sometimes rambled, reliving happy memories, but often she had questions for Thenike.

They were in the kitchen, washing a basket of freshly dug tubers for Kenisi in the huge stone sink, when Marghe asked Thenike when she had first known she was going to be a viajera.

Thenike paused, tuber in one hand, brush in the other. "As soon as I could crawl, I wanted to follow strange paths and talk to different people. Drove my family mad; I was always wandering off. By the time I was seven or eight, my choose-mother had to take me along with her and Hilt, who was old enough to crew by then, whenever they took out the trading ship from North Haven because none of my sisters or mothers would watch me. Too much trouble." She resumed scrubbing. "Whenever we came into a new place, I waylaid strangers and dragged their stories and songs and jokes from them before they even had a chance to find out my name. Then when we were sailing back to North Haven I drove everyone to distraction by repeating the songs and the stories until my mother threatened to unship the dinghy and tow me home behind them. She did that once, when I was nine." Thenike smiled. "It didn't make much difference."

"So who taught you how to be a viajera?"

"Everyone I met. My blood mother taught me to drum. I learned the pipes from a sailor, Jolesset, and a woman called Zabett showed me how to judge when to charge a lot, and when to charge a little. Supply and demand, she called it."

"How old were you?"

"I picked everything up in bits and pieces. When I was fourteen, two years after my deepsearch, I left home on my own for the first time. I was only gone ten days. After that, I went more often, and stayed away longer, until when I was seventeen, my mother moved back from North Haven to Pebble Fleet. I'd been born in North Haven, didn't think of Pebble Fleet as my home. So after that, I wandered."

"And you just go anywhere, whenever you want."

"No, not really. I've been a lot of places, but for now I seem to have settled on an area I travel regularly: North Haven, Sliprock, Three Trees, Cruath. Ollfoss, of course, though I don't get to stay here as often as I'd like. And sometimes I get as far south as Holme Valley, to see T'orre Na and the herders on the grasslands around there. I traveled with T'orre Na for a while, a few years ago."

"I've heard of T'orre Na." Marghe counted the tubers. "I think we've got enough here for today. Put the rest in the cellar." They started cutting the clean tubers into thick slices. "So tell me how you came to be part of Wenn's family."

"Ollfoss was the first place I came to on my own. Wenn was younger then. When I walked out of the forest, she was struggling with an old tree stump on her land. I helped her drag it out. She invited me to share supper with the family. I did. Told them stories and what news there was. I came back many times, often just for the good food. They began to feel like family. Sometimes I brought Hilt. And then when our mother left for Pebble Fleet, it just seemed natural to choose this place as home." She sighed, and pushed a strand of hair out of her eyes with her forearm. "I should spend more time here. But Wenn understands. I get . . . restless."

"Tell me about the others. Tell me about Leifin."

"You don't like her, do you?"

"It's more that I don't quite trust her. Maybe I wouldn't be here if it wasn't for her, but there's something about her that's just too calculated for me. And I don't understand her. I mean, how could someone who can see a beautiful shape in a piece of wood and spend hours lovingly carving it, polishing it, how can that same person then go off and slaughter animals just for their furs? Why can't she see the beauty in the living animal?"

"I think it's that she sees the world differently. For Leifin, a thing is beautiful if she can reach out and put her hand on it any time."

"If she owns it."

"Yes."

By manipulating the family into accepting Marghe, Leifin expected to gain materially from trata: more wealth buys more things. Marghe did not want to think about Leifin anymore.

"So tell me about Gerrel. She used to have a soestre."

"She had two, twins, who died along with their mother, Gerrel's blood mother's lover, when they came too early. We took Gerrel because Kristen couldn't bear to look at her daughter."

SOMETIMES IT would be Thenike who asked the questions, and they would talk until the moons were up. More than once, they wrapped up in furs and cloaks and walked through the garden in the moonlight, still talking. Sometimes they just walked in silence, and Marghe thought she could hear Thenike's heart.

THE FIRST time she saw Thenike with the drums was one night in the family great room, after eating. It had been a good meal, and most of the family were still picking their teeth when Leifin announced she was going on a hunt in a few days.

Marghe went very still. "What will you hunt?"

"Oh, queen daggerhorn, wild taars. Whatever's there."

"Not goth?"

Leifin laughed. "Goth? They only walk through old stories. Not in Moanwood." She turned to the rest of the family. "Have any of you ever seen a goth?"

"I have," Marghe said steadily. "And you were hunting it."

"And when was that?"

"When you found me. At the edge of the forest."

Leifin smiled. "Marghe, you were more than half delirious. You were crawling, crawling mind, in circles. Your eyes were sunken, more than half gummed together with the same blood and mucus that slimed your furs." She laughed, looked at the rest of the family, drawing them in. Gerrel, Marghe was pleased to note, scowled. Thenike was expressionless. The others smiled. "You drew a knife on me, do you remember, Marghe? Thought I was an Echraidhe. Now, if you could think that one Ollfoss woman on foot was a mounted savage, you could have mistaken a tree for a goth, or a chia bird for a . . . dragon."

"It was a goth."

"If you say so. Though, even supposing for just a moment that you're right, what's wrong with that?"

Leifin must know as well as she did what was wrong with hunting goth, Marghe thought, but Gerrel spoke before she could frame an answer.

"You hunt too much!" she burst out. "And we don't need any more meat. We've plenty of furs. I think you just—"

"There're never enough furs for trade up in North Haven," Leifin contradicted gently.

"But . . ." Gerrel trailed off in frustration. Marghe sympathized. Leifin made it all sound so reasonable.

Thenike stretched and looked up and down the table. "I think tonight would be a good time for a song."

"Sing the one about how the rivers first decided to run to the sea," Gerrel said instantly.

"I've a mind to sing something special," Thenike said, and looked at Marghe with an indecipherable expression. "I'll need my drums." Her skirts swirled as she stood, and Marghe caught the warm, musky smell of her skin mixed with the sharper, sweeter scent of the herb sachets Kenisi made for the family to lay in with their clothes. The door closed quietly behind her.

The family waited, listening to the crackle of the fire, sipping their wine.

Thenike returned, sending flames leaping in the door's draft. She squatted near the fire and set her drums to warm, turning them occasionally. The rasp of wood on stone as she moved them was the only sound in the room.

When the drums were sufficiently warmed and the skins

stretched tight, Thenike drew her knees up and settled the drums between her skirts. She looked at Marghe with that same indecipherable expression.

"Once upon a time, if there ever was such a time, the world was different. It was round, as it now is round, and the sun rose in the east and set in the west, as now it does, but it was younger, much younger. Where now there is plain, there was forest; where now there is a valley, there once stood a sea. Mountains reared their shoulders high, and were worn away. Rivers formed, grew, and cut through rock as they ran to the ocean. The world turned.

"In these times, upon that raised plain we now know as Tehuantepec there stood a forest. This was the mother of all forests, and her trees stretched east and west from Pebble Fleet to the Oboshi Desert, and south and north from the Trern Swamplands to the northern coast, though there was no woman here to speak those names. This mother of a forest stretched even beyond the north coast, for in those days there was no sea lying between here and what we now call the icy wastes, and those far northern lands were fair and fruitful. On and on the forest stretched, and down and down upon it shone the sun, more strongly than it does today."

While she spoke, Thenike's hands moved gently over the drums, stroking and tapping, cupping the sounds, bringing them to life beneath her long brown fingers. Then she stopped talking, and set the scene to her tale with drums alone. The drums spoke of warm rain and a forest floor steaming with mist, of strange flying creatures whose shrieks rang through the trees and whose feathers flashed purple and gold.

Something about Thenike's utter concentration warned Marghe that she was about to witness something she had never seen before, something that was at the heart of being viajera. Tonight she would hear more than a pretty tale set to a nice tune.

The viajera's eyes glittered with reflected torchlight. Her black hair, wound in a careless knot on top of her head, did nothing to disguise the tautness of her neck. Her head moved slowly from side to side to the beat of her drums, and shadows caught and dissolved in the hollows of her cheeks and temple and skull. Her whole body swayed lightly. The rhythm built.

For one fleeting moment, Marghe wanted to run. Thenike was in some kind of trance. The beat of her drum was pulling Marghe in; she could feel her heart beating with the thud of the viajera's palms on the drumskin, and her breath sucked in and out to the rhythm of Thenike's swaying body. Marghe knew, without knowing how she knew, that what the viajera was about to do was dangerous—for Marghe, and for herself. But then Thenike sang, and Marghe was caught.

She did not hear the words. She was there, living it. Though she knew she was sitting by a fire in Ollfoss, her mind was taken back to a place, a glade, where tall animals that were not animals swung long-handled axes at the trees. She was one of them, uncomfortably warm in her thick ivory-colored fur. She watched, fascinated, as her three-fingered and two-thumbed hand swung the ax and the clearing grew.

The scene shifted: north, where it was pleasantly cool. The one before her had a leather strap over his shoulder; it wound about his waist, then up again over her shoulder and round her waist, and on to the one behind her, and another behind him. They were straining to pull a huge stone. Within hooting distance, on her left, another group of six were struggling with their stone. They had been working for months. The gods would be pleased.

Time moved on. Back to the clearing, at the southern tip of their great nomadic ellipse. The stones were set, twenty-seven of them in a circle. They hummed. Laid in the center of the circle were three six-sided dressed flagstones. A towering green sculpture of woven vegetable stuff—grasses, moss, leaves, vine—stood on the flags. She sang with the others, a great booming hymn to their gods of sky and earth, and set fire to the sculpture. It burned with an acrid stink. With the others, she took her turn walking through the smoke. Colors writhed at the edge of her vision and sounds swam slowly, like live things. A drug. They danced, and boomed, and mated. She wrote the name of her mate in the ashes with her finger.

Time sped up and Marghe leapt centuries, watched while the snows came earlier and earlier and the northern trees began to die and still she and her descendants traveled south and gathered at the stones to mate and worship. Eons passed like heartbeats: a sea surged between the south forest and the ailing north. Years passed; even in summer icebergs floated in the sea, and the north was white and icy. She and her kind were reduced to grubbing under trees for frozen berries and weeping great yellow tears as their younglings died. None of their number had braved the icy water and the floating bergs for generations.

And then one winter the sea froze.

They sang their booming hymns of praise, wrapped their young as warmly as they could, and set out south. South, to the mating place of their ancestors, to build a fire to their gods, to appease their anger and bring back the sun.

The trek was hard. Their feet bled on the ice; there was not enough food. When the younglings curled up and stopped whimpering, and died one by one, each was laid on the ice, with a song for a grave. There were not many left when they reached the snow-shrouded forests on the southern shore of the sea.

None of the survivors had ever been near the stones, but memories buried in their bones showed them the way. They went forward through the trees with sure strides. But they had hardly lost sight of the shore when it seemed the sky was split by light and thunder and a bolt from god thrashed down and through the trees in a trail of noise and fire. They were knocked over by the blast, and the ground trembled under their feet as the black bolt ground and smashed through the trees. There was a great burning, and alien smells.

They fled back north, back across the frozen sea, back past the frozen bodies of their young, back to the cold and ice and stunted trees, for they had received a message, and the message was plain: the gods did not wish for them to journey south. They were to obey the gods' will and return north, return to scratching at the ice for moss and poor shriveled berries, return to their lonely fastness where their numbers would grow fewer and fewer . . .

"Oh, my people," Marghe whispered to the dying fire, then looked up, confused. People? Thenike sat, weary and still, drums on the floor. The glitter was gone from her eyes; they were dark and withdrawn. Leifin's cheeks were bloodless, and she breathed heavily. Gerrel looked bewildered and a little afraid. Wenn and Kenisi were holding hands, drawing comfort from each other. Huellis and Hilt were both looking at Leifin, the former thoughtful, the latter grim. Marghe wondered if she looked the same. She felt Thenike's hooded gaze resting on her, and turned.

"Thenike . . ." She did not have the words. Thenike had done something she did not understand and could barely believe. More than that, she had told a story which, if true—and it fitted the facts that Marghe herself had ascertained—held staggering implications. People . . .

THE NEXT day, Marghe worked in the gardens as usual. Thenike did not come. Marghe went to find her.

The viajera was in her room, sitting cross-legged on the bed. Light streamed in, staining the white walls lemon, picking fire from a picture painted directly onto the northern wall. Thenike looked like a tired, dark smudge in the middle of so much light; the dark circles under her eyes stood out clearly, and her skin looked pale, almost translucent. Marghe could see a faint blue tracery of veins under her skin. The room was cool.

"I was wondering where you were," Marghe said, standing by the half-pulled-back door hanging. Thenike looked insubstantial; Marghe wanted to put her arms around her, make sure she was all there and all right. She cast around for some plausible excuse for intruding and could not find one. "I was worried," she said simply.

Thenike smiled, a tired smile, but warm. "Come. Sit up here with me. I've been thinking about you. Tell me what you thought of my story yesterday."

"It seemed true. Real." Thenike waited. Marghe struggled to give her the truth. "You, the story . . . possessed me."

Thenike nodded slowly. "Many viajeras have sung for your people. Your people smile and say 'Very nice,' but they don't hear, they don't see. We used to think you were all blind. Until you."

Thenike seemed to go away somewhere inside herself for a moment. Marghe set aside her curiosity and waited. "You followed me in deepsearch."

Deepsearch. The Jeep ritual of naming, of conception, of bonding. Deepsearch. She was not sure if she wanted to believe Thenike. "I thought the virus was part of it."

"Perhaps."

Did that mean the virus was already inside her? No, it couldn't be. She tried to remember what Lu Wai had told her about incubation periods; she knew that contracting a virus and displaying symptoms were not simultaneous. But no, it could not be the virus. The FN-17 would still be in her blood, wouldn't it? She remembered waking in Ollfoss and finding that one softgel was missing. Had she taken it or lost it?

Thenike smoothed the coverlet with her palms. "Some viajeras can sing from within trance, from deep inside their own memories. They can bring others into their trance, make them see what they see, feel what they feel. Be what they've been."

"But you've never been a . . ."

"Goth? Perhaps not. But part of what you call the virus may have part of what we call the goth embedded in its essence."

Marghe realized that Thenike was telling her that the virus contained goth DNA and some of their memories. And then the virus became part of human DNA. She shook her head. That was not possible. She was not even sure she believed that goth existed.

But the stones existed; she had been there. And they were impossibly old.

The trance, then, she thought. What about the trance? That was possible; she had not imagined it. Of course sharing a trance was possible. Mass hypnosis was well documented. And what else was a drum but hypnotic? And singing, too. Rhythm, sound, the heat of the fire. Her body was well trained to follow patterns and rhythms; that was essentially the way one learned to control one's own biofeedback.

"It's a matter of training, that's all." She wished she had not said that so loudly.

"Like being a viajera." Thenike eyed her speculatively. "Can you drum?"

"No."

"I'll teach you."

THE SUN had been hidden behind clouds for two days. The fire in Thenike's room roared; the door hanging was closed. Marghe put the drums aside on the bed, pulled off her felt overtunic, wiped the sweat from her face, and settled the drums back between her knees. She tapped the right drum, the treble, with the tip of her right middle finger, then the left drum with what had been the middle finger on her left hand. She was more clumsy with the left.

Thenike, who had been standing by the fire, listening, came over. She took Marghe's left hand in her own. "Do these scars still hurt?"

"No."

"Then stop protecting them. Hit the drum, sharp and swift." She demonstrated, striking out like a snake: hand from wrist, finger from hand. The drum sang once, perfectly. "Again."

So Marghe did it again, and again, until both sides of the drum sang with the same depth and the same volume, no matter which hand she struck with. She hit them faster and faster, pleased with herself.

"Now try this." Thenike played an effortless paradiddle with finger, then palm, both drums. Marghe looked dismayed. "Try it."

She tried. Over and over. "It's no good." She wiped at her sweating face with her forearm.

"Move over, and forward." Marghe gripped the drums between her knees and shuffled forward awkwardly. Thenike climbed onto the bed and sat behind her, arms snaking around to the drums, stomach pressed up against Marghe's back. Marghe felt her nostrils flare slightly and the muscles in her stomach tighten. "Lay your hands on mine. Lightly. Now. Feel what I do." Thenike tapped out the paradiddle very slowly, beat by beat, then again, and again, getting slightly faster. Marghe tried to concentrate on the feel of muscle and tendon under her hands, to gauge at what angle the heel of the hand came down, at what point the hand swung and the finger took the lead, but all she could feel was the slide of warm skin under her own, the ruffle of Thenike's breath at her neck. She tried harder.

"Good. Now, on your own." Thenike laid her arms down on her skirts but stayed behind Marghe. Marghe resisted the urge to lean back into the viajera's warmth and applied herself to her drum lesson.

MARGHE TOOK off her muddy boots and walked barefoot over the warm wooden planking of the bathhouse floor. She loved the Ollfoss bathhouse with its smell of lime and minerals, its high, airy space, and the huge stone tubs that descended in height and water temperature from near the ceiling to close to the floor and were worn smooth by generations of use.

Two women she vaguely recognized, Bejuoen and Terle of Ette's family, were wringing out a coverlet. Only one more garment floated lumpily in the rinse pool; they would be gone soon. She nodded at them, and pumped vigorously at the wooden lever that forced hot water up from the spring and through stone pipes. When the water was flowing, she slid the wooden stream dam over to the left and watched while water began to flow into a shallow basin set at ankle height. She plugged the hole in its bottom with a stopper and began stripping off her clothes, filthy with the rich garden mud. When the basin was half-full, she pumped up some cold water, setting the flow dam to direct it into the basin. She dropped her clothes into the water, piece by piece, and climbed in after them.

She enjoyed trampling the heavy clothes in lukewarm water, feeling mud slide out from between her toes. When the water began to turn reddish brown, she leaned down and pulled the stopper free. She filled the basin again, and resumed her trampling.

She nodded good-bye to Bejuoen and Terle.

When the water stayed clear, and she could feel the fibers beneath her feet again instead of slippery mud, she climbed out of the basin, took out the stopper, and reset the wooden dams near the pumps. The larger basins began to fill while she wrung out her clothes and transferred them to the laundry basin proper, to soak in the cold, biting mineral water that seeped up from the ground beneath Ollfoss. She would not need to use soap.

The big tub was full. Marghe diverted the hot water to a lower tub and climbed up the short ladder toward the steam. She lowered herself in inch by inch, sighing as the heat slid over her skin and enveloped her aching muscles.

"You sound like you need that."

Marghe peered over the edge: Thenike, holding a bowl of the foul medicinal tea.

"Do you want company? I could just leave this down here."

"No, come on up."

After a moment Thenike came up the ladder naked, holding the bowl. She had pinned her braid up on top of her head, and the ladder rungs threw shadows over the tight stomach and lean slabs of muscle over her ribs. Hard muscle, soft skin, taut sinew. Marghe wondered how that would feel. Thenike handed her the bowl. Marghe sighed and drank it down in one long swallow. It was bitter, but it warmed her from the inside as the bath did from the outside.

Thenike slid into the water opposite Marghe, near the wooden tray that held soap cakes and brushes. "Ah, that feels good." She splashed hot water over her shoulders. Marghe watched the play of muscle and shadow. "I see that someone has been digging over the south gardens. Your work?"

Marghe nodded. "And I ache all over to prove it."

The viajera picked up the hand brush, the one with soft bristles. "If you'll come over here, I'll rub your back. Ease some of those muscles."

Marghe sat in front of Thenike, as if they were playing the drums. Only this time, Thenike's legs were naked alongside hers; this time, she felt Thenike's breasts touching the skin just below her shoulder blades. This time, there was no mistaking the slow, heavy wave of desire that rose and sank through her guts. She could not help arching a little as Thenike stroked the brush over the small of her back. One of Thenike's hands lay loosely on Marghe's hips, and she could feel every palm line, every whorl, at the tips of those strong, lean fingers. Desire wrapped its arms around her and held her still, helpless, able only to breathe.

"There. You can do mine now." Thenike put both palms on Marghe's lower back and pushed her away, through the water. Marghe's breath caught.

She made a slow turn, felt the warm water rise up over her belly and breasts. She took the brush. Thenike was studying her.

"Marghe. The vaccine you took, the poisons, the adjuvants, they would have kept away, pushed down, your need for sex." She nodded at the empty wooden bowl. "As this gets rid of the poisons, so your need for sex returns." Marghe watched her. The viajera's lips were very red, very soft. "But I don't think you should make sex with anyone. Not yet. Your body and your mind need to be clear, uncluttered, for what lies ahead. Marghe? Do you understand?"

Marghe felt embarrassed, stupid. She knew she was flushing. This was Thenike's way of saying she was not interested. She nodded. "I understand."

Thenike sighed. "I wonder."

Chapter Twelve

MARGHE PUSHED the stick into the dirt, dropped in a seed from her left hand, and smoothed the dirt over the hole. She sneezed. She jabbed another hole, dropped in a seed. Her hands were cold; the wind had been from the north for the last two days and was bitter, dragging with it heavy gray cloud that shrouded the sun. At least it was not raining.

She made another hole, dropped a seed. It missed. She put down the stick, intending to poke the seed into the hole with her finger. Her hands were stiff and aching; she must be colder than she thought. She sneezed again, which set her head thumping.

Fear stabbed under her ribs. She tried to breathe steadily, and coughed. No, she thought, it cannot possibly be. Not yet. It's only the last third of the Moon of Aches. It should be days yet.

Not if she had not taken that missing softgel.

The pain in her head was getting worse. She levered herself to her feet. Her knees hurt. What was it Lu Wai had said? *My joints ached, knees and hips mostly . . . and then the headache started. It's only about a mile from the station to my mod, but I had difficulty walking those last few yards, it hits that fast* . . . Thenike knew what to do; so did Kenisi. She looked around. No one. Well, it was only a few hundred yards to the house. She started to walk.

After about fifteen steps, she knew she would not make it. The path wavered in front of her, and she was shivering so hard that her head felt like it was going to fall off. After thirty steps, she was staggering. So fast, so fast. Impossibly fast. Keep going, she had to keep going. Warmth, liquids, Lu Wai had said. Warmth. She could not afford to fall down here, in the mud. Could not.

It was hard to breathe now. Ten more steps, she told her legs. Find Thenike.

"Marghe!"

Gerrel's face loomed by her left shoulder. Marghe stood, swaying. Confused. How did she get there? "Sick," she said, then tottered forward another step.

Gerrel caught her as she staggered. Marghe sagged in the girl's arms. "Marghe." Rest. She wanted to rest. "Marghe." Gerrel shook her. "I can't hold you by myself. You're too heavy. You've got to help me."

Marghe felt a dim tugging under her arms. She tried to lift her head. "Warm," she said, then burst into a hacking cough. Gerrel managed to drag her a few yards. It hurt to breathe. "Got to. Keep warm."

"As soon as we get you inside."

Marghe tried to set aside the fire that was in her knees and her hips, that squeezed tight around her head threatening to burst through her eyes. Walk. One leg in front of another.

They moved unsteadily forward. Her lungs burned; she could not breathe.

"Don't struggle. Marghe, don't struggle. I've got you. You'll be warm soon. Just walk. Walk. Left leg first. Come on. Marghe! Left leg. Good. Now the right."

It was like trying to walk through fire. Fire that burned her legs and leapt down her throat to sear her lungs all the way to her stomach; fire, too, that threatened to boil her eyes in her head. But she tried.

"Not far now. Keep your legs moving. Another few steps

and you'll be warm and safe. And then I'll bring Thenike. And Kenisi. You'll be well in no time. No time at all. But we have to get there first." Gerrel's voice seemed to come from a long way off. "Please, Marghe. Please. Just a few more steps."

MARGHE NEVER remembered falling on the bed, or Gerrel crying and trying to wrap her in furs. She did not know it when Kenisi came running. It seemed to her only that some cruel beast with talons and beak steeped in fire and acid ripped at her body, over and over. She screamed, but there was no escape.

Later, days or hours, the beast retreated for a while. Marghe was aware of lying on her back. Her throat was stripped raw and her tongue felt swollen and dry. Thenike was sitting by the bed holding her hand, a hand that seemed miles away, unconnected with the rest of her body. It was difficult to breathe; her chest felt weighed down under a hot stone.

Thenike stroked her hand.

"Thenike . . ." It was a croak.

"Hush. Rest. I'm here."

"I hurt . . . don't leave me . . ." Marghe did not know if Thenike could understand the thick, mucous sounds that struggled out of her mouth. "Don't go. I need you." The beast scored her throat with its claws. She coughed and coughed and suddenly could not breathe through the clump of phlegm in her throat. Thenike let go of her hand. "Don't leave me!" Marghe whispered. "I love you." But Thenike was moving away to bring back a cup for her to spit in, and Marghe could not say any more, for the beast with hot claws had returned with a vengeance.

LATER, MUCH later, Marghe watched the ceiling. She could not move her head, or even her eyes. Now the beast had become a thing of cold, with thin fingers sliding under her skin and beneath her fingernails. She wanted to go away, to a place where she would never hurt again. Go away. Anywhere. She closed her eyes. It would not be hard.

"Marghe!" Thenike's voice. Marghe did not bother to open her eyes. She was already drifting away, to somewhere warm and soft, where she would never hurt again.

"Marghe, I won't let you go. I'm here. I have your hand. Do you hear me? I won't let you go."

Thenike's skirts rustled, then her weight settled next to Marghe on the bed.

"Listen to me. I know you can hear. Feel my hand. I can feel yours. It's warm, alive. Blood is beating along your arm, through your wrist. Just as it does in mine. You're breathing. You're tired, yes, almost worn out. But all you have to do is keep breathing, keep that blood pumping from your heart. You've done it for two days. Just one more, and you'll be strong again. Do that for me, Marghe. For me. And for Gerrel."

But Marghe did not want to return to her body. It was no longer entirely hers. The virus lived in it now, in every pore, every cell, every blood vessel and organ. It slid, cold and in control, through her brain. If she recovered, she would never be sure what dreams and memories were her own, and which were alien. She belonged to Jeep. She wanted to shout, *Don't you see? It'll never let go. I'll never be clean again . . . ?*

"In me," she gasped. "Unclean."

Thenike must have understood. "Unclean? No. Your body is changing, just as it does every time you get sick and another little piece of something else comes to live inside you. If a child gets red fever, then when she is grown and her children get the spots, she will not become ill, because the disease is part of her already, and accepts her. Is this unclean? No. It's life. All life connects. Sometimes, one kind of life is stronger than another. As happened with your mother."

Marghe tried to remember her mother. Could not.

"But, Marghe, you're strong, and what you call virus is weak. Accept it. Let it into the deepest parts of you. It's the fighting that takes your strength. Let it be. Just breathe, listen to your blood sing through your veins. Here. Feel." Thenike lifted Marghe's hand and laid it against her breast. "Feel my heart beat." She put her wrist along the underside of Marghe's other hand. "Feel my blood. Feel yours. Breathe with me. In. Out. That's it. In. Out. In. Out . . ."

Marghe's body responded automatically, taking up the rhythm. She was too tired to fight it. She kept breathing. Too tired. After a while, she slept.

SHE WOKE gradually, without opening her eyes. She ached all over, and her throat was still raw and her chest thick with phlegm, but it seemed that the beast with its hot claws and cold fingers was gone, and her mind was clear. Someone was stroking her head, and humming. She smiled.

"Marghe?"

She opened her eyes. Gerrel was bending over her, looking worried.

"Good morning." It was a creaky whisper, but Marghe was pleased with it.

Gerrel's face split into a wide grin. "It's afternoon. You've slept all yesterday, all night, and most of today."

"Could sleep more."

"I'll go get Thenike. She's been here most of the time. But then I think she got fed up with you always being asleep and went to find something to eat." Gerrel cocked her head. "You're probably hungry. Shall I bring something?"

At the thought of food, Marghe felt ill. "Nothing for me." She was terribly tired.

Gerrel hesitated by the door. "If you're sure? Well, then. I'll be quick."

Marghe listened to her light footsteps turn to a run once she was outside. She smiled again.

Alive. She was alive. She turned her head slowly, looked at the wall. It seemed different. And the bed felt . . . not the same. She looked more carefully. This was not her room. Not the guest room.

Something chittered and sang outside. From the forest. A bird? She wanted to be out there, walking through the trees, smelling the life, hearing animals scuttle and sing and wind riffle through boughs overhead. She wanted so many things, and was surprised at how hard she wanted them. She felt different. Again.

Thenike opened the door, carrying a tray. Gerrel squeezed in behind her.

"I want to see the sky," was the first thing Marghe said. Her voice was stronger already.

"No. First you eat. Then you sleep again. Then you eat again. Then, maybe, you go outside and see the sky."

"Not hungry." She felt tired again.

"I tried to tell her," Gerrel said, leaning forward over Marghe, "but she said—"

"I said," Thenike interrupted, "that you needed food. The fever has burnt the flesh from your bones." She put the tray down on the swept hearth. "But first, I want to have a look at you. No," she said as Marghe struggled to lift herself upright, "you relax. Gerrel and I will lift you."

They lifted her up, propping her with pillows, while Thenike listened to her chest. "Breathe. Deep." Marghe had to lean forward, her weight resting on Gerrel, for Thenike to listen to her lungs from the back. From this angle, she could see a half-finished tapestry on the floor, some folded clothes that she recognized on the shelf: this was Gerrel's room. "Breathe." Thenike tapped and listened. Marghe coughed. "Good. Good." They laid her back against the pillows and pulled the covers back up to her chin. "All that rubbish in your lungs should be gone in a day or two. If you do as I suggest." She gestured to Gerrel, who brought the tray. "So first, eat."

Marghe only managed about half the soup, then, to her chagrin, felt her eyes begin to roll. Thenike made her drink a bowl of lukewarm water before she lay down again. She was asleep before Gerrel could lift the soup dish back onto the tray.

She woke again just before evening. This time she stayed awake long enough to eat a large bowl of stew, and to ask Thenike why she was in Gerrel's room: because Gerrel had panicked and brought her to the safest place she could think of, her own room, explained Thenike. Marghe fell asleep with a smile on her face. Gerrel was her sister.

HER RECOVERY was rapid. Almost too rapid, Marghe thought. It seemed as though there was a fountain, a hot spring of energy inside her fizzing and bubbling and demanding to be let out.

"I feel different," she said to Thenike.

"You are different."

"No, I feel . . ." she hunted for a way to describe the incredible well-being she felt, "like I could live for a year on sunshine and fresh air, like I might never get sick again."

Thenike laughed, and Marghe listened to that laugh: rich, smoky, warm, it rolled like the breaking waves on a flat beach, as if it could go on forever, changeless. "Oh, you will," the viajera said, and Marghe heard music in her many-layered voice.

"You even sound different. And I can smell . . ." Everything. She could smell everything, and the scent was excitement: her own, Thenike's. She watched Thenike's dark brow tighten a little in the center, noticed for the first time how the lines were slightly asymmetrical, canting down toward her right eyebrow, like old timbers sagging at one end. Except it was not just sight and sound and smell, it was something else—a different kind of sensitivity that made Thenike's voice almost visible, that sharpened Marghe's sight so that what she saw seemed to have texture, more meaning than mere color or shape.

"It may be that the poisons fed to you as part of the vaccine are out of your system now, that the virus has cleaned you."

Symbiosis, Marghe thought. Like allowing spiders to spin their webs in a house so that the flies and mosquitos were kept to a minimum. Like the *E. coli* that flourished in her gut and helped her digest proteins and process fibers, the result of some bacterial in-fection in a million-years-distant ancestor.

Outside, something sang, a long call that started out yellow,

dipped in the middle to blue, then rose to scintillating gold and orange, as though the caller had decided that it was not, after all, sad.
Marghe smiled. "What was that?"

"The chia bird. She's been singing for two days now. A little
early: today is only the first day of the Bird Moon."

"What does she look like?"

"Come see for yourself."

The chia, perched on top of the house, was like a palm-sized
replica of the pictures of herd birds Marghe had studied at Port
Central: bony crest, grayish, slippery-looking skin blushing to pink
where the capillaries webbed the near surface, stringy pectorals
that powered two true wings like those of a bat, and a fixed gliding wing like delicate parchment. When it turned to examine its
observers, Marghe saw that its eyes were startling and green, like
a cat's.

THE DAYS got warmer, and Marghe moved back into the
guest room. There was more sun, and she heard more chia
birds calling and more wirrels chittering from the forest. There were
insect noises and the soughing of wind in trees, though it was not
the same as hearing wind in Earth trees; the leaves were stiffer, the
sound higher pitched. Sometimes it hissed.

Marghe turned the soil in the garden and listened to the wind.
So many sounds twined into that hissing: insect carapaces scraping
the undersides of dead leaves, living leaves shivering in the wind,
an empty nutshell rolling up against a tree trunk with a soft *tck*. It
would be a long time before she grew tired of her newly virus-
sharp senses.

As she worked, she thought about what Thenike had taught
her, about deepsearching, about patterning, about pregnancy. They
were all part of the same process. She rooted out a weed and tossed
it onto the pile she would use for compost. Deepsearch. Something that all did, once they thought they were ready. Often some
time around puberty, though earlier or later was not too unusual.
The searcher looked within, to find out . . . what?

"Whatever she looks for," Thenike had said unhelpfully. "Almost always a name. Sometimes what she would like to do with her life."

It intrigued Marghe. What did they see, and how did they see it? Like a movie, an interactive net holo, an abstract painting? Maybe it was audio, or tactile. Olfactory.

"All," Thenike said, and added, just when Marghe was beginning to feel satisfied with that answer, "or none, or a mix."

The more Marghe had pressed, the less clear the viajera's answers had seemed. "You're not being clear," she had said, frustrated. "How do you mean, exactly, 'listen to what's inside you'?"

"Try it for yourself," Thenike had said. "Then you explain it to me."

That had been yesterday. Marghe did not want to take the viajera up on her suggestion. She was afraid.

She pondered that as she dug and rooted. Now and again she moved one plant away from another, or closer to its neighbor. She was not sure why she did this, only that it was good for the different plants; it felt right. When the plants were wrongly ordered, it felt on some dim level as though someone were screeching metal down metal, setting her teeth on edge. When she moved the plants, the discomfort stopped. At first she had been disturbed by the fact that she was behaving without identifiable empiric reason, and had tried not to do so. But the feeling became unpleasant. Now she allowed herself to act automatically and tried not to worry about it.

She stood up and stretched, moved to the patch of garden she wanted to break in for the jaellum seedlings growing indoors in the nursery, just off the great room. The ground was hard, still frosty in places. She dug until she was damp with sweat inside her tunic.

She straightened her back. Something was not right. She sat quietly, letting her mind idle, and then she knew: the jaellum seedlings would do better over on the south side of the garden, in the more sandy soil. Which meant she had broken this ground for nothing. She swore softly. It would take hours to dig over a new patch, and she would have to transfer the goura bulbs she had planted earlier in the sandy patch.

Maybe she was wrong. It would be easier if she was wrong. She would continue breaking this ground. Yes. After all, she had no real reason, no good reason, to believe they would flourish better in a different location.

By gritting her teeth, she managed to work for about another half an hour, but eventually she had to stop; her discomfort was almost painful. She admitted defeat. Whether or not she knew how she knew it, the seedlings would fare better in the sandy south garden. All she was doing was wasting time and energy. What needed doing needed doing.

She sighed, climbed to her feet, and took her taar-skin mat and roll of wet felt over to the goura. She starting digging up the shoots, one by one, and laying them carefully on the unrolled felt. Next time she would listen more attentively to her instincts.

She paused, trowel in hand. *What needed doing needed doing.*

Deepsearch. If Marghe was honest, she herself knew she ought to do it. Ignoring the need did not make it go away.

She thrust her trowel deep into the soil and took her hand away. The handle gleamed, rounded and polished by a hundred human hands. She wondered how old it was, whether a woman of Ollfoss using the trowel could look inside her past and see her mother or grandmother or many-times-great-grandmother handling the same trowel, bending over the same patch of dirt. The thought terrified her, but what scared her more was the idea that she might look inside herself and find nothing.

EIGHT WOMEN pattern-sang for Marghe; she made the ninth. When she had asked Thenike why always nine, Thenike shrugged. "Nine is the right number."

Marghe decided not to take that any further. "How long does it take?"

"A few moments, or the whole day. Everyone's different. It depends how far you go, and how easy it is. Many of the young ones are frightened, which makes it harder. You'll go in fast, I think. How long you stay is up to you."

Not long, Marghe thought, not long.

They gathered outside in the early afternoon. It was almost warm, but Thenike had warned her to wrap up well. Standing motionless for hours did not produce much body heat. Two chia birds sang back and forth to each other.

Six of her family were there: Thenike, Gerrel, Hilt, Leifin, Wenn, Huellis. Kenisi and the two youngsters were with Namri, who had put her back out. Kristen and Ette made up the eight.

Thenike would keep her safe.

Gerrel, who had made her first deepsearch only last midsummer, started the singing. She hummed deep, tunelessly. The others took up the hum until it sounded like a creaky tree song, the rubbing together of branches. It wove back and forth like the wind high in the forest, apparently aimless. The singers took breaths according to their own rhythms and exhaled in the wavering hum that climbed and sank and wandered without apparent form. Marghe closed her eyes. Two, then three women began to breathe and hum at the same time, then a fourth, and a fifth. Marghe imagined she could hear their hearts thumping together. Her own breath ran with theirs.

Between one heartbeat and another, they all breathed and sang together, great powerful gusts of sound beating at Marghe like rain, rain that grew in intensity, spattering her face, running then pouring over her, pooling at her feet, until she felt she was standing under a waterfall of sound. The sound pulsed endlessly, like the world. Deep inside her cells, something responded.

Thenike will keep me safe.

She followed the plunging water down, where it wanted to go.

MARGHE CAME up from her not-dream. She felt stiff from standing still so long, and her pattern singers were gone, except for Thenike. Marghe smiled at her, but said nothing; she did not want to talk yet.

In silence, Thenike helped her walk through the evening shadow of the trees until her joints unstiffened. Undergrowth rustled beneath their feet.

Marghe felt she had been gone a long time, much longer than the two or three hours it had taken for the world to turn away from the sun and toward the arms of evening. She had been inside herself in a way she had never thought possible; listening to her body as a whole, a magnificent, healthy whole. And she had done more: reliving memories of her childhood she had forgotten, experiencing again days she had never been wholly aware of. Now she knew how it felt to be a baby just ten days old, and that baby had been as alien to her as any species she had encountered since. There had been more: what felt like days of communication between herself now and herself of many thens. She had sent a question down all the avenues that opened before her: what is my name? And echoing back had come: Marghe. And again: Marghe. And then, whispered in a voice she knew: Marghe, and more.

She was on a thin and misty beach; her mother walked from the shadows and held out her hand. On her palm was the ammonite.

"Primitive cultures thought they were coiled snakes, petrified, and called them snake-stones," Acquila said. "But the word 'ammonite' comes, of course, from the medieval Latin, *cornu Ammonis,* horn of Ammon, due to its resemblance to the involuted horn of Ammon, or Amun, the ram-headed god of Thebes."

She put the cold thing in Marghe's whole right hand. "His name, Amun, means 'complete one.' He acquired the power of fertility formerly invested in Min, the ancient Egyptian god of reproduction." She looked amused. "Min was very popular. But his time passed."

Her mother had faded, leaving the ammonite. Marghe had not been surprised when it sank into her hand. And now she was herself, and more. The complete one.

Marghe smiled. "I have been so many places . . ."

"Yes," Thenike said. "Mind this root here."

"I see it."

Two more chia birds called back and forth. The same ones? Marghe stopped and tilted her head to listen. "Do many women keep their child names?" she asked.

"Some. Not many."

"What was yours?"

"Gilraen."

"Gilraen . . ." She considered the woman next to her, with her rich hair, pinned up, her soft brown eyes and strong fingers. "A nice name, but not yours."

"No."

They started walking again. After a moment, Marghe said softly, "My name is Marghe Amun."

The complete one.

No one suggested that Marghe move out of the guest room, but she wondered if she should. There was something she needed to do, she was sure of it. But what?

Marghe felt the need to do this unspecified something as a subtle pressure against her skin, as when the weather was about to change. She did not mention it to anyone. She gardened, and ate, and talked to Thenike and Gerrel and, now and again, Wenn or Huellis. Leifin disappeared on a hunt.

Marghe became restless. When she dug in the garden, she dug with hard, vicious jabs, and took pleasure in her aching muscles when she sank into the hot tub in the evening. She lay in the almost-scalding water hoping, longing for the heat to soothe her. It did not. It was as though she had a muscle, somewhere, that had not been exercised.

She dried herself off thoughtfully. A muscle that needed exercising. Perhaps that was it. She had to find out what she could do now, now that she had part of Jeep living inside every cell of her body; she had to find out how she had changed.

In the guest room—she could not think of it as hers—she lit a small fire, did some gentle stretching and breathing to ease her sore muscles, and then settled down cross-legged on the warm flags near the hearth.

Three breaths triggered a trance easily. Too easily. She jerked herself out, frightened. Such a deep meditative state should normally take twenty minutes or more.

She smoothed her heart rhythm, thought about that. Was it

anything to be scared of? She was not sure. Was it something that she could control? Probably. Then she would try again.

As easily as before, she sank into a trance, her breathing slow and deep and regular. Her electrical rhythms, her brain activity, began to cycle hugely and slowly, like an enormous skipping rope. Behind her eyelids, she imagined her blood as a thick red river full of amoeba-like creatures: T cells, lymphocytes, phagocytes, doughnut-shaped hemoglobin, tumbling over and over, rushing past. The overwhelming impression was one of vigor, a good, cleaned-out feeling. No sluggish streams or narrow places, no dead-seeming backwaters where toxins gathered.

She had never been so healthy, or seen it so clearly.

She moved her mind's eye on, roaming glandular production, the lymph system, her gut. She paused by an *E. coli*, moved on, settled on a cheek cell. She remembered a long-ago biology lesson: scraping cheek cells onto a slide, examining them under a microscope. It had been nothing like this.

The cell was like an enormous helium balloon in which she floated, swimming through cytoplasm and around mitochondria, bumping gently against the nucleic mass where DNA writhed like a nest of snakes. She moved inward. There, running through the center of the DNA like a bright electrum thread, was the virus. It thrummed like a tuning fork. She glided around it, examining it. So small. She reached out to touch it, pulled back at the last moment. Another time.

When she withdrew back up to conscious level, she found that the fire was long dead and she was shaking with cold.

SHE DISCOVERED that it was too tiring to trance more than once every three or four days, and too frightening. She persevered. Now that she had started, she needed to know more, much more. This was herself she was exploring, uncovering. Discovering. If she was ever to be truly Marghe Amun, the complete one, then she needed to know what she could do, who she was.

The more she discovered, the more she realized there were places she wanted to go, things she needed to do and see, that might be dangerous for her to attempt now, alone.

One day, eating lunch with Gerrel, she remembered Thenike using the drums to take her to an impossible memory vision of the goth, and the way she had used her own body rhythms to keep Marghe alive.

Early the next morning, shivering slightly because it was cold under the trees, she went to find the viajera. The grass was still wet with dew; she followed Thenike's bootprints and found her some way into the forest, gathering nuts for the family's breakfast. Marghe watched her for a while. Thenike seemed separate from everything around her, distinct, as though coated in crystal; she moved here and there in the forest, stooping, tossing nuts into her basket, pausing now and again to look up at some wirrel's chitter or chia's call. Her hair was loose on her shoulders, like a wood-colored waterfall.

Marghe stepped out from the shadow.

"Marghe! It's a beautiful morning. Come and help me with these nuts."

"I need your help," Marghe blurted.

Thenike put down her basket of nuts, sat down by a smooth-barked tree. "Tell me."

Marghe stepped further into the clearing. "There's so much I need to know, and I can't do it on my own. Link with me in search."

Thenike selected a nut, cracked the shell, and chewed. "Why me?"

"Because you're a viajera. You're skilled in these matters." She was standing right next to Thenike now. "And because I trust you."

Thenike nodded slowly, then gestured for Marghe to sit next to her. She took Marghe's hand and seemed to study her a long time. "Very well."

 LINKING WAS hard, Thenike said, and required preparation. They fasted one day, ate lightly of the same things at the same times the next, repeated the cycle, over and over. Fast, eat, fast, eat. As much as possible, they did everything together: walked, ate, cooked, bathed. They slept next to each other in the same bed; sometimes Marghe lay awake listening to their matched breath, and sometimes she fell asleep immediately, knowing that Thenike listened. Day after day, night after night they spent together, and Marghe began to feel a fierce energy building between them, heating and shrinking, pulling them in, like a star about to go nova.

A morning came that filled their room with streaks of shadow and lemon sun, and birds sang, and women laughed outside their window, but the thing between them had pulled them close and all either heard was the sound of the other's breath as it moved in the same rhythm as her own.

They lay facing each other, naked, skin to skin. They stroked each other's face, hands, arms. Rested fingertips on the pulse at the other's wrist. Marghe's forehead was damp with perspiration, and they were both breathing fast. Thenike's eyes were black as olla, her sharp cheeks underpainted with red.

"Is this it?" Marghe asked. She was scared.

"No. This is something different. Do you feel it?" She touched Marghe's forehead with a fingertip. Marghe's bones seemed full of hot, liquid gold. She could feel the heat of Thenike's belly and groin close to her own.

Thenike traced Marghe's lips with her fingertip, then her chin, her throat. Marghe tilted her head back, mouth opening, arching. Thenike slid a hand under her hip, ran the other over Marghe's back, fingers spreading over ribs, thumb brushing her breast. Marghe made a noise deep in her throat, trembled. Thenike slid on top of her, muscle against muscle, slick skin on skin, her hair trailing over Marghe's face.

Marghe reached up and sank both hands into that hair, hair that was dark with all the shades of brown Marghe could name, and many she could not: brown like mahogany and teak, like dry oak leaves, like fresh-turned loam and the shining chestnut of a sweating horse; locks and tresses and strand upon strand. Marghe wanted to lose herself in that hair, lose herself in Thenike.

They searched blindly for each other's mouth, clinging like fish, swimming slowly closer and closer, breast on breast, belly on belly, arms wrapped around the other's ribs like great hoops of oak, breath coming in powerful tearing gasps. Marghe was not sure whose mouth was whose, where her thigh ended and Thenike's belly began, all she knew was heat, a heat like the core of the world, like the energy of all living things as they broke down food and burned oxygen and fueled more life, more heat.

They moved, breath coming in sobs, muscles taut and plump beneath wet skin, until need burned like a sun between their bellies, flaming hotter and hotter, orange to yellow to white, then roared out over them, searing, magnesium-hot under their skin, unbearable.

THE ROOM was full of sunshine and smelled of the minerals Thenike had washed her sheets in, and sweat, and the soft musky scent of their skin. They lay side by side, Marghe still on her back, Thenike on her stomach. Marghe was rolling a coil of Thenike's hair between her fingers, enjoying its strong, coarse feel as they talked.

"I think everyone, everywhere, should choose their own name, when they're ready," Marghe said.

"Who chose your child name?"

"My father, I think. At least, he had an aunt called Marguerite. And I can't see my mother picking a name like Angelica. Although . . ." Marghe smiled. You never knew.

"But now you have a new name."

"Yes."

"Amun."

It was strange to hear it from another's mouth. "Do you like it?"

"Explain it to me."

"It started with a dream." She told Thenike about the dream of shells, and the ammonite, the way it sank into her hand, became part of her. Was her, really.

Thenike frowned. "I can't imagine what it looks like. The ammonite."

Marghe hopped off the bed, brushed a pile of ashes together on the hearth, and smoothed them. She drew with her finger. Thenike leaned over to watch. "They're smaller than this, but they curve around and around, in on themselves. Many-chambered. And they're slate blue." She rested her hands on her thighs, careless of the ash. "I found one on the beach once, in England. Carried it around for days. It felt so good in my hand."

"Like a stone that fits just right."

"Yes. Exactly." She jumped back on the bed. "So what does your name mean?"

"In the Trern Swamplands they make boats from hollow tree trunks and they have many words to describe the kind of sound a log makes when hit. That's how they test the strength of the wood, by the sound it makes when they tap it. Thenike means something like 'ring true' or 'deep and clear.' " She smiled at Marghe. "It's how I like to think of myself."

Marghe smiled back. From what she knew of Thenike, the name suited her exactly . . . and she knew a great deal now, more than she had known about anyone in her life. And Thenike knew more about her, Marghe, than anyone else ever had.

Marghe felt the first faint stirrings of panic. Thenike knew too much about her. Too much. She moved restlessly.

"Marghe, Amun, what's the matter?"

"I'm fine." Her throat felt tight. "I'm fine," she said again, too loudly. "It's just too hot in here. And I'm hungry."

"Then we'll get breakfast." Thenike sat up.

"No." Too fierce. "No," she said again, more quietly. "I want to be on my own for a while." She could not meet Thenike's gaze. She got up, found her clothes, pulled on her tunic. "I need to . . . walk, breathe some fresh air. Think about all this." She gestured helplessly at the crumpled bed and fled, trying not to see the hurt in Thenike's eyes.

ALL THAT day, and the next, Marghe avoided Thenike, eating and gardening alone. She spent the nights in the guest room, trying not to remember Thenike rolling on top of her, the feel of muscle warm and hard under her belly, the way their mouths met. No one bothered her. Most of the family was busy; Leifin had returned from a hunt and they were helping her tan the skins and cure the meat.

The third night, Marghe tossed and turned for hours, too tense to sleep. She got up and pulled a cloak around her shoulders; she needed fresh air. Outside, only one moon was visible, blurred behind clouds. She walked hard, fast, stamping through the trees, glad when she startled a pair of wirrels into shrieking and running.

She missed Thenike. But she was scared. If she went back, it meant deliberately putting aside her barriers, letting Thenike right inside, right in where she could see those parts of herself that Marghe had never shown anyone. Those parts she barely knew herself.

Parts she never would know, if she stopped now.

She paused, then strode on, angry. She could not stop now. Not after surviving Tehuantepec, not after fighting off the virus, choosing her name, discovering so much about herself . . .

She had to choose: Thenike, and the knowledge of who she really was or might be, or old habits that stemmed from fear that no longer had any foundation.

She turned around, marched back toward the house. She wanted Thenike—wanted to earn the name she had chosen for herself, to find out what it meant to be Marghe Amun, to be complete, whole. She'd be damned if she would give up now.

She knocked on Thenike's door, then knocked again when there was no reply.

Thenike opened it, a coverlet draped over her shoulders and her face creased with sleep. They looked at one another.

"Come in," Thenike said, and stepped to one side. The room was dim. Thenike lit a candle from the banked fire.

They faced one another. Thenike looked soft and smelled of sleep. Marghe wanted to gather her up in her arms. "I'm sorry," she said. "I'm sorry. I'm just so scared." And burst into tears.

 THE CANDLE was guttering, and Marghe's face was tight with dried tears. They lay in each other's arms, breathing easily, softly. Flame and shadow flickered over Thenike's skin, turning it reddish bronze and tinting her hair with copper. Marghe knew that she could match her lover's heartbeat whenever she wanted, match her breath, her pulse; that their rhythms were still connected.

"I want to do it now," she said suddenly. "Before I get too scared."

"PUT YOUR hand on mine. Feel the pulse in each fingertip, mine and yours. Yours and mine." Thenike slid on top of her, muscle on muscle, her mouth an inch from Marghe's. "Breathe with me. Breathe my breath."

It was hot; their skin was hot, and their breath. In and out, in and out. And Marghe gave up everything, gave her breath to Thenike, took Thenike's into her lungs. Then their arms were wrapped around each other, eyes open, staring deep, and Marghe let herself slide down that long deep slope, that slippery slope, sinking in, right in, right down until she *was* Thenike, was Thenike's pulse, Thenike's breath, until she could skip back and forth: her breath, Thenike's breath, back and forth. Back and forth.

They slid past each other like slippery same-pole magnets, going in.

And Marghe was standing before the cathedral that was Thenike's body and all its systems, as Thenike stood before hers. She stepped inside.

It stretched far over her head, a vast, echoing space. She wandered, laying a hand here, against the muscles sheathing the stomach, a hand there, between ribs. She stopped and looked in a side chapel where bronchioles narrowed to alveoli. She wandered on, noting cells and bones and connective tissue, glands and tubes. Ovaries.

One ovary felt different from the other. Marghe stopped. She felt its heat, and something else, a bulge, a ripe readiness. The bulge swelled. Marghe watched, fascinated, as it split, opened, released its egg. Marghe followed the egg as waving cilia gentled it down the oviduct.

Thenike was ovulating, and because Marghe knew their rhythms were matched, she knew that this would be happening in her body, too, and that Thenike would be watching. Marghe stepped closer, reached out cautiously. The electrum thread inside shimmered and sang, and the ovum almost . . . changed. Marghe withdrew her hand.

The virus had altered everything. She saw how she could change the chromosomes, how she could rearrange the pairs of alleles on each one. If she reached in and touched *this*, enfolded *that*, the cell would begin to divide. And she could control it—she and Thenike could control it.

Marghe felt the connecting tension as Thenike stood waiting.

She could do it. She would do it; Thenike would match her.

She reached out again, and the thrumming electrum strand that was the virus coiled and flexed and the cell divided. Marghe searched her memory of those long-ago biology lessons: mitosis. But altered, tightly controlled and compressed by the snaking virus until it resembled a truncated meiosis. Chromosomes began their stately dance, pairing and parting, chromatids joining and breaking again at their chiasmata, each with slightly rearranged genetic material. But the chromatids did not then separate again and migrate to the cellular poles in a second anaphase; instead they replicated. This daughter would be diploid, able to have her own daughter.

It was like watching beads on a string rearrange themselves. Gorgeous colors, intricate steps, every bead knowing just the right distance to travel. Precision choreography, again and again, as cells divided, normally now, and the one-celled ova became two-celled, four-celled, eight-celled.

As they multiplied, Marghe felt the tight tension, the connection between these cells that would divide and multiply inside Thenike, and those that would grow inside her own body: fetuses. Fetuses that might one day be born as soestre.

 MARGHE SAT up in bed, the coverlet wrapped around her, watching Thenike coax the fire back to life. The candle, forgotten, had long since burned out. The only light was the dull red of the hearth, sending Thenike's shadow high over the ceiling.

She watched her lover in silence; words would have been too big, too solid, for what they had done together.

Thenike added some dry sticks. The flames leapt, sending her shadow swaying and jumping over the walls. She examined her handiwork and added a log. "You could be a viajera. If you chose. You have the skill."

Marghe cradled her stomach with her right hand. She had done this. They had done this. She did not want to think about anything else. "They'll be soestre," she said. A new thought struck her. "How would I travel as a viajera with a baby?"

Thenike turned to look over her shoulder. "We'd travel together. While they're young, we'll travel smaller distances at a time, and less often. And when we get there, we'll stay longer. We'd be safe, together."

Marghe imagined the *Nid-Nod* tossed by a storm, Thenike wrestling with the tiller, Marghe trying to reef the sail and stop both babies from being washed overboard.

"What are you smiling at?"

"The future." And Marghe knew then that she did want to be a viajera, a teacher and wanderer, a newsbearer, arbitrator, and traveler. "Wenn will be disappointed. I think she'd rather I stayed as a gardener."

"More useful to her way of thinking," Thenike agreed.

"I can't sing."

"Not necessary."

"Teach me what to do."

"I have been doing."

WHEN THEY woke up the next morning, they hugged each other tight, then let go.

"Thenike, I need to get a message to Danner, at Port Central. Tell her where I am, what's happening." Now that she herself knew, finally, what she wanted, she owed it to them, to Danner and to Sara Hiam, to let them know the vaccine worked, that she had chosen to discontinue taking it; that she was going to stay here with Thenike and have a child.

"It's a long journey from here to there. Will it wait until the weather's better, until we can send by herd bird?"

"I should have sent word weeks ago."

"I'll talk to Hilt."

THENIKE POINTED at the map on the wall of Rathell's great room. "Hilt plans to leave for North Haven in the last third of this moon." It was already the Moon of New Grass. Spring. "From there, her ship takes her south and east"—her fingernail swung out into the blue-painted Eye of Ocean—"through the Summer Island channels. Then south and west, pat the Gray Horn, out into Silverfish Deeps and on, down to Pebble Fleet. From there, she'll be able to find a messenger willing to travel north and west up the Huipil and over the hills to your Port Central."

Marghe frowned, and studied the wide-swinging route. "Why doesn't she sail through here?" She pointed to a narrow channel between the largest of the Summer Islands. "Wouldn't that cut more than a few days off the voyage?"

"No ship could get through the Mouth of the Grave at this time of year."

"And there's no other way to get the message to Danner?"

Thenike shook her head. "The herd birds can only fly long distances when the air gets hot enough to lift them, let them glide."

"When will that be?"

"Depends on the weather. Perhaps early during Lazy Moon. It would take . . . ten, fifteen days, maybe more, depending on who was herding where, and how much their birds were needed. If you're in a hurry, sending a message with Hilt on her ship would be faster."

Marghe sighed, and accepted the situation. "How much can I say with a message knot?"

"What do you want to say?" Thenike took a cord and several different threads from a bundle that lay on a shelf.

"That I stopped taking the vaccine. That I contracted the virus about a month later. That I'm here at Ollfoss, I'm well, and I'm pregnant."

Thenike knotted rapidly, weaving sometimes one color, sometimes several, into elegantly shaped knots. When she ran out of cord, she took up another, tied it to the first, and continued.

"That's it?" Marghe took the rope, ran the knots and colors through her fingers. "You'd better teach me to do that."

Chapter Thirteen

DANNER, THOUGH she would not have admitted it to another soul, was enjoying herself.

She stood on a slight rise, eight kilometers from what was left of the Port Central perimeter, and watched the four groups of Mirrors pacing off their marks, pausing a moment to wipe the sweat from their brows with wristbands, aiming, loosing the cross-bow quarrels, and trudging back to check their accuracy. Now and again, the late spring breeze carried the dull *chunk* of quarrel hit-ting mark, then the drifting curses after a poor aim, or the crows of accuracy.

Her Mirrors.

She had thirty-two of them down below on the plain, shooting with a mix of differently tipped quarrels—ceramic, plastic, sharp-ened wood—and competing on a team basis. They seemed to be enjoying it, too.

Spring was spring on any world; soldiers got restless. Danner had talked to unit commanders, subs and higher: keep them busy, get their morale up. So here they were, being told only that they were testing the research of various specialists, Mirror and civilian, who were experimenting with the possibilities of local materials. As she overheard one of them say: crossbows were crazy when you had state-of-the-art firepower, but it beat standing pointless guard eight hours out of twenty-four.

Other specialists were busy, too. Botanists were roped in to select trees for their wood, and the geologists, dubious at first, were now happy to use their previously mothballed talents—one did not test-drill and core-mine around burnstone—to track likely deposits of clay and olla. They and the soil specialist were happily muttering about geest and marl, fuller's earth and alluvium. Climatologists and ecologists were off with Ato Teng, surveying for possible resettlement sites. If Company abandoned them, they had to find a better place than Port Central, somewhere fertile and warm, with good access to trade routes. Somewhere defensible.

Danner breathed the soft warm air of Jeep and smiled. Right now there were probably several reports waiting to be downloaded for her attention, but she was happy to stay here, just be. Be herself, Hannah Danner, feeling sunshine and an alien breeze on her face.

South, just visible if she shaded her eyes with her hand and squinted against the sun, was the thready glint of the Huipil, the river that drained the Trern Swamplands. West was the Ho valley, its wide bottom sliding with the river in its slow-moving middle phase; well over a thousand kilometers long, that river. East, half-a-day's journey across the plain by sled—perhaps a week on foot—was the sea, Silverfish Deeps.

She turned north. Representative Marguerite Angelica Taishan was somewhere up there. Danner compressed her lips. She would give a great deal to have Marghe in her office right now, alive and healthy, answering questions. So much depended upon the health of one woman. If the FN-17 worked, then Company would simply vaccinate their employees and all the potential vacationers and real estate agents and miners who could turn Jeep from a financial embarrassment to a reasonable investment. Then all this surveying and crossbow practice and examination of local materials for possible practical use would be no more than an exercise in morale.

North was the direction Danner faced every morning, unconsciously waiting for news.

The wind died and the sun suddenly felt much stronger. Danner sighed. There was work to be done. Teng might have the preliminary site reports ready. Previous satellite surveys indicated several possibilities on the western bank of the Ho valley, both north and south. South would be better—warmer. Damn Marghe, Danner thought. She could have been useful. Take that trata stuff, now. They could have used that to bargain some breeding animals from the locals, if she had stayed here instead of running off on a wild-goose chase.

Danner walked down the hill, moving slowly, wanting to savor the last few minutes of sunshine and fresh air before closing herself up in her office. A faint cry soared up the rise. She turned to look. A figure was jogging toward the Mirrors from the north. Past that she could see something, moving fast. Maybe a sled.

Down below, the jogger reached the clump of Mirrors in the foreground. One dropped her crossbow, raised her wrist to her mouth. Danner's wristcom beeped.

"Commander, this is Sergeant Leap."

"Go ahead."

"Commander, one of my Mirrors reports there's a sled approaching from the north. Four occupants."

That would be Lu Wai and Letitia, with Day. But that made only three. "Four? You're sure?"

Danner watched as the tiny figures below conferred. "Yes ma'am. Four. That's what the observer said."

In the distance, the sled suddenly slowed. Danner nodded to herself: Lu Wai was giving them a chance to prepare a reception committee. She was glad that the lieutenant had had the sense not to comm ahead the identity of her passengers; Danner would not be able to keep Day's presence unofficial if Company got to hear of it. And they would hear of it if the spy was still monitoring communications. "Thank you, Sergeant. Select two officers, ones who look reasonably presentable if that's possible, and detail them to meet me at the bottom of this hill. I want you to take the rest of your troop west two kilometers and continue weapons exercise. Out."

No point taking chances. Whoever that fourth passenger was, Danner wanted to know here, now, with only one or two witnesses.

She wiped the sweat from her face, snapped her collar tight, and started deliberately down the hill. Whoever was in that sled might be important; it would not do to present a bad image.

One of the officers waiting at the bottom of the hill was old to be still a private posted to off-Earth duty. Danner compared the short gray hair and hard face with the files in her head and made a match: Pat Twissel. Two disciplinary hearings, one suspension. Made sergeant once, almost made it to lieutenant before that first hearing busted her back to private. Efficient, but adamantine. If an order fitted with Twissel's particular worldview, then that order would be carried out flawlessly, tirelessly, brilliantly. If Twissel did not agree with what had to be done, she was never overtly disobedient, but things somehow kept going wrong. Willful, too independent for Company Security. Danner was tempted to dismiss her and just keep the younger officer, whose name she could not recall. But willfulness and independence were traits she might need sometime.

They saluted. "Officers Twissel and Chauhan reporting as ordered, ma'am."

Twissel's voice was surprisingly soft. Danner nodded approval of their tidy hair and tight collars.

"Good turnout on short notice. But, Chauhan, see if you can get that muck off your left boot."

Chauhan blushed, which made her look startlingly young, and scrubbed hurriedly at the offending boot with a handful of grass.

The whine of a sled going slower than it should cut through the slight hiss of the wind on grass.

"There are four people on that sled," Danner said conversationally. "Two are Sublieutenant Lu Wai and Technician Letitia Dogias. You may or may not recognize one or more of the others. If you do recognize them, you are not to display that recognition, or comment upon it, either now or to anyone else at any future time. Is that clear?"

"Clear, ma'am," Twissel said, and Danner hoped that whatever was going on under that gray hair was in her favor.

"Chauhan?"

"Oh. Clear, ma'am. Sorry, ma'am."

"Stay behind me. If either of our visitors requires assistance, you will render it without being asked." The sled was just two hundred meters away. "When I have escorted the visitors to Port Central, you will wait for my debriefing, or that of Lieutenant Lu Wai. You may have to wait several hours. Clear?"

"Unobtrusive assistance, don't recognize anyone but Dogias and Lu Wai, wait for the lieutenant's or your debriefing only. Yes, ma'am."

The sled grounded and began to power down. The hatch flipped up. The first out was Dogias, then a stocky woman with long hair going gray. She moved easily enough, but was looking around too much; tense. Day. Danner caught Twissel's jerk of surprise from the corner of her eye.

The third figure was slight, but jumped down to the grass easily and pushed back her hood. The slight woman looked around, saw Danner, held out her hands in welcome.

"Hannah."

"T'orre Na."

"They tell me you're commander, now."

"It's been a long time." Danner was smiling. "Too long." She took the journeywoman's hand. There were one or two new lines on T'orre Na's face, but not much else to show that five years had passed. "You look well."

"You look older. And worried. I have news that you must hear."

"As soon as I can. For now, welcome." Danner squeezed T'orre Na's hand, then let go. She turned to Day, bowed slightly in formal greeting. "Day, welcome."

Day looked older, thicker around the waist. "Commander."

"Call me Hannah, if you would; I have promised to relinquish my command over you. My thanks for coming."

Day did not relax. "Letitia said it was urgent, but I'd feel happier continuing this once we're under cover. Not that I'm very sure what it is you think I can do to help."

Trust is earned, Danner reminded herself. "Very well. We'll take the sled."

THEY WERE in Danner's mod. Day finished her coffee, poured more. "So, in the absence of the representative, you want me to be a sort of cultural interpreter."

"Exactly."

"But you say you already have trata with Cassil in Holme Valley. I don't see why you need me."

"Holme Valley is a long way from here. There are locals closer that we should be dealing with. And you know what we want, you can understand our needs."

"I'm not sure I can anymore. Living out there for five years changes you." She sipped at her coffee. It had been a long time since Danner had seen anyone savour coffee that way. "Besides, now that you have trata with Cassil, you're more or less obliged to put things their way first. Coming to me is breach of protocol."

"That's exactly the kind of information I need! Look, just say you'll stay here for a few months, six months. In return I'll—"

"You'll what? Agree not to throw me in the brig for going AWOL?"

Danner kept her temper. "I believe I have already agreed that you will remain officially missing. You could walk out of here right now, and that would still be the case. I keep my promises, where possible."

"It's that 'where possible' that bothers me. I know how it is to be a Mirror; if it becomes expedient to suddenly reopen my file and query my status, then you will. Oh, don't get all righteously angry. You know it's true."

Danner was angry, but saw no point in protesting Day's statement. "Perhaps. But what I was about to say was that I would help you in any way I could. We have metal you could use for trade goods, or we could pass information on weather systems along to you at critical times. During the herd's birthing season, for example."

They were silent. The air system hummed. "I need some sunshine," Day said abruptly. "I don't know how you stand it in this box without windows." She stood up, then startled Danner by smiling—a brief, wry smile. "I know what's wrong with me. It's the coffee. I need to go for a walk. I'll come back in an hour or two." She paused. "You know, Danner, we might be able to work something out, but whatever we decide, you really should talk to T'orre Na first."

"I will, thank you. I'll detail an officer to find her, but if you see her first, please ask her to come and find me as soon as she can."

Day looked thoughtful. "Communications not reliable, Commander?"

"A question of security."

Day looked around. "Letitia told me some of it. Company has big ears. This room?"

"As secure as we can make it."

"I gather 'we' includes Letitia and Lu Wai. They mentioned a Sergeant Kahn. Twissel?"

"No."

"You might like to consider her. She knows I'm here now, and that something's happening. She's bright, should have made captain a long time ago, and she'll put two and two together. Better to have her on your side than against you."

"I'll take that under advisement. And, Day, when you've finished your walk, I'd like you to come back and sit in on my talk with the journeywoman. I'd like your input. Sometimes T'orre Na can be a bit, well, a bit alien."

"I imagine she feels the same way about you."

T'ORRE NA sat cross-legged on the bed, just as she had all those years ago when she had come to Port Central with Jink and Oriyest to demand that Company make recompense for the burn they had started, the burn that had destroyed Jink and Oriyest's grazing grounds. Danner had been a lieutenant then. It seemed longer, much longer than five years ago, but some things never changed: Danner had been as off balance then as she was now.

"Cassil wants what?"

"Your help. The tribes are raiding everything north of Singing Pastures. It's only a matter of time before they spread south."

"What does she think I can do from down here? And why should I?"

"Cassil demands a return on trata. She helped you, your family, through Marghe. Now she wants you to help her."

"You know that we're not a family, no matter what Cassil thinks."

"The trata was made in good faith. I was there. So was one of your Mirrors, Lu Wai. She is under your direct command, which makes you responsible."

Danner chose to ignore that for a moment. "It sounds like a territorial squabble. Surely Cassil and the others can sort that out themselves."

"If they could deal with it, they would. That's the way of trata, to always keep the advantage. They lose it by asking your help."

Danner set aside trata and its promise of Byzantine complexities and concentrated instead on what she could understand. "These tribes . . ."

"The Echraidhe and Briogannon."

"Echraidhe and Briogannon. Yes. Is this something they do a lot? Attack people? Tell me about them."

"This has never happened before. It's new. Something's changed, but I don't know what, or why. No one does. It seems that the Echraidhe have some sort of new leader who has bypassed the authority of the Levarch. Her name is Uaithne, but she's calling herself the Death Spirit, riding at the front of her tribe, and killing, killing, killing. She killed half the Briogannon first, to make them join her, and now she slaughters the flocks and herds of Singing Pastures. The pasture women have fled to Holme Valley, but without the herds the people will die. If Uaithne does not kill them first herself."

"Just killing? That's senseless."

"Not to them. It's one of their legends, that the Death Spirit will come and destroy the people. Uaithne has proclaimed herself that spirit."

Danner had been caught in one religious war, on her second tour of duty as a cadet, patrolling Company's interests in Aotearoa in the Tasman sea. Vicious, bloody, incomprehensible. Not about territory or livelihood, but about ideas she could not begin to grasp. "Dirty business, religion. But you said only the herds of Singing Pastures have been affected. Why does Cassil come to me?"

"Singing Pastures has trata with Holme Valley."

"And Cassil has trata with me." Damn Marghe. "Let me think. How about this: I'll be happy to advise the women of Singing Pastures and Holme Valley on how to organize a militia, but I'm not prepared to make the journey myself, or send any personnel."

"You must."

"I can't, T'orre Na. You've no idea of my situation here."

"I think I do. Bluntly, you're on your own."

"Well, that's not quite how I'd—"

T'orre Na talked right over her. "You need all the help you can get. Allies. Support. The best way is through trata. You must honor your bargain." Her voice was low, intense, totally focused on Danner. "You must. For Cassil, for yourselves. Go to Holme Valley and stop Uaithne."

In the silence, Danner's screen bleeped. Glad of the excuse to look away, she swiveled her chair to her terminal and punched accept.

"I hope this is urgent, Vincio."

"Ma'am, a patrol picked up a native heading for Port Central. She's here. Calls herself Sehanol, says she's a messenger, from a place called Scatterdell."

"Between the Huipil and swamplands, two days south of here," T'orre Na interjected.

"Ma'am, she says she has a message from Marghe, I assume she means Representative Taishan, who is at Ollfoss. I think. It's hard to understand her. The bad news is that the vaccine didn't work. Apparently, Taishan got the vir—"

"Enough, Vincio." It had taken Danner a second to understand what Vincio was blabbing all over the net. She gathered her wits too late. "Is the messenger still there?"

"Yes, ma'am."

"I'll send an escort for her. I want a code five on this, effective immediately."

The code-five silence was bolting the stable door after the horse had run. Damn T'orre Na, damn Cassil. If she had not been thinking about this trata, she might have stopped Vincio in time. Now the spy would already have the information on its way to the *Kurst*: the vaccine did not work. Already, Company would be making decisions. It was all over now. No more time.

T'orre Na opened her mouth with a question. Danner held up a hand. "A moment. I need to think." She punched in Lu Wai's code. "Lu Wai? Detail Kahn to go to my office, to escort a native, Sehanol, to my quarters. I want you to implement start of Operation Ascent. Immediately. It's happening, Lu Wai."

She got hold of Dogias next. "This is Danner. Top priority. Track and jam any off-world communication, excluding my channel to *Estrade*. Move fast, Letitia. It may already be too late." She signed off and punched in Sara Hiam's code, drumming her fingers impatiently.

The doctor looked tousled, sleepy. "What—"

"Sara, it's happened. I don't have all the details yet, but I'm setting things in motion at my end. Are you ready?"

Watching Hiam absorb the news was like seeing a slow-motion picture: the doctor's face seemed to contract muscle by muscle until it was hard and tight. "There's no way I could be ready for this. But we'll manage."

Danner knew how much it must be costing the doctor to not ask questions; Hiam had worked hard on that vaccine. She must be as full of professional curiosity and disbelief as Danner would have been if she had heard that a fully armed troop had been routed by five-year-olds armed with sticks. Danner could not think of anything comforting to say.

They looked at each other helplessly. Danner cut the connection and stared at nothing. It was really happening.

She lifted her head, saw the quick compassion in T'orre Na's eyes, and wondered what her face must look like. She felt ravaged, bereft. If only the vaccine had worked. This was it. All over. The full weight of what would happen next fell on Danner like a boulder. She felt as though her world were whirling away out of reach.

"How long will it take Sehanol to get here?" T'orre Na asked.

"What? Oh, twenty minutes."

"And how long would it take me to find and bring back refreshments?"

"Refreshments?"

"Eating or drinking is good for shock."

"I'm not hungry. But if you need something"—she waved her arm vaguely—"I can have someone bring it."

"I would rather go myself."

"Fine."

"But I need directions."

Danner pulled herself together briefly. "Left. About four hundred . . . paces. Third door. Any argument about payment, have them call me."

When T'orre Na was gone, Danner sat and stared at nothing. There was so much to do. So much. Later, later. For now, she wanted to grieve but felt nothing, nothing at all. It was as though she were swaddled in cotton wool.

T'orre Na came back with a hot rice dish and four cans.

Danner looked at it incredulously. "Beer?"

"I like Terrene beer." T'orre Na popped the can efficiently, drank deep. "Here, the rice is for you."

"I couldn't."

"Have some beer, then."

It suddenly struck Danner as funny. Why not? There was nothing else to do for the moment. They sat in contemplative silence, drinking.

"Try some rice. You might be too busy later."

T'orre Na was right, of course, it just seemed . . . inappropriate to eat and drink and make merry as everything threatened to fall to pieces around her. But there was no good reason why she should not.

They both ate. Danner felt better for the food, more in control. "Perhaps when the messenger comes, T'orre Na, she would respond better to questions from you."

DANNER WAS glad T'orre Na was there. She had a working knowledge of the basic language, but the messenger's accent or dialect was so thick Danner could barely understand one word in six. She made a mental note to ask Day which would be the most important dialects to learn—yet another thing Marghe could have helped them with.

After several minutes of question and answer, the messenger accepted a beer, tasted it cautiously, and put it down. Danner noticed she did not drink from it again. Not all natives liked beer, then. She was obscurely glad, though she could not have said why. Perhaps she was already experiencing the faint beginnings of the need to keep her culture separate, like all immigrant peoples on all worlds. For that's what she and the other Mirrors and technicians were now—immigrants.

She listened harder.

It seemed that the messenger was uncertain about something, and the journeywoman was questioning her hard. Eventually, T'orre Na seemed satisfied, and had the messenger repeat something twice. She nodded and turned to Danner.

"The message goes like this. *Marghe Amun, now of Wenn's family at Ollfoss, to Danner, at Port Central. Greetings. I became ill with this world's sickness during the Moon of Aches*—that's the Moon of Rain, as we would reckon it, some sixty or seventy days ago—*and made myself with child thirty days later. The viajera Thenike and I will bear soestre next spring. I am well and happy. Give my regrets and apologies to the healer.*" She repeated it while Danner taped it, for the record.

"Sehanol says the message knot came via ship to Pebble Fleet. Message stones were left by the banks of the Huipil by one of their herders and read by her daughter, Puiell. The stones had been disturbed. Sehanol thinks that some of the message may be missing."

"Not the important part: Marghe got the virus; the vaccine didn't work." The end of everything. *"Marghe Amun,"* Danner said slowly. "I wonder why she did that." Perhaps the virus had affected the representative's mind. Danner had heard vague rumors of Company personnel going crazy when they contracted the virus. They were usually the ones who died.

"Marghe Amun. And she's with child. Soestre to the viajera Thenike." Danner could not identify T'orre Na's expression. It looked like something akin to wonder.

Sehanol said something.

"She wants to leave now," T'orre Na said. "There's work to be done in Scatterdell."

Danner looked at Sehanol, whose eyes were very bright and who had obviously been following what they said. Danner spoke clearly and carefully. "Before you leave, Sehanol, I want you to know that you have my personal thanks and gratitude. If you and yours at Scatterdell need some small favor in the future, ask."

"We will. You are gracious."

T'orre Na punched the door lock. It hissed open and the native slipped through and was gone.

"Gracious indeed," the journeywoman said to Danner, "considering that the message was already paid for."

"I stressed a *small* service. And I thought it was important to cement good relations." Now that they were here for good.

"You did right. Perhaps now that your circumstances have changed a little, you'll be prepared to change your mind with regard to your other obligations in the north."

"T'orre Na, I can't, believe me. More than ever, I've too much to do here. I have to catch someone, a spy. It's now or never. If she isn't caught now, she'll go underground. We'll never be sure who we can trust again. I'm responsible for the evacuation of Port Central, just in case the *Kurst* decides to eradicate this position. Nearly a thousand personnel and our stores and munitions have to go somewhere; and we don't even know where, yet. I have to . . ." She pulled herself up with an effort. T'orre Na did not want to hear all her troubles. "There's enough work here for every woman twice over—work that's vital for our survival. I can't, I absolutely cannot, spare anyone at this time. Please tell this to Cassil and the others of Holme Valley."

"I urge you to reconsider. The Echraidhe are destroying herds and crops and people now. And trata is trata."

"And if I don't do all that needs doing here, right now, there won't *be* any Mirrors to keep trata! Please, try and believe me."

"Oh, I do," T'orre Na said sadly, "but that makes no difference. Cassil needs help, you refuse it. You break trata. There is nothing more to be said."

Chapter Fourteen

HILT LEFT for North Haven, taking the message with her. The Moon of Flowers came, but Marghe Amun's monthly bleeding did not. It was then that she realized that what she and Thenike had done would affect her whole life. In a few months—a year, by Jeep standards—she would bear a child. A daughter. It was strange to think that soon she would be responsible for another human being. It made her feel restless, trapped.

Marghe paused, weed in one hand, trowel in the other. The ovum—the *blastosphere*, her enhanced memory whispered to her— was just cells. She could abort them, it, as easily as she had induced cell division. She could be just herself; she did not need to be responsible.

But she was responsible already. The child growing inside Thenike was partially of her doing. They would be soestre. There was already a bond.

Marghe knelt on the damp ground. She had a child growing in her belly. Did she want it?

Yes. She wanted to bear it—her; she wanted to name her,

watch her learn to crawl, speak, think. Wanted her to have a home, belong.

She went back to her gardening.

The clear air of Ollfoss grew warmer daily, and Marghe and Gerrel spent their mornings and afternoons, and sometimes early evenings when the sun lay like an amber cloak over the tops of the trees, digging out weeds on their knees, trimming back excessive growth of jaellums and soca and neat's-foot.

When she was not on her knees in the garden, Marghe was with Thenike. They helped Wenn weave, gathered herbs with old Kenisi, took turns looking after Moss and Otter while Leifin and Namri were choosing a tree to cut to make a new door and Huellis made candles. They ate together, slept together, talked together; and Marghe learned.

When she took up the drums, it was to learn from Thenike how to use them to drive a story deep into the hearts of her listeners. When she took up a rope, she learned how the knots spelled out shorthand versions of concepts and phrases, how the colored threads made the words, or added emphasis. She was not a good singer, she did not have that smoky voice of Thenike's, but she learned how to give a story rhythm and pacing, how to make it live in the mind's eye of her listener. She was good at that.

She practiced on Thenike, telling her the story of her life, of her mother's life, and her father's, of how Company stole what it could not cheat from people, of the worlds she had visited, and the places of which she only knew rumor.

Her skin browned, and her arms thickened and grew strong. The room where Marghe had stayed became the guest room once more, and at night, before she fell asleep, she would look at their hands lying together, Thenike's long, all sinew and bone, with that white scar snaking over the back of the thumb, her own blunt and spatulate, and feel full of the wonder of their differences. Sometimes she had strange dreams in which her belly swelled so much that she could not get through the doorway, and she felt trapped. She woke on those mornings to sunshine and Thenike's hair spread over her pillow, and a feeling of restlessness she could not explain.

That restlessness grew like an unreachable itch as the Moon of Flowers passed into the beginning of Lazy Moon, and spring became early summer.

ONE EVENING, Thenike was sitting behind Marghe in the tub, rinsing Marghe's hair. It had been windy that day, and the hair was tangled.

"Ouch." Marghe felt irritable. "Be careful."

"I am careful, but a knot is a knot."

Marghe sat stiffly; Thenike worked in silence. Marghe felt restlessness and tension building up inside her until it was almost unbearable. "Stop. Just stop." She pushed Thenike's hands away. "We'll cut it off. It'll be easier."

"Another few minutes and the tangles will all be gone."

"I don't want to wait another few minutes. And tomorrow it'll only be all tangled again." She twisted around to face Thenike. "I want it cut."

"Well, how do you suggest we proceed? Shall I use my teeth?"

Thenike's exasperation was understandable but did nothing to curb Marghe's irritation. "I'm sorry," she said, not sounding sorry at all. "It's just . . ." She slapped at the water in frustration, sending it slopping over the edge of the tub. She would have to clean that later; it made her even more cross.

Thenike reached out and touched her hand. "I've watched you the last few days, winding up tighter and tighter, like a bow. Talk to me, and perhaps we can sort something out that does not rely upon cutting your beautiful hair."

"I feel . . . trapped. No, that's not the right word. It's just that this place, Ollfoss, is so small. I see the same people, who talk about the same things. And every day I go into the garden, and I pull up the weeds from a different patch. And then I eat the same food. It's . . . I want to know what's happening in other places. Has my message got to Danner yet, and what does she think? How will Sara Hiam feel about me not testing the vaccine to the limit? And there's so much I want to know. Here I am, stuck up here in the north—" She broke off, remembering that this was Thenike's home. *And yours.*

Thenike merely gestured for her to go on.

"I'm here, in this small place, when there's a whole world to see! The deserts and mountains, the swamplands and canyons. And the seas. Talking to you, before, while I was recovering from frostbite and exposure, before I got the virus, you made me realize who I really am, what it is that I like: new places, new people, discovering both, and how they influence each other. And since I realized that, all I've done is stay here, in one place. I need to be out there"—she waved her arm—"seeing a different horizon. I want to see old Ollfoss. The place where everything began, where all these different societies started. You've no idea how exciting that would be for me. To actually see the one place from which all this spread! I know, I know, there's nothing there, probably, but I just want to *see* it. It's history." She wanted to go, taste the air, touch the dirt, imagine how it had felt for those people.

"And I haven't even seen the forest. Not really. And soon I won't be able to get out and about. I'll be stuck here."

Thenike was quiet awhile, seemingly absorbed in watching her hands slide through the water under the suds. Marghe wondered what she was thinking.

"Your message," she said at last, "should be in Danner's hands by now. How she feels, what she's doing, how your other friends are, that I can't tell you." She looked up from the water. Marghe saw herself reflected in the dark brown eyes. "But I can help a little with the rest. How you feel sounds familiar. It's spring, the season for wandering, for adventure. For love and danger and new things. Probably everyone here in Ollfoss feels it. But you feel it more keenly, because you're becoming a viajera. I feel it, too. That's why we *are* viajera. Journeywomen. We travel because it's in our blood: to see new things, always. To find out why a thing is, but not always interested in the how." She nodded. "Yes, I know how you feel. Perhaps it's time for us to travel."

To travel, to see new places, smell new air, see new skies . . .

But Thenike was not finished. "But you and I have a debt, to this family, to this place. Wenn and Leifin, and Gerrel and Huellis and Kenisi, took you in. You've yet to repay them. We'll travel just a little, this summer, to North Haven, perhaps."

"And old Ollfoss."

"It's on the way," Thenike agreed. "We'll go to old Ollfoss, and North Haven, then come back. We'll bear our children here early next spring, and then we'll see. By then you'll have brought in one harvest, and be well on the way to another. You'll have cooked and eaten and slept with the family for more than a year. You'll belong. Then, when we leave, and come back now and again, they will welcome you not with grumbles, but with open arms and smiling faces, as they do me, because you're part of them. Can you do this?"

Marghe looked at Thenike, at her planed face, the hollow by her collarbone where a soap bubble clung, the strand of brown-black hair stuck to her forehead. "Yes," she said, and cupped a hand over her belly, barely beginning to round. She already belonged.

THE PATH through Moanwood was not too bad, even with their packs and heavy water bottles, until the second day, when Thenike stopped on the path—such as it was—and pointed east through the trees.

"Old Ollfoss is that way. Perhaps a day's journey."

The trees looked so thick that Marghe found it hard to imagine anyone had walked through them in a hundred years.

They took turns forcing a path. It was not like an earth forest; the trees seemed to grow in patches of the same species. Marghe saw what looked like broadened, rougher versions of the skelter tree, with precisely ordered branches and symmetrically placed blue-black leaves. Beyond that, there were trees that looked to Marghe as though they were upside down: roots more spread, and thicker, than the branches that sprang from the crown of a trunk whose girth increased with its height. It reminded her of the baobab of Madagascar, but that had evolved in dry conditions. She picked her way over the treacherous root systems that threaded the forest floor like an enormous pit of maggots, forever frozen, and crunched through the dry mosslike growth that covered the roots and made them hard to see and even more dangerous. Perhaps the cold climate meant there was very little free moisture available.

After the shrieking wirrels and chia birds of Ollfoss, Marghe expected the noise under the canopy to be constant, but even to her enhanced hearing there was very little audible life under the trees.

"There's always an abundance of life at the edges of places: where forest meets plain, where water meets land," Thenike said. "Here, the animals are fewer, and more shy." Marghe glanced around but saw nothing.

"There. On that tree. Halfway up the trunk." Thenike pointed. "A whist."

It was long, not much less than a meter, and shaped like one of the ropelike hangings that twined about the trees. Marghe could not tell which way up it should go.

"Touch it," Thenike said, "if you can."

It looked as though it might be slow-moving. Marghe inched cautiously toward it, taking care to make as little noise as possible. When she was two strides away, she lifted her arm to reach out.

The whist disappeared.

Marghe touched the trunk uncertainly. Thenike pointed. At the top of the tree hung a new rope, vibrating slowly.

"When I was a child, I spent hours trying to touch a whist, wondering what they'd feel like under my fingers. I never caught one. Never. I don't know anyone else who has, either. They move too fast."

Marghe wondered what their prey was, that they had to move so quickly. Or their predator.

They walked on. Marghe, paying more attention now, spotted a strange, scuttling thing that raised its head above the mosslike undergrowth for a moment, flicked its tongue once, and disappeared back to its dry, crackling world. Everywhere there were berries, in greens and earthy reds and bluish black, but all had a milky quality, like neat's-foot once it was picked.

Toward dark, they stopped for a rest. "The moons will be almost full this evening," Thenike said as Marghe handed her a handful of dried fruit. "Bright enough to keep walking, if you've the energy. Your choice: we could sleep in old Ollfoss tonight, if you like."

They rested until the moons came up, then set off. After half an hour, the undergrowth began to thin, disappearing in patches here and there. Marghe could sense a breeze coming through the trees from somewhere ahead, and the sound of water, faint but definite.

The clearing, or what had been a clearing, was enormous. It was floored with dark green ting grass instead of the mosslike undergrowth, and the trees were few, scattered here and there. None looked very old. All seemed to have sprung up from the shells of ruined buildings. In the moonlight, the scene looked like an old woodcut washed with silver gilt.

"How long ago was this abandoned?" She fought the urge to whisper.

"Two hundred years ago. Perhaps more. Things grow slowly here."

In the center of the clearing, the sound of rushing water was loud. Marghe turned her head this way and that, trying to pinpoint the direction. "Where is it?"

Thenike smiled. Her teeth and the whites of her eyes gleamed. In the moonlight, all in monochrome, she looked less like a woman than a creature of polished wood, heartwood exposed for a century and honed by wind and rain to a stylized shape, a symbol. "This way, Amun."

They walked through the clearing and past a thin stand of trees, toward the sound of water.

"Menalden Pool."

It was sleek and black in the moonlight. At the western end, water fell endlessly from rock that looked slippery and metaled. Moonlight gave the spray a ghostly quality, and Marghe half expected a nymph to step out from under the sheet of water, singing, wringing her hair.

"This way." Thenike led her around the foss, to the quiet, northern edge of the pool, where a single tree with outspread branches like an enormous candelabra dipped its roots into the gently lapping water. The journeywoman seemed to look around for something. "Here." She sat down on a flat rock slightly behind the tree, and to one side, patted it for Marghe to join her. Marghe did, and gasped.

The tree in front of her was alive with light reflected from the water. Light ran like electricity along the underside of its black glossy branches; the tree flickered and shimmered, like a menorah made of fiber optics, a dendrite flashing with nerve impulses. Like lightning.

"I found it the first time I traveled to Ollfoss from North Haven. I was very young. I stayed up half the night, watching it, half dreaming. Every time I make this journey I stop here."

Marghe nodded, still lost in wonder.

"I think of it as my tree, my levin tree. You're the first person I've ever shown it to."

Marghe wrapped her arms around Thenike. "You give me so much."

"I have something else for you." She reached inside her tunic and untied the belt pouch. "Here."

It was a suke, with a bas-relief carving on both sides: an ammonite.

"I drew it for Leifin. She carved it. I polished it and drilled the hole." Marghe touched the silky raised carving. So much love. "Here's a thong. For your waist or neck."

Marghe threaded the braided leather through the hole.

"Do you want me to tie it?"

Marghe shook her head. "I'd like to just hold it awhile."

They sat side by side, watching the water, listening to the soft thunder of the foss. Marghe held the suke more tightly than she would have clutched a diamond.

"The pool's named after the menalden that used to live here." Thenike leaned forward and traced an outline in the sand with her finger. "A menalden. They're dappled, like forest shadow."

It looked like an awkward-legged deer, with a flat, rudderlike tail and splayed feet. Menalden. Dappled deer. From *menald*, seventeenth-century dialect for "bitten," or "discolored," or "dappled."

Marghe's heart thumped. How did she know that? She had no idea how she knew it, but she did, and suddenly she knew why the women of this world used ancient Greek words and Zapotec words and phrases from Gaelic, languages dead for hundreds of years. The words just came, and they fitted. Whether that particular knowledge of the menalden had lain in her unconscious for years, after a cursory leaf through a dictionary, and then been pulled up by some incredible feat of memory made possible by the actions of the virus, she was not certain. That explanation seemed easier to believe than the only other one she could come up with: that this might be some kind of race memory stirred by the virus, a memory of someone who had lived long ago and used such a dialect.

Marghe looked at the levin tree, and leaned against the warmth of Thenike's shoulder.

"What is it, Amu?"

"Just as I thought I was beginning to know this world and understand it, it throws more magic at me."

"What's life without magic? Turn your magic into a song, share it with others."

"You know I can't sing."

"A story, then."

They found a ruined house with most of its roof still intact. Thenike fell asleep straightaway, but Marghe lay awake, thinking of moonlight and magic, and how she could tell a story about what she had just seen so that others would feel what she had felt.

THENIKE WAS already up and about when Marghe woke. Sunlight worked as well as moonlight on the water and the levin tree, she found, though it did not have the same eerie magic. She splashed her face with water from the pool, then leaned forward a little to admire her reflection and the look of the suke on its thong around her neck.

Thenike laughed. "You'll fall in if you're not careful." She was carrying a freshly caught fish.

After breakfast, when they had damped the fire and rolled up their nightbags, Thenike showed Marghe what she had really come to see of old Ollfoss.

"This is all there is left."

It was a huge valley, gouged out of the side of a hill, ending in a curiously shaped hump; not natural, because it did not follow the gradient, as a stream or glacier might have done. Gouged by human—or at least intelligent, Marghe amended—hands. And so big. It was carpeted with ting grass, and big, bell-shaped blue flowers that nodded in the slight breeze and filled the air with the scent of spring mornings and sunshine.

"What are they?"

"Bemebells. Or bluebells. There's a children's song that tells how at dawn and dusk, fairies creep out from under the eaves of the wood and play upon the bemebells with drumsticks made from grass and the anthers of other flowers."

Marghe contemplated the valley, with its raised hump at the far end, glad that Thenike had not shown her this in the moonlight; there was too much melancholy here.

There was only one thing this could be, only one thing that made immediate sense: this was the landing site of the ship that had brought the women and men of Jeep to this world for the first time. Marghe did not know enough about such things to determine whether or not it was a crash landing, but she thought not. Forced, perhaps, for who would want to land here in the north when there were more hospitable areas south?

How had it felt, she wondered, to land in such a strange place, where they could see nothing but walls of trees and a lid of cloud? It must have seemed that there was not enough room to breathe. And then, when they began to sicken, and it became clear that the men would not recover . . . They had been brave.

"What's under the mound?"

"Nothing," Thenike said. "What there might have been has been dug up and used and reused, long before today."

Nothing. "You're sure? You've dug there yourself?"

"In other times, yes."

Marghe wondered if she would ever get used to the fact that her lover could talk about memories that belonged to women long dead and rely upon them, trust them as she would her own. She did not want to believe Thenike, not this time.

"But that heap, it must have been something."

"Nothing but dirt rucked up like a lover's skirt."

Nothing but dirt. It seemed fitting, somehow.

Marghe sighed, and turned away. She had not expected any-thing useful, had just wanted to find something, some piece of broken ceramic or discarded plastic, something she could hold in her hand and imagine being whole and new. But she did not need artifacts; there were the people themselves, people like Thenike. They carried their history with them. As she herself did now.

They walked out of Ollfoss with their packs on their backs and their water flasks bobbing full at their belts, and Thenike sang the bemebell song for Marghe Amun. It was simple and rhythmic, with lots of repetition and places where children were supposed to clap their hands and slap their thighs and stamp their feet in time to the music. The two women sang, and clapped, and smiled at the echoes in the forest, and walked on through the trees toward North Haven.

ON THE day of their arrival, North Haven was humming with the simultaneous arrival of new ships and an unsea-sonable wind that blew cold and hard from the Ice Sea.

"Though now, during Lazy Moon, the ice will be mostly wa-ter," Thenike said. "At least in the more southerly reaches." Then she pointed out a ship with two masts, whose sails might once have been blue-green. "I think that might be the *Nemora*, out of Southmeet. We'll find out soon enough." She smiled but said no more, and Marghe decided that some old friend must be aboard.

Apart from its size, what struck Marghe about North Haven was its life: women on the stone wharfs, unloading fish and baskets of what looked like turtle shells, mending nets and splicing ropes, toss-ing buckets of water over piles of fish guts while fast cadaverous-looking birds quarreled over the mess. It was noisy; women called greetings and shouted insults, water crashed against the stone wharfs and hissed up to the wattle quays farther down the coast, and bas-kets and ropes creaked as catches were hauled up from the decks.

And everywhere there were children: some busy, some just playing an incomprehensible game of tag that involved running and hiding and getting underfoot, and much whooping and shrieking when someone was caught.

Some of the children recognized Thenike: did she have news? Would she sing? Could she spare a comb of krisbread, or a slice of goura? A tune on her pipe? Who was her confused-looking friend?

Marghe felt bewildered by their rapacity and their hard, bright little voices, but Thenike just kept walking, answering questions as she went: yes, she had news, though how would they pay for it? She would sing, all in the proper time. There was no krisbread in her pack, no goura. No doubt she would play them a tune, if they came with their families, and if their families made it worth her while. Her companion was Marghe Amun, who was only confused because she was not used to such rudeness as displayed by the children of North Haven, and she was a fine player of drums and teller of stories who would, no doubt, not deign to display her talents for such rude daughters of herd birds!

Marghe watched Thenike as she laughed and shouted at the children, loving her. The children, being children, noticed.

"Hai! The journeywomen are in love!" one of the older ones called. "The journeywomen are in love!" the others chanted, pleased with themselves. "The journeywomen are in love!"

Marghe felt her cheeks go red, but Thenike laughed and took her hand. "And we'd be in love with a good meal of something that hasn't been in our packs for five days. Is the inn full?"

"There's lots of ships in," the older one who had started the chant offered. "The wind brought them in all at once. But there's some room, I think."

The children followed them, resuming their game as they went.

The inn turned out to be a cluster of buildings: different shapes and ages, built of different materials and to different standards, growing as North Haven had grown—gradually, and in no particular order. The result was a pleasing mix of old stone and raw wood, mossy shingles and bright tiles, with windows winking higgledy-piggledy into three separate courtyards, one of which had a fountain.

A woman with reddish gold hair down her back was sweeping at the leaves in the fountain yard. She looked up when she heard the giggles of the children, and saw Marghe and Thenike.

"Thenike, is it? About time. That boat of yours needs hauling out of the water and its bottom scraping before it rots down to its timbers. But what are you doing standing there gawping—never seen a woman sweep leaves? Get away!" Marghe jumped, but the woman was shouting at the children. "Away with you. Did they follow you all the way here?" This time she was talking to Thenike. Then she shouted again. "If you've nothing better to do than laugh at a poor working woman, then I'll find you something. Now"—she turned back to her visitors—"what can I do for you Thenike, and your companion."

"Zabett, I'd like you to meet Marghe Amun."

"Marghe Amun, is it? That's a big name. How do you like to be called by ordinary folk?"

"I'm not sure yet. I've not had the name long." Marghe had to struggle not to fall into Zabett's speech patterns.

"Well, now, a new name." Zabett gave the leaves one more sweep. "There's a story there, I'll be bound, and no doubt the two of you will expect to stay here for free in exchange, and eat me out of house and home."

"Why else would we come here, to the finest inn in the north?" Thenike said with a smile.

"Flatterer. But flattery won't get you the best room in the house. In fact, there is only the one room left. Over in the west courtyard. I suppose you'll be wanting to go there right this minute, so you can rest a bit, and wash that journey muck off your feet."

The room in the west courtyard was no more than a lean-to, an afterthought added to a wall. But there was room for a bed and a shelf, and there was a latch on the door. Zabett patted the bed. "It's small for two, but no doubt you won't be spending much time in here, except to sleep, and the bed's newly made up."

Marghe liked it. "It's very nice. Thank you."

"Well," Zabett said grudgingly, "it'll do. Now then, I can have you some food ready in a little while, but not instantly. I've more folk than you to look after, viajeras or no." She left, still holding the broom.

"She likes you," Thenike said, unrolling her pack.

"You've known her a long time." Marghe prowled the room, looked out the tiny window. "She runs this place on her own?"

"With her sister, Scathac."

"Is it fair for us to stay here without payment?"

"Nobody stays here without payment. We'll sing for our supper. She was right: we won't be spending much time in here. We'll be telling the news to a packed common room every night, and many will want us to take messages with us when we go."

Marghe had been looking forward to a few days of rest. "Both of us?"

"There'll be some things only you can tell: about your world, how you were caught by the Echraidhe and escaped, how Uaithne started the tribe feud."

"That's a lot of talking."

Thenike sat down on the bed. "It'll only be in the evenings. During the day, we'll sit in the sun and eat Scathac's fine food, gossip about nothing in particular, and wander the docks and along the coastline. I'll show you the *Nid-Nod*. No doubt Zabett's right and she needs some work done on her." She laid her clothes on the shelf, checked her drum. "There. The food should be ready by now. Are you done?"

Marghe was astonished to find that her hands had automatically gone about their business, unpacking, smoothing out her clothes, laying her nightbag on the bed. "Yes."

They took a seat at the bleached white table in the kitchen. Zabett turned and nodded, busy at the fire. After a moment she brought them hot dap. "Eggs in a moment."

Marghe blinked. This was not Zabett: same hair, same build, but her face was not screwed up in that skeptical way, and she did not bustle and fill the room with noise. Not Zabett. Thenike smiled, enjoying Marghe's surprise.

"Scathac, allow me to introduce Marghe Amun. Marghe, this is Scathac, Zabett's twin, a fine cook, a good listener, and a mind like a wirrel trap."

"Pleased to meet you," Marghe said.

Scathac nodded. "Viajering is hungry work. You're welcome to come into the kitchens and eat at any time. With or without Thenike."

They ate, eggs and bread and fruit, and left for the docks.

The day had warmed a little, though the wind was still from the north, slicing the tops off the waves, flecking the gray sea with white. Alien sea or not, it smelled to Marghe the way the sea should smell: big and wide and full of the promise of adventure.

They stood at the edge of the wharf, looking out. Several small coracles were tied together and then secured to one of the huge olla rings embedded in the stone; they bobbed precariously on the swell. Marghe pointed. "Where do these come from?"

"Two days along the west coast. From Luast. See how they're all tied together? Those two, there and there, the ones with the thwarts, are rowed, one woman in each, and the other four are piled up with furs, and little sacks of blue beads dug near Beston-in-the-Mountains. They paddle along the shallows, never out of sight of the shore."

Marghe was appalled at the thought of such tiny, fragile craft battling the northern seas. All for trade. "What do they take in exchange?"

"All kinds of things: wine from the south, timber—they don't have much where they come from, though normally they bring bigger coracles for that—sometimes fruit, or spices from Oboshi . . . whatever they need, assuming that they timed things right and there are people here who want furs or beads."

Marghe scanned the other ships. There were nine, all different makes: two-masted, one-masted; oars and not; double-ended and having definite bows and sterns; larger and smaller. They looked like brightly colored children's toys. She pointed out the ship Thenike had mentioned earlier, which looked to be just leaving. Tiny figures were hauling on sheets, and the sails were bellying. "The *Nemora*. You know someone aboard?"

"Vine, and her kinswomen. Ah, it's a shame we missed them." Thenike rubbed the white scar on the back of her hand, smiling to herself.

Sixty yards out, a boat pulled away from a lateen-rigger. As it neared the wharf, Marghe heard the breath of women pulling oars and the creak of rowlocks, and the sounds of laughter drifting over the water. It was not long before the sailors' boat was bumping up against the stone.

They threw a rope, which landed at Marghe's feet. She picked it up without thinking, then looked around for something to tie it to.

"Like this." Thenike showed her a knot that would hold. "It's called a fishback." It did look a little like a sinuous fish doubling back upon itself, Marghe supposed.

A woman hauled herself up onto the wharf. A bracelet of small clay disks clicked as she held out her hand. "Roth," she said, "Captain of the *Telwise*. My thanks for the knot."

"Thenike, viajera."

"Marghe Amun—" Marghe hesitated, "also a viajera. But new to it."

"So. We all start sometime." Other women were clambering up onto the wharf, clay disks tinkling around waists and necks. "So, Marghe Amun, where do you call home?"

Home. A long story or none at all. Marghe hesitated. "Have you heard of the women from other worlds?"

Roth nodded. "The viajera Kuorra was in Southmeet. She had the story from Telis, who had it from T'orre Na. Supposed to be from beyond the stars, or somesuch she said. Set off burns, don't know anything about anything, wear funny clothes. Call themselves mirrors." She looked hard at Marghe. "But you're a viajera . . . Kuorra says these mirror women can't deepsearch or remember or even have children." She looked from Marghe to Thenike, back again. "Yours must be a strange story."

Thenike said nothing to defend her. Marghe knew this was up to her. "You're staying at the inn? Then come and hear it. It's even stranger than you think."

"No doubt. No doubt. There's room at the inn?"

"You know Zabett," Marghe said, "if you'll pay double the price she'll find you a floor to sleep on, and make you feel grateful."

Roth laughed. "No doubt." She touched the disks at her wrist. There were more, Marghe saw, around her neck and under her tunic. "But we've done well this voyage, and the last two or three. It won't be hard to part with a few of these in exchange for Scathac's cooking." She nodded. "We'll see you at the inn." She walked away, a strong-looking woman with legs bare from the knee, a roll of clothes hanging crosswise across her chest and bumping at her hip.

"By the time she gets to the inn, half of North Haven will know what you've just said." Marghe just nodded. "Roth reminds me of Vine: with those eyes that look more easily into the distance, and those strong bare legs." Thenike laughed. "Like all sailors." She was rubbing at the scar on her hand again. "Come. Let me show you the *Nid-Nod*."

The *Nid-Nod* was tied fore and aft to one of the double wharves at the south of the seafront. She was a small craft with a stepped mast of about thirteen feet, and one sail, neatly furled. A silhouette of a long-legged bird was painted in dark green on both bows. Marghe pointed to what looked like a tiny handprint next to the port symbol.

"What's that?"

"Gerrel's mark. The summer the boat was finished, Huellis and Leifin came to North Haven to see me off and to trade some of Leifin's carvings. They brought Gerrel. She was about four. I was still painting on the name. Gerrel decided she wanted to help. I left the mark on."

When they got back to the inn they found Roth and her thirteen sailors standing in the northern courtyard, with Zabett pointing an accusing finger at a pile of clay dust in her outstretched hand, shouting.

"See, it's not there. No fish tooth. It's a fake. One of you gave me a false credit, and until I find out who, none of you stay here. None."

Thenike leaned toward Marghe and spoke quietly. "They may ask us to judge this matter."

"Us?"

"We're viajeras."

Roth untied the string around her neck, unthreaded one of the clay tokens. "Here's another. Genuine. I know it's genuine because these are the ones I had from you two years ago when we brought in that cargo of keoshell." She held it out.

"Oh, no, it's not as easy as all that, Roth. One of your number tried to pass me a false credit, and that's robbery." She folded her arms.

Roth looked irritated. "Well, you tell me what I'm supposed to do."

"Find out who the dishonest one is among you. I'd think that that's what you'd be after doing anyhow, for your own peace of mind. But I'm not having a thief stay in my house."

The injured parties glared angrily at each other. Then one of the sailors saw Thenike and Marghe. "Let the viajeras sort it out," she said.

Roth looked over at the two women, hesitating a moment over Marghe. "Well," she said to Zabett, "that's agreeable to me. You?"

Zabett nodded shortly. "But you'll pay the fee, as it's your people who caused the trouble."

They spat on their hands, and shook.

Marghe whispered to Thenike. "Wouldn't it be a good idea if they agreed now, while they still don't know who it is, what the punishment would be?" She had seen too many negotiations, on Earth and off, fall to nothing because not enough was agreed at the start.

"Tell them," Thenike said, and gestured.

Marghe took a deep breath. *Pretend it's just like negotiating something for SEC.* "Shake, too, on the reparation price and the punishment you'll mete," she said, stepping forward. While Roth and Zabett prepared to haggle over that, she turned to Thenike. "Any ideas on how to settle this thing?"

"One or two, but they're not perfect."

Marghe thought fast. "These tokens. Zabett has to smash them to see if they contain a fish tooth, otherwise they're not genuine. So . . . Zabett makes them? Yes. And someone's given her a dud. But . . ." They were one-time use only. "That's the central difficulty of the matter, then: once the credit's smashed, it's invalid. So how do we check?"

Roth and Zabett were still talking. Some of the sailors appeared resigned to a long discussion and had sat down in the dusty courtyard.

Marghe thought hard. There was no perfect solution. "The only thing I can think of is that we ask each sailor to take off all her tokens, and empty her pockets, too, just in case, and put them on the ground in front of her. Then we choose one from each pile and smash it. We keep doing that until we smash a dud."

"Some may only have three or four. Losing even one will be a great hardship to the innocents."

"I know."

They were silent; Roth and Zabett had finished talking, and were waiting.

"I can't think of anything better," Thenike said eventually, "and it may be that you won't have to break many."

"Me?"

"You." Thenike deliberately stepped back. Marghe looked around her. She was Marghe Amun. A viajera. She straightened her shoulders and stepped forward.

"Roth." She motioned for the captain to join her thirteen sailors, then stood before them. "Take off your credits and put them on the ground before you. We'll break them one at a time until we find out who did this."

Roth and two others looked resigned and unfastened anklets and necklaces, dropping them into the dust at their feet. The others glanced at each other.

"Why should we?" one asked, a small fair woman with a chipped front tooth.

Marghe's heart was thumping. There was nothing to make these women do as she said. Nothing at all.

"Juomo's right," said a tall woman the color of rich river mud. "We've done nothing wrong. I don't have enough credits to let them get smashed to pieces for nothing. We could sleep aboard."

Several nodded in agreement, and folded their arms.

Marghe looked at Zabett. "Perhaps Zabett would agree to

replace any genuine tokens that get broken?" Zabett nodded. The innkeeper was on her side, at least. Maybe this would not be so bad after all.

The sailors still looked stubborn. Roth looked at them one by one. "I agreed with Zabett that the journeywomen should sort this dispute, Juomo, Tillis. This is the way they're doing it. If you don't like it, elect another captain."

Marghe saw by Roth's easy stance that the captain knew the sailors would not go that far; she began to enjoy herself. This might work.

The women muttered, but began to strip themselves of their wealth. Marghe set aside the urge to grin and watched carefully.

One woman placed a string with just two clay disks in the dust; Tillis, four. Juomo, with the chipped tooth, offered a necklace of five.

Tillis looked at Juomo's necklace and frowned. Juomo pretended not to notice. But Marghe did.

She stepped up to Juomo, touched the necklace with one foot. "Perhaps you have more credits than this." She watched Juomo's carotid thump as her pulse increased. "We wish to see it all."

"You're seeing it."

"I don't think so."

Juomo stepped back a little, tucked her thin hair behind her ears nervously.

Marghe was no longer enjoying herself. She held out her hand. "Give me the rest."

Juomo bolted, but Tillis shot out a leg and tumbled her into the dust. The big woman hauled Juomo upright by her belt and casually wrapped one arm around her neck. Tillis yanked up Juomo's sleeve. A string of twenty or thirty credits was wrapped around Juomo's biceps. "Knew she had more," Tillis said with satisfaction. She snapped the leather thong and unthreaded one of the clay disks. She dropped it in Marghe's outstretched hand. "Try this."

Zabett was there now, and Roth and Thenike. And the other sailors were picking up their dusty credits.

"Leave them awhile," Marghe said, "until we've tested these."

"You can't smash my credits!" Juomo shouted.

Tillis shook her. "Shut up. If it's real, then you can have one of mine." She grinned at Marghe. "Test it, journeywoman."

Marghe was not sure she would be able to tell a dud from the real thing. She held out the disk to Zabett. "I think we should give Zabett the privilege."

AFTER THE excitement in the courtyard, lunch was late. Marghe and Thenike ate outside. The clouds were thinning, letting afternoon sunshine heat the wood of the table, releasing a spicy, resinous scent. Their plates were almost empty; they were eating fruit.

Thenike had been explaining to Marghe the credit system. Zabett and Scathac gave board and lodgings on a barter system; if an individual or crew had a large item that was worth more than the number of nights or meals needed, then the innkeepers gave them credit, in the form of clay disks. One disk equalled one night. Because of their fixed value, and because the sailors traveled from one place to another, mixing with other travelers, the clay disks had begun to assume the status of portable wealth in those places—ports and well-frequented areas, especially around the coast. Protocurrency. Several years ago, Touk, the innkeeper in Southmeet, had arranged with the two northern innkeepers to honor their credits if Zabett and Scathac would honor hers. They agreed, and now the disks were becoming more popular as currency.

Marghe paused, a goura half-peeled. "But if the disks are being used as currency, then much of it stays in circulation."

"True."

"That's nice for Zabett and Scathac: they only have to honor part of what they receive goods for." She cut several slices from the goura and laid them on a plate. A boatfly hummed near the glistening fruit and Marghe waved it away. "So what effect does this currency have on the trata network?"

"Not much. The clay credits are a coastal phenomenon. Besides, trata is about more than wealth. It's about power, and favors: who is beholden to whom. It's about friendships and enemyhood, a webwork of who is known to be trustworthy and who not. Currency is for strangers."

They chewed on the fruit for a while.

Marghe remembered the panic on Juomo's face as she tried to run, as she tried to get away from her, from Marghe. No one had ever run from her before. "What will happen to her?"

"Juomo? All her credits will be taken and smashed. Those that prove to be genuine will be replaced by Zabett and Scathac. But they won't ever let her stay at their inn again. And Roth will be looking for a new hand. I doubt anyone else will take her on board, unless they're desperate."

"But what will she do?"

Thenike shrugged and ate another piece of fruit.

It was harsh punishment: Juomo would not be able to work from North Haven, no one would give her shelter, and even if all her other credits turned out to be genuine, she would not have enough to buy herself a boat to leave. It seemed there were no second chances when people could afford to lose so little. Marghe wondered if she would have been so quick to judge if she had known.

AFTERNOON TURNED to dusk and brought with it a warm wind from the southeast. Marghe and Thenike ate their evening meal outside in the fountain courtyard, enjoying the warm smells of grass and blossom and forest along with several others. More who were not eating, or who had already eaten, began to drift into the courtyard, sitting on the fountain rim, the stone flags, benches, the roots of trees. Waiting.

Waiting, Marghe realized, for her and Thenike to tell them the news. And more than that: Roth's story would have traveled by now. They wanted to see the viajera from another world.

Her mouth went dry and she had to control her breathing to get her heartrate down to normal.

"It was a good winter in Ollfoss," Thenike began conversationally, "and a better spring. The crops will be early, and big. Marghe here knows about the gardens, about the soil and the seeds." She gestured to Marghe.

Pretend you're talking to one person, Thenike had said, *a person who listens hard and exclaims in all the right places, and imagine what that person would like to hear, how you might make the news more interesting for them. If the person is a fisher, and it's a tale of the plains, tell her what she might need to know to understand the story.* So Marghe looked up at the women gathered in the courtyard at the inn of North Haven and pretended she was telling her story to Holle, of Singing Pastures.

"I can tell you about the gardens on the edge of Moanwood, but my story starts a long way before that. It starts further away than Ollfoss, though that's part of it; it starts further away than the camp of the Echraidhe, though I spent some time there. Indeed," she said, "it was on Tehuantepec that I nearly lost my life and my will. But my story starts beyond even Singing Pastures and Holme Valley; it goes back to that place called Port Central." She waited just a fraction longer than necessary. "You will have heard of it."

Nods. Some grins, some scowls. Marghe looked for Roth's face, found it. Addressed it directly. "That's where I'm from. Port Central. I and all the other women from Port Central come from another world. Some of you already know this from the stories of other viajeras. You will have heard that we are stupid, with less brains than a taar or one of your own children. Taars, you might say, have more sense than to trigger burns. Children can deepsearch."

"And you stay huddled up inside that Port like children stranded in the woods," a woman with leathery brown skin remarked.

"True. But children learn. And we are learning. Look at me. I know better than to tread on burnstone. I deepsearched and chose a name. I carry a child in my belly, soestre to the one growing inside Thenike." She looked around the courtyard of faces: some were skeptical, some interested, one or two cynical, but none were hostile. "Some of you will know that what I say is true: your mothers' many-times-great-grandmothers all came from a world other than this. Probably from the same one as I did." She paused. "How many of you have had strange dreams of falling from the sky, or have walked with your ancestors as they saw this place for the first time?"

There were a few uneasy glances. She heard one clear "Aye" from the back of the crowd.

"Your ancestors learned. As I've learned." General nods.

"You seem to be the only one, though," Roth said. "According to the viajera Kuorra the rest of you are huddling in that Port and not coming out. For anything."

"I don't think I am the *only* one. But I'm one of the first. And when I tell you my story, you'll understand why."

"Tell the story, then," Tillis called, in high good humor. She drank from an olla goblet. "I want to know what's been going on since we left land."

"And when was that?"

"Last Harvest Moon."

"Well, last Harvest Moon, I was just landing here on this world for the first time . . ."

And Marghe told her story. She had learned a great deal from Thenike: in those places where the pain was still too raw she told her story in a ritual cadence that forbade interruption, but most of the time she just talked, and now and again a woman would ask her a question, or add something.

It was not just Marghe's story, of course. Much of the tale was news that these people needed to know: that there was tribe feud between Echraidhe and Briogannon, and it was probably dangerous to cross Tehuantepec for a while; a reiteration of the fact that Marghe, a woman from the other world, had been able to deep-search and make soestre in her belly and Thenike's, which held all kinds of interesting implications for the future; that these foreigners from another place had struck trata with Cassil of Holme Valley—there was much thoughtful rubbing of chins at that news; that the harvest of Ollfoss would be very good this year, which meant good opportunities for traders.

The moons were up when Marghe paused in the middle of a sentence to sip at her water, only to find the cup empty. She looked into the empty cup, letting the pause lengthen. The evening was chill with night breezes.

"I'm tired," she said at last, regretful, "and near the end of my story tonight." She did not want the evening to end. "There will be more tomorrow."

After Marghe and Thenike left the courtyard, they walked for a while quietly, both wrapped under the same cloak. Marghe watched the stars, listening to the far-off hiss and drag of waves on the shore and slapping up against the wharf.

She was a viajera. For the rest of her life she would travel and tell stories and judge disputes. It would rarely be as easy as it had been today, she knew, but she found she did not mind. She had found what it was she had been looking for; she had a place in the world, a place she had made. She touched the suke resting against her breast. She was Marghe Amun. The complete one. She felt at peace.

She stopped and kissed Thenike softly, slowly, running her fingers up through her heavy hair. "Come to bed."

Chapter Fifteen

THE DAYS grew warmer, and the nights soft. Marghe took turns with Thenike to tell the news to the new faces and old that gathered in the courtyard of the inn. Roth and her sailors said goodbye on the fourth day and left to sail east, to the Necklace Islands. Marghe did not know what happened to Juomo.

One hot day, their ninth in North Haven, Marghe and Thenike were in the kitchen getting cool water before Marghe resumed her drumming practice. Zabett found them.

"There's a kinswoman come to see you. She's in the courtyard."

When they stepped back out into the heat of the courtyard, Leifin was sitting with one hand in the fountain, her two large hip packs by her feet, looking about. She was wearing a thin-strapped tunic and Marghe was shocked to see how much weight she had lost in so few days; the tendons in her neck stood out like cables. Leifin watched them as they approached, examining them first from one eye then the other. Like a bird of prey.

"Leifin, what's happened?"

"I was hunting," Leifin said dismissively.

"What brings you here?"

"I've brought some trade goods, and a message." She wiped her hand dry on her trews and opened the pouch at her belt, took out a message cord. "For you. I don't think it's good news."

Marghe took it and read the knots one by one.

To Marghe Amun, and to the viajera Thenike, greetings. Danner, head-woman of the Terrene, has refused trata aid to Cassil of Holme Valley and thereby places herself in peril at a time when she most needs support against those who would seek to harm her and the other Terrene. Holme Valley and Singing Pastures are threatened: by the tribes Echraidhe and Briogannon, united under one they name Uaithne, the Death Spirit. If you have any influence over Danner, use it. May your children come into a peaceful world. By the hand of T'orre Na, viajera.

"What . . ." She read them again, carefully, feeling the knots one by one with her fingertips. Sweet gods. How could Danner be so stupid? And the news about Uaithne . . . Oh gods, please let it not be true.

"What will you do, sister?"

"I don't know." She handed the cord to Thenike. "Does that say what I think it says?"

Thenike read the message out loud. It did.

"Why's Danner doing this, and what does T'orre Na mean by 'at a time when she most need support against those who would seek to harm her'?" She paced. "I think Danner's in trouble."

"She will be, if she disregards trata," Leifin said.

Marghe ignored her and continued pacing. "I think something must have happened to make Company react at last." What, exactly, was relatively unimportant. What mattered was that Danner was in trouble, and about to make it ten times worse for herself if she refused Cassil's request. And Uaithne . . . Why didn't the others, Aoife or the Levarch, stop her? She wiped her forehead. Damn this heat.

She had thought that, maybe, Aoife would see reason before Uaithne's madness swallowed them all. She had hoped that her words had made sense to the fierce, dark tribeswoman, that Aoife would do something to control her soestre. Instead, it seemed the violence within Uaithne had ignited into a flame that was now sweeping across the northern continent.

"I have to go back to Port Central."

Thenike looked troubled. "The journey's long, and not easy."

"Some of this is my fault: I made the trata agreement in the first place. It's my fault that I didn't make the importance of it sufficiently clear to Danner."

"Perhaps."

Marghe did not listen. "And it may well be that Uaithne's madness might not have . . . That my presence there, feeding into that stupid, stupid myth . . . Thenike, I have to go. I might be able to do something." She did not know what, but she had to try. She felt involved.

Thenike put her arm around Marghe's shoulders. "Perhaps we could talk later," she said to Leifin.

"Of course." Leifin stood up. "When you've recovered from this bad news."

"Speak to Zabett about a room. We'll find you later, talk about how things go with the family, about your trade goods."

"Yes." Leifin shouldered her bag, turned to go.

Marghe forced herself to speak. "Leifin?" Leifin turned back, surprised. "I'm glad to see you." And she was. Unfathomable motives or not, Leifin was kin.

Leifin nodded, and strode away.

They went back into the kitchen. It was too warm inside, but Marghe felt safer, more secure, indoors. Scathac was nowhere to be seen. They took their water to the table and sipped for a while without saying anything.

"I have to go, Thenike. Even if the family expects me to remain at Ollfoss. I'm responsible for what I set in motion."

"Responsible, too, to your kin."

"I know. But I have to do this."

"If you feel you must, then you must. I'll come with you."

Marghe reached for Thenike's hand. They were quiet for a moment.

"So," Thenike said eventually. "How will you go to them? As

Marguerite Taishan, the one who should have 'done something,' or as the viajera Marghe Amun, offering advice and mediation on a trata matter?"

Choose, Thenike was saying: choose who you are and where your loyalties lie.

Marghe held the suke that bumped gently against her chest. "How will we get there?"

Thenike seemed to accept the change of mood. "Find out who has a ship going south and is willing to go through the Mouth of the Grave, to High Beaches or Pebble Fleet."

A picture of the Ollfoss map appeared in Marghe's head, clear and sharp. She could remember every detail. *We remember,* Thenike had said, *viajeras remember.* Marghe wondered if she would ever grow tired of this new memory.

"Which would be best?"

"A ship to Pebble Fleet would have to travel around the Horn, which would add time to the journey, but then it's a comparatively short distance overland to Port Central. If we ship to High Beaches, then we can go up the Glass River part of the way . . . About twenty days' travel, either way."

Twenty days. And they would have to wait for a ship. Say a month. What might Danner do in a month?

THENIKE WAS down at the docks, asking after ships south. Marghe stepped out into the sunshine of late morning. There was no breeze and it was already hot. Leifin and two other women were in the fountain courtyard, laughing, talking, drinking wine. Leifin was showing the two women her carvings. She had not noticed Marghe.

The carvings were beautiful. A set of three bowls that fitted together, one inside the other, so perfectly that they appeared to be one bowl instead of three. The wood gleamed softly; Marghe recognized it as the same block Leifin had been carving that morning in the great room when they had discussed her petition to join the family. Next were two hand mirrors, the reflecting surface made of olla. The carving was breathtaking: natural-looking flowers twined around the glass, turned into grasses around the handle. The two women handled the wood carefully, but wistfully; it seemed Leifin was out of luck. They shook their heads and handed the bowls and mirror back. Leifin did not seem dismayed but fished out a large white hip pouch with beautifully worked and braided thongs. She handed it to the nearest woman.

Marghe edged closer to listen. Leifin, with her back turned, would not see her.

"It's very soft. What is it?"

The other woman took it, fingered it. Leifin studied her with that bird-of-prey gaze, one eye then the other. "The bag of a male goth I trapped."

Marghe went still. The scrotal sac of a goth. She remembered Thenike's song, the stones that had been raised so many years ago. Leifin had been there for Thenike's song. She knew what she had done.

Leifin took back the pouch, tipped some small white bones into her palm. "Goth knucklebones. Those big ones there are its thumbs. Two on each hand. Looks like they'd be strong creatures, doesn't it? Like they'd be fearsome to hunt. But they're not. Just like big taars. Docile. But cunning." She glanced up, saw Marghe, and said, in explanation, "I'd heard how white their fur is, I wanted it. I really wanted that fur. You can do a lot with good fur. You've seen what I can do. So I said to myself, how can I get the animal without damaging its fur? A trap, that's how. A pit. It took me three days to dig it—I'd judged by their tracks that they were big, so the pit had to be good and deep. Then I had to make it invisible. I used stuff from the forest floor so after a while I couldn't even tell where the pit was myself. Then I hid and waited. You have to be very patient when you're trapping. It's like carving." She gestured to the bowls sitting on the edge of the fountain. "I waited for days, more days than I can remember. I ran out of food after three."

That helped to explain the weight loss.

"It was dark when it finally came along the trail. It was big, big as a tree, and its eyes glowed in the dark. I think if it hadn't been for its eyes, I wouldn't have known it was there. It moved quietly as the coming of spring, pulling barkweed off the trees with enormous hands and stuffing it right in its mouth like it was feast bread." Leifin nodded to herself, remembering. "Yes, it was very quiet, but I was quieter."

Marghe imagined Leifin waiting, silent and still, patient. Methodical. She watched the women weigh the knuckles in their hands, roll the pale bones between their fingers. Only a few days ago, they had been part of a living, breathing being.

"It walked along the trail, unsuspecting, and fell right down the hole. It hooted and hooted. I've never heard anything like it. I don't mind telling you, I got scared. I thought all its cousins and sisters and mothers and aunts were going to come running and snatch me up with their big hands and stuff me in their big, horny mouths, like barkweed. After a while, though, when nothing happened, it just shut up, so I crawled to the edge of the pit and looked down. It saw me, and hooted, softly, like it was asking a question. I just shook my head and tried to explain that I would take care of its fur better than he could, that I'd make it beautiful, that hundreds of women would admire it." She looked at Marghe. "I told it that perhaps its fur would buy many useful things for my family. It didn't understand, of course."

Leifin broke off, watching the nearest woman hefting the bones thoughtfully. "This is the first goth I know of that's been trapped." *Killed,* Marghe wanted to correct, *killed,* and wondered why she was still listening. But she felt compelled: she was a viajera, she had to bear witness to this. "Those bones are very rare. They might even have special healing properties." But the woman just nodded, and did not yet seem disposed to bargain.

"So, I sat there by the pit and watched the goth die. They're tough. It had no food and no water, but it took ten days to die. Ten days. After three or four days it started scrabbling around. It tried sucking the dirt at one point. Thirst drove it mad, I suppose. I wondered about helping it along a bit, killing it with my spear, but that would've put a hole in the pelt and put blood all over it. That would have been a waste. So I just watched. After a while, it seemed to give up. It just sat in a corner of the pit and sort of hooted to itself." She stopped. "Perhaps it was singing. Anyway, it sounded terrible, so I threw things at it, nothing that would damage it, of course, soft stuff mostly."

Marghe could imagine. Perhaps the goth had been trying to taunt Leifin into killing it. But Leifin herself must have been more than half mad at this point. How many days had she gone without food?

"It hooted on and on and on. I don't mind telling you how relieved I was when it got too weak to make any noise. A day or so after it shut up, it lay down on the floor and didn't move. By this time, of course, I was hungry myself. It would have been easy at this point to relax and go forage in the forest, but I waited."

Marghe imagined a gaunt and more-than-half-crazy Leifin, obsessed with watching the goth starve to death.

"Why not just go away a few days and come back when it was dead?" one of the other women asked.

"You don't understand. I wanted that pelt perfect. Perfect. If I hadn't been there the whole time, who knows what or who might have come along and chewed on it when it was dead. No, I had to stay there, share its death."

Leifin shook her head, as if to clear it. "So, anyway, eventually it lay down and died. But I waited awhile, just to make sure. Then I lowered a noose down, and strangled it for a while. It's always best to make sure. But it didn't move. It was definitely dead. It took me a whole day to get it out of the pit."

Marghe did not want to hear how smart Leifin had been to get the enormous goth out of the pit by herself. Leifin made it all sound so reasonable. It was not reasonable. Leifin was obsessed by perfection and possessions. It was an obsession that prevented her from seeing any difference between carving something beautiful and killing another thinking, feeling being for its fur.

"—and the skull is enormous." Leifin held her hands about two feet apart. "I think I'll lime it clean, carefully, then wax it. Beautiful. Someone will buy it. And the pelt . . . it took me two days' careful cutting just to get it off. The starvation helped, of course. It was virtually hanging off already. I'm going to take my time curing it. It's the most fabulous—"

Marghe walked away. If only she had the same talent Thenike had; if only she could take Leifin's own words, and turn them back on the hunter, make her *see* what she had done, make her *feel* it in heart and gut; show her what that goth had gone through just so Leifin could have a pelt to play with. But maybe she could. Maybe Thenike would teach her how to reach into another's psyche with words and music and a powerful beat. Then she could change people like Leifin.

But would it do any good?

She stopped in midstride. Thenike had already sung for Leifin, had already made her see that killing goth was not the same as killing wirrels. There was something fundamentally twisted inside Leifin. Perhaps nothing, no one, could mend it. Except Leifin herself.

Marghe thought about her mother, of the miners on Beaver, of Danner, of Aoife; of herself. People could not be made to change. It had taken her a long time to learn that. People had to want to change themselves.

"THE *NEMORA'S* due back in port in four days," Thenike said.

"Vine's ship?"

"It's been along the coast to Luast. It's due back here to pick up some pelt and wool"—Marghe thought of the goth—"and continue on to High Beaches."

"Will they take us on board?"

Thenike grinned. "Ships are pleased to have a viajera. Two is twice as good. Being at sea can be boring. We'll tell them stories and sing them songs and they'll take us wherever we want to go out of sheer gratitude."

Marghe smiled. Being a viajera was not all fun and free rides. "We'll have to send messages to Danner, and Cassil."

"And High Beaches. We'll need a guide across the countryside. If the rainfall's been low, the Glass might not support *Nid-Nod's* draft and we'll need the use of one of their punts to get up the river."

THE FIRST day at sea, they kept in sight of land. Thenike was taking a nap—too hot out of the shade, she said—but Marghe stood on *Nemora's* deck, aft of the livestock pen, taking advantage of the cool sea breeze on her neck. The sun streamed down from a dark blue sky and shivered back from the surface of the water, bright enough to hurt her eyes. Thenike's skiff bobbed behind them, secured firmly by two cables.

All the sailors worked bare-chested. Some wore breast straps; some, the younger ones whose hands were not yet callused enough to deal with coarse wet rope without damage, wore leather palm straps. Some wore caps to protect their hair from salt spray; some did not bother. Marghe watched them work to swing the mainsail and the small bowsail into the breeze, and wondered how it was to spend a life on the water.

The shore was a greenish-blue line of forest. That night, or the next day, they would swing out due east to find the safe channel through the Mouth of the Grave. Open sea for a while. Marghe did not look forward to the prospect. She was used to large vessels of alloy and plastic, equipped with satellite navigation, and *Nemora* seemed too small, too frail.

The ship was about seventy feet long; the rudder was fixed, in the stern, and the ship steered by means of a tiller, not a wheel. The top of the mainmast still had twigs attached to the wood; the yard was made of two small lengths of wood lashed together with rope. The deck was not solid, just planks resting on thwarts, easily removed for larger cargo. Some of them looked new, and smelled of raw, fresh lumber. The only cabin was a wicker-walled enclosure in the bows, used mainly as a shade when the sun was fierce. At night, the crew slept on deck. One enormous rope ran from one end of the ship to the other over forked posts and disappeared around the stern and bows. Marghe touched it thoughtfully.

"Big, isn't it?" The accent was not one Marghe had heard before. Southern, perhaps. She turned to find a tall, broad-shouldered woman standing beside her. "I've seen you with Thenike. You must be Marghe Amun. I'm Vine."

She did look a little like Roth: same height and cap, and clinking with clay disks. But her face was more leathery, and her eyes were hazel with white lines in the tan fanning out from the corners. She was not wearing a shirt. Marghe found it hard to keep her eyes off the terrible scars on her bare back: a web of ugly white and pink welts, like worms. "It is big, yes. I've been trying to figure out what it's for."

"Stops the ship hogging." Those eyes scanned the horizon, the deck, the sails, then back again. Marghe found it disconcerting. But the eyes came back to Marghe's face long enough for Vine to see that Marghe did not understand. "Drooping at the ends," she explained.

"Drooping?" They used a rope to tie the ship together?

The white lines around Vine's eyes disappeared as her face wrinkled up in a smile. "Don't worry. It's something all ships do. Or would do if it wasn't for the rope. That's what it's for. Keeps the bows pointing up nicely."

"That doesn't sound too good."

"It's the safest ship in the world," Vine said with confidence. "Look, here." She pointed over the side at the overlapping planks; Marghe looked, too. "Clinker-built. I helped to choose the wood myself." She straightened, scanned the ship again. Marghe was beginning to get used to it. "What do you know about wood? Not much? Well, the first thing about building a ship is getting the right timber. Depending what grain you use, how the wood is sawn, you can just about eliminate the effects of hogging. So for these lengths I chose wood that was quarter-sawn, so it warps against the hogging."

Marghe nodded, understanding the principle if not the details.

"See this"—Vine pointed to the tiller, fixed to an enormous paddlelike rudder—"not many ships have these. They're much better than those side-rigged things you'll see a lot of around here. You can only dock on one side of the boat if the rudder isn't in the stern. The *Nemora* can dock anywhere. Steers better, too. Mind you, that's partly because we've got the artemon. Foresail," she explained, for Marghe's benefit. They went over to the mainmast, picking their way past what seemed to Marghe a jumble of ropes, strung in no particular order. "See these side stays and shrouds?"

She was talking about the thick ropes running from the top of the mast to the decking. "Lots of ships don't have these. Only backstays. But these shrouds mean we can take sideways pressure on the mast, too. We can tack. We don't always have to have the wind right behind us."

Marghe nodded. If Vine said so.

"And when the wind gets too much," Vine was saying, "we can furl the sail. No boom, you see."

The *Nemora* still looked like something from the Bayeux tapestry, but maybe they would survive the Mouth of the Grave after all.

Marghe and Vine stood in companionable silence for a while.

"You found each other, then." Thenike's eyes were soft with sleep, and there were creases on her face. She was wearing a pair of short breeches and her hair was up inside a cap. "Hot out here." She slid one arm around Marghe's waist, the other around Vine's.

"It'll get worse before it gets better." Vine was scanning the horizon again, but Marghe noticed the sailor was leaning into Thenike's arm. They were very comfortable with each other. Old, old friends. Here was a part of Thenike's past; she wanted to know all of it.

"How long have you two known each other?"

"Long enough," Vine said, without turning, but she smiled out at the horizon. "Hasn't she told you how she got that scar on her thumb, yet?"

"No."

"Well, then, story for story, viajera. I'll tell you how I met Thenike, here, if you tell me how she found you."

"Let's find some shade if we're going to talk all afternoon," Thenike suggested.

"I like the heat," Marghe said.

"Good, but sun and water can burn you faster than you think. We need shade."

Marghe wondered if the scars on Vine's back burned more easily than the rest.

"And something to occupy our hands," added Vine. "We can work while we talk."

Soon they were seated in the shadow of the wicker wall, splicing rope. Marghe watched the other two; she did not have their skill and speed born of long practice, but after a while she was able to do a passable job.

"It was fourteen summers ago," Vine said, "and I came into Southmeet after my first voyage to Eye of Ocean. The trading had gone well, and the island was a beautiful place, but the voyage was long and we'd hit some bad weather on the way back. We'd been on short rations for a while, and had had to work hard to get home, which made me bad-tempered. I climbed up out of the ship's boat and onto the wharf, and nearly tripped over a young woman with the thickest, blackest hair I've ever seen."

"Thenike," Marghe guessed.

"Thenike," Vine agreed. "She was lying down in the sunshine on the grass that grows by the wharf, half asleep. Drums getting tight in the heat. Leading the life of leisure, I thought. I was young—"

"And foolish," Thenike said with a smile. "The two generally go together."

"I was young," Vine said, ignoring the interruption, "and not as knowledgeable as I am now, and it seemed to me all of a sudden that viajeras never had to do much for themselves. Always eating other people's food and getting free rides. Just for telling stories. And here was me, having almost starved to bring back things that this young woman would use but not appreciate."

"You made those feelings quite plain, as I recall."

"I made some loud comments about lazy good-for-nothings and how some people had never done a useful day's work in their lives. And this woman, who I thought might have been quite pretty if she hadn't looked so lazy, opened one eye and said, 'Well, sailor, what is it that you think you can do that I can't?' "

"I was angry," Thenike said. "I'd been up all night helping a local healer with a difficult birth, and here was this . . . this lout disturbing my rest. She was good to look at, too, which somehow made it worse."

"So I challenged her to a contest. And she—"

"I was really cross by this time, and wanted to beat her at something she probably thought she was superior at."

"So she challenged me to a fish-gutting contest. She was good, too," Vine said, admiration in her voice for that young woman of long ago, "but I'd spent most of my life gutting fish. There could only be one winner."

"I couldn't accept that, though, and just went faster and faster."

"Until the slick fish guts proved her undoing. The knife slipped, and suddenly there was red everywhere. Blood all over the fish, all over the docks, all over my barrel of fillets. And there was Thenike, hand gaping wide and bleeding like a stuck taar, looking furious."

"I was furious. It hurt. And I knew I'd been stupid."

"But she was still clutching the filleting knife, and I thought she was going to attack me with it, so we both just stood there, while she bled more."

Thenike and Vine were both quiet for a moment, remembering. A sail flapped noisily overhead. The wind was picking up.

"And then?" Marghe prompted.

"She threw down the knife and stalked off, and all I had left of the encounter were two barrels of fish and a puddle of blood and fish guts. I thought that was that, until the next day. We were at the inn, drinking more wine than was good for us to celebrate the fact that we were alive, and rich, when in walked the fish-gutting via-jera with her hand wrapped in bandages. 'I'm going to sing you something,' she said, and snatched Byelli's harp right out of her hands and began to play. And you know what a voice she has."

Marghe did. She loved to listen to Thenike sing, with her smoky, rich voice and multiple harmonics.

"Well, it seemed to me all of a sudden that she was beautiful, and I kept her singing half the night."

"Which is what I wanted, of course," Thenike said smugly.

"And then it seemed that she thought I was beautiful—"

"Which you are."

"—which I am, to some. And I ended up inviting her to come to my room and play the harp. And four days later when we left to sail to the Necklace Islands, I asked her to come along. We sailed together for two years. As lovers, then friends. Then Thenike decided it was time to move on, go where she could work properly as a viajera, where she was most needed, and we've seen each other only five times in the last twelve years." She put down the rope she was working on and leaned over to hug Thenike. "It's good to be sailing with you again, even if it's only for a little while." She released her, held her at arm's length. "You're looking good."

"I'm feeling good, better than I have in years."

And Marghe felt a sudden, fierce love for Thenike, and the heat seemed softer, the sea more blue, and the world more alive than it had been.

THEY TOOK half a day tacking back and forth to find the right current, then shot through the Mouth of the Grave, passing within spitting distance of rocky teeth sharp enough to rip the bottom out of the *Nemora*. Marghe was more exhilarated than scared by the danger and the heady rush of white water.

Once they were past the Summer Islands, the weather changed dramatically: the light breezes were replaced by hot winds heavy with moisture. The days were languorous and thick, and Marghe spent hours at the taffrail, gazing out on a sea that shimmered like a dragon's wing and a sky that was glazed with soft light. Once, Marghe saw a bird with a wingspan of more than three meters skimming the swells; its third, fixed wing was the color of cinnamon.

The *Nemora* plowed steadily southwest, and the sea changed slowly from blues and grays to a deep, sliding palette of greens and azures: Silverfish Deeps. Marghe saw thousands of silverfish, gliding beneath the surface in great shoals that flickered and swung silver like a bead curtain as they changed direction.

Marghe and Thenike were on deck, Marghe sitting comfortably on the sun-warmed planking near enough to the rails to watch the wake curve out behind them, Thenike stretched out with her head on Marghe's thigh. It was morning, and a sailor, Ash, was in the bows with a sandglass and a log attached to a length of rope tied off at intervals with knots. Ash threw the log, counted, and when another sailor in the stern shouted, tipped the sandglass and hauled the log back aboard. They did this three times.

"What are they doing?"

"Judging our speed." Thenike raised herself onto her elbow. "Hoi, Ash! How fast?"

"Nine knots," the sailor called.

"Good speed. And yesterday?"

"About the same."

"My thanks." She lay back down. "If the wind holds, we'll be at High Beaches in three or four days." She closed her eyes.

Marghe stroked her hair. Four days, then perhaps another six or seven to get to Port Central. Very good time. Something bright on the horizon caught her eye. "There's something out there."

"Um," Thenike said without opening her eyes.

"It looks big, and bright. Seems to be traveling towards us." She watched a moment. "I think it's moving faster than we are."

Thenike sat up, peered between the rails, then stood for a better view. The object grew. "A seavane," she breathed, "and it's going to pass us."

The two sailors with the log and sandglass had seen it, too, and paused to watch.

Its submerged body, rolling out of the water now and again, scales glistening, was immense, but it was the vane itself, like a sail twice as tall as the *Nemora*'s mast, that would glide through Marghe's dreams for years afterward. It flared between the sky and sea like an enormous stained-glass window, with slender support-ing ribs like the great vaulting arches of a cathedral roof. Sunlight streamed through the transparent webbing and was split into soft, shimmering azures and indigos and golds and greens that cycled through the spectrum, over and over, endlessly, like a Gregorian chant.

The wind direction altered slightly, and the ribs splayed open like the fingers of a fan, turning the sail, stretching it tight enough to show for a moment the vascular system, like a filigree of tarnished sil-ver among the amethyst and aquamarine, before it picked up speed and hissed through the water away from them.

THE *NEMORA* swung out of the deep channel onto a more westerly heading. The weather changed again, cooling a little, clouding over. By the time the shoreline lay on the horizon, the world had turned gray. Marghe was not looking forward to making landfall; it would be a long, hot walk to Port Central, and she was not sure Danner would welcome her opinion of the Mirror's actions.

High Beaches was a forbidding place, all bleak, liver-colored cliffs and rocky promontories rearing from a choppy and restless sea. The *Nemora* weighed anchor, and Marghe and Thenike took the *Nid-Nod* in to a steeply sloping pebble beach. A woman with the same liver-colored eyes as the cliff rock met them. She was thin, with lank brown hair rising from a high widow's peak and the kind of sallow complexion that made her look grimy. She introduced herself as Gabbro.

"The viajeras Marghe Amun and Thenike, sa?" Marghe nodded. "I'm to be your guide through the burnstone to the west," she said, and set off up the beach in a ground-eating stride. "If we hurry, we can make a good start today."

They did not follow her. "We can use the skiff," Thenike called. Gabbro turned; reluctantly, Marghe thought. "The wind should be steady enough to take us upstream faster than we could walk. That is, if the spring rains were heavy enough."

"Sa, sa. The river's deep enough."

"The skiff will save time," Marghe said.

"Sa, sa." Gabbro headed back down the beach toward the *Nid-Nod*.

"But we'll need to eat before we set out."

"We can eat on the way. The silverfish shoals are due before the end of the moon. I have to be back by then. Come, we'll need ropes."

After so long aboard ship, Marghe struggled to keep up on the sliding pebbles, and she was sure she would be sick of hearing *sa, sa* before dark, but she said nothing. This had been her own idea.

THEY WERE four days on the river Glass, four lazy days of trimming the sail, sitting at the tiller, and watching the banks go past. Marghe spent endless hours trying not to think about how she would persuade Danner to honor trata, concentrating instead on the variety of plants and animals they saw: nutches, knobby dark reptilian predators sunning themselves on stones; sleths, which Marghe at first mistook for bunches of reeds until one exploded into motion as a swarm of boatflies hummed past, catching half the cloud in its sticky fronds; pelmats, slow green amphibious things that crawled on the riverbed, and sometimes up onto the hull of the *Nid-Nod*.

In the evenings, they tied up on the bank and Gabbro caught fish for their supper. Sometimes Thenike told a story.

Marghe hardly tasted the fish, barely listened to the stories. Her stomach felt full of rocks. The closer they came to Port Central, the more she lost herself in trying to find a solution to her problem: how to make Danner do the right thing. How? Danner would do as she thought best for her personnel. The difficulty lay in persuading the Mirror commander that honoring trata was the best thing, in the long term.

Marghe went over and over in her mind that original report on trata to Danner, searching for flaws. She found none. It was all there: long-term and short-term benefits. What more could she add? She had no idea, but she knew she had to try. She just had to hope that presenting the arguments in person would carry more force. The queasy weight in her stomach told her otherwise. No. The problem was not in her arguments, her initial reasoning: something was happening that was forcing Danner into this decision. Something of which Marghe knew nothing. What? She could only assume some kind of Company threats. What had Sara Hiam said? *That cruiser out there isn't hanging around for the view. The* Kurst's *a military vessel . . . Every time I wake up, I wonder, Is this going to be my last day?*

Marghe picked absently at her fish. It was almost cold, but she did not notice. What had changed to turn that ever-present threat into something more urgent, something that made Danner believe trata should take second place?

The only thing she knew of was the fact that she was no longer protected by the vaccine. But that would not precipitate Company action, not of and by itself. If the vaccine had been proven ineffective, maybe. But her message had been quite specific: she had chosen not to continue. As far as Company was concerned, that decision would only result in unpleasant consequences for her personally. It should not affect Company's attitude toward Danner or Hiam. In the long term, Company would be philosophical and simply try the vaccine again with someone else. After all, it was not as though the damn thing did not work . . .

"Amu? Marghe?"

"Um?"

"That fish is beyond eating."

Marghe looked at it. Thenike was right. She threw it onto the pile of leftovers that they would bury in the morning before they set sail again. Gabbro was toasting some gram roots in the embers. They smelled sweet. All of a sudden, Marghe was restless.

"I'm going to walk for a while," she said, scrambling to her feet and brushing sand from her legs. She faced west, where the last bloody rags of sunset lay scattered on the tops of the distant hills.

"Do you want company?"

Marghe nodded. They walked in silence, occasionally stopping to skip stones on the river, or to listen to the steady, reassuring flow of the water. It was warm, and insects hummed and buzzed. The evening gradually seeped into Marghe, loosening her shoulders, straightening her back.

"That's better," Thenike said.

They walked farther, then Marghe stopped to watch the last of the dark red slide from the sky. Inky clouds swept across the sky, and the air stirred with a warm breeze from the hills. "I have seen dawn and sunset on moors and windy hills," she quoted quietly, "coming in solemn beauty like slow old tunes of Spain." A viajera's memory was good for remembering poetry.

They walked back hand in hand, and ate hot, charred gram roots with Gabbro.

ON THE fifth day, at the foot of the Yelland hills, they beached the boat.

"From here, we walk."

Port Central lay southwest, but they had to detour through the Yelland hills, zigzagging northwest then southeast to avoid burnstone and the possibility of triggering a burn that might smolder for a generation. It would add two or three days to their journey, Gabbro said.

Marghe walked behind Thenike, trying to imagine how it would be to feel the ground suddenly split between her feet, hot gases exploding, sending them tumbling into rocks; the eerie silence while they lay stunned, then the molten burnstone bubbling up through the turf, forming pools and sinks, setting the grass on fire . . .

The grass was brown from lack of rain, and the hot winds were scratchy with dust. There were no paths, and they had to clamber over outcroppings of needlestone that glittered under the dust and would cut their feet deeply if they slipped. The vegetation was grotesque, shaped by wind and aridity: thick and stunted, with enormous root systems.

On their second day in the hills, they met a band of seven olla shapers, and Weal, their headwoman, invited them to share a meal. Eager to eat something that was not fish or waybread or dried fruit, they accepted.

It was a seasonal camp; the shelters were simple corner posts supporting a roof of wide leaves. There were no walls, and the floors were beaten earth. But the cookfires were big, sunken pits, they had fresh vegetables and ten newly caught wirrels to offer, and a thin and bitter wine.

In return for their hospitality, the olla shapers got a story from Thenike about the nine riding soestre of Singing Pastures who had lived, loved, and died many years ago.

Firelight played on the women gathered around the cooking pit, reflected from rapt faces shiny with wirrel fat, and as Marghe listened to the ageless rhythms of the story, the repetition and ritual description, she knew a stranger looking at the listeners would be unable to tell her apart from the others.

The story was interrupted by the rustle and thump of a landing herd bird. Thenike fell silent as it waddled into the firecircle. It had a message cord around its leg. The viajeras and Gabbro politely looked away as the headwoman unwound the cord and read it: it could be private kin news, or trata business.

"Part of the message concerns the viajeras," Weal said. "It is addressed to all in the north, and asks that if we meet you, we are to pass on the words of the viajera, T'orre Na. *Thenike and Marghe Amun, greetings. Danner is heading north to Holme Valley and the pastures with sixty of her kith, and more following, to fight the tribes. I go with her.*"

There was silence. One of the women coughed and the herd bird humphed and raised its crest.

"That's all of the message?" Marghe asked.

"All concerning you." Weal tucked the cord into her pocket, gesturing for Thenike to go on.

Thenike continued with the story, but Marghe no longer listened. What had happened to change Danner's mind? Sixty Mirrors was a lot of firepower; she must intend serious fighting.

Later, when Marghe and Thenike were lying side by side, too hot for nightbags, Marghe was still wondering what had happened to involve Danner with the tribes. "I don't understand any of this. But I want to find out."

"Then we'll head north in the morning."

"Gabbro won't like it."

"No. But we don't need Gabbro from here. I know the way to Singing Pastures."

They were quiet for a long time. Just before she fell asleep, Marghe asked, "Were there really ever nine soestre?"

"Maybe there were, somewhere," Thenike said, and Marghe knew she was smiling in the dark.

Chapter Sixteen

DANNER STOOD out on the glaring white concrete, waiting for the gig. She was hot, and getting a headache, which she made worse by looking up into the bright summer sky even though she knew they would hear the gig a long time before they saw it.

Day was there, and T'orre Na—it had seemed polite to ask them as guests—and a small honor guard: Lieutenant Lu Wai, Sergeant Kahn, Officers Twissel and Chauhan. Teng should have been there, but the deputy was miles away, investigating a promising site in the southwest at the foot of the Kaharil hills.

Danner made a deliberate effort to not shift from foot to foot. Anything could happen. When—*if*, she amended, *if*—the *Kurst* found out that the orbital station was being abandoned, they might blow the gig out of the sky. Even if they did not, then its passengers were by no means safe: autopilot was fine for landings not involving people, but risky for human cargo, and although Nyo had basic pilot skills, she had not flown anything in over six years.

The sky cracked with sound. Danner jumped, along with

everyone else except Twissel. Good woman under pressure, Danner thought, and filed that knowledge away. The cracking came again, a broader sound this time, then again, and again, until the noise widened into a flat sheet of sound that climbed the register to a roar, then a scream, then a thin, piercing shriek.

"There!"

They all followed Day's pointing finger. A tiny black speck to the northwest, getting rapidly larger. The two sleds detailed as emergency vehicles hissed up onto their cushions of air as their drivers fed power to the motors. Lu Wai signaled to her three officers, and all four snapped down visors and stood to attention.

And suddenly the gig was tearing a tunnel through the air and landing, and Danner grinned, for the immediate worry was over and now here she was, getting ready to meet in person for the first time a woman she had come to know well over the last few months, who had listened when she had needed an ear, had talked when she needed advice, had faced hard decisions without flinching. An ally and friend.

A friend who was coming to stay. A friend.

The gig landed in a ball of heat and noise, adding a black carbon streak to the dozens already crisscrossing the concrete. Its power systems whined. One of the sleds hummed over grass, then concrete, and a tiny figure leaned from the cab to flip open a small panel on the still-warm hull of the gig, then yank a handle. The hatch popped and hissed open. The Mirror pulled down a ramp. Three figures climbed out shakily and onto the sled. One of them waved, and Day and T'orre Na waved back. They were the only ones who did; Danner and the other Mirrors, after hundreds of hours of parade-ground training, did not think to respond. It saddened Danner. What else had been trained out of them? How many other things, human things, would they have to relearn?

The sled hummed back over the concrete and settled five feet from Danner. Sara Hiam climbed down a little unsteadily. Danner saluted, then dropped her hand and smiled instead.

"Welcome!" She held out both hands. Sara took them. She

seemed smaller in real life than on the screen, and thinner. She was trembling.

"Hell of a journey."

"Looked like a good landing." Nyo and Sigrid climbed out of the cab like old women. They, too, looked too thin; Nyo's skin was gray, like hot charcoal. Sigrid was so pale Danner could see the blue lines of veins around her neck and eyes. They both looked as unsteady on their feet as newborn foals. "Welcome," Danner said, troubled, and turned to Sara Hiam. "Is this the gravity?"

"That's part of it, though we've done nothing but exercise this last month." She drew away from Danner gently and looked up into the sky. "I hated to leave. Five years' work up there. Who knows what those bastards will do with it now."

FOUR DAYS later Danner was sitting in her office with the newly returned Teng.

"As you can see," Teng was saying, as she pointed to the screen, "precipitation patterns look favorable. This site in the foothills would be ideal for grain production and for grazing herd beasts."

"Yes. I see." The deputy was looking tired from her trip, and was being more than usually pedantic. "I hear that this site has a name already."

Teng smiled a little. "My team have been calling it Dentro de un Rato."

" 'In a while,' " Danner translated. "A nice enough name, with a good feeling. Sounds like home. But in just four days it already has an Anglo corruption: 'Dun Rats.' What does that say to you?"

Teng said nothing.

Danner sighed, and wished her deputy was someone with a little more imagination, someone she could talk to. Like Sara Hiam. Or even Day and T'orre Na. She made a quick note to talk to the viajera later in the day, find out if there was any reason using this site would antagonize the natives. "Continue."

Teng looked relieved. "Well, there are several springs. Fa'thezam says they're deepwater springs that won't dry up except in the most severe and prolonged drought. In which case we could always run a line from the Ho." She tapped a key. The map widened to include half the continent. "These blue arrows indicate major native trade routes. We can use the Ho to transport our goods for barter: upstream past Three Trees and Cruath, all the way to Holme Valley; downstream to Southmeet and the coastal trade."

"The soil?"

"McIntyre gave the all-clear." Teng consulted her notes, scrolling rapidly. "Rich, well-drained, well-protected by root systems. That means not much danger of erosion. Apparently the—"

"Give me a separate report on that. Let's keep this general. Anything else?"

"It's easily defensible." The map changed to show elevations. Danner nodded. "Plenty of natural resources: clay, wood, workable stone. Olla."

"Has Gautier finished her report on that?"

"Not yet." Again, Teng scrolled busily. "But it looks promising. She says that the chemical valences of the olla are such that if—"

"Later. All I need to know is that progress is being made, and things are looking good. That there are no substantial snags."

"That about sums it up: the more we know about Dentro de un Rato, the better it looks."

Danner turned off the screen. "Tell me, Teng, do you think we could live there if Company cuts us off? If something happened like, oh, say, we lost all our equipment here."

Teng sucked at her lower lip, but Danner made no sign that it was a habit that had always irritated her. Teng was slow, but methodical. Danner had never known her to make a single major mistake: everything was checked and double-checked before Teng would commit herself. Danner trusted Teng's judgment, no matter how impatient she became with her methods.

"Hard to say."

"Take a shot at it." *Don't think,* she wanted to say, *react. Tell me your gut feeling.* But that would only confuse her stolid deputy.

"Well . . ." Teng sucked her lip some more. "If we could start sowing crops now, and if nothing untoward happened—no fires or floods or droughts—and if we had help from the natives: seed stock, a breeding herd, advice, good trade relations . . . then, maybe. Maybe we could." She looked pleased with herself. "Yes, I really think we could."

Danner smiled. "Good. That's good. I want a copy of every report, with your comments. I'll read them tonight. I'll also consult with Day and the viajera T'orre Na, see if we can get a guarantee of that native cooperation." She drummed her fingers a moment. "Yes." She stood up, decisive. "Teng, if you're not too tired, I'd like you to put in some time today and tomorrow laying down a preliminary evacuation plan. I'll rely on you to deal with the broader logistics. If it turns out we hit a major flaw with this site, though I don't think we will, much of the planning could be translated for another site."

Teng did not stand up but shifted uncomfortably in her chair.

"There's something else?"

"Yes."

Danner sat down, gestured for Teng to go on.

"Several people have approached me about . . . about leaving. About taking the gigs up to the *Estrade*."

"Ah." Danner had hoped this would not happen, but there were always those to whom reason meant nothing, who would not believe what they did not want to be true. "How many?"

"Seventeen."

"Seventeen? That'll strain *Estrade*'s life-support systems to the limit."

"They understand that."

Danner sighed. If they did not want to stay, she did not want to keep them. "Very well. But only one gig goes, the other stays here. If they can stand the overcrowding once they're up there, they can sit on top of each other on the way up. If they don't like those arrangements, then tough. We keep one gig here. You never know." Why did she insist on hanging onto these hopes? When Company went, the gig would be useless. Still . . . "Who wants to leave? Anyone we can't afford to lose?"

"Here's a list."

Danner took the flimsy. It was in alphabetical order in Teng's usual methodical style. A name, second from the end, leapt out at her as if it were in thicker, darker print than the rest. "Vincio? Vincio—you're sure?" She felt as though she had been jabbed lightly in the stomach with stiff fingers. She could not believe that Vincio—her loyal assistant, the one who brought her tea every day, who never seemed to sleep, who always knew when Danner could be disturbed and when she needed to be left alone—was leaving. Abandoning her.

She took a deep breath. If Vincio wanted to go, she would not stop her. She rubbed the bridge of her nose, looked at the list again, frowned. "Relman's not on it."

"No."

Danner sighed. Life never worked out the way it should. "Recommendations?"

"Let them go. Let Relman stay. She's a good officer. She'll be especially eager to please, now."

But we're not officers anymore, not any of us, Danner wanted to say. But she did not, because if they were not officers, then what, who, were they? She knew she was not yet ready to face that question; none of them were. They would live the fiction a little while longer: in confused times, people, especially militarily-trained people, liked orders, firm leadership. If she could provide it.

"Give them ten days to think it over. Meanwhile I'll talk to Sigrid and Nyo about making the platform's functions tamperproof, accessible only from our uplink station. We'll need those facilities, especially the satellites, as long as we can get them. I don't want a bunch of disaffecteds screwing with the programs. If we can lock those systems in, then let's let them go."

After she dismissed Teng, Danner read the geologists' reports on Dentro de un Rato. Her thoughts kept wandering. Why did Vincio want to leave? Why did she think she had anything to gain by going up to an orbital station where she had a good chance of dying, either immediately, courtesy of the *Kurst*, or later, due to failed life support? And if—a big *if*—Company did take them all off, where did Vincio expect to spend the rest of her hopelessly contaminated life?

Danner contemplated calling Vincio into her office and asking her why straight out, but in the end decided not to; she was not sure she could face the answer.

DANNER WALKED slowly across the grass from Rec, her face still red from Kahn's fencing workout. She wiped sweat from her forehead with the back of her hand. It came away sticky with pollen. Damn this planet. It just kept getting hotter—thirty-eight degrees Celsius according to her wristcom.

Her mod was blessedly cool. She had a fast shower, resisting the temptation to stand under the revitalizing water for longer, and pulled on summer-weight fatigues. Her stomach growled, and she glanced at her wristcom. She would have to eat while she talked to Gautier, the ceramicist, about her report. There were not enough hours in the day.

She had just stepped back out into the muggy heat when her wristcom bleeped.

"Danner," she answered, walking toward the cafeteria.

"Vincio, ma'am. Another message from SEC rep Taishan. Do you wish to follow code-five procedure?"

Danner was already changing direction, angling toward her office. "Yes. I'll pick it up personally."

Day and T'orre Na were sitting on the bench along the far wall of the outer office when Danner got there. She nodded to them both. The viajera was running a knotted cord through her fingers; bright threads flickered through her tanned hands. "It came on a herd bird," she said.

"My office."

They sat. Danner felt a vast irritation. She did not have time for this. "What does it say this time?"

"From Marghe Amun to Commander Danner, greetings. Hannah, you must,"—T'orre Na looked at Danner—"there's great emphasis on that word, *you must accede to Cassil's trata demands. Even if you only send half-a-dozen officers. You must be seen to do something. Please review my report. I'm on my way to talk to you personally."*

"But she's pregnant!"

T'orre Na looked at Danner blankly, and Day grinned.

"I mean . . . Oh, curse the woman! This is the last thing I need! A pregnant SEC rep who's gone native, swanning in here stomach-first and telling me what I must and must not do! Well, I can't stop her, she can come and she can say what she likes. But I'm just too damn busy." Danner felt foolish at her outburst, then angry at feeling foolish. Damn it, the day was just too hot for this. "I have an appointment." Then she remembered she needed to talk to the viajera. "If you two could meet with me for dinner? Good."

She got out of the office and took four strides across the grass toward her appointment with Gautier and her lunch before her wristcom beeped again.

What the hell was it now? "Danner!"

"Dogias here. We've got trouble. The northern relay has just gone from the grid."

"Gone? What do you mean, gone?"

"Gone. Phht. Kaput."

Danner felt like strangling the woman. "Explain," she said through gritted teeth.

"The northern relay is no longer accessible. Diagnostics show it does not exist."

"Theories?"

"None. What I need is a satellite scan, or to go up there personally and take a look."

IT TOOK Nyo two hours to send signals through the Port Central uplink to *Estrade* ordering a satellite to scan the right area and send down a data squirt. Sigrid took another half an hour to collate the information. The delay did nothing to soothe Danner's irritation.

The room was crowded: Dogias, Danner, T'orre Na, Sara Hiam, Lu Wai, Day, Nyo; Sigrid at the screen.

"It's a bit fuzzy, but the best I could do with the cloud cover. This is the Holme Valley. Here and here"—she circled areas to the north—"are native dwellings. Here"—further to the north—"is the area where the relay is." She magnified. And again. "Or was."

"Sweet god." Danner stared at the tangled structure that had once been the northern relay.

"Someone trashed it," Dogias said. "They must have fired it

first. Only way to bend those plastics. Can you enlarge it once more?" Nyo did. Dogias studied it intently. "Looks like they've even smashed the dish. See? Those shards there. I can't put that back together. Build another, maybe, but that one's history."

"How the hell did this happen?" Danner turned to T'orre Na. "Is this how Cassil responds when I refuse to help?"

There was a sudden thick silence; Danner had ample time to wish she had not said anything.

"No," T'orre Na said, mildly enough, but Danner knew the viajera was angry.

She did not have the patience to apologize now. "The weather, maybe?"

Dogias shook her head. "A big enough storm with lightning hitting it square on might damage it, but, no, this kind of destruction is deliberate."

They all looked silently at the screen.

"There's something else you might want to see," Sigrid said. The picture changed.

"What the hell is this?"

"Watch." The dark patch that filled a quarter of the screen shifted. "This one was taken one minute later. Let me enlarge."

Horses. It was a hundred or more riders. "It's those damn tribes," Danner said wonderingly.

"It looks that way," Day agreed.

"Assuming they've kept a straight line, extrapolate their origin."

It took less than a minute. The screen showed a purple line running directly from the wrecked relay to the riders.

No one, no one could be allowed to get away with that. "Lu Wai, assemble four sleds. Sixty officers, with full field armor and rations for . . ." she calculated in her head, "thirty days. Field hospital and shelters. And make sure we include the crossbow squad." It would be interesting to see how they performed in a real situation. "I'll command. Other personnel: Dogias and Neuyen and whoever else we need to build another relay. When can you have your gear together, Dogias?"

"Three hours."

"Then we'll leave in four. That gives us two hours' daylight." She turned to Nyo. "I want that satellite moved north. I need communications."

"I can do that. And keep you updated on the weather. There's an unusual weather system building up there. Severe storms."

"Very well. Dr. Hiam, we might need a physician."

"I'd be happy to come along."

"And T'orre Na, and Day. I'll need you to liaise at Holme Valley." She remembered they were guests. "If you're willing."

Danner strode out of her offices, the adrenaline of rage singing light and hot through her veins. Rage that soon became a kind of exhilaration.

She was going to get to do her job. At last.

THE BREEZE blowing cool through the Yelland hills eased off as Marghe and Thenike made their way down the foothills and onto the plain toward Holme Valley. The heat made Marghe feel tired and tense. The air was humid, so thick with moisture that she felt it like spiderwebs across her face, and kept wanting to brush it away, wipe it from her skin.

They stopped at midafternoon. Marghe felt a kind of tension in the air, a tension she might not have been aware of before the virus became part of her.

"I don't like this," Thenike said, standing still and sniffing at the heavy air like a pointer. "There's more than one storm on its way. We need to find shelter."

Marghe remembered the mad ride on the sled, bucking over rocks as Lu Wai raced for shelter. Remembered the wind building, then the awful, fabulous lightning; Letitia Dogias laughing like a madwoman; the sheer excitement of so much raw power.

But the image that kept recurring was not Letitia throwing back her head and laughing with the storm, but Uaithne. Uaithne with her knife and her horse and her pale eyes, holding up hands stained with blood, laughing and laughing and riding into the storm looking for blood.

"We have to go on as long as we can," Marghe said. "Uaithne's going to do something terrible in this storm. We've got to keep going."

They plodded on, on and on, until they felt as though they were wading through heat, alert for the first rising of wind.

Marghe told herself there was nothing Uaithne could do against Danner; no way the tribeswoman could hurt Lu Wai and Letitia. It was not possible for Uaithne with her wooden spears and her sharp stones to get past the sleds and slick armor and firepower of the Mirrors. Not possible. But the image of Uaithne with her knife would not go away.

Marghe walked faster. Last time, Aoife had been there to take the knife from Uaithne's hand. Where was she now? Where was Aoife in all this?

HOLME VALLEY looked like a refugee camp, Danner thought as she stepped out of the field hospital. Women everywhere, talking angrily or sitting apathetically, rocking children, and everywhere dust: dust kicked up by the Singing Pasture horse herds which were skittish and nervous, by the sleds pulling hawsers tight to further secure the field hospital, by Mirrors erecting temporary quarters and technicians hanging solar panels and stringing cable. The dust hung in the still air like particles suspended in a liquid.

The heat, and the way every woman she tried to talk to kept looking nervously at the sky, made Danner irritable. "Later," Cassil had said when they arrived, "we'll talk later. There's a storm on its way. There's much to do." Danner, expecting gratitude, had been annoyed. Now, after a mere six hours in the valley, she was sick of the sight of the place.

Sara Hiam, with Day interpreting, had been talking to the women who had been hurt by the tribes as they swept over the pastureland weeks ago. As Danner passed by, she overheard some of the notes the doctor was making into her wristcom. "Evidence of higher than Earth-normal recuperative powers. Compound fracture of tibia and fibula sustained sixteen days ago already exhibits evidence of—"

Danner walked briskly. She did not want to hear how goddamn healthy these people were. She wanted the entrenchment phase to be over so she could start planning the native containment.

They were waiting for her in her tent: Captain White Moon, Lu Wai, Letitia, and T'orre Na. Danner was brusque.

"My immediate priority, until that satellite moves overhead and gives us communications with Port Central, has to be the reinstatement of the northern relay. Captain White Moon, I want you to take twelve officers to escort Dogias and Neuyen to the damaged site. Take Leap and a handful of her crossbow squad along."

"With the commander's permission—" Lu Wai began.

"No, Lu Wai. I need you here. A dozen officers are more than enough. It's only preliminary reconnaissance by the communications team; there should be no danger." Lu Wai looked like she was struggling with that, obviously unwilling to let Dogias go without her.

"Yes, ma'am."

Danner wondered what she would have done if Lu Wai had refused.

"Do that now, Captain. Take two sleds."

"We'll take the gear," Dogias said, "just in case. We could at least begin to rebuild while we're there."

"No. Examination of the site only. I don't want my forces split for too long. This is reconnaissance only. Both sleds and all personnel to be back here, with a comprehensive report, this time tomorrow."

Though the sun sank toward the horizon in bloody reds and oranges, the evening did not cool. Danner tried to ignore the feeling she had done the wrong thing when she saw the drawn look on Lu Wai's face as the sleds headed north.

She went to find Hiam. The doctor was in the field hospital, sitting on one of the beds, absently tossing something from hand to hand. It was small and, whatever it was, it claimed all the doctor's attention. Danner cleared her throat. Hiam spun around. "Oh. It's you." She dropped the object into the pocket of her white coat.

"You haven't eaten yet, have you? Cassil wants us to dine with her and her kith this evening."

"And is this the kind of place where we're supposed to dress for dinner and overwhelm the natives with our aplomb?" Her voice was high and sharp.

"Are you all right?"

"No." She fiddled absently with the thing in her pocket. "I'm supposed to be a doctor, but Lu Wai probably knows more about practical treatment than I do. I'm a researcher." She pulled out the thing she had been playing with. A softgel. "Take a good look at it. FN-17. My only claim to fame. Except it doesn't work for the whole six months. I still don't know why. I still don't understand why it—" She shook herself. "I decided not to take any before I left *Estrade*," she said, "and on my recommendation neither did Nyo or Sigrid. It's too late now, of course." She dropped the softgel back in her pocket and stood up. "Statistically speaking, one of us is likely to die in a month or two. And that takes away my appetite for dinner."

Danner did not know what to say. "Marghe lived. I lived. Everyone here lived. You should, too. With proper care. We've learned a lot about the virus since it first struck. Talk to Lu Wai about it."

"I already have."

"Then you know that we have a better idea than we did of how to care for its sufferers. The mortality rate dropped as we got more experience."

"But it's still high."

"Yes, it's still high. There's nothing we can do about that. But if you want to talk about statistics, think of it this way: you're much more likely to live than to die."

"I know, I know. But I keep thinking: what will I do if Nyo dies, or Sigrid? I miss them already. The last five or six years, we've lived on top of one another day in, day out. There were times when I came close to killing them both, times when I think I would have given anything to see them make a mistake and explode into a cloud of fatty tissues and globules of blood as they EVAed to some satellite or other. But now that I've not seen them for three days, I miss them. I keep looking around, wondering where they are, why I can't hear them or smell them. I feel lost."

LOST, DANNER thought to herself later as she dressed in her best uniform for the evening; we all feel lost. But we won't always be. We'll make this our home. Somehow.

To her surprise, Danner found that many of the foods Cassil's kith served them at the tables and benches set up outside a house made of a bent-over skelter tree were already familiar. The Port Central cafeteria had been growing and serving native vegetables for years. She sat between Sara and T'orre Na, at the same table as Cassil and Lu Wai and Day, three other valley women, and a woman from the pastures, Holle, who still wore a bandage around her head. She enjoyed showing Sara how to eat the tricky goura with its big seeds, and how to pour from the huge pitchers of water without drowning their small goblets.

"No one seems to be talking much," Sara said as she piled her plate with meat.

"Now is for eating," T'orre Na said, "while the food's hot and the water cold. We'll talk when the food is finished."

"Just one of many sensible arrangements you'll find here," added Day.

Danner's wristcom bleeped. "Please excuse me," she murmured to Cassil, and eased back a little from the table before taking the call.

"Teng here." There was some interference, a thin whine weaving in and out of Teng's words. "The gig's ready to go."

"Good." She was glad they had communication again with Port Central, but wondered why her deputy had bothered her with this. "Is there something else?"

"I've delayed departure; someone's tampered with the second gig."

Danner swore, then realized everyone at her table was looking at her, and modulated her voice. "How badly, Teng?"

"Crippled."

It had to be the other spy, the one Relman had mentioned. Coming out of the woodwork at last.

"Request orders regarding the departure of the first gig." Teng's voice slipped a little. "Commander, it's our only way off this world now. We can't let it go."

"A moment." The wristcom hissed with static while she thought. "Teng, ask Nyo if she can fix the autopilot on the gig so that it's tamperproof." If she could do it to the *Estrade* systems, she should be able to get the gig up and back down safely enough . . .

"That's a negative, Commander. But she says she can do something with the systems, cripple them so they can only be flown from our uplink station." There was a pause. "She says to assure you she'll be able to restore the functions once it gets back."

"Good. Then let them go."

Silence. Then: "Commander, you haven't asked if we caught the saboteur. Don't you want to know who it is?"

And Danner realized she knew, had known all along, who it was. Who it had to be. Who had always been nearby, who had access to privileged communications. Who smiled at her every day in her offices. Vincio.

"Never mind," she whispered.

"What? I didn't get that, Commander. Request—" A burst of static.

"Repeat that last."

". . . firm . . . let . . ."

"You're breaking up."

"It's . . . storm. Think. . . . your direction. Repeat. Please conf . . . let . . . gig go?"

"That's an affirmative." Pause. "Hello? Hello?"

Static crackled.

"Damn!" Danner turned to Lu Wai. "Lieutenant, please contact the repair party. Inform them that the storm seems to be headed in our direction. It'll hit them first. Tell them to take shelter immediately."

Lu Wai stood, bowed slightly to her dinner companions, and

walked a few yards away. Danner watched her talking into her wristcom, then turned back to Sara.

"What's going on?"

Danner picked up her knife but did not reply immediately. Vincio. Vincio who was always so helpful. For whom no request was too great.

"You look ill. Hannah, what's happened?"

Danner shook her head, unable to speak. Vincio.

Lu Wai came back at a run. Her face was set and pale. "Commander, I couldn't get through. There's nothing but static."

MARGHE CRAWLED from the old herder's cot. The morning sky was blue, but the air was tight and hot. Ripe. There was another storm waiting, somewhere. But not today. Today they would walk to Holme Valley.

They walked steadily. Halfway up a rise of sun-dried grass, Thenike stopped abruptly and turned her head this way and that, listening.

"What do you hear?" Not the other storm, surely. There was no shelter here. Marghe's face was still sore from the wind and the rain of the previous night, and her shoulders ached from hunching away from the crashing thunder and lightning.

"I don't know," the viajera said. "Something . . ."

Marghe listened, thought she heard something, lost it, then heard it again: a faint up-and-down hum. She knew that sound. "It's a sled." A sled. They would be eating lunch with Danner. She brushed a stray hair from Thenike's cheek, smiling. "Come on," she said, partly eager, partly shy. She took Thenike's hand and they walked over the rise together.

The sled was heading due south, and moving fast.

"Hoi!" Marghe shouted and waved her arms. The canopied sled turned in a wide hissing curve that flattened the grass. It did not slow down. Marghe and Thenike leapt out of the way.

The sled slammed to a halt and a Mirror leapt out, eyes wild, face smeared with dirt. Marghe crouched. This was not right. She rolled to her left and something thudded into the turf by her feet. A piece of wood. Like an arrow.

The Mirror was sobbing, trying to fit another quarrel to her crossbow.

Marghe came back to her feet, arms spread, ready to roll again. A Mirror with a crossbow? She did not have time to wonder at it: the Mirror was raising the bow to her shoulder again, shouting and crying. "Don't move, you bitches. Just don't move. Don't move. Don't move. Don't—"

"Chauhan!" Another Mirror stepped carefully from the sled. Her hair was gray. One arm hung loose; one pointed a weapon steadily at Marghe.

Chauhan looked confused. The crossbow wavered.

"Chauhan, lower your weapon." The older Mirror came closer. Marghe could see how much that arm hurt. "Identify yourselves."

This Mirror seemed in reasonable command of her faculties. Marghe lifted both arms, spread her legs slightly, waited for Thenike to copy her. The Mirrors were nervous, and hurt. She and Thenike looked like natives. Better act like one, until they calmed down a little. "We have no weapons except a small knife each. I am Marghe Amun, a viajera out of Ollfoss, come to speak with Acting Commander Hannah Danner." The older Mirror nodded. The other one, the crazy one, was staring at the ground, crossbow dangling from her hand. "You might recognize my other name more readily. I'm Marguerite Angelica Taishan, SEC representative." She was surprised at how steady her voice was. "And you are . . . ?"

"Twissel." She pointed her weapon at Thenike. "And this?"

"I am Thenike. We bear soestre."

"What?" Chauhan said. "Is that a weapon?" Her crossbow was back at her shoulder.

"Chauhan!" Then, more quietly, "Chauhan, go tend to Dogias."

"Dogias?" Marghe dropped her arms; Twissel motioned for her to put them up again. "Letitia Dogias?"

Twissel studied them both a moment, then nodded once.

"Was it the storm? Did she have a . . . I mean, did she . . . Is she all right?"

"No," Twissel said bluntly. "I think she's dying."

"Dying? Letitia? What happened?"

"Natives. Ten killed. No, keep still until I say different."

Marghe stopped in midstride and made an effort to not shout at the Mirror. "And Lu Wai?"

"The lieutenant wasn't with us."

"But you do have a medic?"

"Dead."

"Then let us see her, Twissel. Thenike here might be able to help. Please."

"I'll need your knives first. Take them from your belts, two fingers only. Drop them on the grass." Marghe felt a flash of anger and realized this reminded her of the way Aoife had treated her. But this was not Tehuantepec. She tossed down her knife. "Good. Kick them over here."

The sled, all alloys and plastics, felt hard and strange to Marghe. It was air-conditioned and cool, but the smells were still there: alien, manufactured materials mingling with blood and excretia and rank sweat. Chauhan was crouched in the cab, blank-faced. They squeezed past her and into the covered flatbed.

Two women lay side by side on inflated medical pallets. Thenike immediately knelt by the nearest, a blond-haired woman in partial armor.

If Marghe had not known that the other was Letitia Dogias, she was not sure she would have recognized her. Her memory insisted that the communications technician was vibrant, alive, full of irreverence and crackling energy; she was not this, this thing breathing stertorously through an open mouth with a hole in her stomach that oozed dark, dark blood. She smelled terrible.

"She's dead."

For one hanging moment, Marghe thought Thenike meant Dogias, then realized she was talking about the other one, the Mirror. The viajera folded the woman's hands on her breast, closed her eyes, had to use both hands to lift her jaw and close her mouth.

"What was your companion's name?" Thenike asked Twissel.

"Foster. Alice Foster."

"Then we should bury Alice Foster."

"No. We have to take her back."

"The heat . . ."

"We have a bag."

Thenike looked at Marghe, who nodded. "Then put her in a bag." She motioned Marghe away from Dogias and knelt. Marghe marveled at her calm poise; she took Dogias's pulse, listened to her breathing, lifted the tunic away from the awful wound in her stomach, pinched some skin and sniffed it, all as matter-of-factly as tuning a musical instrument. "I'll need to get her outside in the light and air. Then I want water, and clean cloths, bandages if you have any. And I'll need my knife back."

Twissel must have been as impressed as Marghe with Thenike's examination; the Mirror handed Thenike her knife without comment, then picked up one end of the pallet.

When they had Letitia outside, Thenike motioned Marghe over to the pallet lying on the grass. Letitia looked even worse in natural light. "I'll do what I can here, but you must help the other one. Chauhan. She needs to be busy." She opened the medical roll Twissel had found and picked out a swab. "She needs to stop thinking about what happened, just for a little while."

Foster was already stiffening. It took three of them to strip her armor and clothes, her dog tag and wristcom, and get her inside the body bag. Twissel, with her injured arm, could not do much.

It was Foster's left hand Marghe would always remember. It stuck out awkwardly, and Marghe had to wrestle it into the slick black plastic bag: she noticed that two fingernails were broken, that Foster had chewed her cuticles, that there was a pale band of skin around the wrist where she had worn her wristcom. *The mark of civilization,* Marghe thought, then looked at her own, evenly tanned wrist, *and how easily it is lost.*

With the motor off, the sled began to warm. The smell got worse. Marghe left the Mirrors scrubbing at the flatbed with bundles of spare uniform dipped in water and alcohol and went outside.

Thenike was squatting on her heels, running her hands, palm down, through the air an inch or so above Dogias's body. She had stripped Letitia's stained clothing, all of it, and washed her down. The wound was clean, still leaking a little blood, but Dogias looked . . . better. She seemed to be breathing more easily. Marghe crouched down next to the pallet; when Thenike's hands passed near her, she felt as though someone had run a powerful magnet over her skin.

"She's stable now," Thenike said. She sounded shockingly tired. Whatever she had done to help Dogias had taken a great deal of energy. "Help me get a compress on her wound."

Marghe lifted Dogias enough for Thenike to pass the roll of bandage under her ribs. The technician seemed heavier than the last time, when Marghe had dangled her over the rock edge and lowered her into Lu Wai's arms, and her skin felt different: slack, clammy. "Will she be all right?"

Thenike nodded tiredly, tied the bandage, and tested the tightness of the compress.

Chauhan took the stick. The others stayed in the back where it was once again cool and dry. The body bag was tucked out of the way in an overhead storage bin.

Thenike checked Dogias's pulse, then motioned for Twissel to come and sit by her. Marghe helped to get the Mirror's armor off. Thenike examined the swollen forearm and frowned. "Lean forward." She probed at the back of Twissel's head. The Mirror winced, and Thenike's fingers came away with dark flecks of dry blood on the tips. "There's nothing wrong with your head. But the bones in this arm are broken."

Twissel just nodded. "Thought they might be." She watched Thenike clip on splints and start to make a sling. "My own fault, this broken arm," she said to Marghe. "Fell on it, when I got hit by the stone that bloodied my head. I know how to fall. Should have managed not to break my own damned arm."

"You were probably half conscious."

"Still, I know better."

"Shouldn't the suit have protected you?"

"It would have, if it was turned on. If I'd been all armored up. I wasn't. None of us were, not fully. You just don't expect to need full armor on a backward world like this. Anyone wants to play rough and all you have to do is pull one of these." She pointed with her left hand at the weapon on her hip.

"So what happened?"

"I don't really know. Danner sent us, Sergeant Leap's squad, out under Captain White Moon. We were escorting Dogias and that other technician to the relay. To check it over. So we were lounging around, keeping an eye out, you know, while the two techs did their checking. Though I don't know why they bothered; it was just a pile of slag. Useless. So anyway, they were doing that, we were talking, some of us playing a game of chicken with the crossbows—"

"When did Mirrors start using crossbows?"

"One of Danner's ideas. A morale thing. Though now I'm not sure . . . Anyway, we were relaxed, but still keeping an eye open. You know. I mean, we weren't worried, but you never can tell, not on a world like this. And we'd been told there were hostiles in the area."

The tribes. Marghe nodded.

"And then the storm hit. The noise, the wind, it . . . It's different out here, not the same as being safe in Port Central while the wind tries to rip the grass out by the roots and the thunder rolls the hills flat. It was like the sky opened its mouth and roared. And out of the dust and roar, the flash of light, came those natives on horses. Like devils." She shook her head. "We were disoriented, deaf, blind, surrounded by women like demons yelling, riding at us. Still, it takes more than hostiles and a bit of weather. We're professionals. I'd seen worse. I pulled out my weapon. I wasn't the only one. I fired."

Twissel raised her free arm, reliving it.

"I fired, but nothing happened. Nothing. I thought it was a damaged power pack. I had it stripped out and replaced in three seconds." Marghe tried to imagine managing that in the middle of an attack and a storm, failed. "It still didn't work. I couldn't believe it. I just kept pointing that thing and pressing the stud. Nothing. Nothing from anyone else's, either. We all stood there, pointing weapons that wouldn't work. Like a nightmare. The only guess I can come up with is that the storm somehow shorted them. Then I remembered my crossbow. I ran to get it out of the sled, yelled for the others to do the same. They didn't."

She winced as Thenike lifted her arm into position.

"Captain White Moon, Sergeant Leap, all of them, they were shaking their weapons, stripping them down, staring at them unbelievingly. I understood how they felt; weapons don't just stop working. They just don't. Only they did. They couldn't get over that. I mean, it just doesn't happen. And meanwhile they were on us, waving their spears, whirling slings around their heads. Seemed like hundreds of them, coming out of the teeth of the storm, yelling. And you know what, all I could think as they came at us was: they stink. Like rancid grease. That's when I realized they were real. They might not be wearing armor, they might not have beam weapons, but they were armed and they were coming for us, and those funny-looking spears and stones could kill."

Twissel paused. Marghe handed her the water bottle. The old Mirror took a deep swig, wiped her mouth. "I was just about at the sled when I got hit. A stone, from a sling. Fell on my damn arm. A stone, goddammit, a stone! When I was wearing state-of-the-art gear and carrying a weapon that could kill half-a-thousand crazies at two hundred yards. A stone." She shook her head. "But I got up again, and I got into that sled and I managed to carry out two bows. I threw one to Chauhan. And all the time I was yelling, yelling at those people to get their bows, get their bows. They just wouldn't. You know what I saw? Women using their weapons as clubs. Clubs. Do you believe that?"

Marghe shook her head.

"It's hard, winding up a bow and fitting a quarrel with one hand. But I did. And Chauhan did, too. She sort of follows me around, does what I do. Bit like a kid sister. Lucky. So we started firing. Then one or two others got the idea, Foster, Leap . . . and Dogias. She was yelling and laughing fit to bust, but she could fire that bow. And she had a knife. Don't know where that came from." Twissel looked at Thenike. "Most of that blood you washed off her wasn't hers. But then she came up against the maddest native of all, long red hair, weird eyes, walked her horse slow as you please through the mess, leaned sideways out of her saddle, and shoved her spear into Dogias's stomach cool as if it were target practice. I lifted my bow, but then she was gone, off into the wind. They were wrecking one of the sleds, didn't seem bothered with us anymore. Then they whirled off. Gone."

Again, she was quiet.

"It took maybe ten minutes. One minute, it was a quiet evening, the next I was standing there with my arm broken, wind howling and lightning crashing, looking at dead bodies. The only ones alive were Chauhan, me, Dogias, and—" She looked at the body bag, and was quiet. "I don't really remember how I got us all into the sled. But I do remember stopping in the middle of the night and feeling this laughter, this hysteria, trying to crawl up out of my throat, and I knew that if I let it, I'd go mad. So I climbed down out of the cab with my weapon and shot it at the stones and the trees, anything. This time it worked. So it must have been the storm." She shook her head again. "But I don't think Chauhan will ever trust anything but her crossbow again."

Thenike finished with the sling and leaned back.

"Captain White Moon, Leap, the others," Twissel said, "they were my friends. I found Leap, she'd been gutted. Never did find Captain White Moon." She frowned briefly, shook her head, went on. "They're all dead. And I don't know why. There wasn't any *reason* behind any of this. I could maybe accept it if there were. If we'd been defending something important. But they just attacked us because they wanted to."

Marghe did not know how to begin to go about explaining Uaithne, and the legend, and the Echraidhe woman's charismatic madness.

"If there was just a reason. If I could just make sense of it. They rode away laughing. Laughing."

Marghe wondered if Aoife had been laughing.

THE MORNING in Holme Valley dawned blue and hot. Danner listened to a report from Lu Wai: no contact with Captain White Moon's party as yet. She told her to keep trying, then checked the temporary quarters and the sled moorings, finding that everything seemed to have held up well in last night's storm. She found Sara Hiam in the field hospital, taking the equipment through a hypothetical diagnostic run.

Danner watched quietly for a while. The doctor worked steadily, competently. "For a researcher you seem to me to know what you're doing."

"The machine does it all." Hiam hit a couple of studs, watched the display. "You know what the most serious thing is I've dealt with in the last six years? Sigrid's tonsillitis."

"Did you fix it?"

"Yes. Actually, I did more than fix it. I set up a culture and modified those bacteria so that their RNA couldn't do anything. Then I reintroduced— Well, it took me two days. And after that, none of us will get tonsillitis again. It seemed more elegant than using drugs."

"Lu Wai couldn't have done that."

Hiam paused. "No. No, I don't suppose she could." Her half smile turned to a frown as she looked at an anonymous dispenser on the wall. "Now what do you suppose these are? Ah, skin patches." She pulled the lever and examined the slippery square that fell into her hand.

Danner smiled to herself and left her to it. The doctor knew much more than she realized, but there was nothing she, Danner, could say to persuade Hiam of that; the doctor would simply have to learn for herself. Just as a young lieutenant had learned how to be a commander.

She returned a sergeant's salute, feeling good, and headed for the western corrals. She wanted to have a look at the Singing Pasture horses while they were here. Then she would have a word with T'orre Na, or Cassil, about trading for some of them—never too early to think about breeding stock. Perhaps she should have brought along Said, the zoologist. Plenty of time for that. They had reared horses at home; she knew enough to be going on with. Besides, it would be good just to see some horses again, and there was nothing more constructive to be done until they heard back from White Moon.

Her wristcom bleeped. "Danner," she said cheerfully.

"Hannah, you'd better get here right now."

"Sara? Is that you?"

"Just get here." Sara disconnected.

Danner headed back at a run.

FROM THREE hundred yards she could see the hospital was a hive of activity: people were climbing out of a newly arrived sled, Hiam had a stretcher by the hatch, and she and Lu Wai and a native—not from Holme Valley, judging by the clothes— were lifting someone onto it. The stretcher hissed over the grass toward the hospital, Hiam and Lu Wai trotting alongside working feverishly to connect drips to each arm, the native keeping one hand on the injured woman's head. Another stretcher carried a body bag.

Two Mirrors and another native, dressed like the first, climbed down just as Danner got there.

"Officer Twissel reporting, ma'am."

Chauhan looked dreadful. Danner had seen that look before: shock. "You're injured, Officer Twissel. You and Officer Chauhan report to the medic . . ." she stared at the native, "and I'll be there to talk to you in a moment." That native, it could not be . . . "Representative Taishan?"

Marghe nodded.

"With respect, ma'am." Danner dragged her gaze from the woman in native clothes and back to Twissel. "I can wait half an hour for the medic. The viajera fixed it up. I'm ready to make my report."

But I don't want to hear it! Danner wanted to shout. *This isn't possible!* But it was, it had happened, someone had destroyed her people, and she had to hear how. She studied Twissel; the Mirror's face was drawn but her color was good. "Very well. But Chauhan goes to the medics. And we'll find you a chair."

Marghe stayed.

Danner listened carefully to the report of the storm, of weapons malfunction, to Twissel's matter-of-fact recounting of stupidity and heroism, of the unidentified and mutilated bodies. But all the time she listened, her attention kept wandering to the SEC rep, to the missing fingers and scarred face, the bare wrist and strange clothes. What in god's name had happened to the woman?

Twissel had stopped and was looking at her oddly. "Go on," Danner said, and forced herself to concentrate on Twissel's estimate of numbers and speed. Not listening did not make the truth go away: her people, eleven of her people, had been butchered. She should never have sent them. She should not have split her forces. It was her fault. Her people were dead because she had let them down.

But what else could she have done? She could not have foreseen that the storm would lead to malfunction. But maybe she *should* have expected the unknown. They had spent too long down here, too long believing the natives to be harmless. Too long getting soft.

Recriminations would have to wait. For now, she would learn what she could. There were still half-a-hundred personnel here to take care of.

"And you didn't find White Moon's body, you say?"

"No, ma'am. But there were some that . . . well, after the tribes had finished with them, I doubt their mothers would recognize them."

Danner chewed that over. "Why, Twissel? Why did these savages do this?"

"I don't know."

"Take a guess. They must have had reasons." Her voice was harsh.

"I don't think they did." Twissel's voice was flat, dull. "Request permission to see that medic now, ma'am."

"Permission granted."

Twissel stood.

"And, Twissel . . ."

"Yes, ma'am?"

"You did a remarkable job. Without you Dogias would have died, and Chauhan probably. No one will forget what you did. I'll want to talk to you again soon, but try to rest now, and be assured that you did everything you could have done. Everything."

"Thank you, ma'am." Twissel sounded as though she did not care what Acting Commander Hannah Danner thought, and Danner did not blame her.

Danner looked at Marghe, who looked right back. Even the representative's eyes looked different, with that scar above the eyebrow. How did she fit into all this? Perhaps she could explain the massacre. There *had* to be a reason. There was always a reason.

That would have to wait.

She punched Kahn's code into her wristcom. "Sergeant, as soon as communications with Port Central are reestablished, I want you to request satellite tracking of hostiles, estimated number one hundred twenty, last known position at the relay last night during the storm, and heading north. Estimated speed fifteen kilometers per hour. And advise Sigrid that weather information now has top, repeat, top priority."

She hit OFF. "Now," she said, turning to Marghe, "I want you to tell me, as plainly as possible, what has happened to you since you left here and why you're here now, while we walk over to see how Letitia is doing."

"PART OF the message was missing . . ." Danner stopped five feet away from the closed flap of the hospital tent. Marghe watched understanding flatten the Mirror's expression, bring a flush to her cheeks. "You mean all this"—Danner waved at the sleds, the stretchers leaning drunkenly against the walls—"all this was a *mistake?*"

"Yes. But not my mistake."

Hiam stepped out of the tent, wiping her hands on her bloody whites. "What mistake?"

Danner ignored her. "Whose, then? You were the one who deliberately stopped taking the stuff. You. No one else."

"I don't understand," Hiam said, looking from one to the other. "Are you talking about the FN-17?"

"Yes," Marghe said tiredly. "How's Letitia?"

"She's stable. Tell me about the FN-17." Hiam was very still, very white. Marghe knew this was going to be hard.

"The FN-17 worked. Or at least, it worked as long as I took it."

"But you said, your message said . . ." Hiam looked from one to the other. "I don't understand."

"The message that reached Danner wasn't complete. The part that was missing explained that I'd chosen to stop taking the vaccine."

"But why?"

Marghe wondered how long it would take for Sara's puzzlement to turn to anger. "I was alone in Ollfoss, with about thirty days' worth of vaccine left, facing a journey to Port Central that would take longer than that, if it was possible at all, which it wasn't."

"If you hadn't insisted on going there in the first place, this wouldn't have come up." Danner's voice was shaking. "But no, you had to go galloping off there in the dead of winter."

"If I was going to learn anything, I had to go north. And it had to be winter: I only had six months." That all seemed so long ago. *Blame Company,* she wanted to say. *If they hadn't landed me in autumn, I wouldn't have had to go up there in the harshest season.* But she said nothing. Danner knew all this, or ought to.

"But you could have kept taking it," Hiam said. "To see. You could have kept taking it."

"No. Thenike told me—"

"Thenike?"

"My partner. She said the adjuvants were poisoning me, that—"

"What does a savage know about adjuvants?"

"That 'savage' is my partner." She spoke very softly. "And she knew enough to save Letitia's life." There was a small silence while Hiam opened her mouth to argue, then closed it, and Danner slapped her gauntlets against her thigh, over and over. "Thenike said the adjuvants were making my body weak. And I needed to be as strong as I could be, to make sure that the virus, when it came, didn't kill me."

Danner stopped slapping. "It wouldn't have come if you'd taken the damn vaccine."

Marghe did not bother to answer that. "Sara, for you it was months of hard work—"

"Years."

"Years, then. For me it was my life. But it worked, Sara. It worked."

"Yes," Sara said bitterly. "And that does us a lot of good now. Shall I call the *Kurst* tomorrow, and tell them? No? No. Because they wouldn't believe me. Because their spy has already told them it doesn't work, and I'm down here. Contaminated."

"I'm sorry."

"Sorry?" She laughed, a sharp bark. "So am I." She lifted the hospital flap to go back in. "Tomorrow, when I've more time, I want you to tell me everything. About the vaccine, the virus, your pregnancy, everything."

IT WAS evening, and Marghe was leaning against a fence-post, watching the Singing Pasture horses, when Thenike joined her.

"You look tired," Marghe said. "How's Letitia now?"

Thenike slid an arm round Marghe's waist and leaned her cheek on Marghe's shoulder. "Steadier. She's strong, and the doctor knows well enough what to do." Thenike's bare skin felt cool; the night was warm and soft. A fly buzzed nearby. "And you?"

"Angry." *They called you savage.* "At Danner, at Hiam. At whatever disturbed those message stones." Nothing she could do about that now. She let her breath go in a rush. "Danner's going to be even angrier when she hears our idea."

"What do the others make of it—Cassil, Holle, T'orre Na?"

"I don't know yet. I wanted us both to speak to them, together. They're waiting."

But neither of them moved for a while; the night was soft and spicy and peaceful, and the talking that lay ahead would go on until morning. They watched the horses flicking their tails at the flies.

THE LATE afternoon sun was a hot, orangey red, and the shadows of the seven women were beginning to lengthen. Danner stared at the other six one by one, at Cassil and T'orre Na, at Day and the one from Singing Pastures, Holle, at Marghe and Thenike. She could not believe what she was hearing.

"Let me make sure I've got this straight," she said. "These tribeswomen have driven Holle and her kin from their land and slaughtered half their herds. They've butchered eleven of my best people for no reason that makes any sense to me, despite what you've been saying, and maybe taken one hostage. Now they're on their way here to wreak god knows what havoc upon us all. And you want to send Marghe here, and Thenike, unarmed, to talk to them."

No one said anything.

Danner wanted to put them all in a bag and shake them. She turned to Marghe. "Do you want to get yourself killed?"

"You've accused me of suicidal tendencies before, and been wrong."

"But not by much! Look at yourself, for pity's sake: fingers missing, scarred, wearing rags. By your own admission you nearly died at the hands of these same . . . tribeswomen." Savages.

"There's no other real choice."

"There is!"

Danner looked to Day in mute appeal, but the ex-Mirror shook her head. "I think she's right, Commander."

Danner would not accept that. "Look. Just wait until tomorrow. Until midday tomorrow. Nyo should be here by then. She thinks she can find a way to stop a storm disrupting our weaponry. Then we can escort you to this Uaithne, protect you. You can talk to her all you want from behind an armored skirmish line."

Marghe shook her head. "That's the worst thing we could do. Danner, I know these people. Or what they've become. They don't think the way we do—they never did. And now that they're behind Uaithne, they've become unreachable. They're living a legend, can't you see that? They've given something up, call it a sense of reality, to live inside something Uaithne has created. They no longer think of themselves as individuals; they're just the followers of the Death Spirit. They don't care about dying—in fact, they'd welcome death."

Danner shook her head in denial.

Marghe thrust her left hand under Danner's nose. "Look at that, Danner. That hurt. For months I was cold, hungry, treated like an animal. I nearly gave up, laid down, and died. The snow up there does something to you. I've lived there. I know what it's like. They know they can't survive. They're not stupid. Every year fewer and fewer children survive into adulthood. There's more and more deficiency disease. They're dying, their way of life is dying. They know that. But what they can't conceive of is that it's possible to live another way. They live inside themselves in a way it's almost impossible to understand. So now along comes Uaithne, who says, I'm the Death Spirit, death is glory! And they see a way to make it all good again. To die. To kill others."

"But if—"

Marghe ignored her. "Some of them, one or two, perhaps, might still be open to reason. And they know me. But if they see your line, nothing in the world will stop them throwing themselves upon you. Can't you see that? It's what they want: hundreds of deaths."

They talked on, through dusk and into the night, until Danner's teeth ached from clamping her jaw around words she knew she would regret if they were said. When she went to bed, she was too keyed up to sleep.

Damn the woman. How could she risk herself like this? Couldn't she see that she would just be throwing her life away, hers and Thenike's? Throwing them away on a useless gesture. And their deaths would be added to the list of people Danner already felt responsible for. Damn them all.

She fell asleep eventually, and dreamed she was standing alone on a grassy plain facing a hundred riders. She was holding a knife, but as they galloped toward her, she realized the knife was a child's toy, clumsily carved of wood.

She woke before dawn, hooves still thundering through her head. She got dressed and walked barefoot through the dewy grass toward the hospital, enjoying the cool wet sliding between her toes.

Lu Wai was sitting patiently by Letitia's bedside. The only noise was the faint hum of a machine at the head of the bed. Lu Wai straightened.

"How is she?"

"Stable, ma'am. And improving. She spoke to me last night." The trace of that miracle was still on Lu Wai's face. She nodded at the machine. "But Dr. Hiam thinks we should keep her asleep as much as possible."

"You agree?"

Lu Wai looked surprised. "Yes. Sleep's a good healer." She paused. "You're not sleeping well, ma'am?"

"No. No I'm not." She pulled a chair up to the bed and sat down. "Lu Wai, how do you decide what to do when you think you're right, but everyone else, who you would have thought should know better, thinks you're wrong?"

Lu Wai took a moment to answer. "That depends. Usually, when what I want is the direct opposite of what everyone else thinks is right, I find fear of some kind, my fear, at the bottom of it. Take my request to be sent with Letitia and Captain White Moon."

"I—"

Lu Wai held up her hand. "No. You were right. What would have happened to Letitia if I'd died out there? But it was fear, fear for Letitia, that prompted my request."

Danner said nothing. She was thinking of her fears: that all the people she knew would die and she was helpless to prevent it. Helpless when all her training had taught her she must be responsible for her people, that their lives were in her hands. But Marghe was not her responsibility anymore; she had chosen to join the natives; and Thenike never had been. "You might be right. You are right. But how do you stop being afraid?"

"You don't." Lu Wai looked at Letitia, festooned with tubes and wires. "But love and responsibility don't give a person the prerogative to be always right. We can't protect people forever. Letitia had a job to do. She went to do it. It wasn't my place at that time to be with her."

Danner absorbed that.

Marghe was a trained negotiator. She knew this Uaithne. Thenike was a viajera, a representative of the other natives. And Marghe was also a SEC rep, better qualified than anybody to do this job.

As she stepped back out into the dawn, Danner punched in Kahn's code. "Kahn, go find out where Marghe and Thenike are sleeping. Wake them up and tell them I'm reconsidering. That if they want transport north, they have it."

"But, Commander, they've already gone. Borrowed horses from the Singing Pastures women and left last night."

Danner closed her eyes and swore. Two women on horses was a very different proposition from two women on a sled that could whisk them out of danger if the natives got ugly. She took a deep breath. To hell with it. She was a soldier, not a diplomat. "Kahn, I want you to go find Cassil, Day, T'orre Na, and Holle, and respectfully request that they be in my quarters in twenty minutes. Tell Lu Wai and Twissel to join us. I want the sleds powered up and all personnel ready to be addressed in forty. I want a message sent to Nyo, to read: 'Am heading with all speed on direct course for last known whereabouts of hostile tribes. Please change course to follow.' That's all."

"Yes, ma'am."

Danner checked the weather reports and thought furiously as she waited for Day and T'orre Na and the others to arrive. When they did, she could tell by their faces that they had already heard her orders.

"You can't do this!" Day said. "You know what Marghe said. If you're there, armed, they'll attack."

"Nyo isn't here," Danner said. "I doubt she'll reach us before we meet with the tribes. And the latest weather report suggests we, the storm, and the tribes will all meet at the same time. Which means none of our weapons will work anyway. So, technically, we won't be armed."

"Then why—"

"We'll rely on our armor. You know what it can do. If we're properly armored up, nothing these savages can throw at us can get through. Modern weapons, yes, because of the heat, but impact weapons, especially low-grade items like stones and spears, will just bounce off. If they got us on the ground, they could probably beat us senseless. Even a helmet can't stop the brain being rattled inside the skull with enough pounding. But if we stand together . . . It should work."

Day opened her mouth to say more, but T'orre Na held up her hand. "Hannah, are you saying that you intend to simply stand, empty-handed, while Uaithne and the massed Echraidhe and Briogannon charge at you?"

"Only if necessary. And we'll have our sleds, and the crossbows. Look, Marghe and Thenike might need us. It's possible that these riders have at least one hostage. Do you want me to let civilians take care of this mess? I'm a Mirror, these are my people. I've been trained to deal with situations like this. And the storm won't last forever. When it's blown out, we'll have our sleds, our weapons, our skills. These tribes need to know that."

She ran a hand through her hair. "Day, T'orre Na . . . We have to make our way on this world. People need to know that we can't be pushed around." She looked at them, unable to tell what they thought. "The sleds might be the only things that save Marghe. And Thenike. I can't not go."

Chapter Seventeen

THE NIGHT wrapped hot and close around Marghe and Thenike as they galloped north and west from Holme Valley toward Singing Pastures. The pastures did not sing with wind now; the clumps of trees and the long grass hung silent and dark and still. The hooves rushing beneath them kicked up dusty scents of parched grass, despite the storm of two days before. Marghe's throat was dry.

This isn't going to work.

She concentrated on urging her mount forward, but with every thud of hoof on turf, the sick feeling in her stomach grew worse. *This just isn't going to work.*

The thud of the horses' hooves changed; they were galloping through a field of flowers, bursting open flower heads closed for the night, crushing the leaves and flattening stalks under hard hooves. They were suddenly drenched with the tight, sweet smell of olla. *The smell of fear.*

Marghe reined in suddenly. She could not do this. Thenike's horse slowed, turned, came back.

"What's wrong?"

"I can't do it. It won't work." Her horse snorted and shifted restlessly.

"He doesn't like the flowers." It was too dark for Marghe to see Thenike's expression. They guided their horses out of the broken blooms.

Marghe broke the silence. "It won't work. It just won't. I can't do it, Thenike, I'm not good enough. They won't listen to me. They'll laugh, or ignore me, or . . ." Or they would kill her, or capture her. *Not again.* "What if we're wrong? What if they won't believe I'm their Death Spirit?"

"If they believe Uaithne, they have to believe that what you say is at least possible. As you said to Danner, they're living a legend now."

"But what if that isn't enough!"

Silence. "Do you want to go back?"

Yes! Marghe wanted to say, and nearly leaned from her saddle and reached out into the soft dark to take Thenike's hand. But if she took Thenike's hand now, all her resolve would crumble, and she would say, *Yes, let's go, I was a fool to even think I could pull this off.* She kept her arms by her sides.

"No." She would go on, she would try. She had to try. If only she had Thenike's skills and could use song and drumbeat to drive her words like barbs into the flesh and minds of the Echraidhe, drive them deep, tangle them about so that they could not escape. Thenike could do it, if she were Marghe. But she was not. Marghe was the only one the Echraidhe might listen to, the only one who had lived with them and who was from another world. The only one they might believe. And all she had was her self, and her story. It did not seem much with which to face a hundred spears.

Thenike looked about her. "Here might be a good place for me to wait for Danner."

Danner would come, they knew. She was a Mirror; she would not be able to help herself. It would be Thenike's job to stop her, if she could.

They dismounted. Marghe felt as though she had swallowed

something so cold it was turning her stomach to ice. She put her hands on Thenike's shoulders; the bone and muscle felt warm and strong. They pulled each other close, and Marghe buried her face in Thenike's hair.

When they remounted, the rim of the sun was just touching the eastern hills with orange. The horses' legs were covered with pinkish yellow pollen. Thenike's saddle leather creaked as she turned this way and that, sniffing the air. "The storm will come today."

Marghe knew Thenike could not be smelling anything through the thick scent of olla; it was another sense she used. Marghe herself could feel that crawling under her skin, that ripe sensation she had felt before the last storm. "The sky's clear."

"I don't think it'll bring rain. Just hot wind and lightning."

"How soon?"

"Afternoon, maybe. We'll need to find shelter before then, some rock. The grass is dry enough to burn, without rain."

They were silent a moment, Marghe's mount facing back the way they had come, Thenike's facing Marghe. Their horses whuffled at each other's necks. Marghe pointed to a clump of trees. "If Danner doesn't come, wait for me down there. I'll be back."

"I'll wait," Thenike agreed. "But before the storm, Danner or no Danner, I'll come looking."

Marghe knew it would be pointless to argue. She gathered the reins awkwardly in her maimed left hand, preparing to wheel and head north. She wanted to tell Thenike to be careful, tell her how much she loved her. She could not find the words. "If she comes, make her wait. Make Danner wait."

"Your wait, at least, is over." Thenike nodded ahead, and Marghe twisted in her saddle to look. The western horizon was hazy with dust, dust kicked up by a hundred horses.

Thenike turned her horse. "Speak well, Marghe Amun. And remember, I'll come looking, before the storm."

Then she was gone.

Marghe turned her own horse to face the dust.

SHE WAS waiting, reins tucked under her thighs, hands free, and the sun almost fully risen behind her, when the riders came over the horizon. Dawn underlit their faces, orange and alien; their sweat-sheened mounts gleamed like creatures of molten metal.

The massed tribes were in a long, straight line—a skirmish line, Danner would call it. Slowly, the line wheeled about its center, where the sun picked fire from Uaithne's braids, and continued to advance, facing Marghe head-on. Next to Uaithne, tied to the saddle and slumping like a gray sack of grain, was a Mirror. Her armor had been ripped off to reveal fatigues, and there was dried blood on one cheek. Captain White Moon. She did not seem more than half conscious.

Marghe breathed slow and deep, keeping a steady rhythm, hands relaxed on her thighs. They would not capture her again. She would make them listen. A slight breeze lifted the mane of her horse and blew it across the backs of her hands, tickling. Her mounted shadow stretched long and umber across the grass between her and the Echraidhe and Briogannon. The tribes would see her as a huge, dark silhouette, backlit by the rising sun.

They halted a hundred and fifty yards away in a whispering of grass and chinking of bits.

Now.

Everything Marghe had learned, from the death of her mother, from the biting cold of Tehuantepec, and at the hands of Thenike— everything that made her who she was—came together in one hot focused point in her center, flooding her with adrenaline, tightening her skin, raising goosebumps. Her hands felt heavy; she remembered the ammonites. She was Marghe Amun, the complete one.

She held out one hand, palm out, as she had in the storytelling tent of the Echraidhe. Her voice cracked across the grass.

"You have amongst you a liar and a deceiver, one whose heart is twisted and empty, who leads you to a destiny that is false. Uaithne, murderer and betrayer, claims to speak for the Death Spirit. She lies. She claims to know my will, *my* will, and lies."

They were listening. Or at least they were not charging at her. Her blood surged powerfully. She nudged her horse to a slow walk, along the line, timed her words to fit her mount's steady hoofbeats, sent them rolling away from her, unstoppable.

"Listen to me now. *I* am the one who has traveled the black void between the stars to come to you; *I* am the one who has wandered the white void, the plain that stretches its hand between the worlds of the living and the dead; *I* am the one who has spoken with the spirits of the ancestors in the sacred stones. *I* am the one who came amongst you and learned, like a child, the ways of my tribe; *I* am the one who left, like a ghost, when I had learned all I needed; and *I* am the one who survived winter alone on Tehuantepec, and who returns to you now."

Her words were steady and hypnotic, falling in a strong cadence, up and down with her breath and the beat of her heart until she found strength building behind those words like a living thing: powerful, straining to be unleashed, to bound away to the tribeswomen astride their horses and tear away their masks.

"Uaithne laid the path. Uaithne brought you together before me. Before *me*, I say. For Uaithne is my tool, no more. A flawed tool. One that would twist in the hand of any who lean upon her promises, and break."

She did not look at Uaithne, but caught the eye of Aelle, of Marac and Scatha sitting together, of Borri. She had their attention. There was no sign of the Levarch. Dead? Then Aoife would be leader, Aoife who was staring at the grass between her mount's legs.

Lift that head, Aoife, look at me.

"You seek death, and I say to you: it comes. I am its herald and its shepherd. But you are *my* tribe, you will die as and when I decree, in the way I shall set down. And I tell you now: this is not the way. For this throwing of yourselves upon strangers is merely seeking death of the flesh." She waved her hand dismissively. "A small thing, an easy thing."

The energy that had been building inside her climbed to the back of her throat, so that she could barely contain it. She rose in the saddle and lifted both hands, palms out. A peremptory gesture demanding attention. "It is *not* the death I have traveled the void to witness!" She slammed the sentence home with a double palm strike to the air. The Echraidhe jerked.

"My journey was hard beyond belief!" All the rage she felt at having been held captive and treated as something inhuman came pouring forth, making her words twist and roar. "The death I demand of you will be harder still! It means nothing to me that you prepare to die one by one in blood and heat. Nothing. I demand of you something more, much, much more. I demand of you the Great Death. The death of change."

She saw a small movement, so tiny she almost missed it: Aoife, lifting her head. *Yes, Aoife. Look at me, listen to what you would not hear before.* The sun was warm on her back now, and the smell of olla overpowering, but she did not care, she was carried away on a tide of her own power and her words were hammer blows.

"The death of change," she said again, "the death of your way of life, the death that is not just an ending but a great and terrible new beginning. *This* is what I ask of you!"

Oh, she had them now. They breathed with her, blinked with her, sat their horses as still as rocks.

"This, then, is my demand." And now her words were implacable. "That you lay aside this crusade, that you move your grazing grounds south and west, that you leave Tehuantepec to the snow scuttlers and creeping plants." She softened slightly. "You are not stones to endure the wind and the ice, you are people. You need light, warmth, food for your children. You need others of your own kind from whom to choose lovers and friends. Ah, but the finding of them will change you."

She surveyed the silent women. Uaithne's eyes glittered.

"You say 'Tribe before self,' and mean 'Tribe before anything,' because deep inside your selves you have a barren place that wails, 'Nothing is real but the tribe, there is no one here but us.' You are wrong." She spoke directly to Aoife now, who was studying her intently. "Lift your eyes from the barren place and open your ears, see and hear the world I have made ready for you. You will find a place where your herds will grow sleek and fat, where your children's hair will be glossy and their eyes bright, where you will not have to listen at night for the breath of the ice wind and the coming of the goth."

Silence.

"It waits for you, if you but have the courage to face this greatest death of all. This death of change."

Aoife frowned, and for one moment Marghe thought she had gotten through, that the tribeswoman had heard, but then Uaithne's laughter splashed over them all like cold, bright water.

"Death," she said lightly, "is no thing of doubt and struggle, but a thing of heat and bright and red glory."

The wind rose again as Uaithne spoke, and stirred the hair on the back of Marghe's neck. The air seemed to hum with it.

Uaithne laughed again and pointed behind Marghe. "And there is our death, come to greet us. We must ride to meet it."

Marghe twisted quickly in her saddle. The hum was not the wind.

Forty or more Mirrors, visors glittering and black armor dusted with pollen like the exoskeletons of alien insects, crested the rise in a lazy, bunched swarm. Sleds hummed, one on each side of the closely packed Mirrors, one behind. In front of them, her back to Marghe, was a single rider. Thenike. When the Mirrors started forward, Thenike did not move. The Mirrors shifted direction; Thenike shifted to meet them. One woman facing down forty.

Thenike. Later.

"No," Marghe said to Uaithne, "not this time."

"Oh, yes," Uaithne said, and couched her spear.

Marghe pulled the reins out from under her thigh and wrapped them around the pommel. The humming changed behind her but she did not dare turn. She breathed deeply, slowly, and sent oxygen fizzing through her arteries into her long muscles. This was not Tehuantepec. She would be ready this time. This time she would fight. She would never give in again.

But Uaithne was not charging. She lowered her spear, slid it into its sheath. For one dizzying moment, Marghe thought she had won after all. But then Uaithne laughed again, snatched out her knife, and in what seemed like one movement pulled White Moon's horse toward her and slit the Mirror's throat.

Blood gushed shockingly red. The Mirror's mount whickered and sidled; blood pattered on the grass.

Uaithne clamped her red, red knife between her teeth and took up her spear in one hand, her reins in the other. Then she thumped her heels into her horse's ribs and was charging across the grass, the tip of her spear coming up, up, pointing straight for Marghe's throat.

Behind Uaithne, the tribal line rippled and tightened. Marghe could not spare a glance for the answering tightening she expected from the Mirrors.

She did not move. She had put everything into her words, and now all that was left were her hands, and it was all going to end in blood.

But then she saw movement behind Uaithne: Aoife, whirling something around her head, straightening her arm with a snap. For a moment nothing happened, and Marghe thought that Aoife, accurate to nine nines of paces with her sling, had missed.

Then Uaithne *oof*ed as though someone had hit her in the back, and the creamy line of scalp showing through the part in her hair bloomed red, redder than her braids. But she managed to hang on and was still coming, and behind Marghe, muffled by the growing hiss of the wind, no doubt the Mirrors were readying their weapons; Aoife had left it too late. Nothing could stop the blood now.

Marghe watched as Uaithne's horse came on, hooves thundering, foam flying from its muzzle. She tightened her thighs, ready to lean, to kick; felt capillaries opening in her shoulders, ready for the strike and twist that would send the spear spinning.

But Uaithne's knuckles were white, and she was slipping, slipping.

Two lengths from where Marghe sat her mount, Uaithne slid sideways and fell in a jumble of weapons and limbs. The riderless horse swerved, passing close enough to spatter Marghe with warm saliva. Uaithne tumbled loosely over the turf to the feet of Marghe's mount.

Marghe jumped from her saddle, panting, trembling with the adrenaline and the effort of not smashing her heel into Uaithne's unprotected throat. She knelt. Uaithne tried to lift her head.

"No. Shh. Keep still."

But Uaithne blew a red bubble of laughter at Marghe's concern, and died.

The grass was making Marghe's knees itch, but she did not move. She did not know what to do. She had been ready and Uaithne had . . . She looked at the body before her. Uaithne had died. The woman who had been about to try to kill her could not hurt her anymore. She did not know how to feel. Everything seemed a long way off.

Something nudged her shoulder: Uaithne's mount, come back for its rider. The grass hissed in the soft morning breeze, then stiffened as the breeze blew hotter and harder. The storm was coming.

Marghe blinked. Everything was quiet, too quiet. Was this shock? She climbed slowly to her feet, expecting the world to burst in on her with sound and fury and mayhem. Nothing happened. She looked around. The Mirrors were still bunched tightly, like a straining muscle. Thenike sat before them, as immovable as rock. The line of tribeswomen was stirring, the horses tossing their heads restlessly; some spears were couched, stone heads catching the sun, and some were held loosely. The tension in the air was thicker than the scent of olla. The wind rose. She breathed carefully; her trembling eased.

Marghe stood alone on the grass between the two hosts for what seemed like an age, while the wind flicked the manes and tails of the two horses and filled her mouth with rushing noise. Then Aoife swung down from her saddle and began to walk toward her, empty-handed, alone. The Mirrors stirred, and a figure detached itself from the ranks, flipping up her visor as she walked. Danner. Also empty-handed.

When Danner passed Thenike, the viajera dismounted and followed, leading her horse.

They all stopped in the middle and looked at one another. The wind was hot and hard now, like the heat from a blast furnace. Thenike laid a hand briefly on Marghe's shoulder.

They were waiting for her, Marghe realized, but her brain felt empty, numbed by the two sudden deaths and the driving wind.

In the end, it was Thenike who spoke first. "The storm's coming. We need to take shelter. The grass is too dry."

Wind. Singing Pastures. Marghe made the effort. "I know a place," she said slowly. "All rocks and scree. There's a cave, and a ravine. No danger of fire there. It's big enough for all of us." Danner looked warily at Aoife. "If tribes and Mirrors can shelter together."

Aoife looked down at the loose tumble of hair and limbs and blood that was Uaithne, then back at the line of Echraidhe and Briogannon, where what was left of Captain White Moon was still tied to the saddle. When she turned back, she fixed flat, hard eyes on Marghe. "My soestre is dead." Then she turned that empty gaze on Danner. "And one of your kin. If more are to die, it should not be in a grass fire."

Danner licked her lips; it was not a very reassuring answer.

Marghe felt sorry for both Danner and Aoife. They were leaders, both of them, solid, conscientious members of their respective societies who were suddenly faced with having to adapt to something new and utterly against their beliefs.

She smiled. Uaithne was dead, and she had been ready. Everything seemed so clear and simple to her now: the tribes could do nothing while their Levarch treated with the enemy over the body of their dead kin; the Mirrors would not dare attack while their commander was in what appeared to be a hostage situation.

The others were looking at her. "Thenike, how long before the storm?"

"It's upon us. Any moment."

"Then we'll have to hurry. Danner, Aoife, you will walk to the Echraidhe line and bring back both Captain White Moon and her mount, and a mount for each for yourselves—you can ride, can't you?" she asked Danner.

"Yes."

"And bring back one of the Briogannon, one of their leaders. Aoife, you will tell your people to follow us. Danner, you will tell your Mirrors to precede us, due south. While you are bringing White Moon and the mounts, Thenike and I will secure Uaithne to her horse."

Danner and Aoife looked sideways at each other.

"Danner. You have a cling?"

Danner looked puzzled. "Yes."

"Give it to me." Danner peeled it loose from her belt and handed it over. "Hold out your arm."

"What—"

"Hold out your arm. Your left. Aoife, you hold out your right." She bound the arms together at the biceps. "Just in case. I'll take it off when you both get back here in one piece. Now go."

Danner took a hesitant step, which Aoife copied, then another. Marghe watched while they pulled each other warily, one step at a time, toward the mounted line.

When they were about halfway there, Thenike put a hand on Marghe's shoulder, turned her around gently, and held her face between the palms of her hands. "You told a good story."

I was ready. "I did, didn't I?"

They smiled at one another, and Marghe wrapped her arms around Thenike and let her breath go in one long, deep rush.

GETTING UAITHNE'S body onto her mount was hard; the horse sidled and snorted and laid its ears back at the smell of blood and excretia. But they managed eventually.

It was Ojo who came back with Danner and Aoife, and who held the leading rein of White Moon's horse. Marghe was tempted to cling all three of them together, but decided to trust them. She directed Thenike to take the lead rein from Ojo, and to walk in front of the three leaders; she herself walked behind them, leading Uaithne's horse.

Ahead, the Mirrors turned and moved south at the march. Behind, the tribes stirred and started at a walk.

All the time, the wind rose, buffeting them in the saddle, and when Marghe had to give Danner directions to pass on to her Mirrors via comm, she had to shout against a gale that wanted to whip away her words like so much smoke.

Marghe kept them heading for the cave and the gully. Shelter first. Then they would talk.

IN THE end, the talking was done at Holme Valley.

When the five leaders had emerged from the cave, they found acres of grassland seared black, still smoking, turning dusk into evening. It was stifling.

Danner touched a stud at her collar. Her suit stopped humming, and she took off her helmet in a spill of cold air. "It's too hot to leave those bodies unburied. We need to get them bagged and cooled immediately."

After several strained hours in the cave, standing between two hundred women who would find it easier to fight than talk, Marghe was irritated by Danner's attitude, but it was Thenike who spoke.

"They're not 'bodies'!" Marghe had never seen Thenike so angry. "They are what's left of your captain and Aoife's soestre. They were real. They had friends, mothers, people here who will pause in the middle of their next meal and miss that unique laugh or the sight of a familiar hand resting on a table. Their deaths helped to buy this." She gestured at the gathered forces, still standing apart suspiciously, but not fighting. Not fighting. "They should be buried out there, where they died. Together. Their grave should be in the place where so many others came close to killing and being killed, on neutral territory so that women can come and visit it and remember why these two women died, and how. Then maybe this . . . this idiocy won't ever happen again."

TOGETHER WITH the massed tribes and a company of Mirrors as escort, Marghe and Thenike, and Aoife, Danner, and Ojo, leading Uaithne's horse and White Moon's and carrying shovels, went back to the place that had nearly become a battlefield.

The olla patch had escaped the fire, and Danner suggested that they bury them under the flowers. They looked at Thenike, but the viajera said nothing; she seemed to have withdrawn inside herself.

"No," Marghe decided, "we'll bury them where they died. We'll put them under the charred grass and the seared soil, and their grave will green when the rest of the plain does."

The funeral was short; there was no ritual that would have been acceptable to both sides. Instead, Aoife stepped forward and told a story about Uaithne, about how she had broken her first pony when she was ten years old, and Danner said a few gruff words about how White Moon had been a brilliant captain, with the respect and trust of her officers. Then Thenike shook herself and began to sing a soft song of harvest time. It seemed an odd choice to Marghe at first, but as the viajera started to clap along with her song, as she raised her voice to sing of harvesting, of threshing, of ground that would be plowed over and seeds that would be sown that the fields would bloom again, Marghe understood. She took up the clapping. As others heard the message of renewal, they clapped, too, and when Thenike stopped singing, the clapping went on and on.

 AFTER THE burial, Aoife sent most of the tribeswomen back north. To gather the scattered herds, she said. Aoife herself and her daughter Marac, representing the Echraidhe, and Ojo for the Briogannon, followed Marghe, Thenike, and Danner to Holme Valley, where the talks were to be held under the great skelter tree that was the home of Cassil's family.

Holle spoke for the women of Singing Pastures, and Cassil for Holme Valley. After much thought, Marghe decided she would act for Danner and the others. She owed them that, at least.

"You're a tribe now," she told Danner. "Try to think in those terms. I'll get what I can for you. Your standing's high right now."

"You mean yours."

Marghe ignored that. "I'm going to secure trata agreements

from the tribes and from Holle, if I can, as well as strengthening the arrangement with Cassil."

"Just as long as we get our seed crop, and some breeding animals."

"I'll do much better for you than that," Marghe promised.

THE FINAL trata agreements were reached in the presence of the viajeras Thenike and T'orre Na:

The Echraidhe and Briogannon, temporarily merged under the madness of Uaithne, were enjoined to become one people in order to ensure peace for themselves and other settlements, and in order to survive; the herds of both tribes were decimated, their goods scattered, their children malnourished. They were granted joint use of grazing grounds to the north and west of Singing Pastures. From their herds, beginning the first year the animals reached reasonable numbers, they would grant a tithe of horses to Singing Pastures, in part reparation, and a tithe of breeding taars. These breeding taars would go straight from Holle's people to Danner's. Until that time, Danner's people would receive a small number of breeding taars from Cassil, and help from both communities in capturing wild animals for domestication. Also from Cassil, Danner would get seed crop, first trading rights on the valley's harvest, two hand looms, and—Marghe had had to fight hard for this—the fostering of six of the valley's children, along with one or two adults.

"Think, Danner, they'll be invaluable!" she told the Mirror. "What better way to learn the way a world works than to learn with their children?"

Cassil agreed, if volunteers could be found. In return, Danner had to promise the fostering of a third of any Mirror children in the next five years, again on a volunteer basis. Marghe was not worried about lack of volunteers. There were many on both sides who were curious, and some who would think to turn the arrangement to their personal gain. One way or another, both communities would benefit, in the end.

THEY WENT to the Holme Valley cave for the witnessing song. It was evening. Marghe lifted her spitting torch a little higher; mica and quartz glittered redly as the nine pattern singers walked ahead of the women of Holme Valley, their audience. Fine sand sifted, cool and dry, between Marghe's toes.

"Letitia told me about this place," Danner whispered as she walked deeper into the cavern, "but I only half believed her."

Before them, glimmering with natural phosphorescence, a lake slid in blues and greens. They were standing on a wide, natural shelf that ran around the walls of the cavern. Thin-waisted columns plunged into the water from the lower parts of the uneven roof. The lake poured with light, throwing shadows on the wall at Marghe's back, sheathing the columns in shimmering cloaks of color.

T'orre Na began the song. Marghe took it up, followed by Thenike and Holle and Cassil; then Aoife, Day, and Ojo. Danner was the last to join her voice to the eight others and close the circle of nine. To Marghe's surprise, the Mirror had a light, clear soprano.

They joined hands: Ojo's rough, dry hand in Marghe's left, Day's—warm and soft—in her right. Marghe smiled as she sang the wordless song, enjoying the way harmonies split off and raced over the water, echoing back from the walls. It felt as though the whole population of the valley was singing.

One by one, the voices dropped out. At the edges of the lake tiny pebbles rocked in a slight current.

They ate together outside, with children crying from fatigue and Ojo and Aoife sitting as far apart from each other as possible. Marghe chewed her bread deliberately, determined not to worry about it; no agreement was perfect.

Later, lying next to Thenike, she fell asleep wondering if some deep, quiet place in the cavern still echoed with the song they had made, and dreamed of small pebbles rocking in the water.

Chapter Eighteen

HARVEST IN Holme Valley began two days after the trata agreement was reached. The year was beginning its steady turn toward winter and it was time for the pattern singers to go their separate ways.

Day left first, with T'orre Na. "I want to go home," she said to Marghe. "I want to watch Jink and Oriyest sitting by our fire. I want to see how the younglings in the flock are doing, and what grass we've got left." She hitched her pack higher on her shoulders, then suddenly thrust out her hand. "It was good meeting you," she said awkwardly, "but better than that, you've . . . well, you've given me hope. Sort of. T'orre Na says that if you can get pregnant, there's no reason I can't." Then she grinned. "Not that I'm sure I *want* to have a child, you know? We've enough to deal with, with Jink's two. But it would be nice to have the choice. It would make me feel as though I belong."

Thenike went with Day and T'orre Na. "Only for a few days, Amu. To see their part of the world again. To hear T'orre Na's stories. I'll be back when you've finished your business with your kin, here."

Marghe knew that Thenike was giving her time alone to have that talk with Hiam and say her good-byes, but when she waved the three of them off, it was hard not to feel as though someone had ripped loose one of her limbs. Thenike would be back, Marghe told herself as she walked through the dry grass. She would be back.

That night she dreamed of Thenike running her hands through the air over her body, cupping and smoothing vast tides of electromagnetic energy over her skin, until Marghe felt herself changing, lengthening, growing fur. Becoming a goth. And then Letitia Dogias was laughing, saying, Now you understand, then running out into a storm, onto a spire of rock while lightning jagged through her, again and again.

Marghe woke feeling as though something she should know was dancing tantalizingly out of reach. She shook her head and got up. Hiam might be able to help. But when she went to the hospital, Hiam was not available. Marghe left a message.

Further down the valley, she found the women of Singing Pastures mounted, their packhorses weighed down with their possessions and what was left of their herds standing, heads hanging, beneath a cloud of dust. Marghe ran a hand over the muzzle of Holle's horse, remembering Pella, and looked up. "So soon?"

"There's maybe thirty days of good grazing left up north. Every mouthful helps. It'll be a hard winter. You'll be going back to Ollfoss?"

"It's my home now." Home. Last time she had been here, with Cassil, she had had no home.

"Don't be too late setting out. Winter won't be long coming this year. And come see us in the spring. With your youngster. Maybe we'll lend you another horse."

Holle knew she would not get Pella back. The debt had been written off as part of the trata agreement, but a horse was not an inanimate object. Marghe hoped the mare was still alive up north somewhere, grown shaggy against the cold, running with the remnants of the Echraidhe herd. Perhaps with a leggy colt running beside her.

Marghe laid a hand on her own belly. This time next year, her daughter would be three months old. A spring child. Born at the same time of year as young taars and foals, when birds began to sing and wirrels ate the last of their hoards. A time when the world smelled fresh and new. She wished Thenike were there to share the thought. But she would be back in three or four days.

Holle and her people urged their sweating horses here and there, closing up the taar herd for travel, then moved out in a swirl of drovers' whistles and whipcracks. Marghe watched until there was nothing left but the hanging dust.

THE HARVEST at Holme Valley was not the orderly cutting of fields in a straight-line pattern that Marghe had observed in cultures all over the world. Instead, the women started harvesting in the outer fields and cut to the accompaniment of children singing, clapping hands, and beating drums; almost as if they were herding some small animals toward the center of the fields.

"But of course," Cassil said when Marghe asked her about it, "we keep the soul of the rice going inward, so that it concentrates, instead of leaving the grain."

And Marghe, when she stood still listening to the stamp of bare feet and the hissing thresh of olla scythes against stalks, felt . . . *something* moving inward with the beaters and reapers. It grew stronger, more focused—like a storm gathering, but warmer, more yellow.

She walked away from the fields thoughtfully and punched in Hiam's code. The doctor was still not talking. She went to find Danner.

Marghe spent the next two days at Danner's screen, downloading huge chunks of biology and physics data and comparing the information with what she knew of Thenike's abilities and her own, with Letitia's and Uaithne's strange behavior during severe storms, with what she had learned during her biofeedback training. It made for some interesting theories.

MARGHE SET off for the hospital, trudging through the muggy heat under an overcast sky. There would not be many clear skies again at Holme Valley until spring. She thought of the bright, hard skies of Ollfoss and wished she and Thenike were starting their journey back the very next day.

When she got to the hospital, the doctor was not there, but Lu Wai was, holding Letitia's hand. Letitia was awake.

"Letitia!" Marghe tried to smile, but the technician looked thin and fragile, like a dark brittle stick against the white bed.

"Don't look like that. I feel better than I look. Pretty good, in fact. I won't be turning cartwheels for a week or two, but I'm alive, Lu Wai's alive. And it looks like things are going to get pretty interesting from now on."

This time Marghe's smile was genuine. "You do sound better than you look."

Letitia grinned. Her face was terribly thin. "I hear I missed a good storm."

"The first one was better."

"Yes." She smiled at Marghe, that thin, stretched smile. "The way Twissel tells it, I'm some kind of hero." But Marghe saw Letitia's knuckles whiten as she squeezed Lu Wai's hand, and realized the technician was not really talking to her. Marghe felt as though she was intruding on something private.

"Well, I'd better go find Hiam."

"No, wait." Letitia reached out a hand to Marghe. "I haven't thanked you. You and Thenike. Hiam says you saved my life."

Marghe did not know what to say. Thenike deserved most of the credit, but Thenike was not here to accept the thanks that Letitia needed to give. "Anytime."

They were quiet. A machine bleeped softly.

"So, rumor has it you're pregnant."

"Yes."

"You don't look pregnant." The machine bleeped again. "When's it due?"

A green light blinked, and Letitia's eyes rolled. Marghe looked anxiously at Lu Wai. The Mirror held a finger to her lips. Letitia closed her eyes and fell asleep with a faint smile on her lips.

Lu Wai motioned Marghe outside. "She'll be asleep for about four hours. It's the only way we can get her to have enough rest. You know what she's like."

In the natural light Marghe could see how drawn and tired the Mirror looked. "Are you all right?"

"Yes. It's just . . ." She dug her boot toe into the turf, ground out a hole. "I look at her, lying there, and I wonder how it would be if she'd died. I don't think I could . . . I don't think . . ."

Marghe touched her shoulder. "I know."

"But she's healing. She's tough." Now Lu Wai smiled, a private, proud smile, and lifted her head. "She'll wake up still wanting to know when your child is due."

"Tell her the Moon of New Grass. Next spring. And tell her that if you would both like to come for the birth, for the births, Thenike and I will send a message."

"I'd like that," Lu Wai said softly. "I'd like that very much."

AOIFE AND Marac, along with the Briogannon, Ojo, stayed a little longer. They wanted to study the ways of the Holme Valley community, Marac said; how they shaped the skelter trees, plowed their fields, used the river. For three days Marghe watched them as they went out and about—the hard, lean Levarch and the younger, softer daughter—fingering an olla bowl, thumping the tendons of a breeding taar, or asking short hard questions on the length of the seasons this far south. Once, she saw them both lift their hands and rub at their chins thoughtfully while Cassil explained a harvest technique. Ojo drifted behind them, a dark-eyed shadow.

But summer was short on Tehuantepec, and Aoife and Marac had to get back north to join their people. "There's not much time to bring our herds south before the snows. Winter comes early this year," Aoife said from her horse.

"That's what Holle said." The sun was bright, and Marghe had to shade her eyes with her hand to look up at Aoife. Marac and Ojo waited on their small, shaggy ponies some distance away.

Aoife looked diminished, Marghe realized. She wondered how it must feel, to kill a soestre.

"You did the right thing," she said suddenly. "It's best for your people."

"I am Levarch. I always do what is best for the Echraidhe." Her eyes were bleak. "Sometimes it is not easy. For me or others."

An apology?

"You were right when you said the Echraidhe must change. I listen to truth and those who speak it. But I'll never forget that it was you who made me kill my soestre. You will never be welcome in my tent."

Aoife looked at her without expression, then wheeled her horse and was gone, Marac and Ojo thundering along beside her.

You will never be welcome in my tent. There was an Echraidhe curse: *You will never be welcome on our grazing grounds or in our tents, neither you nor your daughters nor the daughters of your daughters. May your taars lose their fur and your horses their teeth, and may your land be frozen for a thousand years.* But Aoife had restrained herself. *My tent,* she had said, not *our grazing grounds* or *our tents.* Even now, the Levarch was keeping the tribe's best interests over her own: the Echraidhe would need all the help they could get in the next few years, and it would be foolish to declare a powerful viajera and her even-more-powerful friends anathema. Instead, Aoife had declared a personal animosity.

Marghe watched the three galloping horses dwindle into the distance. It would not be long before their strange tribal code eased as the harsh winters of Tehuantepec that had made it a necessity for survival became a thing of the past. She was surprised to find she would mourn the passing of that fierce Echraidhe insularity.

Marghe wished Thenike would come back. She needed to feel strong arms around her; she wanted to lay her head against Thenike's belly and listen to see if she could hear the child that would grow up as soestre to the one living inside her own body. She wanted to talk and think about something other than Aoife's unforgiving words, something other than change and death.

THAT NIGHT, Marghe found Sara Hiam sitting on the dry, dusty-smelling grass outside the hospital. She joined her.

"It smells good out here," Hiam said.

Marghe nodded, then realized Hiam would not see that. "Yes."

They sat quietly. The breeze blew warm, then cool; autumn was coming. In the distance a horse snorted.

"I like the nights," Hiam said. "After six years on *Estrade*, the days down here seem too big, too intimidating. All that sky, and air. Sometimes I get nervous when a breeze swirls. I'm so used to air coming from one direction at a time, and always the same temperature."

"The storms must have been hard for you."

"Yes."

Silence.

"Marghe, this world . . . You seem at home here. But it scares me. The wind scares me, the people. The virus. You scare me."

"Me?"

"You've changed."

Marghe did not know what to say. "Yes."

Hiam moved restlessly. "There's so much I don't understand. Like your friend, Thenike. I'm sorry I called her a savage. I don't know what she did, or how, but whatever it was, she saved Letitia's life. How did she do that? She was right about the adjuvants, too." A tiny silence. They understood each other: apologies given and accepted on both sides. "And you're pregnant. And I don't understand any of it. I want to know. I want you to tell me."

Marghe wondered where to begin. She picked a long stem of grass and sniffed it, smelling the familiar spice of Jeep. "It's the virus. It changes everything. It's . . . Well, I have a theory about Thenike's healing. I felt something, when she was running her hands over Letitia. Over the air around Letitia, really. I was trained to be sensitive to my own body; I think I'm more sensitive than most. Then when the virus became part of me, it was like that sensitivity increased a thousandfold. More. So when Thenike did what she did, I could feel it." She stripped away the brownish outer layer of the stalk of grass. "I wonder if I might not, in time, learn to do it myself."

"You're not making much sense."

Under the outer covering, the stem was green and juicy. Marghe put it in her mouth, chewed awhile. "I've been doing some reading lately. It turns out that every cell in the human body—in every other body, too, plant and animal—and every molecule and atom in that cell, is in a constant state of vibration. All this cell-by-cell excitation adds up to produce enough energy to change the electrical and magnetic properties of the space they occupy."

"That's nothing new."

"No. Anyway, we all resonate on a particular, unique frequency, but because all humans radiate within a narrow wave band we all receive and transmit those signals. All the time. We're in constant communication with each other and with the outside world. Patterns of these waves explore everything close by, so all the time we're with other people we're unconsciously probing them. And being probed." She picked a shred of grass from her teeth. "I imagine if a person was sensitive enough, it would just be a matter of training to bring that kind of probing under conscious control." She stared out at the dark, heaving sky. Thenike could probably explain this better. "Sara, how would you define healing?"

"Making someone better. Or, rather, helping—tricking, persuading—a body to heal itself."

"Right. Modern medicine does it mechanically, like stitching, and chemically—antibiotics and things. But what about electrically? Magnetically? Electrochemically?"

"We do that already," Sara said thoughtfully. "Strap a power pack around a break and it heals anywhere up to six times as fast."

Marghe nodded. "According to what I've been reading, injury, like Letitia's, produces a disorganization of the normal, healthy electrical pattern. Are you with me?"

"Yes."

"Now what if, what if a person has enough control over her magnetic field, her transmissions, to affect another's? What if the healthy person's patterns could interact with the sick person's?"

Hiam looked dubious.

"Sara, when Thenike ran her hands around Letitia, my body could feel it! It was like her pattern was talking to mine, to all the eddies and flows of my cells, saying: See? See how you should be? Like this, this is how you're supposed to go."

"But how? I don't understand how she can do it!"

"The virus, that's how. Oh, Sara, the things I've seen! When I woke up after being sick, it was like becoming conscious for the first time, like a blind person seeing color . . . No, that's not right. It was just *more*. Like I could see better and hear better and smell better, like my kinesthetic sense was more highly developed. There's so much out there to notice, to feel. It's almost as if the virus is part of this world, so that when the virus became part of me, I could see the world and feel it more clearly. . . ."

Sara Hiam sat in obstinate silence.

"It's the virus," Marghe repeated more quietly. "It gets all tangled up in the DNA somehow, and changes things. Maybe it intensifies the semiconducting properties of our nervous systems. I don't know. That's something you'll have to find out. Viruses are what you know. I can only tell you that it's my belief that the virus allows us greater control—much, much greater control—over the autonomic nervous system, and other things."

Sara was still silent. Marghe decided to change tactics.

"I've been thinking about Letitia Dogias. You've heard about her behavior during storms?"

"Yes," Sara said unwillingly.

"Have you had the opportunity to find out why?"

"I've run some tests."

"And?"

"And I can't find anything wrong with her. Nothing."

"I think I know what's wrong with her: she's very sensitive to the buildup of energy around storms, but doesn't know what it is she feels, or how to deal with it. She's got no biofeedback training at all. She overloads."

"It could be a psychiatric condition."

"It could. But it isn't."

The sky lit up in a long, vivid flash, then died back to inky black.

"What was that?" Sara asked.

"I don't know. I've never seen anything like it before."

They listened, but there was no noise except the wind in the grass and, from a long way off down the valley, a trail of laughter.

"I'm afraid," Sara said from the dark. "Everything's so different. You're so different. I remember you up on *Estrade*. You were so . . . ordinary."

"I'm different, yes."

There was no way to explain how it felt. How it was to be able to remember in a way she would have thought impossible a year ago; how it felt to only have three fingers on her left hand, to have nearly died. How it felt to have another life growing inside her, to have a partner. A home.

"Change is just change, Sara. Not all good, not all bad. Just different."

They were quiet a long time, listening to the wind in the grass.

"I'm still afraid. Soon the virus will come for me, for Nyo and Sigrid. And I can do nothing to stop it. Nothing. I'm a doctor and I can't stop it."

"You can't stop the common cold, either."

"But that won't kill me."

"No."

"Hiam!" The call came clear through the dark.

Hiam started, then stood up. "Over here! Who is it?"

They heard the running footsteps, surprisingly close. "Me. Danner."

"What is it? What's happened?"

"Out of breath. A moment." Danner bent over, straightened, sucked air into her lungs. Marghe could not see her face, but something was very wrong. They waited. "Sigrid just called. *Estrade's* gone."

"Gone?"

"They blew it up."

"That flash . . ."

"Yes."

"The people on board?"

"They didn't take them off first."

Marghe imagined a corona of plasma floating and frozen, orbiting the planet forever. "The *Kurst*?"

Danner seemed to notice Marghe for the first time. "Gone. Peeled out of orbit just before detonating the platform."

"Sweet god," Sara said.

"At least they didn't kill us."

"Not yet."

Marghe stared at her. They were gone, weren't they? "What about the gig?"

"Also gone. We're cut off now. Completely on our own."

"Not for long," Hiam said. Now they both stared at her. "Don't you understand yet? There's a whole world here, and Company won't forget it. They might be gone for now, but they haven't given up. Company never gives up. They'll keep at it, on and on, until they find a vaccine, or a cure, and then they'll be back. It might be five years, or it might not be until that daughter of yours is grown, Marghe. But they'll be back. And when they do, they'll be holding our destruction, the destruction of all the communities of this world, in their syringes or their sprays. Without the virus, the people of this world don't have children. No children and we die."

We die. While they were standing there, looking at each other, wondering how they could ever be ready against that day, Thenike came back.

DAWN WAS cool and the sky ragged with cloud. Danner and Hiam had walked through the trees with Marghe and Thenike as far as the river.

"Come north when you can," Marghe said to Sara. "The goth

are there, somewhere. You more than anyone would know what to
do, how to find out more. The virus has something to do with
them, I think. And I need help with those records. Letitia and Lu
Wai are going to come for the births; Letitia's promised to do what
she can with the disk I found. You could travel together. The more
we can learn, the better. The goth, the virus, the records . . . they
all tie in somehow, and we need to find out what we can before
Company returns. Will you come?"

"I . . . Perhaps."

"It gets better, Sara. Believe me." In time, Sara would learn that
the world was not hostile, that one only had to take the proper
care and give the weather proper respect, and travel did not have to
be fatal. "And you, Hannah?"

"I'd like to. But I don't know. Whatever we become, tribe or
community or kith or kindred or a howling mob, it's my job to
steer us onto the right track. Worrying about breeding herds and
seed crop and irrigation isn't that different from worrying about
surgical supplies and duty rosters. I'm good at that."

"Too good, maybe." Danner was scared, too. Scared of losing
her authority and finding there was nothing else. "Perhaps you
should leave the burden in someone else's hands."

"One of these days they'll get someone else to do it, but not
for a year or two. Until then, travel's a luxury I won't be able to
afford."

"In a year or two, then." They both knew it would be longer
than that. Or maybe not. Marghe looked from Danner to Hiam.
Maybe they would be good for each other.

Danner held out her hand. "Good luck, Marghe Amun. And
when you come south again, viajering, swing by Dentro de un
Rato and tell us the news."

Marghe hugged her, hugged Sara, and then stepped away from
them. The wind that blew from the river was cold. Thenike picked
up her pack and slung the strap of her leather drumcase over her
shoulder. Marghe picked up hers, then hesitated.

"No more goodbyes," Sara said. "It's cold enough to freeze a
bird out of the sky. Get walking. And when you brew up your next

cup of dap, think of us. Come on, Hannah." She took the Mirror's arm and led her away, back toward the trees.

Marghe hefted her pack and looked at Thenike. They started walking.

By MIDDAY the sun had burned the clouds away; they walked at a good pace, and by the time the grass became striped with streaks and patches of burn they were sweating. They detoured around the field of nodding olla flowers, but the thick, sweet scent made breathing difficult. They tied scarves around their noses and mouths and slowed their pace a little. They were in no rush.

Evening. The grave was visible from a good distance: a brown mound rising from black. Their footsteps were loud as they crunched over the plain of cinder.

In the eight days since the grave had been dug, there had been winds from the southwest, and the base of the mound was lightly dusted with pinkish yellow pollen. Marghe knelt, pulled down her scarf, laid a hand on the mound; under the powdery burned smell lurked the scent of sun-dried dirt, a light, end-of-summer scent.

The end of many things.

There was something sharp under her palm. She poked at the dirt with an index finger, then picked up several tiny white shards. Broken shells.

Thenike knelt and wrapped her arms around Marghe from behind. "This used to be a lake, an inland sea. Long, long ago."

They listened to the soughing of their breath, feeling muscles warm and alive over strong bones. After a while, Marghe put the shells back; the grave did not seem complete without them.

When the sun set, the night turned cold, and they built a fire. Marghe set two bowls of dap to warm by the fire, then settled down to toast a piece of soca on her knife.

After a while, Thenike dipped a thumb into the nearest bowl. "Dap's hot." They sipped, staring into the flames.

"They're like the sea," Marghe said, "always changing. I never get tired of watching."

Thenike put her bowl down by the fire to keep warm and took her drums from their case.

"A song?"

"For you, Marghe Amun."

She sang softly of a woman who walked the shore of a long-forgotten sea, collecting seashells, shells she would string to make a necklace for her love. The woman took the shells home and washed them carefully, and dried them. Some glimmered blue and pearl, like her lover's eyes; others glowed pink and caramel, like her skin; one shimmered blue-black, as mysterious as the sea at midnight . . .

Marghe thought of the suke hanging around her neck, the ammonite Thenike had carefully remembered and reproduced for Leifin to carve, and smiled.

Thenike sang on, and while the drum beat softly and the flames danced, Marghe set her face north, toward Ollfoss. Toward home.

Nicola Griffith Talks about Writing *Ammonite*

"ARE WOMEN human?" That question forms the subtext of more speculative fiction novels—fantasy, SF, horror, utopia and dystopia—than I can count. I intended *Ammonite* as a body blow to those who feel the question has any relevance in today's world.

I am tired of token women being strong in a man's world by taking on male attributes: strutting around in black leather, spike heels and wraparound shades, killing people; or riding a horse, swearing a lot, carrying a big sword, and killing people; or piloting a ship through hyperspace, drinking whatever pours, slapping boys on the back, and killing people. I am equally tired of women-only worlds where all the characters are wise, kind, beautiful, stern seven-feet-tall vegetarian amazons who would never dream of killing anyone. I am tired of reading about aliens who are really women, or women who are really aliens.

Women are not aliens. Take away men and we do not automatically lose our fire and intelligence and sex drive; we do not form hierarchical, static, insectlike societies that are dreadfully inefficient. We do not turn into a homogeneous Thought Police culture where meat-eating is banned and men are burned in effigy every full moon. Women are not inherently passive or dominant, maternal or vicious. We are all different. We are people.

A women-only world, it seems to me, would shine with the entire spectrum of human behavior: there would be capitalists and collectivists, hermits and clan members, sailors and cooks, idealists and tyrants; they would be generous and mean, smart and stupid, strong and weak; they would approach life bravely, fearfully and thoughtlessly. Some might still engage in fights, wars and territorial squabbles; individuals and cultures would still display insanity and greed and indifference. And they would change and grow, just like anyone else. Because women *are* anyone else. We are more than half of humanity. We are not imitation people, or chameleons taking on protective male coloration, longing for the day when men go away and we can return to being our true, insectlike, static, vacuous selves. We are here, now. We are just like you.

But *Ammonite* is much more than an attempt to redress the balance. It's a novel. One about people—how they look at the world and how the world makes them change; one that attempts to look at biology, and wonder *What if . . .* ; one that shows readers different ways to be; one that takes them to other places, where the air and the temperature and the myths are not the same. If, a week after reading *Ammonite*, you pause over lunch, fork halfway to your mouth, and remember the scent of Jeep's night air, or on your way to work daydream about the endless snow of Tehuantepec, or wonder for a moment as you climb into bed whether or not a virus *could* enhance our senses—then I've done my job.

Atlanta, 1992

Glossary

Abersayesh	busy settlement at the mouth of the Sash River
Agelast	heir apparent to the Levarch of the Echraidhe
auricul	edible fungus
baby fever	the Echraidhe term for the virus of Jeep
Beaver/BV 4	Company's mining planet; site of Marghe's unfortunate tour as SEC rep
bemebell	flower, most often blue
bezoar	a remedy
boatfly	large, slow-moving insect
bollo	game, similar to polo
Briogannon	a nomadic tribe of Tehuantepec
burn	patch of ground devastated by the ignition (by lightning, or a fire, or mining) of a naturally occurring peatlike substance; when triggered, a burn can smolder for a generation
cetrar	herbaceous plant often used as a febrifuge
chessel	wooden cheese vat
chia	migratory bird
choose mother	a child's preferred caregiver in the household

corax	succulent-leaved plant of the northern forest; harvested in summer, its leaves make a powerful bleaching agent
Cruath	settlement on the river Ho
cuirm	bitter-tasting ale
cyarnac	large four-footed predator, possibly marsupial, snow dweller
dap	tea, mild stimulant
days of dark	the nine days of mid-winter when the sun does not climb over the horizon on Tehuantepec
deepsearch	ritual trance
Dentro de un Rato	(a.k.a. Dun Rats) the proposed site of the new settlement for ex-Company employees
Durallium Company	(a.k.a. Company) a vast interstellar conglomerate
Echraidhe	tribe of nomads on the Tehuantepec Plateau (pronouned Eck-RAYV)
ellum root	tuber, infusion of which is used medicinally to treat bowel rot
erimon	delicately scented spring blossom
Estrade	Company's orbital station; control center for microwave relays, intra-orbital gigs, communications, quarantine
Eye of Ocean	resource-rich island in the middle of Silverfish Deep
flickvine	also known as clingvine, lianalike organism whose sap is both sticky and acidic
FN-17	experimental vaccine created by Dr. Sara Hiam against Jeep's virus
Gallipoli	Company planet
gaver	pepper, used as nutritional supplement
gavesam	knobby tuber, used medicinally as infusion to treat eye infection
gig	ground-to-orbit transport vessel
Glass	river running from the Yelland Hills to High Beaches
glimmer fly	flying insect, found near water, appearing only at dawn and dusk
goth	large two-footed sentient, semi-mythical
goura	a fruit
Grenchstom's Planet	see Jeep
herd bird	large avian, semi-domesticated

High Beaches	settlement at the mouth of the river Glass
Ho	largest river east of the Kaharil Mountains
Holme Valley	one of the largest settlements on Jeep
Huipil	river that runs north of the Trern Swamplands to Pebble Fleet
hyrat	jackal-sized carnivore, hunts and scavenges in packs
Ice Sea	narrow channel between Luast and the Wastelands, almost always frozen
irrillil	medicinal herb, foul-smelling, usually applied as paste
ixtle	flower, prized for its fibrous stem
jaellum	food plant with high carbohydrate content; seeds planted in spring mature into fruit-bearing vines in summer
Jeep	a.k.a. Grenchstom's Planet; world discovered and settled several hundred years before the beginning of the present narrative; mineral and other exploitable rights currently leased by Company. Also the name of a deadly virus
jewelfeet	wraithlike tree-dwellers of the northern forest whose chitinous toe coverings refract light like peacock feathers
Kaharil Mountains	mountain range west of the river Ho; old, geologically speaking
kris fly	native insectoid, attracted to olla pollen, travels in swarms, mild sting
krisbread	bread, slightly sweet
Kurst	Company security ship, in orbit around Jeep
Levarch	leader of the Echraidhe, non-hereditary position; the Levarch usually resigns in old age and is succeeded by the chosen Agelast
limegrass	aromatic herb
locha	fermented taar milk
Luast	port west of North Haven
marac dubh	healer's black knife (pronounced marac-DOOV)
menalden	dappled, deer-like mammals
Menalden Pool	pool of Old Ollfoss
mimic bird	fabled bird of the south
Mirror	member of Company's security force, so called because of mirror-visored helmet

Moanwood	great northern forest of Tehuantepec
Mouth of the Grave	opening to the Summer Island channels, made impassable by reefs most of the year
mustard fly	native insectoid
neat's foot	aromatic leaf, used to flavor soups and stews
Necklace Islands	to be found in the eastern reaches of Silverfish Deep
needlestone	quartzlike mineral
Nemora	deep sea trading ship, out of Southmeet
nerka	salt-water fish
n'gus	a.k.a. queen daggerhorn; large herbivore of the northern forest
nid-nod	wetland bird, also name of Thenike's boat
nitta	nutrient-rich gourd whose seeds are used as a dietary supplement
North Haven	sea port north of Moanwood
nutch	reptile
Oboshi Desert	desert, west of Kaharil Mountains
Old Ollfoss	site of original colonist landing on Jeep
olla	vitreous substance used for a variety of purposes from crockery to knife blades; must be mined and processed
olla flower	native flower, ivory petals, golden pollen, grows in abundance over buried olla patches
Ollfoss	large, prosperous settlement in the north of Moanwood, famed for its gardens
palo	telescoping wooden baton used as a herding switch by nomadic tribes
pattern singing	vocal net woven by family and friends, usually nine women, to aid a young woman's first deepsearch
Pebble Fleet	fishing port at the mouth of the river Huipil
Pella	Marghe's horse, obtained via trata from Singing Pastures
pelmat	very slow-moving amphibian
pensel	spear pennant
Port Central	Company headquarters on Jeep
ringstones	twenty-seven megaliths on Tehuantepec, of uncertain origin
ruk	snow crab; edible, though oily and vile-tasting

Sash	big river far west of the Kaharil Mountains
Scatterdell	settlement on river Glass
scrophy	a skin disease
seavane	vast marine mammal that dwells in the surface waters, possibly related to the weblike organisms to be found on the grassland
SEC	joint Settlement and Education Councils: Earth body overseeing human rights on settled planets
Silverfish Deep	ocean east of Fisher's Bay
Singing Pastures	home of taar herders; north of Holme Valley
skelter tree	native tree with a long life span
sled	surface transport vehicle
sleth	aquatic insectivore
SLIC	Search, Locate, and Identify Code; combination ID and GPS transmitter; usually incorporated into wristcom, but also implantable subcutaneously
Sliprock	coastal settlement west of Luast
snow worm	annelid dwelling in the supra-permafrost layer
soca	small, round fruit
soestre	two or more children conceived simultaneously by mothers who bond in deepsearch (term probably derives etymologically from both *sister* and *oestrus*)
Southmeet	settlement on estuary of river Ho
suke	carved belt ornament
Summer Islands	three islands east of High Beaches, whose main port is Kull
taar	herd animal
tanglethorn	thorny bush, found in windy places
Tehuantepec	icy northern plateau; home of Echraidhe and Briogannon tribes; long winters and brief but hot summers
Telwise	trading boat, captained by Roth
tent mother	any woman over the age of about twenty who shares a child's tent
tent sisters	women of roughly contemporary age who share a tent
Terragin	Company-owned interstellar transport
Three Trees	settlement on river Ho
ting grass	almost ubiquitous vegetation; hollow-stemmed

trata	a kind of trade; a network of mutual obligation
Trern Swampland	coastal marsh south of the river Huipil and east of Southmeet
tris bark	prized for its resin
viajera	native journeywoman teller of news, arbiter of disputes, rememberer
whist	fast-moving arboreal
wirrel	tree-dwelling rodent
wristcom	combination SLIC, data storage and retrieval, and communications device worn on the wrist
yanomao	tree-dwelling marsupial
Yelland Hills	home of the olla shapers
yurt	tent, made of taar felt

Characters

SEC Employees

Marguerite Angelica Taishan, a.k.a. Marghe (pronounced with emphasis
on the first syllable, a hard 'g', and no 'e': MAR-g) Amun; representative of the joint Settlement and Education Councils to Grenchstom's
Planet, also known as Jeep

Maurice Courtivron, SEC rep, deceased

Janet Eagan, assistant SEC rep

Winnie Kimura, assistant SEC rep

Company Employees

ABOARD ORBITAL STATION *ESTRADE*:

Sara Hiam, physician, creator of the FN-17 vaccine

Sigrid, remote communications specialist

Nyo, satellite systems specialist

ON JEEP:

Hannah Danner, acting commander of the Mirrors

Ato Teng, her deputy

Vincio, Danner's administrative assistant
Lu Wai, Mirror sergeant, partner of Letitia Dogias
Letitia Dogias, senior communications technician, partner of Sgt. Lu Wai
Ana Kahn, Mirror private
Day, a Mirror private, currently AWOL and living with the herders Jink
    and Oriyest
Helen Relman, Mirror lieutenant, partner of Bella Cardos
Bella Cardos, cartographer, partner of Lt. Helen Relman
Pat Twissel, Mirror private
Chauhan, Mirror private
Ude Neuyen, communications technician
Alice Foster, Mirror private
Fa'thezam, Mirror lieutenant
Gautier, ceramicist
Hurro, Mirror captain, deceased
Leap, Mirror sergeant
Margaret, Mirror private
McIntyre, soil chemist
Said, zoologist
Sevin, plastics engineer, deceased
White Moon, Mirror captain

Native Inhabitants of Jeep

THE ECHRAIDHE:
Aoife (pronounced EE-fee), Agelast of the Echraidhe
Uaithne (pronounced WAITH-nee), estranged soestre to Aoife, messianic
    Death Spirit
Borri, healer, tent sister to Aoife
Marac, Aoife's daughter
Scatha, Marac's tent sister
Aelle, mother of Scatha
Mairu, mother of Kaitlin
Kaitlin, soestre to Licha
Licha, soestre to Kaitlin
Fion
Nehu, an elder, the former Levarch
Macha, deceased

INHABITANTS OF OLLFOSS:
Wenn's household:
Leifin, trapper and wood carver, partner to Huellis, blood sister to
   Kristen, mother of Moss, daughter of Jess and Bejuoen and Rolyn
Huellis, partner to Leifin, mother of Otter
Otter and Moss: infant soestre
Gerrel, daughter of Kristen
Thenike, viajera, Gerrel's choose-mother
Hilt, a sailor of North Haven, Thenike's blood sister
Kenisi, cook and herbalist
Wenn, the eldest of the household, Kenisi's partner

   Rathell's household:
Kristen, Gerrel's blood mother, Leifin's blood sister, one of Marghe's
   pattern singers
Namri
Ellyr
Hanner
baby Gin
Rathell, who owns the map

   Ette's household:
Ette, one of Marghe's pattern singers
Bejoen
Terle

OTHERS:
Cassil, farmer of the largest field in Holme Valley, Rhedan's choose-
   mother
Rhedan, daughter of Cassil and her kith
Holle, herder of Singing Pastures
Shill, herder of Singing Pastures
Jink and Oriyest, herders on the plains, original plaintiffs in *Jink and
   Oriyest v. Company*
Sehanol, woman of Scatterdell
Puiell, daughter of Sehanol
T'orre Na, viajera to the herders
Kuorra, southern viajera
Telis, viajera on the western banks of the river Ho
Zabett, innkeeper in North Haven

Scathac, Zabett's sister
Vine, sailor aboard *Nemora*
Byelli, sailor aboard *Nemora*, amateur harpist
Ash, sailor aboard *Nemora*
Roth, sailor, captain of *Telwise*
Juomo, sailor aboard *Telwise*
Tillis, sailor aboard *Telwise*
Touk, innkeeper in Southmeet
Jolesset, sailor who taught Thenike the pipes
Gabbro, a woman of High Beaches
Weal, head olla shaper in the Yelland Hills
Fellyr, a.k.a. Ojo, of the Briogannon, Uaithne's former lover, enemy of
the Echraidhe

© Kelley Eskridge

About the Author

NICOLA GRIFFITH is a native of Yorkshire, England, where she taught self-defense and fronted a band before discovering writing and moving to the U.S. She is the author of the novels *Slow River*, *The Blue Place*, and *Stay*, and coeditor of the Bending the Landscape series. Her work has been translated into eight languages and has won many awards, including the Nebula Award, the World Fantasy Award, the James Tiptree, Jr. Memorial Prize, and the Lambda Literary Award (five times). She lives in Seattle with writer Kelley Eskridge, and takes enormous delight in just about everything.

For more information, visit www.nicolagriffith.com.

STAY
(an excerpt)

by Nicola Griffith

from Nan A. Talese/Doubleday, April 2002

Chapter One

FROM THE roof of my cabin I can see only forest, an endless canopy of pecan and hickory, ash and beech and sugar maple. Wind flows through the trees and down the mountain, and the clearing seems like nothing but a step in a great green waterfall. Even the freshly split shingles make me think of water. Cedar is an aromatic wood; warmed by the autumn sunlight of a late North Carolina afternoon, it smells ancient and exotic, like the spice-laden hold of a quinquereme of Nineveh. It would be easy to close my eyes and imagine a long ago ocean cut by oars—water whispering along the hull, the taste of spray—but there's no point. There's no one to tell, no longer a Julia to listen.

Grief changes everything. It's a brutal metamorphosis. A caterpillar at least gets the time to spin a cocoon before its internal organs dissolve and its skin sloughs off. I had no warning: one minute Julia was walking down the street, sun shining on black hair and blue dress, the next she lay mewling in her own blood. The bullet wound was bigger than my fist. Then she was on a white bed in a white room, surrounded by rhythmically pumping machines. She lasted six days. Then she had a massive stroke. They turned the machines off. The technician stripped off his gloves, and grief stripped me raw.

I set the point of a roofing nail against a shingle, lifted my hammer, and swang. The steel bit through the cedar right on a hidden imperfection, and the shingle split. The hammer shook in my fist. I put it down and laid my hands on my thighs. The shaking got worse.

A plane droned over the forest, out of sight even though the sky was clear, a hard October blue. Birds sang; a squirrel shrieked. The droning note deepened abruptly, grew louder, and resolved into a laboring car engine. There was only one road. I didn't want anything to do with visitors.

The ladder creaked under my boots, but once on the turf I moved silently. Truck and trailer were locked, and the cabin did not yet have windows to break. I collected the most valuable of the hand tools—the froe and drawing knife by the sawhorse, the foot adze and broadaxe by the sections of split cedar—stowed them in the old hogpen, and walked into the forest.

Parts of the southern Appalachian forests have been growing uninterrupted for two hundred million years. Unlike the north, this area has never been scoured to its rock bones by glaciers. It has been a haven for every species, plant and animal, that has fled the tides of ice which creep across the continent every few thousand years: the ark from which the rest of the East is reseeded after the ice melts. A refuge, my refuge.

On my right, brilliant white-spotted orange puffballs bloomed from the horizontal trunk of some huge tree that had fallen so long ago it was impossible to identify. It was being absorbed back into the forest: carpenter ants and fungi broke down the cellulose; raccoons and possums lived in the cavities and salamanders in the shade; deer and wild pigs ate the mushrooms. When the whole thing collapsed into rotted punk, more microbes would turn it into rich soil from which a new tree would grow. I touched its mossy bark as I passed. This was the world I belonged to now, this one, where when a living thing died it fed others, where the scents were of mouse droppings and sap, not exhaust fumes and cordite, and the air hummed with insects rather than screams and the roar of flame.

Ninety feet over my head the canopy of ash and white basswood shivered in the constant mountain breeze; it was never quiet, not even at night. I stood for a while and just listened. The sudden, rapid drumming of a pileated woodpecker echoed from the dense growth ahead. I pushed through fetterbush and fern and skirted a tangle of dogwoods, trying to pin down the source. It drummed again. North.

I found it forty feet up a huge yellow buckeye on a stream bank orange with jewelweed: big as a crow, clamped onto the bark by its strange backward-and-forward claws, and braced against the tree with its tail. Its scarlet head crest flashed forward and back in an eight-inch arc, over and over, a black-and-red jackhammer, and almost as noisy. Wood chips and plates of bark as big as my hand showered the weeds. When it reached softer wood, its tongue went to work, probing for carpenter ants, licking them up like a child dipping her tongue in sugar. Perhaps woodpeckers developed an instinct for which trees were rotten with ants, the way a police officer can spot the criminal in a crowd. It was efficient and brutal. When it was done, it launched itself from the tree and disappeared downstream, leaving the remaining ants wandering about in the wreckage of their shattered community. I wondered if the bird ever gave any thought to those left behind. I never had.

I emerged from the jewelweed and sat on a boulder by the rushing stream. Damselflies hummed; a chipmunk chup-chup-chupped next to a fallen pecan; birds began their evening song. Tree shadow crept to the edge of the far bank, then across the water. I let it all pour through my head, emptying it.

When I stirred, it was twilight under the trees; in the valley it would be full dark. If my visitors had been smart, they would have turned their lights on to drive back down the mountain. I stretched, then walked along the stream bank, savoring the cool scent of moss and mud, following its curve north until it met the trail that led south and west to my cabin.

Three hundred yards from the clearing there were no birds singing, no squirrels scuttling through the undergrowth. The long muscles in my arms and legs and down my back suddenly plumped and warmed as adrenaline dilated blood vessels. I flexed my hands, moved silently to the tree line.

Woods surround three quarters of the clearing, but the southern quarter falls down the mountain as a heath bald and, unhindered by trees, the last of the evening sun slanted over the grass and splashed gold on the windscreen of a dark blue Isuzu Trooper parked by the trailer. A man sat on the log by the fire pit, one leg crossed over the other, an unlabeled bottle by his foot. He was slight, with black hair long enough to hint at ringlets where it touched his collar, and although I couldn't see his eyes I knew what color they would be: Irish blue. He was whistling "Kevin Barry" through his teeth as though he might sit there forever.

I know how to look after myself; I have the money to buy whatever I need. Neither of these things is any protection for the raw wound that is grief, and this man sat like a sack of sharp salt in the middle of the only safe place I knew.

He didn't hear me step from the trees, didn't hear me cross the turf. It would be easy to break his neck, or pull the hatchet from its stump and chop through his spine at the sixth vertebra. But he had met Julia, once.

I stood behind him for nearly a minute—close enough to smell the familiar bitter hint of coffee grounds—before he jerked around and whipped off his shades.

"Aud!"

Aud rhymes with shroud. After a moment I said, "Dornan."

"I was beginning to think . . . But here you are."

There were dark circles around his usually bright eyes but I didn't want to see them. "What do you want?"

"Would you sit down at least? I brought a drink." He held up the bottle.

"Say what you have to say."

"For the love of god, Aud, just sit for one minute and have a drink. Please."

I didn't move. "It's almost dark."

"We'd best make a fire then." He stood, tried to look cheerful. "Well, now, hmm, I'm no expert but that looks like a fire pit, and this, over here, is no doubt firewood. If I put this in here, then—"

I took the hickory log from him. "Kindling first."

"And where would I find that?"

"You make it."

"I see. And how do I go about doing that?"

His forehead glistened. He knew me, what I might do if he pushed too hard. Something was so important to him that he thought it worth the risk; I would have to hurt him or listen. Briefly, I hated him. "Bring the bottle."

Inside the trailer, I turned on lights and opened cupboards.

"Well, would you look at this! You do yourself proud." He ventured in, patted the oak cabinets and admired the Italian leather upholstery, then stepped through the galley to the dining area. "A satellite television!" He pushed buttons. "It doesn't work." I had never bothered to connect it. "And a real bathroom." The trailer, fifth-wheel rig, was a treasure trove of hidden, high-tech delights. I let him wander about while I assembled plates, bowls, cutlery. "I had no idea these things could be such little palaces," he said when he came back. "There's even a queen bed."

After five months of solitude, his prattle was almost unbearable. I handed him a chopping board and knife, and he frowned.

"So where's the food?"

I picked up a cast-iron pot. "Bring that flashlight."

"There's no electricity?"

Only when I ran the generator, and I preferred the peace and quiet. He followed me to the water pump, where I handed him the pot. "Fill this. Less than a third."

While he pumped inexpertly I jerked the hatchet from the chopping stump, split the hickory into kindling, and carried it to the fire pit. Beneath the ash, the embers were sluggish. I blew them to a glow. When the kindling caught I added a couple of logs and went to the bearproof hogpen to get the food. The sky was now bloody, the trees behind us to the north and east a soft black wall.

Dornan handed me the pot and I hung it over the fire.

"Pumping's thirsty work," he said, and uncorked the bottle. He drank and gave it to me. The poteen smoked in my mouth and burned my gullet. I shuddered. We passed the bottle back and forth until the water came to a boil. My forebrain felt strange, as though someone were squeezing it. I added rice, and opened plastic tubs of sun-dried tomatoes, green olives, olive oil, and cashew nuts.

"No meat I see."

"You're the café owner. Next time call ahead."

"I tried. Do you even know where your phone is?"

It was around somewhere, battery long dead. The fire burned hotter. I drank more whiskey. When the rice was done I handed him the slotted spoon. "Scoop the rice into the big bowl. Don't throw away the water. It's good to drink cold."

He gave me a sideways look but spooned in silence. Sudden squealing from under the trees made him jump. "Mother of god!"

"Wild pigs," I said. The rice he had split in the fire hissed and popped.

"Would they be dangerous?"

"Not to us."

He handed me a bowl of rice. I added the dried ingredients and olives, a little oil, and salt and pepper.

We sat on the log side by side and ate quietly while the sky darkened from dull red to indigo. Firelight gleamed on my fork and, later, when we set the plates aside, on the bottle as we passed it back and forth. I rubbed the scar that ran from my left shoulder blade and along the underside of my arm to the elbow.

"Still hurt?"

Only inside. "Tell me why you came, Dornan."

He turned the bottle in his hands, around and around. "It's Tammy. She's missing. I want you to find her."

He had disturbed me for this. Tammy. "Maybe she doesn't want to be found."

"I think she's in trouble."

Overhead, the first star popped out, as though someone had poked a hole in a screen.

"Now, look, I'm not a fool. I know you're hiding up here, eating this, this rabbit food, because you want to be left alone. But I've tried everything, phoned everyone: police, family, her friends"—Tammy didn't have friends, only male lovers and female competition—"and I've nowhere else to turn."

His face was drawn, with deep lines etched on either side of his mouth, but I turned away. I didn't want to know, didn't want to care. *Stay in the world, Aud,* Julia had said from that metal bed in that white room. . . .

Stay alive inside. Promise me. And I had promised, but I didn't know how. . . .

Printed in the United States
by Baker & Taylor Publisher Services